NieR:Automata

ニーア オートマタ

YoRHa Boys

Written by Jun Eishima

Original Story by Yoko Taro

Translated by Stephen Kohler

NieR:Automata

YoRHa Boys

NieR:Automata—YoRHa Boys
© 2018 Jun Eishima / SQUARE ENIX CO., LTD.
© 2018 SQUARE ENIX CO., LTD. All Rights Reserved.

First published in Japan in 2018 by SQUARE ENIX CO., LTD.
English translation rights arranged with SQUARE ENIX CO.,
LTD. and SQUARE ENIX, INC.
English translation © 2020 by SQUARE ENIX CO., LTD.

Based on the video game *NieR:Automata* for PlayStation 4.
© 2017 SQUARE ENIX CO., LTD. All Rights Reserved.
Also based on the stage play *Shonen YoRHa Ver. 1.0*.
© 2018 SQUARE ENIX CO., LTD. All Rights Reserved.

ISBN: 978-1-64609-075-4

Library of Congress Cataloging-in-Publication Data is on file
with the publisher.

Printed in the U.S.A.
First printing, October 2020
10 9 8 7 6 5 4 3 2 1

SQUARE ENIX
BOOKS

www.square-enix-books.com

NieR:Automata
YoRHa Boys

CONTENTS

YORHA BOYS VER. 1.05

YoRHa Boys Ver. 1.05

PROLOGUE

HER PACE WAS BRISK. I had to hurry just to keep up. Unlike the "outside," there was atmosphere here. Gravity, too. As I trotted along, the soles of my feet struck the floor, producing a peculiar sound. *Pit-pat. Pit-pat.* At first, I thought maybe the sound would draw her attention. But she didn't turn. She didn't even slow down. She just continued on her way.

In the end, I had to resort to a more typical method: I shouted out to her.

"No. 2! Hey! Don't ignore me!"

She finally stopped. "What is it, No. 9?"

She whirled around to face me, and the hem of her white skirt billowed out slightly. It brought to mind a scene I'd witnessed in a video recording, of a flower unfurling its petals to the world. But I wasn't able to remember the name of that particular species of plant.

"Is there something you need?" she continued.

"Well . . . no. I wouldn't exactly say 'need.'"

"If you don't need anything, then you're wasting our time."

No. 2 turned and resumed walking. The hem of her skirt billowed out once more, offering a glimpse of her long, straight legs.

"C'mon," I pleaded. "You're being too harsh. Didn't you just get a lecture on how important it is for androids to engage in communication? You know, during the motor functions assessment. Or did you already forget about that?"

". . . I remember just fine."

Her response was curt. I'd come to expect that of her. It probably just boiled down to the type of personality she'd been outfitted with. Just like how I was always brimming over with curiosity, dying to learn more about everything I encountered. Androids came in all different kinds and were diversified in every possible aspect, from personality and capability to physical appearance. It was variety like that which enabled humans to develop highly advanced civilizations. So if you asked me, we probably did it to take after them.

I returned my attention to No. 2. "So, um, where are you headed? Oh, wait! Don't tell me."

I waved both hands in protest before she could respond.

"Let me guess. Based on the general time of day and our present location, I'd say . . . you're on your way to see Zinnia! Am I right?"

"Given our present location, do you really need to *guess*?"

No. 2 pointed to a door immediately adjacent to us. Zinnia's quarters. We were already a lot closer than I'd realized.

Zinnia was the Chief of Research and Development for humanity's armed forces. As indicated by his title, he was the one in charge of designing the new generation of androids. So to us YoRHa units, he was kind of like a father. And he was kind of like our teacher, too, always running us through all kinds of tests and making adjustments.

I continued to plead with No. 2. "C'mon, work with me, here. I'm just trying to have some fun."

"You're too easily swayed by your need for 'fun.' Didn't you just get a lecture on being more careful about avoiding distractions? You know, during a certain assessment we just finished. Or did you already forget about that?"

Touché. It stung a little, having my own words thrown back at me, but still, I was enjoying myself. I liked this rapport—taking little jabs at each other and laughing, sometimes being the one to make the joke, and other times having to bear the brunt of it with a grin. This had to be close to that concept I'd come across in the records—the thing humans referred to as a "family."

The door beside No. 2 had opened, and Zinnia leaned out. "Think you could make any *more* noise out here?"

"Zinnia!" I exclaimed. "Hey, I've got a question for you."

Zinnia looked from me to No. 2 and chuckled.

"I have to say, if I didn't know any better, I'd think you two were inseparable."

No. 2 seemed mortified by the suggestion. "I assure you, the fact that we're together is mere coincidence."

I couldn't help but note that it wasn't actually as coincidental as she believed, although I kept that observation to myself.

"I'm simply here to deliver the documents you requested," No. 2 said.

"Oh, thanks," Zinnia responded. He then turned to me. "And you, No. 9? What brings you here?"

"I just happened to see No. 2 walking by, so I decided to follow her."

I heard No. 2 mumble under her breath, "Are you *stalking* me now?"

"Hey, that's just mean!"

No. 2 turned away from me. I'd been snubbed. No surprise there.

"Look, if you two are gonna flirt," Zinnia interrupted, "do it somewhere else. You don't have to remind me that I'm single."

The way he said it, it was hard to tell if he was joking. It was fascinating, really. Zinnia had a certain way about him that made it difficult to distinguish where his earnest comments ended and his humor began. Not that I minded. It didn't bother me not to know what someone was thinking. If anything, it just excited my curiosity and made me want to ask questions. Like the one that was currently on my mind.

"Wait!" I protested. "You can't just send us away. What about my question? It's about the name Zinnia. That's a kind of flower, right? How'd you get a name like that?"

According to everything I'd read, humanity seemed to have a clear preference for assigning names derived from flowers to females. But Zinnia's frame was that of an adult male.

"My name?" he replied. "Well, it's not like I chose it myself. It was given to me by my superiors at my first assignment."

"But why a flower?"

The zinnia flower was known for its longevity. It stayed in

bloom for days on end. In fact, I seemed to remember it being known by another name as well—the "hundred-day flower."

"Beats me," replied Zinnia the android. "Maybe that's just what people were into at the time. There were quite a few of us named after flowers."

"You mean your name was chosen according to a fad?" I asked. "I had no idea a name was something that could be given so casually."

"Formal designations require Command approval. It has to be that way, to keep things running smoothly. But if it's a nickname, you don't necessarily have to put a lot of thought into it."

Ah. So there *was* a rigorous process in place for assigning names. A formal request filed with Command's upper ranks—just *imagining* the process had me tired out.

"Hey . . . What about us?" No. 2 broke in.

She seemed enthralled, leaning forward as if hanging on Zinnia's every word. It was completely out of character for her.

"Do you think maybe . . . we could get names, too?"

Imagine that. So No. 2 wanted a name. Maybe Zinnia's comment about other androids had sparked some envy in her. Maybe she wanted to be named after a flower. I was about to ask but stopped myself when I noticed Zinnia's reply taking a few milliseconds too long to arrive.

Hesitation. I seemed to recall that being the human term for these empty stretches of time between question and answer.

"Sure," Zinnia finally said. "Once you've cleared all your assessments and it's time for you to receive your first assignment, I imagine whoever's in charge of your squadron will probably give you a name."

"Ah. That's good to know." No. 2's expression softened.

But Zinnia's face seemed to cloud over ever so slightly. I couldn't fathom why he'd be anything other than pleased by No. 2's apparent happiness.

Something about Zinnia's hesitation nagged at me, but . . . was I just overthinking things?

"Oh, uh, No. 2?" I asked. I tugged at her sleeve, hoping my

interruption didn't seem too forced. "We should probably get on our way to the server administration room. We've got a memory diagnostic scheduled today, remember?"

"Right."

I flicked my gaze over No. 2's shoulder to find Zinnia wearing a look of relief. He seemed glad that the conversation had been cut short.

There was definitely something going on there.

We were on the sixth orbital base, site of R&D for the new android models: the Lab. To those of us in YoRHa, I guess it was what you'd call a "home." Or maybe "school" would be a more fitting term, given all the tests we had to endure—enough to drive you to exhaustion. In fact, from the way we were always having parts of our bodies checked and adjusted, describing the Lab as a kind of "hospital" might not have been too far off the mark, either.

According to Zinnia, the Lab contained every cutting-edge development tool you could imagine, along with the most talented minds to make use of them. It had to, as development of new weapons was humanity's top priority. The androids on the surface were locked in a desperate struggle. We—the YoRHa units—were to be the ace in the hole that would finally turn the tide of war.

At the moment, I was busy secretly accessing information about that struggle.

"Wow, so it's true," I mumbled to myself. "The whole eastern portion of the Eurasian continent . . ."

Based on reports from the surface, two weeks ago the machine lifeforms had managed to seize an area of considerable size. Our front lines were constantly falling back, and the fact that we were unable to dispatch the dragoons to the daylands wasn't helping.

I'd heard that our surface units were locked in a desperate struggle, but I never could have imagined how bad it really was. "Considerable size" didn't cut it. The eastern portion of Eurasia was huge. Depressingly huge. It made me wonder if we were going to be all right. I wanted to ask more about what was happening on the ground.

I *wanted* to, but it wasn't like I could turn to Zinnia, or to anyone else for that matter. It was imperative that no one find out I'd read this report. I'd only come across it because I was inside the Lab's server, and my presence there wasn't exactly authorized.

I hadn't been able to stop thinking about the way Zinnia had reacted the other day when the subject of names came up. It wasn't the only time I'd felt like something was off. When I took a moment to observe Zinnia carefully, I'd see it every now and again: that same sad expression. And whenever it appeared, he'd exhale. A small puff of air. Apparently it was known as a "sigh." Was Zinnia upset because of the state of the war? What if those feelings were because of the *other* possibility I'd considered?

Zinnia was hiding something. And the thing he was hiding was something unpleasant. At least, that was my hunch—but it was only a hunch, and it was certainly conceivable that I was mistaken. To be honest, I didn't really want to consider the possibility that Zinnia was one to tell lies or hide truths.

So I'd got it into my head to look into the matter. I would simply run a thorough search, top to bottom, and when nothing turned up, that would be the end of it. It would all be a simple misunderstanding. The way Zinnia spoke—the way you were never really sure if he was joking or being serious—was just part of his personality, and I'd merely read too much into it . . .

That's what I'd hoped, anyway.

"Huh? What's all this empty space?"

I'd stumbled upon a huge void in the server. It seemed like the kind of gap you'd find after deleting some files, but the scope was way too huge. It was as if someone had taken a massive portion of the server and gouged it right out, or had ripped it to shreds and thrown it away or something.

What in the world could have been stored in that space?

The mystery piqued my interest. I decided to try recovering whatever data had been there. I knew the work would be tedious, but my curiosity had gotten the better of me.

I'd managed to complete about 80% of the recovery when I started reading what I'd found.

"Thirteenth . . . satellite orbit . . . ? Huh. They must have been planning to build another base. I guess this is a draft of the plan. But . . . what's this about a 'Council of Humanity'? Why so many references to the surface of the moon?"

At 80%, I still couldn't make heads or tails of most of what I'd found. It was strange. I'd have thought being able to skim the recurring terms would be enough to get the gist of what the document was about. Instead, I was completely lost.

"Forget this one," I decided. "I'll just move on."

Plans regarding construction of a new base didn't seem like the kind of secret that would weigh on Zinnia's mind. I kept searching.

"Hmm. Wonder what this one is?"

Within the same folder was another file, entitled "Outline for the Implementation of a New Model." It seemed like someone had intended to encrypt its contents but did a shoddy job of it, only for the file to be deleted before proper security measures were implemented.

"Huh? Is this what I think it is?"

When I opened the file up, design specs for YoRHa-type androids poured forth. Zinnia's name was there, too. The designs were credited to him.

I knew in a general sense how we YoRHa units were created and the mechanisms by which we functioned, but the explanations I'd received in the past didn't delve into specifics. Whenever I asked for more information, the replies I got were something along the lines of, "The rest of it starts to get complicated, so let's just leave it at that."

As I skimmed through the pages, one diagram in particular caught my eye.

"This is a schematic of our reactor core . . . What the . . . ?!"

I started again from the beginning, this time reading more carefully. The words and formulas began to blur and distort, a bizarre dance unfolding before my eyes. That, too, seemed beyond reason. They were just letters and numbers. My inability to focus must have been a result of my own agitation.

"No," I reassured myself. "It's just an early concept design. That's all this is."

The specifications had been revised. Obviously. That was why the file had been deleted. That had to be the case, because the information before me now was impossible. According to the file, we were essentially . . .

Was it really impossible, though? I remembered the strange melancholy haunting Zinnia's face when No. 2 had looked so happy. What if *this* was the explanation for his reaction?

"Wait. What about that other proposal? What if . . ."

The draft flashed back into mind—the one that I couldn't make sense of even at 80% recovered, with all its unfathomable terms like "Council of Humanity" and "surface of the moon."

I set back to work recovering the data. Identifying and squishing bugs one by one no longer felt like a chore. I wanted desperately to believe in our father. Our teacher. Zinnia, the very creator of YoRHa. Perhaps somewhere among the unrecovered words was a passage that would clear everything up. Something that would make everything right again. I yearned to find it.

But when the draft was entirely restored, my heart only sank deeper.

My hands began to tremble. I couldn't believe it. That was the only human expression able to sum up the storm of feelings inside me. Bewilderment and turmoil flooded my mind, threatening to steal away any capacity for rational judgment. *I couldn't believe it.*

"Why? Why? *Why*?!"

I couldn't comprehend it. I wasn't malfunctioning. My AI was working just fine. But I didn't *want* to comprehend.

Zinnia had lied. He'd deceived us all.

"How could he?! How . . . ?!"

A new sensation coursed through my circuits. An emotion I'd never experienced before.

"Zinnia . . . He . . . he betrayed us."

This must have been the feeling that humanity knew as "hatred."

A few dozen hours after my unauthorized foray into the Lab's server, I executed my plan.

I'd wanted to start sooner. The more time that passed, the greater the chance that Zinnia would notice traces of my hacking and data recovery work. But it took several dozen hours until the conditions were right. I had one stipulation in particular on which I absolutely could not compromise.

No. 2 had to be outside the base, and she had to be alone. That meant my plan had to wait until the day of her atmospheric entry test.

When the day finally came, I went to watch as No. 2 boarded the descent training unit and shot out of the launcher. Once I'd confirmed her departure with my own two eyes, I was ready. I exited the hangar and set about my work.

First was the server administration room. That was where most of my peers would be, busy undergoing a memory diagnostic.

When I walked in, the researcher working the console turned and looked at me. "No. 9? Aren't you supposed to be taking a motor functions assessment?"

"I was, but I seem to be exhibiting some irregular behavior."

It wasn't a lie. I was the only unit scheduled to have my motor faculties evaluated that day. I'd say the fact that I'd killed the assessor certainly qualified as irregular behavior.

"Is something wrong? What exactly—"

The researcher crumpled to the ground, an expression of surprise still plastered across his face. Dispatching old models was easy. Their response times were abysmally slow and their strength hopelessly inferior.

What I had to watch out for were other YoRHa units. Fortunately, the ones in the server administration room were all inside the diagnostic booth. None of them would have any idea what had just occurred. I interrupted the diagnostic routine, executing a different program that would reset their memory banks to their default values. For the duration of the program, they'd all be completely powerless to intervene. For good measure, I set the reboot timer for one hour following program completion. They'd lie comatose indefinitely, waiting for sixty minutes that would never elapse—an impossibly distant future they'd never be able to see.

"Uh-oh . . . Guess I ruined this outfit."

I'd looked down to find my clothes stained with red. It must have happened when I stabbed the researcher. When I'd dispatched the assessor at my test, I'd elected to use my hands, sneaking up behind him and applying pressure to the neck, then snapping his cervical vertebrae for good measure. It was effective, but the process had taken longer than anticipated. A more rapid method was required. So this time I'd decided to try using my sword.

The mess was a drawback I hadn't considered. On a white outfit, red stains would stick out like a sore thumb. They'd give me away before I could make it down the corridor. I entered the diagnostic booth to strip the clothes from one of my peers. Fortunately, one of the androids undergoing the diagnostic happened to be using the same young male frame as me.

"Sorry about this," I apologized to the android, "but I don't have time to get you dressed again."

I laid my red-stained shirt and shorts atop his motionless frame. He might have been unconscious, but he deserved at least a shred of decency.

After briefly stopping once more to place an incendiary device on the inside of the door, I stepped out into the corridor. I'd already rigged up similar devices in several other locations:

NieR:Automata YoRHa Boys

the test site, the control room, the residential block, and the materials storage area.

I had to hurry. No. 2 would remain outside on standby only for so long. When she didn't receive orders to commence her test, she'd undoubtedly assume a malfunctioning comm system and return to the Lab. At best, I probably had about fifteen minutes to get everything ready.

As I rushed down the corridor, I caught sight of another android.

"No. 4!" I called out.

She turned around, and I continued to run toward her. I pretended to be in a panic.

"There's something wrong with No. 2," I blurted. "She's in a descent unit, outside the base."

I pointed to one window and urged, "Look!"

No. 4 glanced out the window. After a moment, she tilted her head.

"You see it, too, right?" I asked.

Led on by my words, No. 4 walked closer to the window, now craning her neck to see outside. Fool. Little did she realize, there was nothing to see. No. 2 was on the opposite side of the base.

Her face was now nearly pressed up against the glass.

"I don't see anything," she muttered.

Those were her last words. My sword slid straight through her back. Compared to the other YoRHa units, I wasn't too good with weapons, but an android with her back left wide open was still an easy target.

"You have to understand, No. 4. It had to be this way. We were all . . ."

She crumpled to the floor before I could finish. A pool of red slowly spread across the corridor floor. I gingerly stepped around it and headed to the nearest door. Zinnia's quarters. He'd be inside right now, discussing tomorrow's calculation speed diagnostic with No. 21.

The door slid open, and I hurled myself inside. Zinnia began to look up and No. 21 began to turn. Both were still oblivious to what was happening on the base. I angled myself toward No. 21 and went in for a tackle before he could notice the flecks of red on my newly acquired, newly stained outfit. I held my sword in a reverse grip as I went in for the kill.

"No. 21!" Zinnia screamed. His voice was shrill.

No. 21 didn't even have a chance to get a word out. He lay on the floor, already nonfunctional.

Zinnia stared at me. "No. 9, why . . . ?" he asked.

"Why? Why? *Why*?!" A grin snaked across my face as I mimicked Zinnia's words.

I raised my sword once more. Zinnia didn't move. Perhaps he *couldn't* move. After all, no one knew the capabilities of the YoRHa units more thoroughly than he did. He'd realized right away that he could never hope to overpower me or flee.

"Are you really asking me that?" I said. "*You*, of all people?"

I closed the distance between us. It was all so easy, I could have done it with my eyes closed.

"You know exactly why," I sneered.

I slashed once. I didn't aim for his neck or his heart. My blade sliced down diagonally from chest to stomach, his solar plexus right at the center of the wound.

Zinnia's eyes widened. His face contorted. His abdominal unit peeked out from the red gash across his torso. I knew that given the location of my strike, the pain lancing through his receptors must have been unbearable.

"Don't think for a second that I'm going to let you die easy," I said.

Suddenly, the interior illumination cut out. For just one moment, the room was in darkness. Emergency lights soon switched on, bathing the room in red. The timer on my incendiaries must have run out. Flames would be spreading throughout every corner of the Lab now.

"What . . . have you done . . . ?" Zinnia groaned.

"Do you honestly think I owe you an explanation?"

I slashed him with my sword again. Chest to stomach, diagonal. Shallow. I didn't want him dying on me quite yet. The wounds on his torso now formed an 'x.' Zinnia would suffer, right up until the moment the Lab began to crash. I'd see to that.

"No. 2 sure is taking her sweet time," I said. "I thought she'd be here by now."

Panic joined pain in Zinnia's expression.

"What's that?" I taunted. "Are you worried about her? Still playing the doting father, even in your final hour?"

I paused, then added, "Or is it something else? Maybe you can't bear the thought of her ever finding out what you've done."

It all made sense now. I understood Zinnia's many hesitations. There was a truth he desperately needed to hide. The YoRHa units would never be given names. It had already been decided that we would live out our lives referred to by code number alone. And it was all because—

Zinnia made a move. He turned toward his desk, arm outstretched.

"Still clinging to hope?" I asked.

My sword went through his shoulder, then continued downward, pinning him to the floor. An earsplitting shriek filled the room. He wouldn't be going anywhere now.

"Give it up already," I said. "The control room is a sea of flames by now. Power is long gone, and so is the network connection."

Why hadn't No. 2 come running in yet? I'd purposely avoided placing firebombs near the launch hatch and hangar in order to leave her a clear path.

I approached the door, intending to inspect the corridor. It slid open, only to reveal a dark figure obstructing my view. No. 4's corpse. It took a moment before I realized how it could have moved, and why it was floating in midair: with the base on fire, gravity control had gone haywire.

The dead android's frame floated over my head and into Zinnia's room. On top of the gravity issues, the whole base had begun shuddering sporadically as the fire spread. I finally understood what was taking No. 2 so long.

Under normal conditions, the distance from the hangar to

Zinnia's room could be sprinted in five minutes or less. But a headlong sprint wasn't possible given the current state of the base.

I shrugged. "Guess we'll just have to put our faith in her motor faculties, won't we?"

I closed the door once more and drew my backup sword, then concealed myself in one corner nearest the doorframe. In terms of combat ability, No. 2 easily surpassed me. A surprise attack was my only chance. Otherwise *I'd* be the one cut down.

I placed an ear against the wall. From the corridor came a series of thumps at gradual, irregular intervals.

"Sounds like footsteps," I said. "Maybe our guest has finally arrived."

She was probably making her way along by kicking from one wall to the other. Little by little, the sounds grew louder, a countdown timer heard but not seen. I grabbed hold of the emergency handle on the wall, steeling myself for the moment to come.

"Zinnia! Are you in there?!" No. 2 shouted.

The door slid open. A wave of sweltering air rushed into the room. It seemed the fire had already spread to the corridor.

A note of panic entered No. 2's voice as she surveyed the scene. "No. 4! No. 21! What *happened* here?!"

"Stay back . . ." Zinnia groaned. "You have to . . . get out of here . . ."

The desperation in Zinnia's face was plain. He wanted more than anything to warn No. 2 of the danger. It was exactly what I'd hoped he do. No. 2 followed the sound of Zinnia's voice, and when she found him, she froze.

"Zinnia?! How—"

I launched myself through the air, slamming No. 2 against the wall. This way, neither the failing gravity nor the shuddering of the base could throw me off. My blade would go *exactly* where I intended.

When No. 2 finally processed what had happened, she gasped, "No. 9 . . . ?!"

I slowly pushed myself away. The tip of my blade came free, and red droplets sprayed into the air.

"Your battle reflexes really are amazing," I said. "You managed to twist away from what would've been a fatal wound."

It was a lie, of course. I'd made certain not to strike anything vital.

"What . . . what's going on?" she asked.

Don't worry, I thought. *I'll tell you everything. But we have to do things in order.*

"Tell me, No. 2," I began. "Did you know there's a secret about us YoRHa units? Something they don't want us to know?"

"Don't!" Zinnia shouted, his voice strained.

"Shut up!"

I kicked Zinnia's side. His frame lurched upward, now freed from the floor, and smashed into the wall, sword and all. The sound that escaped his throat was somewhere between a groan and a whimper.

"Stop it!" No. 2 yelled. "What did Zinnia do to deserve this?"

What had he done? Plenty. No number of kicks to bruise his body or gashes drawn across his skin would be punishment enough.

"Our designer here had some very *unorthodox* ideas when it came to creating us."

The deleted spec sheet had left me speechless. It truly was beyond belief.

"You know those black boxes inside us? The ones they claim are some new type of fusion reactor, with efficiency levels off the charts?"

I paused. Waited. Drew in one slow, deep breath.

"Let me tell you about them. They're an energy source, all right. But they're built out of repurposed cores. Cores they harvested from machine lifeforms."

I used to love reading through data from the old world. I pored over every description of human civilization, determined to learn all I could about mankind to better imitate their behavior. It had brought me so much joy. I'd dreamt that someday I might get to live like a human. But that was never meant to be.

"Do you get it now?" I asked. "We're not would-be humans. We're not even androids. Everything we are is based on machine technology. We're *monsters*!"

Of course they'd never give us names. Who would bother to make a monster happy? As far as the other androids were concerned, numbers were already far more than we YoRHa units deserved.

"But . . ." No. 2's voice was a thin whisper. "That's no reason to . . . to do something like *this* . . ."

Ah, my sweet No. 2. So gentle. So kind. Knowing all this, she'd still forgive Zinnia and stand up for him. But that was only because she had yet to hear the rest.

"Believe me, I'm only just getting started. Let me tell you about Zinnia's *other* project."

Our forces on the surface were losing ground day by day, suffering defeat after miserable defeat. Low morale was to blame. The androids on the front lines and everyone else had lost their human creators. There was no one left to protect. No reason to go on fighting.

In stepped Zinnia, convinced something had to be done to turn the tide. And so he came up with his insidious solution.

"It's a project to raise morale among androids by faking the presence of human survivors on the moon," I said.

First, fabricated records would be spread, suggesting that the remnants of humanity had fled to the moon and were still there, alive and well. Then, a new server would be established in an unmanned lunar base, dubbed the "Council of Humanity." The server would send periodic broadcasts to Earth, all to maintain the ruse that humanity continued to exist and watch over its android army.

The final stage involved the creation of a dedicated android squadron, along with its very own orbital base, which would act as the sole conduit for contact between androids and the Council—or, more plainly, it would maintain the fake server on the moon. *That* was Zinnia's proposal.

"But there was one fatal flaw," I explained. "As long as the Bunker continued to maintain the Council of Humanity, there was always the possibility that the secret could get out. That's where I stepped in."

If there was any concern about information being leaked by the Bunker, the solution was simple: make leaks impossible. Destroy the evidence before it came to light.

"I installed a backdoor in the newly built base. After a certain amount of time passes, it activates, leaving the Bunker vulnerable. The machines will infiltrate, and everyone aboard will be annihilated. Once the base is destroyed, all that will remain of the project are the transmissions from the server on the moon. Everyone aware of the project will be gone, and the truth can never get out. The secret will be safe forever, and humanity will persist for time eternal, far out of reach on the lunar surface. We'll have created a god for androids everywhere."

The necessary programs had already been sent to the lunar server: the schematics for the new orbital base, the design specs for YoRHa-type androids, and orders for the automated production line. Everything necessary to the project's execution was already in place. The whole process could be left entirely alone and it would go on mass-producing YoRHa forces.

"Just imagine. A god born of a self-perpetuating YoRHa squadron, and a YoRHa squadron that lays down its lives for the sake of that god!"

The humans we androids worshipped so dearly were gone forever. A colossal lie had been fashioned to conceal that fact. But Zinnia, our creator, would not be the one to complete it. That duty fell to us. It was the YoRHa androids themselves who would ensure that the lie never came unraveled.

"I'd like to give our plan a name," I told No. 2. "I'm thinking 'Project YoRHa.'"

What do you think?, I'd intended to add. But I never got a chance to say the words. I had a vague impression of her shouting, "Enough!" And then my mouth was hanging slack, and what spilled out were not words but low, guttural moans.

"Enough of this . . ." she whispered. "No. 9 . . . This has to end . . . You're not well . . ."

Her face was heavy with grief. A pattern of red dots slowly unfurled across my vision. The dots hung there gently until all was engulfed in flame. Eventually, it occurred to me that I'd been stabbed. And that was fine. I'd avoided striking anything vital when I lunged at No. 2. If I'd had the option, I wouldn't have hurt her at all. But she was too gentle. Too kind. If I hadn't struck first, she would have never found the resolve to kill me. And if a sentence had to be delivered, I wanted her to be the one to do it.

"It's too late," I told her. "The project . . . can't be stopped . . ."

It doesn't matter if I die at your hands, or if the Lab burns away to nothing. All the parts are already in motion.

"But know . . . that we'll both . . . be rebuilt . . ."

Specifications for the No. 2 model and the No. 9 model were safe on the lunar server. Both she and I would be created again. We'd meet again. And we'd die again. Over and over, time and again, until one day, we'd finally fade away, the secret of humanity still held tightly to our chests.

"I'm . . ."

My vision wavered. It was bright. And red.

"I'm glad, though . . . At least this me . . . got to . . . got to be killed by . . . you . . ."

I felt warm. The darkness deepened, but the warmth enveloped me and held me close. I hoped we'd be somewhere warm the next time we met, too. Maybe somewhere brighter. Somewhere where the light was overflowing . . .

I'd like to see you again. Wouldn't that be nice? Don't you think so, No. 2?

YoRHa Boys Ver. 1.05

CHAPTER 1

[Log Entry: No. 2 / Orbital Base "Bunker"—Residential Block]

"NO. 9."

On murmuring the name, I was overtaken by a strange sensation. It took me a moment to pinpoint why: it was the first time I'd ever spoken a code number out loud. I had yet to come face-to-face with any of my future squadmates.

"Engaging in unproductive personal conversation is inadvisable."

I pointedly ignored the voice emanating from my wrist and returned my attention to the display screen hanging in the air before me. This time, I read with purpose, in a voice several times louder than my initial mumbling.

"No. 9. Healer. Squad recovery. Low combat specification."

Naturally, this unit wasn't expected to be handling weaponry. He was designed to provide support functions. But while he wasn't meant to get directly involved in battles, he was also the only Healer in the YoRHa Experimental M Squadron. If No. 9 were to fall, the operational capability of the entire squad would be severely limited.

"No. 21. Scanner. Battlefield reconnaissance and intel acquisition. Low combat specification."

As with No. 9, nobody was expecting No. 21 to be spearheading assaults. But unlike No. 9, he'd be directly engaged in facilitating other squad members' duties. A Scanner couldn't just sit around on the back lines. His specific role could vary depending on the squad's precise configuration, but it was conceivable that he'd be tasked with working alongside offensive units, right where the action was at its hottest.

"No. 2." The voice from my wrist had grown stern.

I ignored the rebuke and continued reading aloud.

"No. 22. Gunner. Long-range attacks. Notable performance in rifle marksmanship. No. 6. Attacker. Close-range assaults. Proficient in use of swords. Boasts exemplary agility. These four units are hereby assigned to M002."

All four androids were configured with male frames designed with an adolescent appearance. Boys. Just like me.

"So this the new face of M Squadron. The second batch of recruits."

YoRHa M Squadron was the first experimental squadron composed entirely of male-type units. It was quite a novel thing, really, given the fact that the overwhelming majority of YoRHa-type androids were configured with adult female frames.

"Vocalization is unnecessary for retaining the presented information. Unnecessary actions waste resources and increase likelihood of delay in completing assigned duties. Proposal: Cease reading aloud."

The voice droned on. The pronouncements of the Support System unit outfitted on my wrist were as long-winded as the device's official designation: Support System Model Delta Code 153.

"Tone it down a little," I muttered.

The unit was meant to provide us with all manner of necessary support when we carried out operations. But I'd quickly discovered that sometimes it provided a level of support far beyond what was necessary. In other words, it had a tendency to nag.

I'd have been hard-pressed to name anything more annoying than the constant stream of commentary emanating from my wrist. The thing was so obnoxious, in fact, that I'd recently decided to try drowning it out with the sound of my own voice—hence my reading the new squad assignments out loud. Unfortunately, this particular plan had backfired.

"Alert: Calibration of the No. 2 unit's auditory systems is already complete. At present volume, voice communication should be within tolerable—"

"What I meant was, *shut up*!"

But I'd already lost my train of thought. My auditory systems might have been deemed ready to go, but much of my other training and calibration was far behind schedule. I didn't need my SSU to remind me of that.

Originally, I'd been scheduled for assignment to M001. I was supposed to make my descent alongside No. 3 and No. 4, two offensive units who, like me, were part of the first batch of recruits. As was standard for M Squadron, they both had male-type frames. However, unlike me, they had the appearance of full-grown adults.

I looked down at my palms. The hands on No. 3 and No. 4 were probably a full size larger. And their wrists and biceps were undoubtedly much thicker than my scrawny arms. Contrary to what our physical appearances suggested, there wasn't any age difference between us. Still, my body was that of a boy's. I was shorter, and my physique more slender.

Of course, differences in physical build didn't reliably correspond to differences in physical capability. The other M002 units had the same kind of frame as me, the same short, slender build. But as far as their test results were concerned, the second set of offensive units—No. 6 and No. 22—didn't display the slightest functional inferiority compared to the first. If there *was* any difference, I imagined it wouldn't amount to much more than the first-batch units having a slightly longer reach during close combat encounters.

The thought did little to console me. While No. 3 and No. 4 were sailing through their preparations, I was here marking time in orbit. Not literally marking time, of course. That was just a figure of speech.

Training, tests, and calibration. That was my life up here. And once I finished with a cycle, it was rinse and repeat: More training. More tests. More calibration.

I'd heard that No. 3 and No. 4 got to perform their combat training as a pair. I was always on my own. Of course, I had to admit that the nature of my training didn't exactly make it the kind of thing you did with a partner.

Memorizing the data in front of my face now—these details about the squadmates I'd eventually rendezvous with on the surface—was one more vital step in ensuring my own operational success. Still, I couldn't help but sigh.

Another page of data appeared on the screen.

"No. 2 Type D, huh?" I muttered to myself.

Defender. An experimental model built to withstand attacks, both physical and otherwise, equipped with a defensive barrier that would protect against logic viruses. That was why I had more physical strength than other models, and why I was equipped to resist viral infection . . . If any of my squadmates were to ask about my unusual specs, that's what I was supposed to tell them. I wondered if it would really be enough to stem their curiosity.

I continued reading. "Type D units position themselves on the front lines, absorbing enemy attacks amidst the fray, and are prepared to lay down their lives to keep their comrades safe."

"Well, that's ironic."

My comrades? The other members of my squad were no more than still images on a screen. I hadn't interacted with any of them, not even once, from the moment I rolled off the production line. I'd spent days on end without anyone to talk to except my SSU. I was *always* alone. Solitude was the definition of my life in orbit.

Maybe my frustration explained why my progress was so slow. I'd fallen so far behind that it seemed like even the second set of units might overtake me. No . . . Surely it wasn't possible that feelings as trivial as that had held me back.

As I stood in contemplation, the grating voice of the SSU cut in once again.

"Alert: Dynamic load test to begin in 300 seconds. Proposal: Proceed immediately to the testing block."

"Yeah, yeah."

Even I had to admit that my response was a little rude.

Pistol reports echoed in the darkness. Three discharges in rapid succession. Then another set. A total of six shots fired. The pings of the third and fifth shots sounded higher than the others. My guess was that they'd failed to hit their targets.

"Shooter: No. 3. Four targets hit," came the assessor's report.

Six shots, two misses. No. 3's previous performance had been similar: six shots, one miss. A subtle reminder of how unsuited he was to the Gunner role.

"No. 4, swap in."

At the instructor's command, No. 3 left the booth, and I stepped in.

We'd had 120 minutes of firearms training, followed by a fifteen-minute rest, and now this test. In the initial round, there were both stationary and moving targets, and luminance and reflectivity values matched the standard lighting conditions throughout the Bunker, in order to establish a baseline for each unit's firearms proficiency.

After that, we were asked to fire again, this time in the presence of a single, harsh light. On the surface, we could be forced to operate in "blinding daylight"—that is, in areas that received intense amounts of sun, like deserts or ocean shores. The second round was meant to simulate those conditions.

Finally, there was a round in complete darkness. The insertion of M Squadron would take place somewhere in the daylands, where the darkness of night didn't obtain. But that didn't mean every op was guaranteed to happen in daylight. Apparently, there were plenty of locations on the surface with minimal light conditions, places like underground passages, caves, and ancient ruins.

I picked up the handgun and got into position. The display inside my visor adjusted in response to the sudden darkness.

A disc-like target sprang upward from the bottom left. I aimed my gun toward the estimated endpoint of the target's trajectory and squeezed the trigger. At that precise moment, another target shot out from the top right. I rapidly calculated an endpoint for the new target and fired again. Sparing no time to confirm the hit, I lined up my sights once more, firing to hit a third target that had also emerged from the right almost immediately after the second.

The reason behind No. 3's inferior performance was starting to become clear. He had a bad habit of relaxing his attention between each executed procedure. A test like this required actions made in quick succession. It was designed that way precisely to catch a wandering mind off guard. Up against a demand like that, his performance would suffer.

No. 3 concentrated too much effort into each thing he did. Too much focused tension in one moment meant not enough in the next. Gunners were constantly forced into situations demanding sustained fire at a large number of targets. Inability to let one's focus flow from one shot to the next was a fatal flaw.

The next targets came as a trio, simultaneously launched from three different directions. Each moved at a slightly different speed. This was another test pattern that No. 3 would have had trouble with.

When you're processing multiple simultaneous tasks, your mind has to assign an order of priority. As long as you're operating an AI with an upper limit on processing capacity, it's something you just can't avoid. Prioritization is determined by levels of necessity: the things that have to happen, the things that should happen if the situation allows, and the things that can be safely left alone.

No. 3 always tried to give every demand equal attention. If it was in front of his eyes, he couldn't leave it alone. If you spent any time with him, you'd pick up on that real fast. He was the kind who valued action over thought. Shoot first, ask questions later.

I'd heard that carnivores on the surface exhibited behavior like that. The lower brain was already passing signals to all four limbs before the creature had a chance to think. When it came to hunting, getting the jump on prey—even by a matter of milliseconds—was the difference between dinner and an empty stomach.

"Shooter: No. 4. All targets hit."

Once the assessor had made his report, I placed the handgun back down. When I exited the shooting booth, No. 3 clicked his tongue in a noise of disgust. This, too, was typical. If a thought entered his mind, you'd be hearing it. He was incredibly transparent, which I guessed was a quality to be thankful for in someone I'd be operating alongside.

"So you got lucky, big deal. Just wait until next time," No. 3 grumbled.

Still, everything had to be a competition with him. I could put up with a sore loser, but that wasn't the only consideration here. The real problem was that stubbornness like his had a way of clouding judgment.

"Didn't realize we were keeping score," I said. "Aren't we on the same side? The more dead machines, the better."

"Excuse me?!"

It was a shame. If he'd fix his attitude, his marks in battle simulations would undoubtedly skyrocket. At the very least, you'd think he could quit routing every spare processing resource into motor functions. A few spared for logic would have made a world of difference.

"Are you saying I'm not even worth your time?" he demanded. "Huh?! Is that it?!"

When No. 3 pressed in, it was the instructor who intervened. "That's enough, you two."

"Sir!"

I immediately stood at attention, bringing my left fist up to my chest. It took a moment, but No. 3 followed suit. Instructor Black wasn't just in charge of our training. He was the commanding officer for all of M Squadron. His orders were absolute.

The instructor lifted his right hand casually, signaling for us to be at ease. No. 3 and I each lowered our arms, but kept our rigid posture intact, awaiting the instructor's next words.

"Get some rest," he ordered. "Six hours from now, you'll both undergo final calibrations."

"*Final* calibrations?!" No. 3 exclaimed. "Does that mean what I think it does?!"

Even from the corner of my eye, I could see the way No. 3's face lit up. Final calibrations could mean only one thing: we were done with our preliminary training at the Bunker.

"Once final calibrations are complete, you'll head down to the surface for on-the-ground exercises."

Currently, the enemy dominated the airspace over almost every region on the planet, which meant that making a descent trip was practically the same thing as dropping straight into battle. Just *getting* to the surface would put us in extreme danger, and here No. 3 was, treating it like a dream vacation.

"Hell yeah! Did you hear that?! We're going to the surface!"

I wasn't sure whether he'd failed to understand the situation, or if he *did* understand it and was delighted at the thought of days spent in all-out war against the machines. Maybe a little of both. In any case, the surface wasn't a place you showed up at feeling like a kid in a candy store. I wished for the umpteenth time that my companion might try diverting a few resources to his logic circuits. As usual, my wish was in vain.

"Oh, and one more thing," the instructor continued. "You may have already caught word, but be advised that the YoRHa Experimental M Squadron will consist of seven units. The others will join once their training and calibration are complete."

"So there's seven more aside from us?"

"Great math," I said. "No. That's seven *including* the two of us."

No. 3 looked away as he muttered his response. "Wise-ass."

"Sir. Permission to ask a question," I said.

"Go ahead."

"Will you be accompanying us for on-the-ground training, sir?"

"That's the plan."

If the instructor was traveling with us, that meant he didn't need to be around for the training and calibration of the other units. There were probably other Attackers and Gunners among the remaining five, and I doubted their regimen would vary much from ours. It put all the training No. 3 and I had completed into perspective. Clearly, the real work was yet to come.

"On-the-ground" training was probably as close to actual battle conditions as possible, including the degree of danger. Apparently, there wasn't a single place left on the surface that could be considered completely safe from enemy assault.

I continued to consider the implications after I'd returned to my own quarters to rest. The surface. We'd be training as two isolated units in a hostile environment rampant with machines. Eventually, we'd move on to real combat operations. I wondered what our mission might be, once our seven-unit team was finally assembled.

No. 3 probably would have laughed at me if he could hear my thoughts. "God, you worry too much," he'd say. "It's still so far off. What's the point of stressing about it?" Not the kind of thing I wanted to hear from someone who couldn't even manage to think three minutes ahead.

For the time being, No. 3 was the only partner I had. What was so wrong about teammates seriously evaluating each other's faults and weaknesses? Why shouldn't we try to stamp them out?

A single major shortcoming would cancel out any significant strengths we might possess. Conversely, if we eliminated all our major shortcomings, we'd manage to survive, even in the absence of particular strengths. That was the endpoint of the target. That was what we needed to be aiming for. What could I do to make sure it happened?

I thought, and thought, and thought some more.

[Log Entry: No. 9 / Orbital Base "Bunker"—Server Administration Room]

"Glad to make your acquaintance, No. 9. 'Course, I guess an introduction's pretty long overdue."

No. 22 gave me a sheepish grin as he said it. Next to him stood No. 21, who wore a faint smile. We'd actually encountered each other before in the training area. Several times, in fact. We'd even had a few brief conversations.

No. 21 was a Scanner, and No. 22 was an Attacker. Though their specialties differed, the two always seemed to do everything together—probably because they were designed as twin models.

"Hold up. I'm glad you've all met, but *I* don't know these two yet."

"Oops, you're right. Sorry, No. 6."

I'd been part of a battle simulation with No. 6, another Attacker, once before. It involved a scenario in which he had been wounded, and as the Healer I had to provide emergency aid. So for me, all three of the other units present were familiar to some degree. But it seemed today was No. 6's first encounter with the twins.

Presently, No. 6, No. 21, No. 22, and I were undergoing our final checks and calibrations in the server administration room. It was also an unofficial chance for us to meet and interact before the formal establishment of M002.

As to why this wasn't an official introduction, that was because at present, the leader of the YoRHa Experimental M Squadron wasn't aboard the Bunker. He'd gone on ahead to the surface with M001. So we M002 units wouldn't officially be a part of M Squadron until we descended and received our commanding officer's approval.

That said, here we were, talking to each other and introducing ourselves. It might not have been official, but in a way, we already felt like part of a team.

"Nice to meet you, No. 6. I'm Scanner No. 21. Um . . . Let's see, you must be a . . ."

"An Attacker."

No. 6 answered with a grin. His always-pleasant smile belied an incredible degree of strength. His motor faculties were top-rate, and his movements swift. Like the crack of a whip—that might have been the most accurate way to sum him up. No. 21 and No. 22 would probably be blown away the first time they observed his performance up close.

"And I'm Gunner No. 22. My specialty is long-range precision fire."

Huh? Wasn't No. 22 supposed to be an Attacker? It seemed I'd misremembered. I was thankful at least to have avoided slipping up and referring to him as an Attacker in person. I imagined that having one's role mistaken wouldn't be a very pleasant experience.

"Hey. Cut the chatter."

The rebuke came from a member of the R&D team. All four of us shrugged our shoulders in unison. No. 6 poked his tongue out ever so slightly, and No. 22, on seeing it, burst out laughing.

"Enough!"

"All right, all right. Sorry, sir."

Having comrades was pretty fun. Every other time I'd come in for checks and calibrations, I'd been bored to tears, but today it didn't feel tedious at all. Before I knew it, the whole thing was over and the four of us were walking down the corridor, the server administration room at our backs.

We'd been given six hours to rest. But using the time to actually sleep seemed like an enormous waste. So instead, the four of us wandered the Bunker, excitedly talking away.

"Wonder how long it'll be before we're back to the Bunker."

"Ha ha! Don't tell me you're already feeling homesick, No. 22. Can't handle spending a night away from home sweet home?" No. 6 teased.

No. 22, clearly flustered, shook his head vigorously.

"Th-that's not what I meant! I just wondered how long our mission on the surface was gonna take."

Speaking of which, I hadn't heard a word about our mission, either. And if No. 22 didn't know what we were going to be doing, that meant No. 21 was probably in the dark, too.

"No. 6," I began, "Have you heard anything?"

"Not a word. Probably hasn't been decided yet."

"What makes you say that?"

"Doesn't seem like the kind of call you can make from up

here. Missions have to be planned based on the enemy's latest movements."

His logic seemed sound. No. 6 always came across as highly intelligent. Of course we couldn't decide something like that ahead of time. The length of our deployment—the length of time we had to spend in battle—would depend entirely on what the enemy was up to. Any plans we made up here could be rendered obsolete during the time it took us to complete our descent.

No. 22 snapped his fingers and exclaimed, "Hey, let's go take a look at Earth!"

The planet wasn't visible from the residential block; it could only be seen from the side of the Bunker that housed facilities like the hangar and the command center.

"What's the point of doing that?" No. 21 seemed puzzled. "I mean, why go out of our way to look at it when we'll be heading there in person soon enough?"

"Once we're down on the surface," No. 22 explained, "we won't be able to see the whole planet all at once. The way it looks from up here, I mean."

"Good point. And I guess there's no telling when we might be back to see it like that again," I responded, to which No. 22 nodded in apparent delight.

"Yeah! Like, just in case. But who knows? Maybe we won't even be gone that long. Maybe they'll send us back right away."

"Sure hope they don't," No. 6 said, in a slightly sardonic tone.

No. 21 pretended to headbutt No. 6 as he retorted, "Hey! What's that supposed to mean?!"

We made our way to the block containing the hangar, all the while intentionally bumping shoulders and playfully chasing each other down. Along the way, we were reprimanded by a member of the maintenance team, who called out, "You lot settle down before I have to write you up!"

On my own, the idea of running down the hallway wouldn't have even occurred to me. Yet as a group, suddenly there were all kinds of new things we wanted to try. It was strange, but also exhilarating.

If No. 22 had been on his own, I imagine he'd have never come up with the idea of one last moment spent observing Earth. Well, maybe that was a moot point—it was hard to imagine No. 22 ever being alone, since No. 21 was always right by his side.

Setting that thought aside for the moment, I stepped up to a window. We'd all lined up along the corridor's wall, staring out at the planet as it hung there in space, perfectly round and lit with a faint blue glow.

"It's so pretty . . ."

Humanity's home. The world we were fighting to reclaim.

"Kinda feels like we're saying farewell."

"No. 6! How could you say such a thing?!"

We YoRHa units were the ace in the hole. We were going to turn the tide of the war. It was the whole purpose of our experimental squadron. At least, that's what everyone was saying.

"Hey, what's the first thing you want to see once we get to the surface?" I asked. "C'mon, everyone give an answer."

I pointedly didn't ask about the first thing they wanted to *do*. After all, once we descended, we'd be occupied with one thing and one thing only: fighting the machines.

No. 22 gave a dry laugh. "How are any of us supposed to answer something like that on the spot?"

I considered his response. Was my question really so difficult?

"You go first, No. 9. What do *you* want to see?"

No. 6 added, "Yeah, you can't just throw it out there. You have to get the ball rolling."

"Umm . . ." I began. "Well, stuff like birds and insects, I guess. And maybe plants? Oh! And I'd really like to see fish swimming through the water. And animals as they run across the ground."

The other three stared at me. They looked baffled. Was my answer really so strange? Was I asking for too much? But I was just being honest. The surface was surely full of all kinds of living organisms, and I wanted to protect them and see them flourish again, for humanity's sake.

Maybe a dream like that was far too big for an android like me. I frightened easily, and I was honestly a pretty clumsy fighter. Yet I truly wanted to see that dream through, with all my heart.

YoRHa Boys Ver. 1.05

CHAPTER 2

[Log Entry: No. 3 / Base Camp]

A SMALL BREEZE BLEW PAST MY EAR. I'd barely managed to avoid it. Not the breeze, I mean, but the bullet that made it. I was locked in a frenzied battle. Blade against gun. Attacker versus Gunner. Me and No. 4.

"Grah!"

My sword arced back and forth through the air, deflecting a hail of gunfire. The bullets, now cut in half, clattered as they hit the ground. Heh. Too easy. I closed the distance to my enemy in a single leap.

Like a bunch of random gunfire could ever hope to hit me. Guns only have an advantage at the outset of a battle. Once you're up close and personal, the advantage swings to a melee fighter. Now *I* was the fast one.

"Take this! And this! And this!"

I wasn't gonna let him get a hit in on me. Not a single shot.

"Hrah!"

I brought my sword down, aiming for No. 4's right hand. His handgun went flying. He was unarmed. Now I had him. I swung my blade once more, intending to stop it at the last moment, when it was right up against his neck.

A shock ran through both my arms, and my sword suddenly went spiraling through the air. It was all so fast, I had no idea what had happened.

Then I saw No. 4's left hand.

"Hey!"

A handgun. A *second* handgun, different from the one I'd just knocked out of his grip.

"The hell?! No fair!"

No. 4 just scoffed at me. On his face was the same stuck-up look he always wore when he pulled this shit. He could've at least tried to look proud of his victory. Or, y'know, at least done *something* to make himself more likeable.

"Don't expect to get by like that on the battlefield. You can't afford to hesitate when you go in for the kill."

What a goddamn pain in the ass. Everything about the guy pissed me off.

"If this were a *real* fight," I growled, "you'd have been dead the first time I brought my sword down."

I knew he wouldn't be able to leave it. He was bound to come back with some kind of snide remark.

But it was the instructor who cut in. "If you really believe you're capable of it, then do it. Kill him right here during training."

After eyeing me for a second, the instructor continued, "Words aren't going to convince a machine lifeform. Our enemy has no concept of restraint. If you aren't prepared for that, the only thing that awaits you is defeat."

If No. 4 had been the one to say them, the words would've grated on me like nothing else. But since the observation was coming from the instructor, any notion of protest I might've had died just as fast as I could blurt out, "Yes, sir!"

I brought my left hand to my chest in salute.

"As you were," the instructor ordered.

I lowered my salute and was struck with the tiniest urge to argue with the instructor. Or maybe not to argue so much as say something that had been on my mind.

"Sir!" I said. "How long are we going to continue training by ourselves?"

Here we were, finally on the surface, the whole place crawling with machines, and yet we spent day after day in training. Training, and more training, and even more training after that. And always just me and No. 4. Honestly, it was starting to get a little boring.

"Well, what else can we do?" No. 4 responded. "Can't exactly form a platoon with just the two of us."

That was No. 4 for you. Always negative. "Nothin' we can do" was a favorite of his, along with "Never gonna happen." I was so sick of listening to him shoot things down.

"The hell are you talkin' about? There're all kinds of things a two-unit team could manage. Y'know, like, raids on enemy installations or whatever."

"A Gunner and an Attacker, all by themselves? No recon support? The machines'd have us surrounded in seconds. We'd be annihilated. If you ever stopped to *think*, you could probably figure that out all by yourself. Try using your head for once."

"Excuse me?!"

Dammit all! I wanted to deck him. One good punch square in the jaw.

"No. 3."

At the instructor's curt warning I relaxed my hands, which had been balled into fists.

"Work on that temper of yours. And No. 4, watch your words. Quit trying to egg him on."

To my mind, the issue still hadn't been put to bed, but I knew well enough when to call it quits. I lowered my arms and let out a deep breath.

"That's better," the instructor said. Then his tone brightened. "Now, I've got some welcome news for you both."

News? For us? I wondered what it could be.

I took a quick glance to my side. No. 4 was staring at the instructor in rapt attention. Good. He was just as in the dark about this as I was.

The instructor looked back over his shoulder. Apparently, it was a signal. In jogged several other androids—YoRHa units, just like us. There were four in total. It dawned on me who they probably were.

"These are your new squadmates, assigned as of today. M002 models. In other words, your juniors."

My intuition had been right on the mark! I knew that No. 4 and I couldn't be the only members of the YoRHa Experimental M Squadron. It made no sense. We'd need other members to help with things like recon and rear support. I'd heard somewhere that those other members were gonna arrive soon, and that we'd ultimately form up into a seven-man team.

"All right! Glad you guys finally made it!" I exclaimed. "Check it out, No. 4. Our very own crew of rookies to train."

"Rookies, huh?" No. 4 said. "Don't give yourself too much credit. We only got here a couple weeks ago."

"Jeez! Do you *ever* quit with the nitpicking? Listen to yourself!"

I swear, No. 4 could swap his AI for a rock and he'd be better off. The things that came out of his mouth left me speechless.

Except . . . Wait a minute. There was me, and No. 4, and now the four units that just arrived. Something felt off. It was like the math didn't add up or something.

"M002," the instructor ordered, "sound off for your comrades here."

Whatever. It probably didn't matter. The fact that No. 4 was dumber than a rock didn't add up, either. I cooled my head and took a better look at the rookies.

The first one introduced himself. "Scanner No. 21 reporting. Newly assigned to the YoRHa Experimental M Squadron. Proficient in recon and data analysis."

Recon! That meant we finally had a scout! He was little and kinda scrawny, but I figured that was par for the course when it came to Scanners. So . . . did that mean the one standing next to him would be running recon, too? The two of them sure looked an awful lot alike.

The lookalike fumbled with his words. "Uh . . . I'm, um . . . No. 22. Gunner. Newly assigned to the YoRHa Experimental M Squadron."

A Gunner? Like No. 4? *This* shrimp?

He continued, "My specialty is precision fire, so, um . . ."

"Whoa, whoa. Are we supposed to believe this bitty little thing can actually fight?" I demanded.

No. 22 was a full head shorter than No. 4, and his arms were so skinny, it was honestly hard to say whether there was any muscle on them at all. His legs poked out from his shorts like little twigs.

"Put a lid on it," No. 4 hissed, "before you embarrass yourself."

"*You* put a lid on it," I muttered under my breath. The way a frame looked on the outside wasn't always a good indicator of its basic functionality. I knew that just as well as anyone else. The fact had just . . . slipped my mind for a moment.

"Next," the instructor called.

"No. 6. Newly assigned to the YoRHa Experimental M Squadron. I specialize as an Attacker, but there's plenty of other stuff I can handle, too."

Other stuff he could handle? The hell was *that* supposed to mean?

I could tell already that this one was a real piece of work. It was the way he smiled, arrogant as shit. There was more going on with this creep than met the eye. Maybe he had an axe to grind. All I knew was that I wasn't about to let my guard down as long as he was around.

The final kid spoke up. "I'm Healer No. 9, newly assigned to the YoRHa Experimental M Squadron. My main responsibilities are mechanical repair and backup of consciousness data."

Wait. Backing up *consciousness data*? What the . . . ? I didn't remember anyone mentioning a procedure like that anywhere in our training.

"Backup, huh? Haven't heard of functionality like that before." No. 4 was looking as confused as I felt. Good. That meant it wasn't something I'd just forgotten.

"That's correct," No. 9 confirmed with a nod. Unlike No. 6, this one seemed so honest, I felt like I was seeing straight into his brain every time he opened his mouth.

"I'm designed to maintain a full copy of each squad member's consciousness data and memory banks in case of damage or complete destruction."

A full copy? Of *everything*, including our memory banks?

What in the world was he talking about? I mean, the words themselves made sense. I understood those. The part I didn't get was *why*.

Our consciousness data, as far as I understood it, referred to every thought we'd ever had, and every piece of information we'd bothered to remember. In a way, it was our entire being, I guess. And this kid was saying he was gonna make a backup of all of that? Was that even possible?

I didn't ask it out loud, but my question must have been written all over my face, because No. 9 nodded his head slightly and continued, "In order to facilitate that, my own personal storage capacity is approximately ten times larger than the standard for units in our squad."

"*Ten times* more storage?! Holy . . ."

That was basically like saying he could store ten full copies of everything inside me!

No. 9 continued, "That extra capacity is for emergency use only. It's not available to me during normal functioning."

Yeah, yeah. Emergency use and unavailable normally, whatever. The thought of him walking around with storage capacity like that still blew my mind.

Now that the four rookies were finished, the instructor turned to me and No. 4. "You, too, M001," he said. "Sound off."

I put my thoughts about the backups aside. Let No. 4 ask the boring follow-up questions. I knew he wouldn't be able to help himself anyway.

"Attacker No. 3 of the YoRHa Experimental M Squadron. Happy to have you. It's great to see some new faces around here."

Starting today, these little shrimps were our new squadmates. So what if they were scrawny or arrogant or had crazy amounts of storage. I could look past all that. Having some new allies around was a good thing.

No. 4 gave his introduction next. "Gunner No. 4 of the YoRHa Experimental M Squadron."

That was it. A real class act, as usual. You'd think he could bother adding a friendly word or two, but nope, not No. 4.

I was still shaking my head when No. 4 turned to face the instructor.

"Sir. A question, if I may."

"What is it?"

"There appears to be a total of four M002 units here today. I'd understood our team was to be composed of seven members. Counting me and No. 3, that still leaves us one unit short, sir."

Right! Yeah! I'd been thinking the same thing. So that was why the numbers didn't seem to add up!

"The final unit is running behind on his calibrations. It was decided he'd be assigned at a later date."

Huh. So it was the two of us, these four runts, and one mystery unit still to come. And then we'd have seven. Yeah. Now the math made sense.

"For the time being, you six will be conducting combat simulations."

"Understood, sir!" responded No. 4.

The instructor looked us all over and added, "As you're no doubt aware, a YoRHa special ops squad composed entirely of female models has already been dispatched from the Bunker to begin actual combat operations."

Right. How could I forget? While we were stuck in this endless, boring training routine, the female squad was churning out results. I couldn't stand the fact that we were already losing to a bunch of girls.

"We are a newly introduced experimental squadron—a test case, composed entirely of male YoRHa units. Command has high hopes for us. They're expecting battlefield results superior to anything they've seen thus far. I want each of you to remember that M Squadron has been entrusted with breaking this long deadlock and leading humanity to victory. Carve that message deep inside your memory banks."

The instructor brought his left hand to his chest.

"Glory to mankind."

I followed his lead, my left hand coming up to my own chest as I echoed the same three words.

"Form up!"

Break time was over. I heard the instructor's call and stood, patting my clothes to get the dust off. Really, they weren't very dirty in the first place, as I'd been sitting on top of a boulder. I guess I just went through the motions for peace of mind.

Here on the surface, if you didn't pay attention to where you were sitting, you could end up with serious consequences. During the first few days, I managed to get my uniform absolutely covered in mud. Another time, I sat right on an insect, squishing it and creating a huge mess for myself.

Up on the Bunker, we'd had training areas that simulated surface terrain, with stuff like soil and sand. But they didn't have any organisms in them. No insects or reptiles. No thickets of tall grass to release clouds of pollen when you brushed by, or vines with prickly thorn-covered fruit on them.

That was the big difference between orbital life and surface life—whether or not there were living organisms around. It was a fact that had occurred to me long before our descent, but it wasn't until I set foot down here that it really sank in. The surface was brimming with life. It was bewildering. The sounds, the smells, the *presence* it all exuded. None of that existed up on the Bunker.

There were some creatures whose colors and forms I recognized from video footage, but now that I was here, seeing them up close, it was like encountering something else entirely. It seemed the state of "knowing" something wasn't a simple binary like I'd assumed. Familiarity seemed to be a gradual process, like great piles of information built up over time.

And that didn't only apply to the world's many organisms. It was the same way with the other members of my own squadron. Days had passed since we'd arrived and begun training together, but I still found myself making constant tiny updates to the records I kept on each of them. It seemed that many of my squadmates had other sides to them that I was just beginning to discover. All sorts of unexpected details kept emerging, and

I'd set myself to the task of thoroughly understanding each discovery I made. It was like going down a list, adding check marks one by one.

Take No. 3 for example. I'd once watched as he interacted with the young offspring of a bird. The creature had fallen from its nest, and No. 3 picked it up, placing it back where it belonged. Outwardly, he admonished the creature, saying, "Damn bird. You're in my way." But the action suggested that in truth, No. 3 was quite considerate of those around him. Given how loud and abrasive his speech was, I'd always found him a little intimidating. So that particular discovery came as quite a surprise.

Another example was No. 6. I'd come to realize he had a bit of a mean streak. I suspected he was probably too smart for his own good. Perhaps he felt frustrated by the constraints of the role assigned to him.

And then there were No. 21 and No. 22. The two of them were . . .

I'd become so buried in thought that my pace had slowed.

"No. 9!"

I looked up. The other units were already formed up in front of the instructor.

"Huh?!" I blurted. "Oh! B-be right there, sir!"

Flustered, I ran the remaining distance. I'd really screwed up this time.

Once I'd drawn near, I bowed my head and added, "Apologies for the delay, sir."

I lined up next to No. 6. It was clear I'd need to stay a little more conscious of my own actions.

"Now that we're all here," the instructor said, "I've got something for you. As of today, you're being outfitted with a new piece of equipment."

The instructor began handing out devices to us. They appeared to be information terminals, but each sported a different design. I surmised that they were tailored to each of us: a streamlined construction that wouldn't interfere with our individual combat functions.

"Support System Model Delta Code 153," the instructor said.

Apparently, that was what these things were called. No. 3 scrunched up his face and responded, "Jeez, that's a mouthful."

I thought so, too.

"You may refer to them as simply 'Support System unit' or 'SSU,' if you like," the instructor responded.

Ah. I'd wondered if there might be an acronym like that. Overly long names didn't exactly lend themselves well to chatter on the battlefield.

"Now pay attention. This is how they operate."

The instructor called out, "SSU," then ordered, "Tomorrow's weather."

The units now attached to each of us responded in unison.

"For the immediate vicinity, partly cloudy in the morning, followed by probable afternoon showers."

I had to admit that having answers instantly provided like that was a pretty handy feature, but at the same time, I had to wonder when we'd ever actually use the things. Couldn't we figure that stuff out for ourselves? I'd barely formed the thought when No. 6 made the same observation.

"Pretty sure our internal comm system is more than sufficient for simple information queries."

"The Support System unit serves as an extension of a YoRHa unit's capabilities," the instructor responded. "That includes long-range communications support and real-time tactical advice, as well as the provision of regular maintenance checks."

Maintenance checks? On us? Access to regular diagnostics while out on missions could, in a word, revolutionize our battlefield performance. Every spare cycle I had was now focused on the instructor. I didn't want to miss a single word he said.

"SSU," he ordered. "Run a diagnostic for any motor-function viruses in the No. 6 unit."

As soon as the instructor's order was issued, No. 6's expression changed to one of confusion.

"Huh?" he said. "What . . . what's going on?"

Parts of his body jerked unpredictably. It kind of looked like he was being tickled.

"Abort diagnostic," the instructor ordered.

No. 6 immediately ceased his fidgeting and let out an audible sigh. He turned to the instructor and asked, "All right, what just happened?"

"I initiated a diagnostic routine designed to identify and remove any physical viruses present in your motor systems."

A means of finding and removing physical viruses? Now *that* was something impressive.

No. 6 asked, "So does that mean we'll be able to halt an enemy infection?"

"The Support System is capable of nullifying physical virus infections localized in any system outside of the brain unit."

"So, what about logic viruses? Does that mean it can't help us against those?"

"Analysis of feasibility is currently underway. You can probably expect to see support for it in a future update."

So it wasn't possible now, but R&D was busy working on it. Once the Support System was able to help us fight off enemy logic viruses, it would considerably reduce the threat those attacks posed to us.

"Support System functionality is identical across all units, but the device's physical construction is tailored specifically to each of you. Spend some time trying yours out so you're ready to deploy it in the field.

"That about sums everything up." The instructor seemed ready to dismiss us, but at the last moment, No. 6 raised his hand.

"Hold up, sir. Got a question."

"What is it?"

"That diagnostic you initiated. It tickled. Felt kinda good even. Permission to have that run on me again, sir? Maybe we could do it in private this time?"

I'd learned that this was typical of No. 6. He'd chime in with some odd comment, and I'd have no idea whether he was being sincere or not.

But the instructor cut the inquiry off with a curt, "Denied."

No. 6 didn't look terribly upset at the response, so I surmised that perhaps this time he'd been making a joke.

At any rate, this apparently wasn't the time for idle speculation. The instructor turned his attention back to the rest of us and announced, "We move out in 196 minutes."

Move out. The words ushered in a momentary silence across the entire squad. Training was over. We'd be engaging the enemy for real now. It filled me with a strange new sensation; it occurred to me that it must have been what humans described as "tension."

I'd had a hunch that this moment wasn't far away. After all, quite a few days had passed since we'd joined up with the M001 units, and I was beginning to feel like we were running out of training scenarios. We'd practiced for just about any situation I could imagine us getting into.

"All units, perform a final check of your equipment. Dismissed."

The moment the instructor was out of sight, we were all in motion. No. 3, for his part, seemed to remember something he'd wanted to ask about. He turned to No. 6, intense curiosity written all over his face.

"Are you into guys, too?" he asked.

"I'm not sure," No. 6 replied. "To be honest, it never occurred to me to evaluate a partner based on criteria like that. But one thing I *am* sure about is that anyone as vulgar and brainless as you wouldn't be my type, No. 3."

"That's No. 3, *sir*, to you! Show some respect."

"Yeah, yeah."

I recognized this type of response from No. 6. I felt pretty certain that the next time these two interacted, No. 6 would again fail to address No. 3 with "sir." Although No. 6's verbal response seemed to indicate confirmation, when coupled with the expression he wore now, it often actually signaled a negative. I'd figured that out just recently.

No. 3 seemed to know it, too. He watched as No. 6 turned and walked away, letting out an audible "Hmph."

"Let's go get our gear, No. 3."

At No. 4's invitation, No. 3 fell in step with him, and the two walked off together. I watched the M001 units as they left. They both possessed a certain intensity. It was something I didn't see when I observed the M002 units, and it wasn't due merely to the fact that No. 3 and No. 4 were taller.

As they walked away, I heard No. 3 say, "Hey, No. 4. I've been thinkin'. You really oughta roll out as the Attacker instead of being the Gunner. It's more your speed, y'know?"

Change to an Attacker? And what did No. 3 mean about it being more No. 4's speed? No. 4 was supposed to be a Gunner. No. 3 was the one who was an Attacker.

"I thought we already settled this."

When No. 4 responded in this manner, I heard a heavy, drawn-out sigh from No. 3. Honestly, to me, No. 3 didn't seem like the type to sigh. What did their exchange mean? I waited until they were far enough away and then turned to No. 21.

"Do you have any idea what they meant by that just now?"

As a Scanner, No. 21 specialized in information. Perhaps because of that, he always seemed like a font of knowledge on almost any subject. The current situation was no stranger to him, either, and he quickly summed it up for me.

"No. 4 is designated as a Gunner, which means he's currently outfitted with firearms. But his original designation was as an Attacker."

"You're saying he used to have the same role as No. 3?"

"That's right. He let No. 3 keep the role and switched over to being a Gunner."

No. 22 seemed to have a good handle on these kinds of conundrums, too, seeing as he and No. 21 were always together. He added, "But actually, I hear that No. 4 is the better of the two when it comes to handling a sword."

I'd opened my mouth to express my surprise, but before I could, No. 3 shouted out from the other side of camp, "I heard that, No. 22!"

We couldn't see him anymore, but his voice was so loud and clear, it felt like he was still standing right next to us.

"You're gonna pay for that comment!" No. 3 added.

No. 22's shoulders jerked upward, and No. 21 slapped his back playfully with one palm. The two of them certainly were close. I almost felt envious. It must have been nice having a twin.

With our mouths still tightly shut, we carefully observed our surroundings. All was quiet. It seemed to me that there was no way No. 3 could *still* be listening in on us. Finally, we looked back at one another and let out sighs of relief.

Somehow the whole episode came across as quite funny. But we didn't dare laugh out loud, so the three of us sat there, shaking with the effort of stifling the urge to giggle. In the end, however, we were unable to hold back. I wasn't certain which of us was the first to explode in laughter, but by the time I realized what was happening, all three of us were rolling on the ground, clutching our sides.

Our bout of laughter eventually subsided, and we sat back up. Suddenly, everything was awkwardly quiet. We found ourselves itching for something to do.

The instructor had ordered us to re-check our equipment, but there was a reason the three of us were dawdling. In truth, we were all well beyond a re-check at this point. Even before the instructor's order, we'd all completed re-re-checks. Some of us had already finished a re-re-re-check. We all felt it, deep in our bones, every moment of every waking day: the time for battle was drawing near. Our minds were racing. We couldn't settle down. And at some point, we found ourselves constantly checking over our equipment, making sure we were ready to go at a moment's notice.

"Not long now until our first combat assignment. Are you nervous?" I asked the others.

I couldn't help but ask, considering how nervous *I* was. But No. 21 shook his head.

"All you have to do at times like these is stay focused and act like usual."

No. 21 was the calmest one among us. He always was.

"You're so strong," No. 22 replied. "Honestly, I'm terrified."

Of the two of them, I'd always felt like No. 22 had a personality closer to mine.

Even now that we were down here on the surface, he'd sometimes say out loud the precise things that I was thinking.

"There's nothing to be afraid of," No. 21 said and smiled. However, it didn't seem to be enough to dispel No. 22's anxiety.

"I bet dying in battle is awful. It must be so painful."

No. 22 cast his gaze downward.

"Dying in agony. It sounds terrible. I . . . I don't want to go through that."

I couldn't say how much agony would accompany death, or how terrible it would be. After all, I hadn't experienced death yet—none of us had. But suddenly, I felt a wave of remorse wash through me.

"Sorry," I told them. "It's not fair, is it? I'm always going to be on the back lines where it's safe, while you guys . . ."

"Huh?! No, that's not what I meant!"

No. 22's expression seemed to say, *Oh, shoot. I've really done it this time*.

"You back up our data for us," No. 21 interjected. "That's a major responsibility! If we didn't keep you in a safe position, well away from the fray, we'd *all* be in big trouble."

And No. 22 added, "And if you weren't around, who would fix up our injuries?"

It was nice of them to say that. The two of them were very kind.

"Thank you," I replied. "I'll do everything I can to make sure you stay safe. You just concentrate on the fight."

"That's the spirit," said No. 22 with a decisive nod.

No. 21 added with a smile, "Of course, don't expect us to let there be any injuries for you to treat in the first place.

"After all," he continued, "I'll be observing the enemy and putting together the best strategies possible."

He turned to look his twin directly in the eyes. "All you need to do is follow my instructions, No. 22, and you'll be fine. I'll keep you safe. I swear it."

No. 22 nodded, looking pleased. This must have been the

very definition of "trust." Since the two were always together, they must have been very special to each other.

"All right, then. Let's go take care of that 'final' equipment check."

"Right. See you around, No. 9."

I waved my hand as I told them both, "See you soon."

There were 175 minutes left until we moved out. I realized once more that I really was quite nervous. To tell the truth, fighting wasn't exactly my thing. I tended to get frightened easily, and I wasn't great at handling weapons. But there had to be other ways I'd be able to contribute. I knew it.

At the very least, our days spent training on the surface had been a lot more enjoyable than my time in orbit, which, aside from brief interactions, I'd spent almost entirely alone. Perhaps our experience here was a good approximation of the group life humans experienced when attending the facilities they referred to as "schools."

It was that new sense of being part of a group that made me want to be helpful. They were my squadmates. They were important to me. And in turn, I'd be able to rely on the M001 units, so much more experienced than the rest of us, and No. 6, with his intelligence and strength, and No. 22, always calm and composed, and No. 21, so kind and thoughtful.

I wouldn't be able to say anything nearly as inspiring as No. 21's vow to keep his twin safe. Nonetheless, I was determined to help out in every way that I could.

YoRHa Boys Ver. 1.05

CHAPTER 3

[Log Entry: No. 6 / Wetlands Zone]

AN EXPLOSION RUMBLED IN THE DISTANCE. Then an-other. And another. Over and over at regular intervals. Most annoying sound in the world. Could've been bombs or land-mines, but whatever they were, there was about one metric fuckton too many of the things, and none of them were doing a damn bit of good. We were long gone from whatever loca-tion was being targeted.

I swatted an insect stupid enough to fly up close to my face. I loathed the wetlands. You could never find solid footing, it was a pain and a half trying to find any cover, and the air was always thick with the mingled stench of mud and moss. I was so done with this whole damn region.

Somehow, I'd managed to find a small depression over-grown with a thicket of low trees. I'd huddled inside to wait out the machines. That had been . . . about eight hours ago.

"Graaah! Dammit all!"

No. 3 came barreling into the hiding spot with a racket ob-noxious enough to rival the explosions. As usual, the way he spoke was crude. Everything about him betrayed his lack of control. Yet another thing I was done with. I would've told him off, but I knew it'd only make the situation worse. This was No. 3 we were talking about, the hotheaded dimwit extraordinaire.

So I kept silent and rewound the bandage on my left arm. It wasn't looking good. The enemy had sliced right through sleeve and skin. I was just glad it wasn't my right arm. Although, at this point, it probably didn't matter. Either side would've hurt just the same.

"No good," No. 3 grumbled. "The whole northwest gorge is lousy with 'em. Even got some types I've never seen before walkin' around up there."

He made a noise of disgust and kicked off his boots. He tipped one upside down, and a shower of gravel fell out. Ugh. Couldn't he at least *try* to show some class? A moment later, the scent of blood hit my nostrils. Hmph. Apparently he'd had it pretty rough out there. Not that it was any surprise.

I couldn't restrain myself from muttering, "I told you. Waste of time."

He'd run off however many hours ago, hollering like a crazed ape about how he'd find a weak point in the enemy line, some place where the machines weren't so numerous and we could break through. Honestly, I tried to stop him. I gave it a decent shot anyway. Not like it was worth investing a lot of effort. It was already painfully obvious that No. 3 didn't listen to reason, not even when things had clearly gone to shit.

"We've been stuck here for eight hours," I added. "Trust me, the enemy'll pinpoint our location soon enough."

The whole area had to be crawling with machines, all circling in on our position. The sheer volume of gunfire and explosions was proof enough of that. And still, this moron couldn't shut up about how *he* thought the chaos coming from the northwest didn't sound as bad. Great job, detective. You've discovered the phenomenon known as statistical aberration. Either that, or you're deluding yourself.

"No Scanner. No Healer. What, you think our situation's gonna magically improve?" I asked.

At some point, I'd realized that No. 21 was gone. No. 22 as well. They were probably dead. The only others left alive would be No. 9, stationed about as far as you could get from our front line, and No. 4, who had been assigned to keep the Healer safe.

"Well, what the hell are we supposed to do then?!" No. 3 demanded.

Ugh. Couldn't he just *shut up* already? He didn't have to shout. We were right next to each other. And the question he'd asked was so utterly meaningless it didn't even warrant asking. There was only one answer.

"We keep quiet and wait for help. Either it arrives, or we die."

"Say *what*?"

He was starting to look unsettled. Was I going have to spell it out for him? *Again*? We all knew how this was supposed to go down.

"Why are you so upset? No. 9 will take care of everything once it's over."

No. 21 and No. 22 had done their jobs well. And it wasn't like I'd been screwing around, either. Even No. 3, for all his incurable idiocy, carried out his duties reasonably well. We'd all done our part. Now it was No. 9's turn to do his. That's how it went. Division of labor.

"I already told you, I don't wanna! I ain't havin' nothin' to do with that!"

Yup. This again. It wasn't a question of whether we wanted to or not. Why couldn't he get that fact through his thick skull?

"Suit yourself. Makes no difference to me."

I was wasting my breath. It wasn't the first time we'd had this conversation. Unlike No. 3, I had the ability to learn from past experience. Still, I never could've predicted what happened next. I was about to witness a whole new level of stupid.

"Suppost System!" he shouted in his obnoxious voice. "Send out a distress signal on all standard communication channels! Full strength! Keep it blaring!"

"The hell are you doing?! You're gonna draw the machines right to us!"

A full-strength, sustained signal? He might as well throw out a welcome mat and invite the enemy to come on over. What would possess him to try something like that?

"Hey!" I hissed. "Remember all those machines scouring the area? We're surrounded! Have you *still* not figured that out?"

"So we lure them to us, look for a weak point in their formation, then charge and break through."

"And how are we going to get clear of them without a Scanner?"

"Simple. Intuition."

Had I heard him correctly? *Intuition? That* was his plan?!

"I knew your brain unit was barely functional, but I had no idea it was about to fail completely."

I sighed and got to my feet. He was a lost cause. Just my luck that it had to be me and the pinnacle of idiocy together at the end. The sheer absurdity of the situation made me want to laugh.

"Well, at least I'm *doin'* something!" he shouted. "We got better odds tryin' to break through than we do sittin' on our asses until we're out of options!"

He was still talking as if we had any chance of living through this. Why didn't he get it? It was statistically impossible to pull off the kind of stunt he was proposing.

"No. 3," I began quietly, "I'm not going to say this again. Cut the transmission."

I drew my blade, and not just for show. But the dimwit still didn't back down.

"How many times have I told you?" he growled, drawing his own sword.

Right. I'd figured this was how it would go.

"That's 'No. 3, *sir*' to you!" he shouted as his blade whistled through the air.

The arc was wide. Sloppy. Did he really think he could connect like that? I could've dodged one of his downward slashes with my eyes closed.

I sidestepped, then brought my own blade slicing in. There was no way someone as slow-footed as No. 3 was going to evade my attack. But he did manage to parry. Hmph. So he was ready to take the blows he couldn't evade. He'd managed some logical thought after all. Or maybe it was just gut reaction.

He swung again, but I easily avoided the attack.

"You gonna dance around all day?!" he demanded.

"Why wouldn't I? Parrying is for chumps who don't know how to get out of the way. The kinda thing *you'd* do! Hrah!"

Hmph. He managed to block again. Turned out his excessively long sword had some benefits after all: the thick, wide blade was doubling as a shield. If my own blade kept slamming into that thing, it'd chip away into nothing. I needed to wrap up this fight quick.

I switched from slashes to thrusts. Swift and strong, the sword-point driving head-on. He could parry these all he liked. It'd only serve to throw him off-balance, leaving him more and more exposed with each successive strike. Pretty effective strategy, really. The kind of thing an idiot could never hope to come up with.

"Glad we two Attackers finally got to find out who was stronger," I sneered.

I drew my arm back for a final strike.

"Die!" I thrust my sword straight into No. 3's undefended gut, only to see a grin spread across his lips. Huh? Why was he smiling?

"You're mine now."

I felt a hand clamp down onto my right arm, holding it firmly in place. I was unable to withdraw my blade. I couldn't believe it. Had he taken the hit on purpose, just so he could pin me down? Could he get any stupider?

"Let go!" I shouted.

My upper arm was locked in an iron grip. I could only move my wrist, so I did, dragging the sword back and forth and ripping up No. 3's insides. The pain should have been agonizing, but No. 3 didn't make any move to release me.

"I said *let go*!"

What the hell was this? My opponent was *No. 3*. Stupidity incarnate. How had *he* managed to immobilize me?

"Graaaaah!"

More of his crude bellowing . . . Wait. This noise was coming from my own mouth. No. 3 had plunged his sword deep into my shoulder, and I'd let out an earsplitting scream.

I heard his voice. It seemed somehow distant. "Oops. Missed."

Shit. He must have been aiming for the left half of my chest. I gave my body a sudden twist. *Ow, ow, ow, ow!* Damn moron! What did he think he was trying to do? I had to get away, and fast.

It wasn't clear how long we went on like that, but at some point, I realized my right arm was free again. No. 3 was lying faceup on the ground, the gaping hole in his stomach now large enough to fit my fist through. Exposed beneath the shredded skin was his mangled abdominal unit. How had he been able to bear that kind of damage and keep going? I wished he'd just die already.

"*This* is why I didn't want . . . to be paired . . . with such an . . . imbecile . . ."

Pretty soon, I'd lost the strength to stand, too. I wanted to pull out the sword lodged in my chest, but my arms couldn't summon the strength to do so. I slumped to my knees in a disgraceful display. Disgust filled me as I realized I might pitch forward, planting my face in the mud. I'd be covered in filth.

If I'd known this was how it was going to play out, I'd have simply stabbed him dead from behind. Would've been easy. No. 3 was always leaving his back wide open.

"Yeah. Next time . . . that's exactly how I'll . . ."

The rumbling of the explosions faded to nothing, along with the stench of mud and moss.

[Log Entry: No. 22 / Deep-Sea Base]

"What did I do that for?"

No. 6 gave a pained smile. Just moments ago, he'd stumbled over the remains of a dead machine, causing him to pitch forward and slam into No. 21. The accident had saved No. 21's life.

"Not exactly like me to . . . take the hit for somebody else, y'know?"

The Attacker appeared to shrug, but the gesture looked

rather odd thanks to his missing shoulder. A sudden burst of enemy fire had ripped through his right arm, shearing the entire limb from his body and sending it tumbling across the ground. It now lay a short distance away, riddled with holes like a beehive, its hand still clutching No. 6's sword.

"Just hurry up and move!" No. 4 yelled. "We're almost at the server room!"

No. 6 was leaning against one wall, probably using it to support his weight. But instead of continuing down the corridor, he slumped, sliding down the wall until he was sitting on the ground with his legs splayed in front. The rest of us were too busy dealing with the enemy reinforcements still pressing in on our position. We couldn't afford to offer a shoulder to hoist him back to his feet or even drag him down the corridor.

"Go! Leave this to me!" No. 4 barked.

"Are you sure?" I protested. "The enemy'll . . ."

I knew he was right, though. No matter how many rounds I fired, the enemy's numbers never seemed to thin. If anything, it felt like the opposite: for each one I shot down, more inexplicably appeared. The deep-sea base wasn't even that large to begin with. Where had all these machines been hiding?

We'd been tasked with neutralizing the enemy's undersea server. This single server provided orders for all the enemy's forces in the vicinity; if we managed to take it out, the machines themselves would cease to function.

The plan called for No. 21 to hack the server. I was to ensure his safety throughout the mission. No. 4 and No. 6 would provide operational support; they'd hold off enemy forces and secure us an exit route. No. 3 was away from the fray this time, taking care of guard duty for No. 9.

Usually, No. 21 and I were among the first deaths in any given mission. That was how it had been last time in the Desert Zone, and the time before that in the Wetlands Zone. But this time, it was imperative to mission success that we not check out before our objective was complete.

"No. 22! I'm serious! Get going!"

"Y-yes, sir!"

I took a glimpse over my shoulder at No. 21. He was fine. No injuries whatsoever.

"Sorry to put this all on your shoulders, No. 4."

I mumbled my embarrassed apology, and then No. 21 and I took off, dashing down the corridor. If No. 21 was damaged, the op would be a failure. Seeing him to the server room unharmed was my top priority. Nothing else mattered.

I hit a switch on the wall as we ran by. There was a grinding sound, and a bulkhead door slowly sealed off the portion of corridor we'd left behind. The whole base was filled with similar dividers. It was a means to prevent flooding—a ready way to block off any given corridor or section in case of a breach. Our squad had tried closing a few of the bulkhead doors on the way in; we thought they might help cut off pursuing machines, but the strategy brought limited success. This was, after all, their own base.

Still, it was worth a shot. We had to press onward. We had a mission to carry out. As we left the bulkhead door behind, we heard a great roar from the other side. No. 4 had probably attempted to blow the corridor apart, along with any machines bearing down on him. It was a last-ditch measure, but as the squad's other Gunner, I was painfully aware of how low we were running on ammo.

I blocked it from my mind and put everything I had into the final sprint. We didn't stop until the entrance to the server room was just ahead.

When the door was in sight, No. 21 approached slowly and whispered, "Careful. Enemy units inside."

"How many?"

It was a pointless question, one I'd asked on reflex. We stood at the threshold of the enemy's heart. For such a critical location to be unguarded was unthinkable, and given the intensity of the enemy's jamming signal here on the facility's deepest level, No. 21 wouldn't be able to run scans to determine the number or positioning of enemy units. He had visual confirmation of at least one enemy inside. That was all the detail we had.

"Think we can manage a forced entry?"

"Yeah. Let's go for it."

His response was positive, but I knew that wasn't a reflection of our chance of success. It was because we didn't have any other options—we'd have to rush straight in and hope for the best. I was the only one left to handle whatever we encountered inside. Success rested entirely on my shoulders.

"Here we go!"

On my signal, we dove through the door in tandem. I centered my sights on the nearest enemy and let loose. No need to conserve ammo at this point. If it meant getting No. 21 access to the server, I might as well burn through it all.

We kept low, steadily making our way across the room. I was point shooting anything that moved, my gun blazing nonstop. When I'd somehow managed to finish all the enemy units off, I ran back to secure the door, then fired a round into its control panel. That'd buy us some time, at least until the machines broke the door down.

"Shit . . . " I heard No. 21 mutter.

"How's it look?" I asked. "Can you hack it?"

It took everything I had to keep my voice from faltering. I couldn't let No. 21 find out. He needed to concentrate.

He shook his head. "There're too many defensive layers. It'd take forever."

Apparently, a hack was out of the question. Physically destroying the server was our only option.

"But don't worry," he said. "We've got enough juice to blow a system of this size right out of the water."

He pulled out a box of explosives and gave it a light tap.

"Good. Countdown timer's still intact. We'll be long gone before the fireworks start."

"But we don't have an escape route," I protested. "There's no way No. 4 and No. 6 are still alive."

"Not a problem. A site like this usually has some kind of emergency access hatch. And it just so happens that this room is no exception."

No. 21 pointed toward one corner of the ceiling. At first

glance I didn't see anything out of the ordinary. It wasn't until I focused hard that I saw the faint square outline.

"If they've got a hatch, that means they've got another way to get in," I said. "If you crawl through there, you'll come head-to-head with their reinforcements."

"But once the server's dead, the machines stop moving. We'll be fine."

Then No. 21 added, "Of course, I guess that depends on how far along we are when we run into 'em."

I breathed a sigh of relief. "Good . . . You've thought this through."

We'd succeed in destroying the server, and No. 21 would get safely away.

"I'll set the bomb," I told him. "You climb up and start crawling."

"What are you talking about? We'll set it and leave together."

"No. That's, uh . . . not the way this is gonna go."

I carefully lifted the hand that I'd kept pressed hard against my side. No. 21's eyes went wide.

"One of their shots must've grazed me."

In truth, I knew the enemy had hit me dead-on, though I still hadn't ascertained exactly what was injured and to what extent. I was too afraid to look at the wound. That's how much of a coward I was.

"It'll be fine," I told him. "Just go. I can take care of this place all by myself."

There was another issue, which was that after clearing out the server room, I didn't have a single bullet left. So there wasn't much point in my running with him. A Gunner without ammunition was as good as no Gunner at all.

"I don't want to slow you down," I said.

"Don't say that! How could you say something so stupid?!" No. 21 raged.

He threw his arms around me.

"No," I told him. "Please. Don't do this . . ."

You need to hurry and get out of here, is what I wanted to say, but my lips wouldn't form the words. It felt so warm with him beside me. I didn't want to lose that comfort. I didn't want to be parted from him.

"There's no way I'm leaving you behind!"

"I'm sorry. I'm so sorry. This is all my fault. If I wasn't here—"

"Stop. Don't say that," he repeated. This time, it sounded almost gentle.

"What if it had been me?" he asked. "Would you have escaped alone if I was the one injured?"

No. Not in a million years. There was no way I'd be able to leave No. 21 behind and flee on my own.

And that's when I understood why. We'd always been together. Ever since the moment we stepped off the production line.

"I guess those were pretty stupid things to say . . ."

"Yup. And that's why you gotta listen to me. Just do what I tell you."

"Yeah. You're right."

I buried my face in his shoulder and whispered, "Thank you." It was strange. Now that I knew he'd stay with me, my pain seemed to fade into the background.

"Are you cold?" he asked.

"A little. But I'm all right. Everything feels still somehow, almost like when it's snowing."

"That's because we're 2,800 meters under the sea."

"And it's quiet, too," I added. "Like that day on the Bunker, when we looked out at Earth."

No. 21 took my hand and placed it against his cheek. I felt a bloom of warmth under my palm, and I understood that my vitals were fading. My failing auditory processes must have been the reason everything seemed so quiet. My deteriorating vision brought to mind the blackness of space.

Huh?

I heard a new noise. A kind of . . . sniffling.

No. 21? Was he weeping?

"Hey. It's all right, No. 21. I'm . . . I'm not afraid."

I'd always been a coward, but in that moment, I didn't feel the slightest bit of fear.

"You know why?" I said. "Because I have you here with me."

So please, don't cry. It'll be all right. I can't see anymore, and I can't hear. But I know you're still right beside me.

And there's nothing . . . nothing in the world that could make me happier . . .

[Log Entry: No. 9 / Deep-Sea Base]

Once we detected a thermal reaction at the estimated location of the server room, No. 3 and I proceeded to make our way inside the enemy's deep-sea base. Or, more precisely, we made our way inside what was left of the base.

By that point, the facilities were little more than deep-sea ruins. Areas not flooded with seawater were the exception, and now that the server was down, the resident machines had ceased to function—all of them, whether they were busted up or not. The fact that we were able to navigate the ruins in safety was thanks to No. 21 and No. 22. It seemed they'd laid down their lives to set the bomb and ensure its detonation.

In the corridor on the bottommost level, the first thing we came across was No. 6's lifeless body. Next, we found and recovered his black box, suspended in safe mode.

I set his self-repair routine to maximum speed and began assessing his injuries. Once I was done with that, the next step would be to . . .

It occurred to me that I'd grown quite accustomed to this process. It was a painful realization.

The right half of No. 6's frame was shattered and torn. Too bad it hadn't been his left side. His suffering would have been shorter. As it was, I had no doubt that he'd sat in agony for quite some time before the end finally came. His left hand was balled into a fist, fingernails lodged deep in his palm.

We continued down the corridor to find No. 4—or what I assumed to be No. 4. It was hard to tell, considering what little remained. What portion we did find was damaged far worse than No. 6. He seemed to have been caught in an explosion he'd triggered at close range—likely a last-resort measure taken to impede enemy movements and aid No. 21 and No. 22's safe passage to the server room.

I knew how hard they'd all fought. Initially, their comm systems were functioning, and I'd listened to the reports streaming in from the Support System units. The details were so graphic, I'd wanted to press my hands over my ears to block out the words. But eventually the enemy's jamming signal grew strong enough to drown out our equipment, and I'd been left to wonder how the rest of the mission played out.

It was always me alone, living on through mission after mission from the safety of the back lines.

"You doin' okay?"

"Oh. Yes." I turned to No. 3 to answer. "Sorry about that. I just spaced out for a moment."

No. 3 hadn't said much over the course of the operation, either. From the moment the forward units took off, he'd stood next to me in silence, his brow furrowed and ears trained on the choppy transmissions coming in from the SSUs. Assigned to keep me safe, he'd lived through this mission. But in countless previous operations, No. 3 had experienced . . . demise, just like the rest of our squadmates.

The YoRHa Experimental M Squadron, newly established and living up to the implications of its name, was being dispatched on all manner of combat missions so that Command could get an overall sense of our aptitudes. We fought against all sorts of machines—some were flying, some were giant, some were the enemy's latest models, and others came in endless legions. Perhaps precisely because of our experimental nature, the places to which we were dispatched inevitably featured some powerful foe never before encountered by androids. Thus, annihilation of all squad members dispatched to forward positions was the standard outcome in almost every operation we carried out.

I understood that we underwent these trials for the benefit of humanity. Despite our losses, our infiltration of the deep-sea base had been an operational success. We'd destroyed the server, paralyzing all enemies in the vicinity.

But it didn't change the fact that not a single one of our units down here had been able to make it back out.

After picking our way along a debris-filled corridor, No. 3 and I paused in front of a door that looked like it had seen better days.

"I think the server room should be just inside here," I said.

Or rather, that should have been the case, according to the blueprints provided by my SSU, but the door remained stubbornly closed. Unless we found a way to open it, I'd be unable to visually confirm the destruction of the server. To be honest, I was impressed that the door was still there at all, and that the immediate surroundings hadn't flooded. The facility seemed quite solidly built, which made sense, I supposed, considering the fact that it was the enemy's command center for the entire region.

"Damn thing won't open," No. 3 grumbled.

Maybe it had been locked from inside. Or maybe the door's control panel had been destroyed. Either way, it was likely a measure taken by No. 21 and No. 22 to keep the machines out. That's how desperate the situation must have been; the last two members of the squad had no other choice but to seal themselves inside with the bomb.

"Stand back, No. 9. I'll take care of it."

"Understood, sir."

"Already told you. You can quit with the 'sir' business. Call me 'No. 3.'"

Was it my imagination, or did No. 3's tone of voice seem a little more subdued than usual?

After some straining, he managed to pry the door open and declared, "There."

Acrid smoke billowed out from the gaping doorway. I stepped inside to find the server room still uncomfortably warm from the earlier explosion. The ceiling had caved in, and the floor was so littered with unidentifiable shards of metal that I found it difficult to make my way forward. I saw tangles of pipes and cables spilling out from holes in the walls, all half-melted and fused into clumps.

It took quite some time to find the two of them among the wreckage. I finally spotted them on the far side of the room, huddled in a corner, their curled-up figures having long since ceased to function. No. 21's back was charred a cruel black. He seemed to have draped his body over No. 22 in a futile, final protective act. He must have felt determined to keep his twin alive, right up to the bitter end. I remembered the words I'd heard him say to No. 22 time and time again. *I swear I'll keep you safe.*

No. 3 muttered, "Aw, hell," then fell silent once more.

Hell. There really wasn't a more accurate way to describe what we were seeing.

We recovered the two bodies from the server room and laid them faceup in the corridor. I began a more thorough assessment of their condition. While the most notable damage to No. 21 was his completely charred back, No. 22 had endured severe damage to his abdominal unit. Another wound indicated that a bullet had passed clean through his left shoulder, and there were countless nicks and scrapes across his frame where bullets must have grazed it. Clearly, No. 22 had done everything he could to shield his twin from damage until they made it to the server room.

How had No. 21 felt, watching his twin's life drain away? What thoughts had gone through his mind as he set the explosive device?

From the outset, I'd thought the operation absurd. We had no data whatsoever regarding enemy numbers or types inside the base, and we hadn't even been certain if our comm systems would function at all once inside. Sending a small squad of four to a place like this seemed irresponsible at best.

You're so strong. Honestly, I'm terrified.

No. 22's words suddenly flashed back into my mind. He'd said that just before we first rolled out. No. 21 had smiled and responded, *There's nothing to be afraid of.* I remembered his kind gaze as he delivered those words of comfort.

At the time, I don't think any of us really understood. Neither No. 21, nor I, nor even No. 22 in all his terror truly knew what it meant to die.

Only I still didn't know, even now.

I alone continued to live on, ignorant of something that my squadmates had come to know quite well. I was unable to do anything but watch. I was one of them, and yet I was not; they were united in a new circle, one which I would never be allowed to enter. And I would continue to stand by myself, apart from my squadmates. To do so was my job.

[Log Entry: No. 21 / Base Camp]

I was feeling, maybe for the first time ever, a sense of panic. It was like being burned by a flame from the inside, or pricked by hundreds of tiny thorns pressed against my skin. Yes. I was definitely panicking. If things continued to play out this way, I wouldn't be able to guarantee No. 22's safety.

Even worse, I'd already failed to protect him, time and time again.

You're so strong. Honestly, I'm terrified.

I'd sworn to keep him safe back then. I told him he'd never have to feel scared. Yet here I was, failing to keep my promise.

The battlefield was an endless stream of surprises. My recon could be as accurate and detailed as possible, but I'd still never be able to cover all the variables. Enemies far exceeding my best predictions would routinely show up and unleash devastating assaults. It didn't take long for me to learn that the unexpected is par for the course in war.

In fact, my recon and intel were usually close to perfect right up until the fighting began. The problem was that everything came undone as soon as the first enemy appeared or the first shot was fired. Then I'd be back to square one, running recon and gathering data from scratch. I was determined to maintain a perfect picture of the situation, so I dedicated every spare cycle of my AI to make sure it happened. We needed that data.

If I could have it ready one second or even one microsecond faster, all the better.

If I failed to keep up, defeat awaited us. But the machines' tactics got more sophisticated by the day. At first, they'd just relied on their greater numbers as a means to overcome us. Soon, they were making use of the terrain or inclement weather to launch surprise attacks.

The damn things were learning. They were evolving.

Of course, so were we. We learned, and we evolved. Each battle we fought meant an inevitable boost to our skills. Pretty soon, though, it was obvious that increased skill alone wasn't going to cut it. We needed something more. That's where I came in. Taking a combat disadvantage and turning it to our favor, or turning a tiny weakness into something we could exploit—those were the duties of the Scanner.

I needed data. I craved it. Anything, no matter how trivial. Info about the composition and layout of the terrain, or of typical weather patterns at our next insertion point. I'd never be able to finalize intel on enemy types, numbers, and formations until we were in the thick of it, but information about the battlefield itself was something I could amass and analyze beforehand.

Survey data collected from the surface. Survey data collected from orbit. New data. Old data. Any data. I took it all and crammed it into my memory banks.

In the real world, there was no such thing as absolute certainty. Facilitatory conditions could nudge probability exponentially closer to 100% or 0%, but you could never say for certain that something would or wouldn't happen. So no matter how dire the situation was, our chances of success were never actually nil. It was my job was to pull us as far away from zero as I could possibly manage.

If the enemies were so great in number, packed so tight you couldn't see the spaces to maneuver between them, where could you find the aberration that might lead to victory in that situation? In the topography? The weather?

I needed more. Something new. I'd already run simulations like this for every battle we'd been through.

"Hey, do you have a sec?" At some point, No. 22 must have wandered near.

I cut him off. "Sorry. Can it wait until later?"

I had only so much time until the next operation.

"Oh, right. You're working. Sorry. I always bother you like that."

It was an overstatement, of course. He wasn't *always* bothering me. Not by any stretch of the imagination. No. 22 generally knew quite thoroughly what tasks I'd be working on and when. The problem was that my tasks had begun to consume more and more time. With each new sortie, my pool of past data to reference grew larger, and so I had more to work through.

That was when it hit me.

Things to reference. Past battles. Of course.

What if I went back further? I could analyze engagements between androids and machines in past wars. Not on a scale of decades or even centuries. I could go back *thousands* of years. I could take into account every surviving record of every battle that had ever taken place in the geographic location in question. Machine lifeforms learned and evolved through every encounter they had with any group of androids. I could do the same: with comprehensive knowledge of all past engagements, I might find a useful trend or consistent pattern in the enemy's behavior—some key that could turn the tide in our favor. At the very least, I could look for some tiny way to shore up our strategy in time for the next op. It would make our mission that much easier.

My next task, then, was figuring out where combat records like that might be stored. The main server was a good bet, but since data like that likely wasn't accessed often, it'd probably be a real pain to dig up. Still, it was worth a try.

I'd alert the instructor and file an immediate request with Command for access to—

No. If I went through the usual request process, I'd never have the data in time.

"This is a case of act now, report later."

I decided to give myself permission to dive in. This was exactly what they meant when they talked about unauthorized access, but it wouldn't be a problem so long as I didn't get caught. In fact, even if Command *did* figure out what I'd done, I felt certain they wouldn't say a word if it meant the operation went well. Right now, the only thing that mattered was time, and I couldn't afford to waste any more of it.

The main server turned out to be surprisingly easy to hack. Sure, there were a few heavy security measures in place, but compared to the hell I'd been through hacking the machines' servers, it was like pushing my way through a wall made of paper. I made a mental note: sometime when we all had a bit of breathing room, it might be worthwhile to file a report suggesting we reinforce server security.

Once I was in, I began to look around. As expected, the top levels didn't house the combat records I was after. I dove deeper, pushing my way through additional server defenses.

How had this idea not occurred to me earlier? I cursed my own shortsightedness. Or maybe this was how it had to be. Maybe it was *because* we'd suffered so many defeats that the thought first emerged. Wasn't there a human saying to that effect? "Desperation breeds innovation," or something like that? If so, it shed new light on Command's approach with our squadron; they never granted permission to abort an op or withdraw, no matter how hopeless the situation became. Maybe it wasn't as absurd a stance as I'd assumed.

As I made my way deeper into the server, I encountered a sudden increase in security. The barriers weren't just blocking the way anymore; they were actively *attacking* me. It made sense, I guess. This deep, there was bound to be all kinds of highly classified data tucked away.

Still, no server was about to make a fool out of a cutting-edge

Scanner model. I deftly deflected the attacks and continued my search.

"Hm? What's this?"

The files I was after were still nowhere to be found. But I'd stumbled across something else.

"What the . . . ?" I murmured.

Once I started reading what I'd found, I couldn't stop.

YoRHa Boys Ver. 1.05

CHAPTER 4

[Log Entry: No. 9 / Mountain Zone—Military Trench]

THE SKY ABOVE OUR NEWLY DUG TRENCH WAS A
BRILLIANT BLUE. Just beyond the lip of the trench, peeking
above the spoil pile like lace trim, was the mountain's black
ridgeline. From where we stood, the mountain didn't seem
particularly tall, but I knew its peak was over 3,000 meters
above sea level—a towering giant that was right at home here
in the Mountain Zone.

Even this area where we'd dug the trench was at a considerable altitude. Which made sense, since keeping the high
ground in relation to the enemy was one of the ABCs of battlefield strategy. Well, it was according to No. 21, anyway.

No. 22 piped up with, "Hey, No. 21, look! I wonder what
kind of bird that is."

A black shadow soared through the patch of sky beyond
No. 22's outstretched finger. The sound of artillery fire roared
in the distance. No. 21 looked up just a bit too late.

"What bird?"

"Way up high. It's flying around and . . . Oh! It just landed
on that tree over there."

"Does it matter what it's called? This really isn't the time for
bird-watching."

At No. 21's sharp response, No. 22's mood shifted to silent
and sullen. It was hard to say either of them was in the wrong,
but I decided to offer No. 22 support first.

"Hey, no need to be like that. No. 22's just trying to ease
the tension a little. How about we all take a deep breath and
relax?"

But the lines furrowed across No. 21's brow only deepened. I knew he had to be racking his brain, trying to determine the best possible mission strategy; probably more than ever, in fact, considering the unusual nature of our current op. Command had picked up a distress signal inside enemy territory. We were to check it out and extract whoever it was that needed help.

That was the idea in a nutshell, anyway. But there were complications. The signal originated from somewhere deep in the Mountain Zone. Traversing the area would be difficult enough, but to make matters worse, the signal originated in an area particularly rife with hostiles. And the terrain and enemy presence prevented us from establishing communications; as a result, we didn't even know who exactly we were trying to help. I had my own theory, of course: it was probably a member of one the many Resistance groups active down here on the surface.

We were no strangers to fights against overwhelming odds. Nor, at this point, did we lack experience fighting on difficult terrain. But we'd never been tasked with a rescue op, and we'd never made contact with a non-YoRHa android on the surface. So No. 21's consternation didn't surprise me; there were a lot of unknowns for our Scanner to try to account for.

We had to locate the target, proceed with the extraction, and make it back alive. This time, success required survival. Rushing in with a suicide mentality wasn't an option. And yet we still faced the usual quantity of enemies, at their usual strength, and with the terrain generally working in their favor.

So there we were in the trench. No. 3, No. 4, and No. 6 had gone ahead to scout out the area and note possible entry routes. The location we'd inserted at was supposed to have a comparatively low concentration of enemy units—the key word being "comparatively."

No. 22 hadn't accompanied the others on the scouting efforts because No. 21 had been assigned to the rear. Instructor Black felt that we'd be better off having our Scanner perform wide-area scans from the back lines this time around.

It occurred to me that it had been a long time since the three of us were together during an op. For some time now, No. 21 and No. 22 had been consistently assigned to forward roles, which inevitably involved charging headfirst into heavily-occupied enemy territory.

"I just wanted to know what it was called," No. 22 ventured hesitantly.

He was talking about the bird, but the words implied something more. I knew what he meant, and I'd long since realized I felt the same way. We were giving everything we had to a war meant to reclaim a planet we didn't even know.

"And the names of other things, too . . ." No. 22 continued. "I want to know all about the earth. It's our home. We should take the time to get to know it."

Hmm. It seemed his perspective was a little different from mine. Still, our feelings would've come from basically the same place. Of course, I'd never dare speak the conclusion *I'd* come to out loud. I knew it was a pretty negative outlook, the kind of thing that would make anyone who heard me feel uncomfortable. And on top of that—

There was an odd sound, like a faint whistling.

"Do either of you hear that?" I asked.

I put my previous thoughts on hold and examined the area around the trench.

"What are you talking about?" No. 21 replied, head tilted quizzically. "I don't hear anything."

It felt like something was heading toward us, and that it was getting close—like it was almost on top of us.

That was when it clicked for me. It was *literally* almost on top of us. I glanced up to confirm pure terror falling fast.

"Get down!" I shouted. "It's an EMP bomb!"

I didn't think. I just reacted, throwing up my defense shield, praying that I'd been fast enough—that the shield would materialize in time. Out of the corner of my eye, I saw No. 21 tackling No. 22 to the ground. Light exploded everywhere. There was a millisecond of silence, and then the roar of the blast washed over us.

When the explosion subsided, I checked myself over. I didn't appear to be damaged and felt a rush of relief. My shield must have held up.

But a piercing scream drove that relief away. I recognized the voice as No. 22's, yet at the same time, it sounded like the cry of an animal. I whirled around to find him writhing on the ground.

"It's . . . it's inside my circuits! No. 9! Help me!"

"Just stay calm! I'm on it!"

I pulled an injector out of my field repair kit and jammed it into the back of No. 22's neck. I needed to halt the enemy nanomachines before they got too deep into his circuits—that was the standard mechanism for any logic virus. As I observed No. 22's state, I silently prayed that this particular virus wasn't some new variant we'd not encountered.

His arms and legs stopped spasming. He was out cold from the treatment, but we'd been lucky—it looked like this virus was one of the enemy's usual standbys.

"You're all right now," I murmured quietly.

So long as he got enough rest, he'd regain consciousness and be back to normal.

"Wait," No. 21 said, a worried look on his face.

He pulled out his Support System unit.

"Based on the data, every time the enemy launches an EMP attack, they always follow up with—"

The tinny voice of the SSU finished his thought. "Scan complete. Machine lifeforms inbound from all directions. Hostile force exceeds 2,300 units—"

No. 21 exhaled heavily as he muted the SSU. Were we out of options? Surely there had to be *something* we could do.

"Wait. Maybe there's something in our rules of engagement directives that can help."

I directed my SSU to search the documentation for anything applicable to our current situation. I had to control my voice to keep it from breaking.

The unit's robotic response came cold and uncaring. "No applicable resources found."

No. 21 shook his head. "It's no use. No. 22's the only combat model here, and he's non-functional."

"But—" I protested weakly.

"I'm telling you, there isn't a combat strategy in existence that would give a single Healer and a single Scanner a fighting chance against these odds."

We could hear them now: the faint crunching of countless mechanical limbs on rocky terrain. The approaching forces were still a ways off, but I knew it was only a matter of time.

Neither No. 6 nor the M001 units were here to protect us. In a stroke of bad luck, the instructor happened to be away, too. He'd headed off just minutes beforehand, hoping to find a spot with some semblance of proper reception in order to make his regularly scheduled contact with Command.

I looked back at No. 22. There was no way he'd regain consciousness in time. His rifle lay beside him, unceremoniously dumped to the ground during his earlier convulsions. The weapon seemed almost lonely, as if pleading with its downed owner to wake up and bear it once more.

"You're wrong," I announced to No. 21. "There *is* something we can do."

I reached out and lifted the rifle from the ground. Even holding it with both hands, it was so heavy I thought I might tip over. But our enemies were on their way. We couldn't just sit here doing nothing.

It wasn't like I didn't know how to shoot. Even Healers went through basic firearms training. I managed to get the butt of the rifle up and braced against my right shoulder, steadying the forestock with my left hand. The machines had entered visual range. I shifted my right hand into position on the grip.

The moment I pulled the trigger, my shoulder and neck violently jerked back; my balance faltered and I fell, rear end ungracefully planted on the ground. The weapon's kick was a lot stronger than I'd anticipated.

"Don't be stupid! That weapon is designed for *Gunners*! We can't just pick it up and expect to be able to handle it!"

No. 21 ran to my side and helped me up. I knew he was right, but I still didn't want to admit it.

"I . . . I can't just give up."

I rose to my feet, consciously locking both knees as I leveled the rifle once more.

"You really are a fool," No. 21 muttered.

But suddenly the barrel felt lighter. I realized No. 21 was standing beside me, his hand helping me steady the weapon.

"Huh? What are you doing?"

"You just concentrate on bracing and firing. I'll worry about the aiming."

I popped out the weapon's link cable; No. 21 took it and plugged it into his own ear.

"I'm not saying I think this'll work," he said. "But it's got a better chance than you shooting alone."

"Got it."

"All right. Here they come. Gimme two bursts on my mark!"

He began a countdown. When he said "Fire," I pulled the trigger. The barrel shuddered violently. I released the trigger, then squeezed it again. I was holding on for dear life. I couldn't see anything, but I heard several explosions. They seemed to come from somewhere far ahead.

"Did . . . did we get them?"

No. 21 let go of the weapon and straightened up briefly to survey our work. He seemed satisfied and nodded, with a decisive, "That'll do." Our shots had found their mark. We'd managed to thin the enemy's ranks. There was hope after all.

"Let's keep it up," No. 21 ordered. "We'll mow each wave of 'em down as they get clo—"

The crackling hiss of a laser streaking through the air drowned out the rest of his words. The next thing I knew, we were both flung backward and slammed against the ground.

"No. 21!" I shouted, looking around.

I sprang to my feet. I seemed to be uninjured. My companion, however, wasn't so lucky.

"Stay . . . down . . ." he said. "They must have a . . . laser sniper unit somewhere . . ."

No. 21 held his shoulder and grimaced as he spoke. Clearly, we weren't going to be firing the rifle anymore. Aside from No. 22's weapon, we had nothing we could use to resist the machines.

"What now? Is this the end for us?"

No. 22 lay unconscious. No. 21 was now injured. That left me and me alone. The machines were still pressing in on our position. I wasn't even able to defend myself against the enemy, much less launch a counterattack.

What were the machines doing here in the first place? This was supposed to be our rear line. It was supposed to be *safe* here.

The advancing machines came to a sudden halt. I could see and hear them clearly now. They always paused like this just before they opened fire. All I could do was stare as they slowly rotated and readied their armaments.

Just as I'd come to terms with the fact that all was lost, a violent burst of wind blew through our position. Enemy units clattered to the ground one after another, suddenly lifeless.

"Aw, hell. Looks like the machines got you pretty good, huh?"

It took me another moment to process what had happened. That was no mere gust of wind. Another android had swept in, and now he was moving from one end of the enemy line to the other, slashing machines apart with ease.

"No. 3 . . . ?" I gaped. "Is it really you? You came back for us, sir!"

"How many times do I gotta tell ya? Cut the 'sir' crap!"

No. 3 tugged his visor up and wiped the sweat from his brow.

"'Course, I gotta admit, the way you insist on doin' things the right way is kinda charming." He grinned as he spoke.

All I could focus on was the machine lurking just over his shoulder.

"No. 3!" I shouted. "Behind you!"

He turned, only for a blur of metal to rush at his face. It happened so fast, I couldn't tell if it was a punch or a kick, but at any rate, the machine was bearing down on him. No. 3 was done for.

Once more, my dread was cut short; this time, an even-tempo volley of gunfire signaled deliverance. The looming machine burst apart, fragments of metal arcing through the sky before pattering down as steel rain across our surroundings.

"And how many times have I told *you*," a gruff voice said, "to stay focused. You've got a bad habit of letting your attention wander every time you finish something off."

I brought a hand to my chest in relief. No. 4 had come back as well.

"Get your visor back on!" he yelled at No. 3. "The fight's not over yet!"

No. 4 dropped to one knee, fire spitting from his dual guns. Machine lifeforms around us crumpled one by one.

"Are you *ever* gonna stop being so uptight? Quit nagging me," No. 3 retorted, but he pulled his visor back down over his eyes before hefting his sword again. The next wave of approaching machines didn't even have time to shift into attack mode before they were cut down.

"Gotta say, it's painful watching you M001 units work. You could really use a lesson in efficiency. And in *finesse*."

No. 6 appeared as well, the flat of his blade resting against one shoulder. Though he'd said "M001 units," I felt reasonably sure he was referring to No. 3 specifically. Even No. 6 would have to admit that there was no lack of precision in No. 4's shots.

The enemy forces continued to grow in number, as they always did, but somehow I felt like things were going to be okay. No. 6 and the two M001 units were with us now. They'd probably seen the EMP bomb in the sky and estimated it hit somewhere near our position, or perhaps they'd suspected something was up when our comms cut out. In either case, what mattered is that they'd rushed back to check on us.

"Hey!" No. 3 yelled, his eyes on No. 6. "Less talking, more killing. Get to it!"

"Yeah, yeah."

And then, before he could be bothered to add another word, No. 6 was leaping through the air. Two more machines were sputtering sparks by the time his feet touched the ground, but his show was just getting started. The length of his sword gleamed through his deadly dance, and before I knew it, he'd mopped up every single machine in the vicinity.

"Happy now, tough guy?"

"That's 'tough guy, *sir*,' to you!"

"In your dreams."

The fact that they had time to banter signaled that the tide had turned; the enemy had begun to withdraw.

"No. 9! Deal with No. 21's wounds before the machines regroup!" No. 4 ordered.

"Yes, sir!"

I turned back to No. 21 to assess his injuries. This wasn't a time to be basking in relief. The machines often acted this way—when they realized they were outmatched, they'd withdraw just long enough to replenish their ranks. They'd be back, and in greater numbers. Out here on the battlefield, we couldn't afford to let our guard down for even a moment.

"Shit. Machines got you pretty good, didn't they?" No. 6 said as he peered over my shoulder.

No. 21's face was contorted in pain. Now that we were out of the woods—for the time being, anyway—his body had probably begun to register the pain.

The wound went a lot deeper than I'd imagined.

"Instructor!" No. 3 shouted.

A sense of relief washed through me. The instructor had returned. He quickly sized up the situation and immediately walked toward me.

"Status report," he ordered.

"Sir! Immediately following an enemy EMP attack, we realized No. 22's circuits had been flooded with a logic virus. I managed to stabilize him. No. 21 then sustained an injury while—"

No. 21 hastily stood, interrupting my explanation with, "I was hit by enemy sniper fire, but I'm fine. I can keep going, sir."

"Very good," the instructor replied, sweeping his gaze over

the lot of us. "Command has been able to pinpoint the broadcast location of the distress signal. It's about five klicks from our current position. The signal is still active, so we assume the distressed party is alive. The mission is to go ahead as planned. Make sure your equipment's ready to go. We move out in fifteen minutes."

Fifteen minutes. That was all the time I had. Was I going to be able to have both No. 21 and No. 22 up and running?

"It'd save us all a lot of trouble if this 'distressed party' could just kick the bucket already," No. 6 muttered. He didn't say it so loud as to suggest open defiance, but at the same time, I had a hard time believing the instructor wasn't meant to catch it. I assumed his comments weren't about personal objection so much as relaying the general sentiment that this mission was hopeless.

"Sir!"

"What is it, No. 21?" the instructor responded.

"Considering M Squadron's experimental nature, it would stand to reason that we are not currently suited for a rescue operation. Perhaps we could put in a request with Command for some backup, sir?"

No. 21 seemed to have chosen his words carefully. Every time we'd asked for permission to withdraw or abort an operation, the request had been immediately denied. Asking for support was a new approach. I had to at least give him credit for ingenuity, even though everyone present knew the new angle was unlikely to yield any new results.

"I already tried that." No. 4 made the comment in a matter-of-fact way, even though internally he must have wanted to sigh.

"There's been no response to that request as of yet from Command," the instructor said.

"Hmm, now I wonder why that might be?" No. 6's sarcastic remark was accompanied by a sinister smile.

"I can think of two reasons," No. 4 replied. The fact that he bothered to respond to No. 6's quip underscored his excessively earnest nature.

"Either there's a problem with the communications equipment," he continued, "or their failure to respond is . . . intentional."

"But why would they ignore us?" I asked.

It was a question I knew no one here could answer. I couldn't help but ask it anyway.

"Who knows?" No. 4 responded. "Too many variables at work, and I don't really feel like playing a guessing game anyway."

All this while, the instructor had stood in silence, listening to our exchange. Finally, he spoke. "Whatever the answer, it's irrelevant. We are to follow protocol and prepare for the rescue operation."

He added a terse, "Now get yourselves ready. *On the double.*"

And with that, he walked away.

I heard a small sigh, though I wasn't sure who it came from. Based on No. 3's next comment, I could at least assume it wasn't him.

"How 'bout we quit arguin' over stupid details and get on with it? Let's bust our way in and kill some damn machines."

After our recovery work in the deep-sea base, something about No. 3's attitude seemed to have shifted. He'd become a little too eager to fight, and it didn't sit right with me. How could somebody be anxious to rush into battle again after witnessing the carnage of the other day? Maybe he'd snapped. Maybe the experience had steeled some inner resolve.

"If you wanna throw your life away with some piss-poor excuse for a strategy, be my guest. But keep the rest of us out of it," No. 4 sniffed.

"Yeah?! Well, if the machines haven't killed you by the time this is over, you can bet your ass I'll be happy to finish the job."

I doubted that No. 4 actually wished for No. 3 to head off to certain death, just as I didn't think No. 3 would ever really follow through on his threats to kill No. 4. Probably not, anyway.

"Radio silence from Command, an instructor so rigid he'd snap before he bent a rule, and a stream of constant bickering from the two senior-most members of the squad. Got dealt a real winning hand here, didn't I?"

I'd heard enough from No. 6 that comments like this no longer surprised me. Still, I'd noted a change in him, too. His quips seemed to be growing more acerbic by the day.

"C'mon, No. 22. Time to gear up," No. 21 said. He attempted to haul his downed twin to his feet.

I tried to intervene. "Stop! No. 22 needs rest. He still hasn't—"

Regained consciousness, I'd intended to say, but right at that moment, No. 22's eyelids fluttered ever so slightly.

"Are you okay?" I asked.

"Yeah," he replied weakly. "Sorry for the trouble, No. 9."

He still seemed to be in quite a bit of pain. Forget combat—in his current state, *walking* would still be a battle. When I suggested as much, No. 21 answered for his twin.

"He's fine. A few more minutes and he'll be good to go."

"You can't be serious! He needs to lie down! His auto-repair function will be able to restore the damaged circuits, but the process will take time to—"

"Well, we can't delay the op! Not 'cause we were careless enough to get hurt!"

There was nothing more I could say. Nobody would be more worried about No. 22's safety than his twin.

"I'm . . . I'm fine. Really. I'll . . . be ready to go . . . any second now . . ." No. 22 said.

The way he struggled to get the words out made me certain that he was in excruciating pain. Still, I could only nod in response.

And for who knew how many times in just as many days, I repeated the same question that was stuck in my mind.

What in the world is Command thinking?

[Log Entry: Phlox / Mountain Zone—Cave]

In my dream, I was digging a well.

The location seemed familiar. We were at a campsite. When had I been here last?

The lake we'd been using as our source of potable water had dried up overnight; it seemed the machines had cooked up a new plot to kill us. Honestly, it was our own fault for not having a secondary source of water planned out. With no other options, we decided to see if we could manage to dig a well. I think it was the captain who came up with the idea. Or was it? I was hazy on the details.

At any rate, we were making progress until Lotus came along with his explosive charge. I tried to warn him. The fastest way to get to water—the surest way—was through good old-fashioned shoveling. But Lotus just couldn't accept that fact.

I heard the roar of the explosion and felt the tremor shake the ground. That was when I knew he was really going through with it. He'd undo all our work; the shaft we'd dug would collapse and fill back up, and we'd be back to square one. I had to stop him. I had to get the captain . . . *Captain!*

"Help! Somebody help!"

Captain Cactus's screaming brought me back to the waking world. The well-digging had been part of the dream, but his panicked cry definitely was not.

"What's the fuss, Cap? You having nightmares again?"

I rubbed the sleep from my own eyes and sat up. Next to me, the captain was trembling, still wrapped up in his sleeping bag. Even in the dim of the cave, I could clearly make out the beads of sweat oozing from his forehead.

"Phlox? Is that you? Oh, thank goodness . . . It was just a dream."

The dull roar of an explosion came from somewhere outside. Now I knew how Lotus's explosive charge had found its way into my dream. The sound was probably the source of the captain's nightmare, too.

"Just some survey bombing, Cap. Remember? They carpet the area, trying to use a bunch of noise and light to flush us out. Nothing to be worried about."

We'd spent three days hiding out in our makeshift stronghold. Honestly, I was getting a little fed up with the captain's touchy nerves—I thought he would have settled by now.

For his part, the captain seemed to be just as fed up with himself as I was.

"You don't have to explain. I know what it is," he pouted, cheeks puffed out like a sulky kid.

I figured I'd just wait until he calmed down and then try to go back to sleep. It wasn't like there was anything else to do down here. To tell the truth, pretending the cave was some kind of stronghold was optimistic at best. We were surrounded by the enemy. We couldn't have moved even if we wanted to.

A strange muttering echoed throughout the cave.

"So big. So big. So big!"

It took me a moment to realize it was Lotus. He was clutching a large box, tottering his way around the cave. The box was full of junk he'd apparently collected outside. He was *supposed* to have been scouting the area to get an update on enemy numbers. Instead, he'd been collecting garbage.

"So *big!* Yes, yes," he mumbled on.

"A big *catch*! A big *haul*! A big *trove* of treasures!" he continued, but it was all nonsense to me. The only thing I knew for sure was that his stash of junk had him just about as excited as I'd ever seen him before.

"A thermosensor, yes, yes, and a gravitational control unit. Quite costly, though. Not many chances to see these in action."

"Hey, um, Lotus?"

He didn't seem to hear me. He mumbled a bit more, then started laughing—a maniacal little giggle—which he followed with, "Fascinating! These must be the sights for an FFCS!"

"Hey! Lotus!" I shouted, loud enough to echo throughout the cave this time. I finally managed to catch his attention.

"Yes, yes. What is it?"

He didn't, however, bother to turn and face me. He continued gazing at his box of junk.

"How were things outside?"

"Isn't it obvious? Just look at it. Quite the haul! And no trouble gathering it. No, no. Very smooth. So many treasures in here. All quite uncommon. Quite uncommon, indeed."

"I'm talking about our *enemies*! The machines! What do their numbers look like? You *did* remember to check, right?"

"Goodness. Is that all you're interested in?"

Lotus glanced at me, his gaze now dreary.

"No change. No. Not much at all," he said.

Thank heaven. He hadn't abandoned his duties, despite the fervent attention he poured into his inane little hobby. I supposed, generally speaking, Lotus pulled his own weight despite his eccentricities; you just had to put up with his frequent miscommunications and puzzle out the odd explanations he gave.

A long time ago, someone had explained to me that humans referred to individuals exhibiting that kind of behavior as "socially awkward." The fact that the term existed at all told me there'd always been a few oddballs like Lotus around, ever since the dawn of human civilization.

Lotus wandered over to me with a piece of scrap in hand.

"Imagine that this here is our cave," he began, drawing a circle in the dirt.

"Now, this represents a five-kilometer radius," he continued, drawing another, much larger circle to encompass the first. "It's packed with machines. All active. All hostile. You get the picture, yes?"

Right. So not much had changed.

"Of course, there is the notable addition of the autoturrets." Lotus added a number of dots at irregular intervals around the smaller circle. Apparently they were supposed to represent turrets. "I modified several of our fallen foes and placed them strategically, you see. In the general vicinity of the entrance to the cave."

"Which means," he concluded in triumph, "we are quite safe here for the time being."

"U-um! But what happens when the enemy takes out the turrets? Won't they storm in and kill us all?!" The captain had crawled over to peer at Lotus's makeshift map. He pointed at the inner circle as he posed his uncomfortable question.

It seemed he'd given up on the idea of getting back to sleep. Maybe the scenes of his latest nightmare were still floating around his mind.

"Of course not. The turrets are distributed quite randomly. No way to deduce our position. None at all."

That explained the peculiar spacing of the dots. Lotus had undoubtedly also set each turret facing in a random direction. They'd have scored more kills if aimed strategically along the likely enemy approach lines, but that kind of positioning would be a dead giveaway of *who*, *where*, and *what* the emplacement was meant to protect. What seemed to be an inefficient method at first would in the end provide us with the surest results.

It was the same logic behind digging a well by hand.

"Oh! And there's more," Lotus continued. "If the enemy manages to take down a turret? Not a problem. None at all. A lovely virus infects whichever machine happens to attack last. One turret lost, another one gained!"

Did that mean the virus could keep taking out enemies one by one until the whole area was clear? With every machine in the vicinity dead or turned into a friendly autoturret, maybe we could just waltz on out.

My idea was shot down before I could voice it.

"Of course, with each additional casualty," Lotus clarified, "the machines will place themselves on higher alert, until eventually the whole region will simply be carpet bombed. They have very large bombs, you know. Extremely large. Will blast craters a few dozen meters deep. Yes, yes. This little cave of ours won't stand a chance."

I hadn't given the machines enough credit. The Resistance had been locked in battle with them for ages, and it wasn't like the things were gonna fold thanks to one measly virus.

The captain tilted his head skyward and muttered, "Heaven help us."

Not that you could see the sky from in here.

Lotus cleared his throat. "Do try to keep in mind that our whole predicament is your fault, dear captain."

"*My* fault? How do you figure that?"

"Leading us deep into enemy territory. Eyes lusting after treasure, unable to resist."

"Wh-what?! I'm doing everything I can to . . . "

The captain faltered and his gaze fell bit by bit. Lotus's remark seemed to have hit home. Our resident eccentric was intelligent enough—I'd give him that. But he never seemed to understand when not to cross the line.

"That's enough, Lotus," I chided.

Yeah, it was true that the captain had been a little too focused on his prize. But the blame for our situation didn't rest entirely on his shoulders.

I eyed Lotus and said, "When we first arrived in the area, all the machines were dormant. No activity to show up on our scans. There was no way we could've known what we were walking into."

"Yes, yes," Lotus nodded, calmly acquiescing to my point. "I suppose that's true."

He didn't know when to hold back, but at the same time, when explicitly told to lay off, he didn't continue to push. Lotus was a lot to deal with, but that didn't mean he was a bad guy. It was just all those little miscommunications and the fact that you always had to puzzle out the things he said—in other words, all the social awkwardness.

The captain looked at me with the eyes of an abandoned puppy. "What are we supposed to do now, Phlox?"

I suppressed an urge to snap back that *he* was supposed to be the one in charge.

"Well, Lotus's autoturrets will keep us safe for now, but apparently we can't afford to just sit tight forever. At the same time, we don't exactly have any tricks up our sleeve for getting out of here. And then there's the issue of this little item . . ."

I flicked my gaze toward the large container positioned at the very center of the cave.

"I'd say our only real option is to wait it out and hope that *someone* happens to notice the signal this thing's been blaring nonstop."

The container was tall and narrow, standing about the same height as me, and damn heavy. Not that we'd weighed it or anything, but I was willing to bet it had to be at least seven or eight hundred kilos.

"Ah, yes. The signal. Who knows? Hard to tell," Lotus said, as he eyed it doubtfully.

We had no idea what was actually inside the container. It had a panel that looked like it might open—some kind of lid or door—but it required a passcode. The code had us stumped, and the container itself was impregnable. We couldn't even put a scratch on the thing with the equipment we had on hand, much less break it open.

"If you ask me," Lotus continued, "pinning all our hopes onto this mystery box is a bit misguided."

"How could you say that?!" the captain cried. He jumped to his feet and puffed out his chest.

"This right here is a product of the Council of Humanity. Grade-A equipment from the moon itself!"

Of course, that was just speculation—or, more bluntly, the captain's hopeful longing.

"Think of how much money we could make selling the contents off to some other Resistance group!" he continued. "We'd be living the high life then. Open your eyes, you nitwit!"

"Uh, Cap?" I began. "Don't forget that we're part of the Council's army too. I mean, I appreciate a good, honest opinion as much as the next guy, but maybe you oughta be a little more discreet with your intentions? Y'know, dress up the words a bit?"

Though I was aware of that particular human-coined expression—"to dress up one's words"—I had to admit I didn't really understand how you'd ever put clothing on words. I mean, I guess it had to be figurative—plenty of human expressions were. Logically, I supposed it implied choosing fancier words to mitigate the kind of offense more direct terms might cause, in the same way that proper attire could make a better impression. It struck me as a fascinating point of inquiry.

While I was lost pondering the trivialities of language, Lotus had begun tapping away at his tablet. I heard him add, "Well, I for one appreciate the captain's clarity. His down-to-earth—"

Something seemed to catch him off guard. He tilted his head to the right and gave a puzzled, "Hrm?"

"What is it?" I asked.

"One of the turrets. It appears to have been destroyed."

"Oh. Right. So now whatever machine destroyed it is getting infected, and that becomes the new turret, right?"

"Yes . . . about that . . ." Lotus murmured. "The newly infected unit's signal has also been terminated. And now—"

He tilted his head to the other side and murmured again, "Hrm?"

His head bobbed back to the right.

"Something unusual?" I asked, peering over at the tablet.

Red lights dotted the display, apparently representing the autoturrets. Several blinked out, replaced by new lights immediately adjacent to them, only for the new lights to go out, be replaced once more, and on and on in a cascade of red dots. And then, suddenly, the lights were disappearing from the display altogether, at an almost blinding rate.

What was going on? The mystery had me tilting my head just like Lotus.

That was when the explosion hit. A huge roar from somewhere close.

"Whoa! What was that? What was that? *What was that*?!" The captain was on all fours, crawling with unbelievable speed to one far corner of the cave. When he reached the rock wall, he curled up like a pill bug.

"Lotus, what's going on?!"

Lotus was busily tapping away on his device.

"The machines! They're vanishing," he replied. "Not just the hacked ones. All of them. And it's happening *fast*!"

Another explosive roar shook our surroundings, this one even closer than before.

"Whoa, whoa, whoa! We're all gonna *die*!" The captain's wailing was about as earsplitting as the explosions.

"Captain!" I yelled. "No disrespect, sir, but *please*! Shut. Up."

The latest blast had sent a shower of dirt and pebbles clattering to the rocky floor. The cave was a natural formation. Unreinforced. I doubted it would stand up to much more abuse.

"Lotus!" I yelled. "How about finding us a safe route outta here?!"

Lotus didn't seem to be listening.

"What in the . . . Oh! Oh, this isn't good at all!" he yelped.

"What *now*?!"

"Something's headed this way! Straight into the cave!"

More explosions quaked around us. I put a hand to my rifle.

"Captain! Get your weapon ready!"

When he failed to respond, I grabbed each of his hands with my own and slapped them onto the barrel and grip of his weapon. I clicked his safety off. Lotus was right. I could sense something drawing near.

"Lotus!" I yelled again. "Get to the back of the cave! Keep your head down!"

I readied my weapon. But I never got the chance to aim or shoot; the next explosion was easily a magnitude larger than the last. Visibility went to nil with the blast. I heard something flying through the air. I tried to wave away the billowing dust and smoke that had filled the cave.

There was a body on the ground. Maybe our intruder had underestimated the toll the forced entry would take on him.

"Who is that? Who is that? *Who is that?*"

The captain was now completely gripped by panic. I saw his hands tighten on his weapon, like he was ready to start spraying fire indiscriminately. I shouted with everything I had.

"Stop! It's an android! Don't shoot!"

Lotus muttered, "An android. Lovely. The perfect vector for an enemy logic infection."

His caution was warranted. But I didn't feel comfortable letting the new arrival lie unexamined on the floor, either. With my rifle still held at the ready, I approached slowly, one careful step at a time. The android was dressed head to toe in black. Judging by the frame, it was a model I was unfamiliar with. No telling what kind of specs it had. If I assumed the worst, and this new arrival was indeed carrying a virus, would the three of us and the firepower we had on hand be enough to take him down?

And if it came to that, would I be able to go through with it? It didn't feel right killing a fellow android, even if it was one I'd never interacted with. I found myself almost wishing he'd died on impact to spare us the quandary.

"Aghhhhh! Dammit all, that *hurt*!"

I jumped back at the sudden exclamation. The intruder sprang up from the floor, still shouting.

"Hey! What about my cover? Thought you said you had my back!"

"How are we supposed to provide cover for dumbass tactics like that?"

The second voice alerted me to the fact that another figure all in black had arrived. This one wore a black coat with a hood.

"Barreling straight in like some kinda lunatic . . ." the second android continued, shaking his head.

Both androids had black blindfolds over their eyes. It struck me as highly strange. How did they manage to get anything done like that? Echolocation or something? Were these two supposed to be *bats*?

The second android turned to address me.

"You the ones sending out the distress signal?"

Apparently, they could see just fine from under those things. He looked directly at me, then turned his head slightly to look at the captain and finally at Lotus.

"We've come to get you outta here," he said.

My mind was reeling from the events of the past few minutes. I still half-expected the two strangers to declare they were here to kill us.

"You . . . uh . . ." I faltered. "You made it through the enemy lines? That's a lot of machines to get past."

Too many machines. There were only two of these androids. No, scratch that. Now more figures in black were making their way inside. Four more, all smaller than the first two.

Still, a squad of six wasn't remotely enough to break through the enemy perimeter.

"Plenty of 'em out there, sure. But most of the types you got around here are real pushovers." It was the first one—the one who had come tumbling in with the explosion—who replied. He seemed very pleased with himself as he made the announcement.

The second android—the hooded one—proceeded to take his companion down a notch.

"Remind me: who was it that almost got cornered by a swarm of those pushovers? Maybe if you could admit your screw-ups, you'd learn something from them."

"Excuse me?!"

The two larger androids seemed ready to go for each other's throats. Surprisingly, it was Lotus who stepped in to defuse the situation.

"Hey! Hello, hi! A question, if I may. Are you saying you *dispatched* the enemies you came across on your way in?"

"That's right. Cleared the whole area. Sent the unlucky bastards flyin' left and right."

I saw, for the briefest moment, a furrow cross Lotus's brow. But I didn't have time to puzzle out his thoughts as yet *another* black-clad visitor arrived. From the way this last one held himself, I could tell he was in charge, but for whatever reason, he wasn't wearing a blindfold like the others.

"Everyone unharmed?" His voice was crisp.

The captain sensed the aura of leadership, too. He piped up with, "Yes, and you are?"

I could tell Cactus was trying as hard as he could to project his own air of authority. Unfortunately for his attempt, he was still huddled in his corner.

"M Squadron," the leader announced. "We're a team composed of new YoRHa-type models, here to provide assistance."

Lotus tried to interject with an "Um . . ." but was ignored by both our captain and the leader of this M-whatever.

"You're here to rescue us?" the captain asked.

"That's correct. We picked up your distress signal."

One of the shorter black-clad soldiers—er, rather, "YoRHa models"—poked his head out from behind his commander.

"And it wasn't easy. You wouldn't believe what we went through to get here."

He was smiling as he said it, but something about his tone felt accusatory. I found myself scrambling to deflect the blame.

"It wasn't us," I said.

"Huh?"

"The signal. We aren't the ones sending it. It's coming from this thing."

All of us—or, all of us with the exception of Lotus—turned our attention to the container. Lotus stuck doggedly to the captain's side, fidgeting and continuing to throw out the occasional "Erm . . ." and "Um . . ." The captain, of course, ignored him.

Cactus's priority was to cement the claim he'd staked on the container. "Oh! But, uh, see . . . *we* discovered the object. It's obviously very valuable, but I'm afraid we won't be able to split the spoils with you. But, um, I guess if you just want to *look* at it, we could consider allowing you to do so."

I had no idea why the captain felt like he was in any position to put up a front. For their part, the strangers didn't seem to find him the least bit intimidating—though I supposed we were just lucky that they didn't take offense. They walked over to examine the container as if permission had never been an issue to consider.

"ID number . . . 219432D, it looks like."

The leader read out the tiny number inscribed on one surface of the container. We'd seen it, too; for a while, we'd hoped it was a clue to solving the passcode needed to open the thing, but it hadn't gotten us anywhere.

"Don't bother," I said. "Thing won't open. We even tried to force the lid, and it didn't budge. Whatever the hell it's made out of, it can sure take a beating."

"ID number 219432D."

My helpful advice went unheeded. The guy simply recited the number again while standing in front of the crate, as if beginning some kind of fancy voice activation sequence.

"Requesting unlock. Identify voice signature: YoRHa M Squadron, Instructor Black."

So the leader's name was "Black." Hmph. Couldn't have been any more on the nose if you tried. And apparently he was some kind of instructor, to boot.

A new voice emanated from the crate itself. "Voice signature confirmed. Commencing unlock procedure."

"H-hold on . . . ! What did you just do?!"

The captain's attempt at an authoritative demeanor slipped into flustered confusion. Normally, I'd have found it funny. But I wasn't laughing this time. I was just as confounded as the captain. What was going on?

There was a hiss, and white smoke trickled from the seams in the container's exterior. The panel slid open, and something fell out. Something humanoid and dressed all in black. It happened so quickly, it took me a second to process. The new arrival seemed to be unconscious; he lay facedown on the ground, completely motionless.

"That's YoRHa gear!" one of the strangers exclaimed.

"Is this soldier one of yours?" the captain demanded, his voice uncharacteristically forceful. "Who exactly *are* you YoRHa units?!"

"It's him . . . He's here . . . No. 2 Type D . . ."

Now it was this Instructor Black guy who was stumbling over his words. You'd think recovering a lost comrade would be a cause for celebration. Instead, his reaction seemed almost conflicted. I took it to mean that there was something unusual about the guy they'd recovered.

"Umm . . . !"

Lotus was *still* at it.

"Enough!" I shouted. "Can't you see we've got bigger things to deal with than whatever you're on about?!"

I was getting pretty sick of his constant mumbling. I figured a few sharp words would be enough to shut him up, but my attention had the opposite effect.

"Yes, yes," he began prattling on, more frantic than ever. "I can see you're all quite busy, but I really do think we ought to reassess the most pressing issue at hand. I have what could very well be a matter of great importance. Very great. And you do like to emphasize the value of good communication, yes, Phlox? I admit, I tend to get wrapped up in my collection. So many fascinating parts, you see. Quite easy for the need to relay information to slip my mind. Still, this particular thought does seem quite pertinent. A time to be proactive, really. Get everyone up to speed, so to speak. Yes, so that's why I'd very much like to—"

Seemed I'd hit the wrong switch. It'd be almost impossible to shut him up now.

"Fine! Whatever!" I pleaded. "We're listening, so *what is it*?"

A faint noise filled the air—an unusual sound, like the beating wings of a swarm of insects. I wasn't sure if I was really hearing it or if it was my imagination. But I didn't have time to think about it. Lotus thrust a finger toward the first of the so-called YoRHa units to arrive—the one that came barreling in with the explosion.

"That one! The one in black! Erm . . . I suppose they're all in black," Lotus hesitated. "The, um, the one with the short hair and shorter temper. He said it himself."

Lotus's words, as usual, were poorly chosen. The specified android was understandably upset, and he took a threatening step toward Lotus.

"What did you just say about me?"

But Lotus wasn't the least bit perturbed. If anything, it was those of us watching the scene unfold that were the most on edge. Lotus probably didn't even register the man's words as a threat.

"'Sent the unlucky bastards flying left and right.' That's what he said, yes?"

"And what of it?"

"Phlox, Captain Cactus, and I have spent nearly three full days holed up and surrounded. We've been very cautious. Established a threshold. Never destroy more than a few machines at once."

"Sounds like a hell of a lot of trouble to go to. Why bother?" This question came from the hooded man.

"Mm, yes, well, in areas with a high concentration of machine lifeforms, any extremes in action tend to get one noticed. Marked, even. By the enemy forces, of course."

Oh no. How had I forgotten? We'd even had a serious discussion about it when our situation became clear. We needed to observe a careful limit on takedowns to avoid drawing attention. It was precisely *why* we were stuck, unable to fight our way home.

The strange noise I'd been unable to place returned to the forefront of my mind. It most certainly *wasn't* my imagination.

"What do you mean, 'marked'?" the hooded android asked.

"Yes, well, there are a number of possible patterns. But when the enemy forces suspect the presence of an android squadron of significant strength, then based on existing experience, collected data, and so on and so forth, we know they have a particular penchant for bombs. Wide-area aerial bombardment, specifically."

This was bad. The buzzing sound grew louder. Now it was something I definitely recognized. Enemy bombers, inbound on our position.

"Ah! The sound you hear now, yes? I believe this perfectly illustrates my point."

Lotus pointed up at the cave's ceiling. Now there was a sudden, intermittent whooshing sound coming from overhead. Dozens upon dozens of enemy units. By the time we realized the bombs were falling, it was too late. Everything had gone dark.

[Log Entry: Lotus / Mountain Zone—Cave]

It's been a while since I've had such a restful sleep.

I must have been down for quite an extended period. My neck is still cracking and popping with every movement.

What was it I'd been working on?

Let's see . . . It must have been . . . Ah, yes! The autoturrets. The design still needed improvement. I'd decided I'd very much like to see their range extended. They really ought to be able to fire just a teensy bit further.

Time to get back to work, then. Erm . . . Oh dear. Oh dear, indeed. Just look at this part. All twisted and warped. Well, I suppose it would be. Lots of wear and tear near the barrel. Yes, yes. All those rapid temperature fluctuations to contend with, too. But we can't simply leave it. No. Not like this. The whole turret will suffer. Terrible reduction in accuracy. That won't do at all. I suppose I ought to start here, then. Improved range won't mean a thing if it never gets a hit off!

Now, the simplest solution is a more robust part. I could alter its shape, yes, or select a different material. But if I alter the shape, hrmm . . . I'd have to run the numbers all over again, wouldn't I? And oh what a bother that would be. No. It absolutely must fit perfectly in place. Even the slightest gap could produce such nasty vibrations. It could throw the whole turret into disarray. Yes, so a change in materials it is, then. Fashion the same shape out of something new. Yes, yes. That's the sound and simple approach.

But then, what material to use? Quite a demanding set of specifications. Is there nothing in my collection that's up to the task? But I had such a big haul! A big catch! How can there not be a single item that meets my needs? Augh! Emptiness among such vast riches! What irony!

I really must resolve this as quickly as possible. I suppose that means venturing outside yet again. More searching. More collecting. But what if I'm unable to locate the remains of a suitable machine? Does any such material exist in the types lurking near our cave?

Ouch! What was that? It felt like something hit me on the head . . .

Hrmmm?

I-I don't believe it! A machine part! And its makeup, why, it's perfectly suited for my needs!

And . . . is that another part over there? And one over here, too? What in the world?! Here's *another*! And another one over there! I don't believe it! Is such expediency possible?

Well, I shouldn't look a gift horse in the mouth. This is big. A big catch! Big haul! Big trove of treasures! My autoturrets will shoot farther and more accurately than ever before. And they'll be energy efficient, too!

Hrm?

But wait. Wait, wait, wait. Assuming I first go with the . . . and then the . . .

Yes. Of course. It can be even *better* than I imagined! I'll just have to make some adjustments. I'll move *that* like so, and then tinker a bit with *this* . . .

Ah, my heart races at the thought! Modding machines is the greatest thing ever!

And there are so many more mods I'd like to make. But alas, this area doesn't have the number of machines I'd need to make it happen. Or, rather, it's not an issue of population. It's the imposed limit: I can only harvest so many. Too many units down all at once, and we could find our whole location marked for bombardment. Wouldn't like that. No, no. Why, just a few moments ago . . .

Hrm? What, what? It feels like I'm on the verge of remembering something. Something important. It's on the tip of my tongue, but—

"Dearest Loootus!"

Hm? What was that? Someone calling my name? Why, that looks like a . . .

Whaaat?!

Machines! A whole horde of them!

I'm done for! They'll tear me to parts!

"Dearest Loootus!"

Preposterous! The machines! They're . . . *speaking*?! What an astounding evolutionary—

No! That's not the issue right now! Why are they calling me their *dearest*?! Why are they sidling up beside me?!

"Dearest Lotus! We *need* you. ♥ Hurry up and *mod us*. ♥"

There are so many of them! Little ones! Medium ones! Big ones! Flying ones! Every type of machine I could imagine, right here before my eyes! And they're baring everything—they've got their brain unit compartments popped right open, as if inviting me inside. They're telling me to take a peek. To look anywhere I like. To, erm . . . *touch* them, if I wish!

I-it's like that thing I read about in human civilization! The harem trope! A cast of tempting morsels all circled around an inexplicably irresistible main character!

. . . Oh dear.

Oh dear, oh dear, oh dear.

No! Stop! This isn't right! Reality isn't supposed to work like this. I'm certain of it!

I need to set them straight!

"Ahem! Excuse me, but . . . that language is *not* appropriate. A machine would never say things like that. Do you hear me?!"

They're machines! *Not* human girls! Most certainly not!

"dEArEst . . . LoTuS . . . dEaReSt LoTuS . . . mOd us. PLeaSe!"

This! This is exactly what I'm talking about! This suggestive language! This power disparity! Do they not see it?! *This* is the problem!

. . . Well, now. With that settled, which one of these delicious little units shall I mod first? I could start by taking the sights from that flying model, or perhaps the brain unit from this mid-sized cutie . . .

"pICk me! I wAnt tO Be mODdEd, tOO!"

"mE fIRst!"

"No! *i* wANt To bE fIrST!"

Ah, this is the life. Not like when those ruffians in black

showed up. What a nuisance. Wiping out every single ma-chine lifeform in the vicinity of our cave, ensuring our location would be marked and bombed to smithereens.

Finally, I've found true happiness. It's so perfect, in fact, it's almost like a dr . . .

Hm?

Marked by the enemy?

Bombed to smithereens?

Erm . . .

Yes, on second thought, this entire situation does seem a little *too* expedient. All the hallmarks of indulgent slumber.

. . . No. No, no, no! I refuse! This cannot be a dream. I forbid it! I will *not* wake up from this. I swear it on my life!

Just look at all these pretty machines gathered around me. So many of them, and they're all . . . all gone? Hm? Honestly? Is this *really* a dream?

Wait! Just one! That's all I ask! Let me mod one single ma-chine before I wake up! Pleeeeease!

"Grngh! Nooooo!"

. . . I looked around to find myself in the cave. I'd awoken to the sound of my own yelling.

Drat.

[Log Entry: No. 9 / Mountain Zone—Cave Ruins]

"Do we have to? My uniform's gonna get dirt all over it."

It sounded like No. 6's voice. But I couldn't see. Everything was dark. Pitch black. Was I dreaming? Had I actually heard anything at all? My chest felt a bit tight. It was hard to breathe.

A vague thought formed in my mind.

You'd think a dream could at least be pleasant.

"Ah. You're alive, too. How very nice. Yes, yes."

"Yeah. Guess the cave wasn't at the epicenter of the bombing."

"Oh, is that so? Hmm. Quite fortunate."

Now I was sure the voices I heard were real. This wasn't a dream. No. 6 was speaking with one of the Resistance members we'd encountered. What was his name? Lotus, or something like that.

"And the rest of your companions? What about them?"

"Beats me."

"Beats you . . . ? Aren't you concerned for their safety?" This new voice belonged to another Resistance member we'd met. Phlox.

It was all starting to come back to me. We'd finally made it to the source of the distress signal, only for the whole area to get blasted by enemy forces. Everything after that was a blank.

"Doesn't really make a difference, does it? I can be concerned all I want, but if they're dead, they're dead, and if they're alive, they're alive."

I'm alive! Right over here! I wanted to answer, but I couldn't make the words come out. My arms and legs wouldn't budge. It was as if they were frozen in place. No. Not frozen. Stuck. The reality of my situation finally dawned on me. The cave had partially collapsed, and I'd been buried alive in the rubble.

"No. 9. Can you hear me?"

It was the instructor. Suddenly, I felt my body being tugged free. Air rushed violently into my mouth and nose, so much so that it left me in a coughing fit.

When the fit subsided, I was finally able to respond.

"Y . . . yes, sir. Th-thank you."

The inside of my mouth was rough with grit.

"No. 4. Keep up the search for the rest of our squad," the instructor ordered.

"Yes, sir."

I looked around. No. 3, No. 21, and No. 22 were nowhere to be found. I was filled with the urge to join in the search, but I was unable to stand. A considerable length of time seemed to have passed since the bombing. My joints were painfully stiff and my body was uncomfortably cold.

"You wouldn't happen to know where our captain is, would you?" Phlox asked.

"Yeah. He's lazing about somewhere around here."

"Ah, good. So he's safe."

As I listened to the exchange between Phlox and the instructor, I managed to get my arms and legs to move by small degrees. My body ached all over.

"Captain! Captain, wake up! It's morning!" Phlox called.

Cactus continued to snore away happily.

Lotus intervened.

"No, no. That won't suffice. Not at all," he said, picking up a large stone from the cave floor.

Oh, no. He wasn't planning to . . .

Was he?

Phlox exclaimed, "Whoa, whoa, whoa! Lotus!"

"Dieeeee!" Lotus screamed.

It was as I'd feared. Lotus aimed the stone right at Cactus's forehead, his arm sweeping down. It happened so quickly, none of us were able to step in.

I felt positive that, had the captain been human, the assault would have claimed his life.

"Ngaaaah!"

Instead, Cactus sprang awake with a shriek of pain.

"Lotus!" he shouted. "What'd you do that for?! Ever heard of being *gentle*? And I could've sworn I heard you scream 'Die!' You did, didn't you?!"

When the captain pressed him to answer, Lotus blithely admitted, "Why, yes. I believe I did."

I began to suspect the three of them might forever be beyond my comprehension.

"Now, now, captain. We have guests, remember? The YoR-whatever Squad."

"YoRHa Squadron," the instructor corrected. He seemed exasperated, as if he'd already had to say it many times over.

A shout from No. 4 drew our attention.

"Found No. 2!" he called.

I got to my feet. I was still shaky, but I managed to stand. And now I remembered: there'd been another. Just before the bombing commenced, we'd made contact with the seventh member of our squadron, designated No. 2. Another senior M001 unit.

"No. 9. Prep him for activation."

"Right away, sir!"

I hurried to No. 2's side. My joints creaked and protested with the sudden movement, but I tried to put it out of mind.

No. 2's body was caked in mud. I knelt down beside him and began checking him over. I couldn't have said whether it was because he'd been buried or because he was in suspend mode, but his limbs were even colder than mine.

As I performed my duties, I overheard No. 4 speaking with the instructor.

"Sir, if I could ask, who exactly is this No. 2, anyway?"

"The final member of YoRHa M Squadron."

I didn't know very much about this new squadmate of ours, either, so I strained to hear the instructor's response.

"No. 2 Type D," he continued. "A defense-oriented model. Initially, he was scheduled to descend as part of M001. His calibrations were taking more time than expected, however, so Command decided to send him down later. By the look of things, he must have been en route aboard a transport, and the enemy intercepted and took it down, forcing No. 2 to board an escape pod. I assume that's how he ended up here."

"So this guy's definitely one of yours?" Cactus interrupted.

The instructor didn't seem to mind. "That's correct."

He added, "Sorry to disappoint. Turns out your find wasn't full of treasure after all."

Cactus shook his head in disappointment. "Damn. Just our luck . . . We had big plans. Sell the contents off, make bank, and go retire in luxury somewhere far away from any machines."

Now that I was aware of the three Resistance members' plan, I was glad we'd fought our way in. I wouldn't have wanted No. 2 to be sold off.

"Sir, No. 2 is ready to boot." I announced.

His limbs were still cold, and there were a number of scratches across his frame, perhaps suggesting he'd been jostled around inside the pod on impact. But his condition wasn't so severe as to interfere with the activation sequence. Once he was up and running, it wouldn't take him long to recover, either.

"Activating now."

No. 2's body jerked as if shocked by a violent surge of electricity. He began to cough and hack. And then, before I knew it, he was on his feet, scanning the surroundings, seemingly ready to take on any imminent threat. The speed with which he moved reminded me of No. 6's agility.

"Where am I?" he asked.

He continued to look about, wary of the unfamiliar location. If his transport really had been shot down, I couldn't blame him for being cautious. It was hard to say at what point he'd lost consciousness, but regardless, he'd almost certainly been surrounded by the enemy and in dire straits immediately prior to entering suspend mode.

The instructor replied, "A cave in the northwest sector of the Mountain Zone. Or what's left of it, anyway."

"Are you are?"

"Assembled before you are the members of YoRHa M Squadron. I am Instructor Black, the squadron's commanding officer."

No. 2's eyes widened slightly. Yeah, I'd have been just as surprised. His escape pod would have been launched in the general direction of our base camp, and it had been broadcasting a distress signal. All the right pieces were in place for us to eventually link up. But that said, the arc of potential landing sites for the escape pod still encompassed a vast area. To wake up and find your squadmates standing in front of you would seem like an extraordinary stroke of good luck—and an event of extremely low probability.

"I'm guessing your transport must have been shot down en route. Is that right? We're going run a check on your vitals and scan for any trace of a logic virus just to be safe. No. 9, get to it."

"Yes, sir!"

As soon as I'd responded, the instructor turned to address No. 4.

"I'm still not seeing the rest of the team. What's the holdup, No. 4? We're YoRHa units. It's going to take more than a few falling rocks to wipe us out."

"It'd be a lot easier if we had our Scanner around, sir."

The instructor began to look about the cave. He shouted, "No. 21! Do you hear me?"

A faint groan came from a short distance away. "Over . . . here . . . sir."

The voice was hoarse, but it was definitely that of No. 21. I breathed a sigh of relief.

"Are you injured?"

"My leg seems a little off . . ."

"No. 9, go take a look."

"Right away, sir," I replied. But I'd barely begun treating No. 2. What was I supposed to do?

No. 2 picked up on my hesitation. "I'll be all right," he said. "This, uh . . . No. 21, was it? Go ahead and attend to him first."

It seemed our newest squadmate was a very kind-hearted individual. I bowed my head slightly in a mixture of appreciation and apology, then hurried over to No. 21's side.

"I'm going to be touching your leg now," I informed him. "Tell me where it hurts."

No. 21 nodded. I very slowly worked my way along his limb. It was smeared with mud, but fortunately it didn't seem to show any obvious lacerations or breaks. I pressed down carefully, inch by inch, watching my patient for any reaction. I started with the ankle, carefully bending it back and forth. Nothing. Next came the knee. No. 21 grimaced. He must have been in a great deal of pain; I knew from experience that he didn't so much as wince for mild or even moderate injuries.

"This is no time to act tough," I chided. "If there's pain, you have to tell me."

" . . . Yeah. I know, I know."

"Does it hurt when I do this?"

"A little bit."

It was as I feared. His frame was significantly damaged,

which would impair his motor functions. This was a major issue. The kinds of parts I'd need to repair it were all the way back at base camp. There was only so much I could do for him in the field.

I turned to address the instructor. "Sir! In regard to No. 21's leg, I've provided makeshift repairs, but unfortunately, a full recovery will require replacements that I don't have access to out here."

"Understood. No. 21, in your current condition, are you able to run scans for us?"

"I'm ready to go, sir," No. 21 answered, struggling to his feet. I hurriedly slipped my shoulder under one of his arms to help him keep the weight off his damaged knee. The more he used it, the worse the pain would get.

"It's okay to sit this out, No. 21," I pleaded.

"I'll . . . be fine." His voice and expression were obviously strained.

As he began his scan, I saw a faint sheen of sweat appear across his brow. We still hadn't located No. 3 or No. 22. That was probably why No. 21 was so intent on fulfilling his duty despite the pain.

"I'm detecting faint black box signals . . . One there . . . and another over there." He raised an arm to point out the locations as he spoke.

"But . . ." he added, only to falter and fall silent.

I knew I wasn't the only one who could guess the words he was unwilling to say. The instructor, No. 4, and No. 6 would have all understood, too.

"No. 6 and No. 4, get them out of the debris."

"And what, No. 9's just gonna sit there and watch? That's real fair," No. 6 complained.

The instructor came to my defense. "You two are Attackers. You'll dig more efficiently with your superior strength."

Still, I understood No. 6's feelings.

"I'd like to help!" I announced.

I might not make a big difference, but right now, every minute counted. We needed to get our squadmates free as soon as possible. I reached down to begin lifting handfuls of cold earth away. The sensation reminded me of my own chill prison of just moments ago. I shuddered involuntarily. It wasn't right to allow our comrades to remain buried under the earth any longer. And there was another reason for my discomfort: I had a feeling we weren't going to like what we found.

No. 6 and I managed to pull No. 3 free from the fallen dirt and rocks, while No. 4 got No. 22 loose. Both bodies were limp. They hadn't moved in the slightest as the rubble was cleared away. My premonition had been correct.

"Assessing black box status," I said, checking each recovered squadmate over. " . . . It appears they've both gone into emergency shutdown."

No. 21 had been anxiously peering over my shoulder as I worked. At my words, his features stiffened. No. 6 let out a very audible sigh, and No. 4 just looked at the ground in silence.

Cactus watched, a perplexed expression on his own face.

"What's the problem?" he asked. "Aren't you gonna fix these two up? Y'know, reboot 'em real quick, just like you did for the other guy."

I only wished it were that simple. A quick reboot, and No. 3 and No. 22 back with us, good as new. That'd be nice. Nothing in the world would have made me happier at that moment.

"You don't get it, do you?" No. 6 replied, giving an exaggerated shrug.

"The black box is a critical part of our system. It's like our heart. When it goes into emergency shutdown, we enter safe mode and all our functions cease."

"Well, what's so different about the fella you pulled out of the crate? He wasn't moving much."

"No. 2 was just in suspend mode, awaiting reactivation. That's totally different from an emergency shutdown. No. 3 and No. 22 aren't getting any power to their brain units right now. That means their memory banks have gone unstable."

"Their *memory* is starting to fail? Won't they die if that happens?"

"Well, that's how it works for a normal android . . . Hey, No. 9? When you're done with your chores over there, try and bring them up to speed. I'm kinda sick of explaining this stuff."

And with that, No. 6 turned away from Cactus and the others. I continued working on my "chores" in silence. First, I needed to get No. 3's self-repair routine operating at max speed. Then I needed to disable his black box's safe mode. And after that, the list just went on . . .

It took a while, but eventually I was done. No. 3 sprang up as if he'd been pinched. He coughed violently just as No. 2 had, shoulders heaving up and down with each spasm.

When he'd caught his breath, he demanded, "The time! How many hours?!"

It was the same exchange we had every time I revived him. I read aloud from the display on my SSU.

"Thirty-five hours and thirty-two minutes."

"Shit! It's been that long?!"

He slammed a fist against the ground. Cactus looked on with the same perplexed expression as before. Of course he had no idea what this was about, and neither did his comrades Phlox or Lotus, so to them, No. 3's preoccupation with the time and his violent reaction would seem bizarre.

"But you're back with us, yes?" Cactus asked. "I don't see what the problem is."

"It has to do with a new feature present in YoRHa units," I explained. "Something that hasn't been seen in androids before. You see, we're able to back up our consciousness data."

"What do you mean, your 'consciousness data'?"

"Memories, combat proficiencies, personal quirks . . . things like that."

In other words, everything that made us who we were. The essence of our selves.

"As the squad Healer, I'm responsible for backing up each member's data and periodically uploading it to our command server."

"But doesn't that mean you can fix 'em? I still don't see the reason for all the long faces."

The backup process involved encoding each squad member's personal qualities and sending it to the Bunker's server, where it would be stored. That way, even if we ran into unforeseen circumstances on the surface and lost our own internal memories, we could always download the backup for reinsertion, and everything would be restored just the way it was. Or that's how I'd assumed the process would work, until my squadmates actually began dying.

"If only it were that simple," No. 21 said, quietly shaking his head. He continued to gaze at No. 22's still form as he spoke.

"The backup process takes time, and in order to upload it to the server, we need a strong and stable signal."

"Well, yeah, I suppose that makes sense," Cactus conceded. "It does sounds like an awful lot of data."

"That means a good stretch of time without any enemy attacks *or* interruptions to the connection. Two conditions that aren't even common on their own, much less together. The last time I was able to run a complete backup was thirty-five hours ago."

"Ah!" Lotus chimed in, his eyes sparkling with curiosity. "So they'll have lost all memory of everything that occurred in the interim, yes? A thirty-five hour window of amnesia, so to speak?"

Strictly as a definition of what occurred, it wasn't inaccurate. But there was more to it than that.

I continued with No. 22's reactivation procedure. I disengaged the black box's safe mode and began reinstalling his consciousness. How many times had I been through this process? How many times had I witnessed their anguish on reawakening to the world?

When No. 22 stirred, his twin clasped his hand and exclaimed, "No. 22! Are you all right?!"

"I'm . . ."

How many times had I witnessed the sadness that clouded their faces once they realized what had happened?

"It's not amnesia," I said to Cactus. "It's more than that. It's like undoing everything they experienced. For No. 3 and

No. 22, the past thirty-five hours never happened. That data is gone. Erased. Lost forever to the world."

Thirty-five hours between my most recent backup and the moment they were revived. Thirty-five hours. It wasn't a trivial span of time. Nothing they experienced or felt during that period remained with them.

It was why No. 3 kept telling me I could "quit with the 'sir' business." He'd never remember all the times he said it. It was why No. 22 kept wondering aloud about the names of the same birds he'd seen flitting among the trees countless times before. And I felt certain I'd hear those things again. Because *I* was the only one who remembered.

"In other words," I continued, "you can restore the memories, but the person who is revived isn't the same as the one who died."

"And lemme tell you, this sure as hell isn't the first time any of us have died," No. 4 muttered. As he said it, the shadow over his downcast eyes seemed to deepen.

Also erased from their minds were the fear that preceded death and the agony they suffered the moment it closed in. And it was precisely because they couldn't retain that knowledge that I suspected something else might be building up inside them. Each time the squadron was inserted into a new battlefield only to be completely annihilated, I could see their expressions grow a shade darker, a hint more grim.

They were unaware of what they had lost, yet they knew that something was gone. I imagined it must have felt like having a hole inside oneself—one that opened to an impenetrable blackness.

"Sure isn't," No. 6 agreed. "Killed and brought back to life who knows how many times over the past two months. The whole lot of us."

Though he said "the whole lot of us," I knew the expression didn't include me. To ensure everyone else could come back to life, it was imperative that I not be struck down. I would never die. It was the heavy burden of duty that I alone was fated to bear.

When we headed out of the half-collapsed cave, we found a half-collapsed mountain. Before, the peak had been pretty impressive. Now, there was a giant gouge in the landscape. It brought new meaning to the concept of ground zero; a few meters closer and the cave we'd been hiding out in wouldn't have been *half*-collapsed.

At least the fireworks show had cleared the area of enemy units—for the time being, anyway. They'd be back soon enough.

"Why's every place they send us to gotta end up lookin' like a damn wasteland?" I muttered.

This time around, a twist of luck had left us alive to tell the tale. I wasn't sure whether to be thankful or not.

"Surrounded by the enemy just like on every op, and this time we're short on parts for repairs and dragged down by a bunch of worthless Resistance members to boot."

Normally, I wasn't much for complaining, but when you were knee-deep in shit, it was hard not to grumble.

"And to top it off, we gotta welcome some mystery recruit to the outfit."

No. 4 flicked his gaze toward me and said, "Mystery recruit, huh? I assume you mean No. 2." From his expression, I could tell he had an opinion or two to share about my thoughts.

He added, "He's been scheduled for assignment to the squad since the beginning, y'know. He's not some stranger."

"Dammit, you *know* that's not what I meant!"

I should've known better than to mutter my complaints in front of the wrong guy. Now I had to explain what I meant, and I had to find a way to make it so simple that even a guy dumber than a rock could understand. What a pain in my ass.

"I'm talkin' about being squadmates or brothers-in-arms. Y'know, eatin' outta the same pot or whatever. Not that we actually got any pots to begin with, but . . . You get what I'm sayin', right?"

Count back and you'd find that two whole months had

passed since the lot of us formed up into M Squadron. Two months spent blowing shit up together created a certain kind of bond among us. We were comrades now. I'd come to realize that scrawny No. 22 had a pretty steady arm on him, and No. 21's intel was always solid. My ass had been saved by No. 9 who knew how many times, and even No. 6 did all right, for all his goddamn attitude.

But now this No. 2 character was thrown into the mix. Not back at the Bunker, not at base camp, but right here in the field, popping outta some creepy crate like a science experiment.

"The six of us have a good thing goin', and now we gotta throw in some outside element so tiny that it's like it's not even there. But it *is*. Do you get it now?"

"No. I don't."

I gave a massive sigh. Of course he didn't. No. 4 couldn't read a room even if the instructions were painted on the walls.

It occurred to me that of all the squadron's members, No. 4 might be the hardest one to wrap my head around. The hell was his deal? Deciding he was gonna let me have the Attacker spot even though he claimed he was better at the job? And then he says he did it 'cause we gotta have the best people we can get in every role? His reasoning didn't make a damn bit of sense.

Ugh. Time to quit bitching. I wasn't going to figure out No. 4 any time soon, or ever, and I needed to focus now. Just as I had that thought, I heard someone calling from behind.

"Hey! Hey, wait up!"

I turned to look. It was the Resistance's, uh . . . their captain, or whatever. Cactus, I think he said his name was. With him was another one of their guys. Phlox, or something like that. Yeah, that sounded right. The two of them were rushing up to us.

No. 4 stopped and asked, "What's the trouble? Got something you need?"

Typical. Real class act, that No. 4. If he ever spoke politely to someone, I'd probably die from shock.

"No trouble. We just, uh, feel kinda bad. Thought we could at least give you a hand with the scouting. A little thanks for saving our behinds, y'know?"

The way he said it, you'd have thought scouting was supposed to be easy. But it wasn't like the machines just waved little flags to show you where they were. You had to *find* the damn things.

Honestly, the Resistance members would just get in our way. So I gave them a decisive shake of the head.

"We got this. YoRHa models are the latest and greatest. You just sit back and relax. Catch some Z's back in the cave."

"C'mon, now. That's a little harsh," No. 4 interjected.

That was the last thing I wanted to hear from a bolthead like him. But before I could tell No. 4 off, Phlox piped up with, "No worries. You're obviously much stronger than us. If we tried to take down one of the bigger machines around these parts, we'd probably be fighting all day."

Well, look at that! Someone able to own up to his shortcomings. I kinda liked this guy.

"Takin' down machines is what we do," I replied. "It's what YoRHa was designed for. And as an Attacker, I guess you could say I'm the strongest of the bunch. No need to be embarrassed relyin' on us. We're happy to help."

Not to mention, we were sworn to assist and fight alongside any androids we came across in the field. Seemed like a good enough reason to me to keep them safe.

"You'll have to excuse my comrade. He knows how to handle himself in a fight, but he falls a bit short in the intellect department."

"You wanna say that again?!" I shouted back.

But Cactus interrupted before I could really set No. 4 straight.

"I should point out, it's not our first time around the block. The Resistance hasn't been carrying on the fight for however many hundred years just for optics, and I'd say what we lack in strength, we more than make up for in experience. It wouldn't be wise to disregard that."

"Experience? Like what?"

"Y'know. The knowledge we've built up over the years. The focused training. A little bit of this, a little bit of that."

A little bit of this and that? What the hell was this guy talking about? I was lost.

And then, while I was busy trying to wrap my brain around it, Phlox started apologizing for some reason.

"Hey, let's just forget it," he said. "I'll be the first to admit our captain's a coward. He just can't stand being shown up, so he feels like he has to argue a bit."

"What do you mean he's a coward?!" I demanded. "You should be ashamed of yourself, Phlox! He's your superior officer! Treat him with the respect he deserves!"

He shot me a sardonic smile. Ah. Now that was a feeling I could relate to. I totally understood what he was getting at. Apparently this Cactus guy wasn't the sharpest tool in the shed. The kinda guy who didn't have a lot going on upstairs, but you couldn't hold that against him.

"All right. I gotcha. You can tag along. Just don't push yourselves too hard, hear?"

I didn't know exactly why, but I'd started feeling a kind of camaraderie with the Resistance members. I clapped a hand on Cactus's shoulder.

Suddenly, No. 4 had his handgun up at the ready. Had he spotted an enemy?

"Stay sharp, No. 3. Machine inbound. Looks like a scout."

Even without his warning, I'd have figured it out. My visor display was soon flashing a hostile signature.

"I see it. You don't have to tell me," I grumbled.

I began sprinting in the direction indicated by my HUD. There! Dead ahead. It was a pretty hefty-looking one. And a flier, to boot.

I slammed into it with my sword. I wasn't about to let the thing have the spare moment it'd need to shift into attack mode.

"Another on your right!" No. 4 yelled.

Oh, so this machine wasn't working alone, huh? Invited a buddy along to play?

"Yeah, I see it."

I knocked the next machine down, then just for good measure, kicked it as hard as I could. It went spiraling through the air. Time to go bye-bye. You and your buddy can have a nice nap!

"Hmph. I guess that about covers it," I said, sheathing my sword and preparing to rejoin the two Resistance members. But something didn't feel right. I heard a rustle, like movement in the brush.

"Another one?! Where the hell were *you* hiding?!"

It was long and skinny, like some kinda snake or centipede or something, and it was bearing down fast. I reached for my sword. This was gonna be close . . . or . . . no, I wasn't sure if I was gonna draw in time!

Just as despair washed over me, the third machine exploded into pieces. The thing had been right in my face.

"How many times am I gonna have to say it before it sinks in? You've gotta stop letting your attention wander every time you finish something off."

Seemed No. 4 had been the one to take out my assailant.

"Yeah, yeah," I said.

Way to ruin all my fun. So I'd goofed. Big deal.

I couldn't stand the thought of seeing No. 4's smug face, so I made a point of not looking his way. I turned to the Resistance members instead and was met with a pained groan.

"Auuugh! My back!"

Cactus was sitting with his butt on the ground, one hand rubbing his lower back. Maybe that last machine had scared him, and he'd jerked back so suddenly it did a number on his spine.

"*Again*?" Phlox asked. He looked exasperated as he ran over to Cactus's side. "How many times have I warned you not to make sudden movements? Throw out your back once and it'll bother you forever."

Cactus accepted the shoulder Phlox offered and managed to get to his feet, body still awkwardly hunched over. Oh, great. Did this geezer still want to tag along, looking the way he did now?

"Captain, maybe you oughta head back, at least for today," Phlox suggested.

"Well, I really think . . ."

"I can go along on the scouting operation."

To which No. 4 added, "Y'know, captain, one of our squadmates back at camp, No. 9, he'd be able to fix up a problem like that real quick. Go have him take a look at it."

Finally, Cactus seemed to give in.

"Think you can get back by yourself, Cap?" Phlox asked.

"Yeah. I'll be fine."

He tottered away. Or jerked with pain every step, really. The kinda pitiful shuffle I wouldn't wanna be caught dead doing. Phlox's eyes remained on his captain's back. He was probably worried whether the guy would really make it back on his own.

I figured Phlox must've felt the same way about the old man as I'd felt about the Resistance members. To him, having the captain around just meant feeling dragged down.

"Seems like you got a lot to put up with," I offered.

A weird look crossed his face. I wasn't sure how to describe it. Maybe it was kinda like the way you felt when there was a little bit of sand stuck in your boot, but you couldn't get it out, and eventually, it somehow made it from your boots to the insides of your socks.

"I know he doesn't look like it now, but back in the day, the captain used to be a real fighter," he replied.

Guess I'd been wrong. Way off the mark. Oh well. Not like any of my expectations or guesses ever came true in the first place.

"He's a hero. A veteran of countless battles," Phlox added.

And then he started to share the story of Captain Cactus's past or whatever.

Honestly, I found it all pretty hard to believe, considering the way the guy had just limped off hunched over in pain. But apparently Cactus was a real celebrity among the Resistance forces in this area.

And that wasn't all. He was a sort of legend, always fighting his way into locations filled with hundreds of machines and managing to survive the ordeal. I had to admit, it sounded a lot different from us and the way we got annihilated every single time we went out.

Cactus's popularity meant that soon enough, tons of soldiers were flocking to his command. I mean, of course they were. Nobody wants to die, and if there's some captain out there who seems to make it out of every mess alive, well, that's an easy choice to make. Fight alongside that guy, and you have a better chance of survival.

Cactus's command grew pretty sizeable in numbers, and as it did, he was racking up bigger and bigger victories on the battlefield. Pretty soon, wouldn't you know it, expectations for the guy were through the roof.

And then one day, he headed out with a handful of fresh faces on a recon op. Easy stuff. No danger expected. Perfect chance to let the rookies rack up some experience. Or so they thought.

While they were out on the op, Cactus and the kids managed to tail a stray machine. It was a pathetic, rusty old thing. Didn't give the slightest indication that it knew it was being followed. And lo and behold, the thing led them right to the enemy camp, which contained not only the majority of their forces, but their server, too.

Cactus realized that this was his shot. If he could take the server down, every machine connected to that network would stop dead in its tracks. It's a standard approach—as solid a play now as it was however many hundred years ago. Cactus was pumped.

But it was a trap.

The pathetic, rusty old machine; the concentrated forces; and the server itself were all bait. A tasty morsel left out in plain sight to lure in a particularly strong android squadron. And Cactus and his rookies gobbled it right up.

Once they were deep inside enemy territory, a huge swarm of machines swept in from behind to block their exit. That was one of the enemy's standard plays. They loved to do that.

Being a scouting party, they didn't have many units, and to make things even harder, the majority of them were rookies. They were outnumbered and outclassed. But Cactus, war hero of the ages, wasn't going down without a fight. He fought them off tooth and nail and finally broke free of the enemy perimeter. Friendly squadrons raced in to his aid. They ended up finishing off the whole lot of those damn machines, and Cactus claimed victory once again.

Only this time, it came at a high cost: the life of every rookie who was with him that day.

"We were so sure it'd be an easy day's work, perfect for helping the new recruits find their feet," Phlox said and shrugged. "We underestimated the machines."

Something about that look seemed kinda familiar.

"The captain took it the hardest," Phlox continued. "He was the only survivor from the scouting party. Just imagine. Your whole squad annihilated except for you."

Annihilation. It was the same thing our squad had been through, over and over and over and *over* again.

"Anyway, maybe you can see why he is how he is now. He's not a bad guy, honest."

Everyone else annihilated. The only one left standing. I had a pretty good idea how big a toll that took on a person's mind. That time I'd been assigned as No. 9's escort on the back lines, just *looking* at the poor kid was hard enough. It showed me real clear what he was going through.

"I think right now he's just feeling a little lost," Phlox said, still talking about the captain. "He still wonders if there was some other way. Some better strategy he could've used."

Was there a way things could've gone different? I'd wondered the same thing a bunch of times. I hated dwelling on stuff like that, but it still stuck to my brain like old gum that couldn't be scraped off. What if I'd done this or that? What if, what if, what if . . .

My mind kept repeating those questions even though I *knew* no amount of thinking or puzzling would change what'd happened. It was probably the same for both Cactus and Phlox.

[Log Entry: No. 9 / Mountain Zone—Cave Ruins]

No. 21's injuries, it turned out, were even more serious than I'd thought.

"Nothing you can do, I take it?"

"Yeah. No number of patches to your motor functions program will change the fact that your knee's going to have to bear some of the weight."

From off to the side, No. 22 looked on with obvious concern. When it came to repair work, he was completely out of his element. But this time, the damage was so obvious, even he could tell how bad things were. His expression quickly clouded over.

"Hey, you really need to take it easy, No. 21," he said.

Of course, he knew better than anyone that No. 21 wasn't the type to take that advice willingly. Maybe No. 22 just felt compelled to say it out loud, even though he knew it might not make a difference.

An obnoxious rattling noise interrupted my thoughts. I looked over to find Lotus drawing near. The whole time we'd been here, I'd only ever seen him doing one of two things: either poking at junk or staring at his tablet. Right now, it seemed he was doing the former. Except this time, he was pacing around while absorbed in his latest bits of garbage. I hoped he didn't trip or walk into someone.

He suddenly stopped and looked about.

"Hrm? What happened to the captain?" he asked.

"He went off with the others to scout the area for machines."

Though No. 21 had answered his question, Lotus made no effort to go looking for the captain. He merely sat down on the ground and began pulling scraps out of the box he was carrying. It occurred to me that he might not have had any interest in finding his captain in the first place.

"You new androids sure are strange," he mumbled absently.

I found it rather odd that an individual now stacking metal plates to form a haphazard tower should be the one to describe others as strange.

"Really, I can't see why you'd want to stick around here," Lotus continued. "Why not just head home? Leave us deserters to our own devices."

So the three of them were deserters. I'd suspected as much. Three units wasn't a full squad, so they probably hadn't been dispatched to the area, and it didn't seem like the bulk of their group's forces were anywhere nearby.

"YoRHa squadrons," No. 21 replied, in an overly matter-of-fact way, "are sworn to assist and fight alongside any androids we come across in the field."

He tried to pass it off as something a duty-bound soldier might come up with, but he was actually just parroting word for word something the instructor had said before this mission began. In fact, it had been the instructor's reply to No. 21's own complaint; No. 21 had been grumbling that a rescue mission was impossible given our squad size and available equipment.

"Listen," No. 21 said, "tomorrow we're ditching the cave and getting back out of enemy territory. And we're taking you three with us."

"Oh? Well, that's very brave. Do take care."

That seemed a little harsh. Lotus was talking like the matter didn't even concern him.

No. 21 seemed to have the same reaction. He lifted one eyebrow just slightly at Lotus's latest declaration, then added,

"Though, to be honest, I'll be glad once we part ways. I never would've guessed there were Resistance members that scurry away from the enemy like cowards. Kinda grosses me out."

No. 21 was angry. *Really* angry.

"I think that's going a little far," No. 22 said timidly. I was pretty sure this hesitant rejoinder had zero effect.

Lotus, for his part, seemed unfazed. "Yes. Yes, I suppose you would," he replied, as the metal plates in his busy hands continued to clink and rattle.

Suddenly, he asked us, "Are you familiar with the lazy ant theory?"

Now he was spouting off completely unrelated nonsense. I really did not understand this guy.

But No. 21 humored him, perhaps out of morbid curiosity. "No, what is it?"

"It's a theory based on observation of ant colonies. It states that if every member of a society is a worker critical to its function, when something happens to said workers, the system will collapse. But if some of the society's members are idle, they can step in and replace the workers as needed. Thus, in any organization, a buffer naturally forms. Twenty percent of the population turns into layabouts, for the sake of the greater good."

"Sounds exactly like the kind of excuse I'd expect from you," No. 21 retorted. He really wasn't going to cut this guy any slack.

"Perhaps," Lotus said, but he didn't exhibit the slightest trace of embarrassment.

One was just as bad as the other: No. 21, with his merciless jabs, and Lotus, brushing the criticisms off without a thought.

As suddenly as he'd arrived, Lotus stood up and began to walk away.

"And just where do you think you're going?" No. 21 yelled after him, his harsh tone apparently meant to stop Lotus in his tracks.

"Off to set up a sensor array. One that will alert us to any approaching machines so we can all sleep soundly tonight,"

Lotus said. "I built this sensor from repurposed enemy parts, you see? The rate at which the machines have evolved this past while is really quite astounding. Yes, yes. Perhaps you'd like me to elaborate on what makes this particular sensor so spectacular?"

I was beginning to learn that Lotus marched to the beat of his own drum.

"No thanks," No. 21 said. He wasn't about to give in, either.

"Yes. I'd assumed as much," Lotus replied.

The two of them were equally obnoxious. I was ready to throw my hands into the air and leave them both to their own devices. But then, without warning, Lotus whirled to face me in particular.

"Ah. No. 9. Yes. I believe No. 2 was asking for you," he said.

Huh?! When had he bothered to remember my code number? He'd seemed so uninterested in learning the most basic details about us that I'd figured I could repeat my designation to him a hundred times and he still wouldn't remember. But somewhere along the way, it apparently—and unexpectedly—sank in.

"He was saying his logic virus diagnostic was complete."

"I'll be right over!" I said, wishing Lotus could have shared the news a little sooner. No. 21's repairs were a big job, but my work on No. 2 was going to be difficult in its own way.

Our squadron's newest addition was resting in an area just outside the cave. It was a precaution—something I thought was for the best until his virus diagnostic came back all clear. The fact that he'd asked for me meant that everything was all right. Probably.

Aside from the virus diagnostic, there was a long list of other treatments I needed to administer. I had to hurry if I was going to get through them all. I started dashing off in No. 2's direction, but another thought occurred to me that stopped me short: I realized I really ought to make the situation absolutely clear to No. 21. He *had* to take things slow. I didn't know how much of an effect my advice would have, but I knew if I didn't say anything at all, he'd definitely push himself too hard.

When I'd half turned to jog back, I heard a few emphatic admonitions from No. 22. "I'm serious! Lay off! Were you not listening to anything No. 9 just said?!"

It surprised me. No. 22 rarely, if ever, spoke sharply. Maybe I didn't need to be the one to make things clear after all.

"All right, I get it already," No. 21 sulked.

Interesting. I'd considered this possibility before, but I'd never had any real data to support it. It seemed that the two of them indeed acted a little differently with each other when nobody else was around.

I found the discovery a little . . . What was the word? Oh, right. "Humorous."

I stifled a chuckle and turned around. It seemed I could leave this job to No. 22.

As I resumed my dash toward No. 2, I caught one last comment from No. 21.

"Hey, have you thought any more about what we talked about?"

His tone was suddenly hushed. What did he mean? I felt a slight twinge of curiosity, but I couldn't exactly turn around *again* to ask what they were talking about. It'd be obvious that I'd been listening in.

And besides, I needed to attend to No. 2. I didn't have time to waste.

This time, I ran as fast as my legs would take me.

[Log Entry: No. 2 / Mountain Zone—Cave Approach]

It was an odd sensation, having a complete diagnostic workup done in a place that was neither a maintenance booth nor one of R&D's training areas. The fact that it was another YoRHa android running the diagnostic—not a member of the maintenance team—only heightened my dysphoria.

When No. 9 arrived at my side, I could feel the intensity of his gaze even through his visor. The dossier I'd read in the Bunker didn't mention it, but apparently he had a very earnest personality.

"How does it look?" I asked.

"Seems you're clear, sir" he responded. "Nothing shows up on the virus diganostic."

I was glad to hear it. That eliminated my greatest concern. No. 9 seemed relieved, too. Pleased, even. He gave a faint smile. Perhaps I'd judged him too harshly. Perhaps his formal manners were the product of a gentle personality.

"Could you, uh, dispense with the 'sir's, maybe?" I asked.

Terms of address like the one he'd used were a means of showing respect. But No. 9 had no reason or need to pay me any respect.

The request seemed to take him off guard. "Huh? But you're an M001 unit, sir. You're my senior in service."

"And yet I'm the last of the squad to arrive here on the surface. Really, I don't mind."

"I'm still not sure . . ."

His hesitation seemed to stem more from confusion than from deference. I added one more detail to my store of data regarding No. 9: he was exceptionally humble.

"All right," I said, "then consider it a direct order. No. 9, I'd like you to address me informally, please."

"Yes, sir! Uh! I mean . . . sure thing!"

"Perfect. Just like that."

His face brightened, and I felt like I'd finally come to understand what it meant when humans described someone's eyes as "sparkling." Not that I could actually see No. 9's eyes—they were covered by his visor, of course. It was just a figure of speech.

His bashful smile suddenly popped into an audible, "Oh!"

He seemed to have remembered something of importance. After rummaging around in his pockets for a bit, he pulled out a roll of adhesive medical bandages.

"You injured your wrist, if I'm not mistaken."

"Hm? Oh, yes," I responded.

When I awoke after extraction from the escape pod, I realized immediately that my right wrist had sustained damage. It seemed to be a result of the emergency landing, perhaps because I'd failed to properly brace for impact due to my dormant state. Fortunately, the injury was minor. The parts themselves would be fine—I wouldn't require any replacements or firmware patches. In fact, I'd been quite confident that it wasn't in need of medical attention at all.

"I happened to come across some tips on the server archive," No. 9 explained. "One recommended taping as a way to address minor joint injuries. See? Like this."

I was startled when he suddenly took my hand. He'd just completed a full diagnostic of all my systems, so it seemed superfluous to devote additional attention to the wrist. Also, something about the warmth of his hands was unsettling.

"Apparently, there are a lot of different ways to tape an injury," he continued as he worked. "I'm just using the method I know. It'll help keep your artificial muscle tissue in place. The restricted motion is supposed to help speed recovery."

He skillfully wrapped the tape around my wrist. Not wanting to betray my consternation, I forced out a feeble protest. "But won't that interfere with my combat performance?"

"Well, the whole point is to get you fully healed so you're ready to fight at maximum efficiency again."

He was kind. He demonstrated concern for his companions. Through this one brief interaction, I felt I'd come to know everything about No. 9's behavior in regard to his squadmates.

" . . . Thanks," I said.

It was the first time I'd experienced either of those things—the first time I'd been on the receiving end of kindness or concern. It gave me a warm feeling.

I found it very unsettling.

No. 9 finished winding the tape, but he still didn't leave. He didn't seem to *want* to leave. He was visibly eager to continue talking.

"Your designation is No. 2 Type D, correct? I have to admit, I don't know much about your model type. What kind of specialties do you have?"

"The 'D' stands for Defender. Built to withstand attacks, both physical and otherwise, and I'm equipped with a defensive barrier to protect against logic viruses. I'm an experimental model."

"Experimental?"

"Correct. My frame features improved physical strength, so I'm better able to bear physical assaults, and I'm also equipped to withstand viral infection."

"Wow! That's incredible!"

"I'm meant to position myself on the front lines, absorbing enemy attacks amidst the fray, and I'm even prepared, as one of my duties, to lay down my life to keep my comrades safe."

It was just empty talk. A standard description I'd memorized. But as soon as the final sentence was out of my mouth, No. 9 froze.

Right. He was a Healer. Probably overly sensitive to discussions of death. I should've been more careful. I felt bad for making him uncomfortable.

But when he finally responded, he sounded bright and cheerful.

"Well," he said. "Sounds like some extra work for me."

The tone was a little *too* cheerful, in fact. It seemed he was trying hard not to offend me.

"As the Healer," he continued, "I'm responsible for fixing up the squad's injuries. So I'd appreciate it if you didn't get too carried away."

I smiled back. I felt obligated to give some kind of response to acknowledge his tactfulness. I even tried to laugh a bit—something I *never* did. My little show seemed to work; relief swept over No. 9's face.

But a moment later, it was gone. The Healer's voice grew somber as he told me, "Actually . . . I should probably let you know something. All of our other squadmates have already died. *Lots* of times."

Ah. Right. I'd heard them discussing it earlier, with the Resistance members. The three non-YoRHa units were taken aback. But not me. I'd already heard the reports from my SSU. I knew that M Squadron had been annihilated numerous times.

"Whenever it happens," No. 9 confided, "I reinstall their consciousness data. But . . . sometimes I suspect they still feel it inside, as if the pain and sorrow of death somehow stick with them."

This bit of information, however, was new to me. I knew about the casualties insofar as they were recorded as data. I hadn't realized the way they made No. 9 feel as he stood all alone, observing his squadmates die over and over and how they reacted after.

"So, um . . . that's why I'm asking. Please. As best as you're able. Please don't die, No. 2."

For a moment, I was unable to answer. I didn't have any sort of prepared response for someone pleading with me not to die.

"Uh . . . sure. I'll do my best."

It took everything I had to piece together those few words. I was curious to see if he bought them, but No. 9 quickly stood, and I could no longer see his face.

"I'll go get you some water," he said.

"No need. My tank's still—"

"Nonsense. If you happened to run low during a fight, you'd lock right up. It's best to maximize the spare energy you have on hand. Wait right there."

I watched him run off and realized I was relieved to see him go. I knew it would be best if we didn't converse like that any further. Not to mention, I didn't enjoy being eavesdropped on, and I certainly wasn't so dull as to fail to notice it happening.

"No. 2." My eavesdropper spoke up. Instructor Black.

He'd been waiting for No. 9 to leave. I heard his footsteps drawing near, but I didn't turn to face him.

"It's been a while," he said. "Not since our chat in the Bunker's hangar, I suppose."

I hadn't realized you could call that a chat. In my mind, it was more like he'd shown up unannounced to check on my progress.

"When do you start?" he asked.

"You're not authorized to know."

Was he fishing for information? If so, why was he doing it under the pretense of having a casual conversation instead of just issuing me a direct order? Was that just how he operated down here on the surface? Or did it imply something else?

"No. 2 Type D . . . How long do you plan to operate under a false identity?"

"Nor are you authorized to know the timeframe under which I intend to reveal my identity."

It wasn't as if I could refuse to answer a direct question from a superior officer—as much as I hated to admit he was one. So I kept my answers brief and my words vague. After all, you never knew who might be listening in.

"You and I both know who you really are, No. 2 . . . Type E."

With a single stroke, he smashed my careful attempts to keep the conversation discreet. It was upsetting, to say the least. What the hell was he thinking, saying my proper designation out loud like that? He obviously lacked judgment.

"A specialized unit for the express purpose of executing an active YoRHa Squadron, charged with the complete destruction of all units—black boxes included—to prevent dissemination of details regarding YoRHa androids, the Council's most vital secret."

It was poorly considered comments like these that made fools with partial clearance so dangerous. Could he even begin to comprehend the danger of the words coming out of his mouth? And if he did, what was he hoping to get out of me that he was willing to take such a risk?

"Of course, that description is just another lie."

As if he needed to point it out. The Type E model was surrounded by lies. Lies, secrets, and deceit. That described my entire makeup. That was who I was.

"As I understand it, your line was originally intended as a means to quell insurrection among YoRHa units. Suppression duties. A trump card held in reserve by the Council in case everything went wrong."

"I am not authorized to respond to that. However, I would remind you that of YoRHa Experimental M Squadron, you alone have been made aware of my purpose. Allowing that information to leak to the other units is a punishable offense."

I allowed my tone to grow menacing to drive home the point. It was unclear to me where Black's true motives lay, but in any case, casual mention of the Type E designation was absolutely unacceptable.

"I'd be more concerned about your own actions," the instructor replied. "Allowing yourself to become attached to your squadmates could prove a real obstacle when it comes time to kill them."

Bastard. Now he was just trying to provoke me. And he wasn't doing a very good job of it.

"Your concern is unnecessary. I've trained for this."

"Ah."

And then, with nothing more than the briefest acknowledgement, Black pivoted on his heel and walked away.

That was when it finally hit me. The questions he'd been asking—what if there was no ulterior motive to them? No lies. No deceit. Maybe he just wanted to know when it would all begin.

But how would that knowledge change anything? What, was he going to offer a helping hand or something? The thought was absurd.

I was here to kill my squadmates. That job fell to me, and me alone. I was outfitted with everything I'd need to get the job done, and no one would stand in my way.

Out of the corner of my eye, I noticed the taped wrist.

So, um . . . that's why I'm asking. Please. As best as you're able. Please don't die, No. 2.

Why did he have to be the one to say that?

What would he do if he knew what I really was? Would he hate me for it? Would he try to kill me? Or would he—

No. Leave it. Best not to entertain irrelevant thoughts. The only thing I needed to think about was my mission . . . And my mission was to kill all of my comrades.

CHAPTER 5

[Log Entry: No. 2 / Mountain Zone—Campsite]

"AND SO I TELL HIM, GO ON, GET TO WORK ON THE TRENCH. And Lotus comes back all like . . ."

Cactus formed two rings with the thumb and index finger of each hand, then brought them to his eyes and peered through them. Apparently, he was simulating a pair of glasses to round out his impersonation of Lotus.

"The trench is ready, yes, yes!" Cactus spoke in a high-pitched screech to make sure we got the point.

I had to give him some credit. The portrayal wasn't entirely inaccurate.

He continued in his normal voice. "And so I follow him back, expecting to check it out, right? And it turns out the thing's only knee-deep! I mean, what, is it supposed to be a trench or a *pit trap*? I hop in to show him why it won't work, but he starts pouring *cement* into the thing! The stuff hardens right up, and wouldn't you know it, just then a buncha machines decide to show up. So now I'm batting away enemies, stuck in a knee-deep trench . . . I tell ya, I thought I was done for!"

As he spoke, Cactus swept his arms wide and dramatically reenacted the motions of the story. I didn't find the tale particularly interesting, but the rest of the squad seemed to love it. They were sprawled out comfortably, erupting in great fits of laughter at each twist.

Despite my disinterest, I maintained the appearance of a captivated listener. To do otherwise would have been careless. I was certainly capable of feigning a laugh, even when faced with dismally uninspired material.

And to be honest, I wasn't alone. No. 4's smile seemed a bit forced, too. At first, he'd listened attentively, but partway through Cactus's tale, it seemed to click for him that this wasn't the kind of thing you were meant to take seriously.

In contrast, No. 3 was very literally clutching his sides with laughter. At a glance, it seemed he and Cactus got along quite well, and I'd noticed he was also pretty friendly with Phlox.

Phlox, for his part, had probably heard the current story dozens of times. His laugh was pained, as if the humor for him was in the fact that the captain was *still* getting mileage out of this particular standby.

On the other hand, No. 6's laugh seemed slightly condescending. I'd discovered him to be a bit standoffish, though I knew from his profile that he'd scored staggeringly well on all of his tests. The discrepancy between the data and the way he conducted himself in person was surprising; I'd need to keep my guard up around No. 6.

Next to him, No. 9 and No. 22 sat side by side. Both were smiling and seemed to be enjoying themselves, if not to the extent of No. 3. One could tell at a glance that they had honest, straightforward personalities.

According to the reports I'd been provided with, No. 22 was supposed to have a bit of a timid side. That might have stemmed from a lack of confidence. Perhaps what faith he lacked in himself he instead placed in those around him. Or maybe he acted the way he did out of habit, long used to following the lead of his twin model, No. 21.

No. 9's smile, though . . . That betrayed his sincere nature. The more contact I had with the Healer, the more my initial impression solidified into certainty.

He was also exasperatingly kind. Just earlier, for example, I'd bent over to pick up some materials with my injured hand. No. 9 had dashed over to admonish me. "Stop! You mustn't lift anything heavy until it heals! Here, I'll carry those for you." He then gently took the items from my grip. Honestly, they weren't of any notable weight to begin with.

No. 9 acted that way not just toward me but toward everyone. He was always carefully watching the other members of the squadron, making sure nobody was feeling unwell or overexerting themselves. No. 9 seemed intent on finding any way he could to contribute to the squad. I attributed it to feelings of inferiority for being unable to participate in combat, even though such feelings were wholly unnecessary.

No. 9 didn't need to feel inferior for being unable to fight, as he was the very lifeline holding the YoRHa Experimental M Squadron together. If he were to die, all the squadron's members would lose their means of resurrection.

But putting speculation aside, here we were—myself, No. 3, No. 4, No. 6, No. 9, No. 22, and the Resistance members Cactus and Phlox—all sitting together listening to the captain's story. Black, No. 21, and Lotus were not present. The three had gone off to (according to Black) conduct a strategy meeting: No. 21 because of his role in providing squad reconnaissance and Lotus because, despite his quirks, he was thoroughly familiar with the area. Black's choices seemed reasonable enough.

However, I had reservations about Black spending much time in close proximity to No. 21. The Scanner might be more perceptive than Black gave him credit for. A single slipped word or miniscule shift in expression might be more than enough to trigger No. 21's suspicion. Ultimately, it was a matter of whether Black was sufficiently in control of his actions or not. This was, after all, the same man reckless enough to utter my formal designation aloud.

"Lemme tell ya, things were shapin' up real bad for yours truly! As soon as we take out the machines, this whole pack of wild boar storms in and *wham*! I'm all like, 'look at the pretty stripes on the piggies, mommy,' and then the world's goin' hazy and all I can focus on are the pretty flowers and that nice clear river just over there . . ."

As another round of laughter erupted, in walked the man I'd written off as trouble, No. 21 at his side and Lotus trailing just behind.

"Everyone, listen up."

The sound of Black's voice flipped a switch in the room. The laughter abruptly stopped. With the loss of attention from his audience, Cactus stopped his charades, instantly looking more serious.

No. Maybe it was the other way around. Everyone had stopped laughing and regained their focus *because* Cactus dropped his act.

"We've plotted an exit route," Black said. "However, it won't be easy. I'd like to ask for your undivided attention."

He raised his arm and pointed into the air at his side. Just beyond the tip of his finger, a map flickered into view. It appeared to show the surrounding area. The small blinking dot in the center, then, would denote our current position.

"We're currently located here," Black said, pointing at the blinking dot.

Bingo. One point for me.

New lights began to dot the map, all surrounding ours. They were red, and there were a lot of them. I didn't have to wait for the explanation for these, either; I knew immediately that they represented enemy units.

"As you can see, the surrounding area is full of hostile machine lifeforms. The cave and our present campsite just happen to be situated in a tiny gap in their coverage. We remain undetected for now, but it's only a matter of time before the machines discover our presence."

No. 4 raised a hand.

"Sir! Any chance we could request backup or aerial support?"

I hated to dash his hopes, but nope. Not a chance. I found out why firsthand: the moment I'd entered the atmosphere on my descent, enemy units had swept in to intercept. The assault was so intense, as I'd climbed inside the escape pod, I figured there was a good chance it'd be my coffin.

"No good, No. 4," Black responded. "The enemy has the air-space around here locked down tight. There's no way for a transport carrying an extraction unit to approach and safely touch down."

Black's response was word for word what I'd predicted. But

No. 4 didn't look disappointed. It seemed he'd asked just for the sake of asking, anticipating the answer just like I had.

Next, No. 22 raised a hand. "Couldn't we fry 'em with a satellite laser strike?"

Again, Black shook his head.

"I'm afraid the area's just too large. It isn't possible to take out the number of enemies we're facing with a single strike. Not to mention, Command won't authorize use of a satellite laser to begin with."

"And why the hell not?" No. 3 asked, clearly dissatisfied.

"As one of the most powerful weapons in our arsenal, we can only afford to use it sparingly. Indiscriminate firing would give the machines too much opportunity to analyze its properties and develop a way to resist it."

"Swell. So in other words, we're not important enough to risk their precious baby."

No. 3 spat the words out, but somewhere among the distaste, I sensed another feeling: resignation. I could easily guess why. This undoubtedly was not the first time they'd been rebuffed by Command.

"I didn't call this briefing just to deliver bad news," continued Black, trying to soothe his audience. He turned to Lotus. "The report, please."

Lotus stepped forward, a little too eagerly, ending up with his face poking through the projected map. He didn't seem to notice or care, instead just barreling on with his presentation.

"Yes. Hrm. Well, in short, the present region used to be Resistance-controlled territory. But, you see, four years ago, the machine lifeforms swept in and ravaged everything. Since then, it's remained uninhabited. Yes. So, with that in mind, I should very much like to introduce to you all a most fascinating characteristic of machine lifeform behavior. Truly, I cannot overstate how intriguing this particular facet is. Caught your attention, have I? Hmm. Now, you see, it turns out that the machine lifeforms are quite aware of the differences between androids, including the Resistance, and the weapons they employ. And that, of course, is why . . ."

How long was he going to babble on for?

Apparently, I wasn't the only one losing my patience. No. 4 tried to hurry Lotus along, asking, "And your point is?"

"Precisely this: when we treat our weapons like thus . . ."

Lotus grabbed Cactus's rifle.

"Hey! What're you . . . ?! That's mine!"

Lotus ignored his captain's protests and placed the weapon on the ground, then slowly backed away from it.

"Voilà. You see, the machines show not the slightest interest in our weapons when left unattended like so. They focus their attention solely on us."

No. 3 interjected, "Just imagine, gettin' rushed by a bunch of machines when we're unarmed . . . Sounds like a damn nightmare."

It was perhaps the most obvious and unnecessary observation ever made.

But Lotus stretched his arms wide, a knowing smile on his face.

"The point is, the focus of their attention is on *us*. They leave the *weapons* alone."

No. 3's mouth hung open in confusion, and he wasn't alone. To tell the truth, I hadn't the slightest idea what Lotus was implying, either. Black and No. 21 would have clarified the details in the strategy meeting, but aside from those two, everyone present looked absolutely lost.

Phlox walked over and clapped a friendly hand on Lotus's shoulder. "So, uh, I've been meaning to talk to you about this, but . . . the way you explain things. It always comes across as pretty damn disjointed. How about you try once more, laying it out for us step-by-step?"

"Disjointed? Me?"

Lotus tilted his head to one side, mystified. Clearly, he'd believed his explanation was more than sufficient.

"All right. Erm. Let's see . . . Yes. Well, as this area was formerly under Resistance control, it was obviously outfitted with an airfield. For the purpose of transporting goods to and from the area, naturally."

Suddenly he was talking about an airfield. Where had this come from? I was getting more confused by the second.

Unable to bear watching the spectacle any longer, No. 21 stepped in.

"Here's an aerial photo showing the old airfield," the Scanner said.

The map displaying the hordes of enemies around us shifted to a view of one tiny swatch of level terrain in the Mountain Zone. I could make out the contours of what had once been a runway; the entire length was scarred with bomb craters.

"As you can see, a few undamaged transport vessels remain on site."

I was finally starting to understand what Lotus was getting at. The machine lifeforms could clearly distinguish between androids and their equipment. A transport ship with androids aboard was a prime target: the machines would smash it to pieces. But one sitting idly on a runway or in a hangar with no androids in sight—things like that, they left be.

So the plan was to commandeer an old transport long ignored by the machines and make a break for it. That seemed to be the gist of what Lotus was trying to say.

"But I thought the enemy had control of the skies in this area?

At No. 9's question, No. 21 flicked the display to a different aerial photograph. The runway was still visible, but this time, it was surrounded by a slew of red dots: enemies in the vicinity of the airfield. And I was willing to bet they were all flying ones.

A short distance away blinked a single white light, much brighter than the enemy dots. No. 21 placed a finger on it.

"This is the enemy control tower."

"And what about it?"

"It manages the flight paths of airborne machines. So if we neutralize the tower . . ."

The light indicating the control tower winked out, and the red dots surrounding the airfield soon followed.

" . . . we eliminate guidance for all flying enemies, effectively paralyzing them."

Several questions remained. Would destroying the tower be as simple a task as their briefing made it out to be? And would the long-neglected transport be operational? Still, it was a plan, and given our current situation, it seemed to be our only real option for escaping the area. Nobody was about to protest.

"We have Lotus and No. 21 to thank for this proposal," said Black. "However, it is not within my authority to issue orders to Resistance members. So instead, I ask: will you join us?"

At Black's appeal, a curtain of uncertainty fell over Cactus's face. He started shaking so bad, it almost hurt just to watch the guy.

"Uh . . . Wh-what should we do?"

He looked to Phlox for help. It wasn't the first time I'd seen Cactus like this in our short time together. While he was supposed to be the leader of their little group, he often leaned on his subordinate Phlox for assistance. Lotus, the lowest rank on their little team, was generally left to do as he pleased. I had no idea how Cactus could stand to run things that way.

"You're the captain. You gotta make the call," Phlox responded.

"Oh. Yeah. I guess you're right."

This was another mystery to me. Phlox would drop a casual comment like that, and Cactus would magically find his composure again. Their whole organizational structure was beyond me: I couldn't wrap my head around their convoluted chain of command, or the relationships they had with each other.

"All right. Yeah! Count us in," Cactus concluded. "Er . . . I guess I should say, please take us with you!"

The three Resistance members bowed their heads in unison.

Black responded, "Very well," and segued into the details.

"We'll be operating in three teams," he explained. "Team A will conduct an assault on the tower, starting with the elimination of all surrounding enemies at long range. The team will consist of No. 4 and No. 22, and I'd like to ask our three Resistance allies to accompany and assist, given their familiarity with the terrain."

So the plan was to split up and let each group do its thing, huh? I carefully committed to memory the rosters of each team. I'd need a firm grasp on everyone's whereabouts.

"Next, Team B will take control of the transport. Considering the high concentration of enemies on the grounds of the airfield itself, I want No. 21 leading the way, spotting enemies for No. 3 and No. 6 to dispatch as they follow closely behind."

"Think you're up for that?" Black asked, looking at No. 3.

The Attacker seemed pleased. "Up for it? Hell, I was born for that shit."

No. 6 gave a dismissive shrug, his expression conveying both his disdain for No. 3 and a desire that we all know No. 3's crass comment did not speak for him.

"Finally," Black continued, "Team C will keep the squadron backup safe by escorting No. 9 to the transport. Escort will be provided by myself . . . and Defender No. 2."

He glanced toward me as if implying something. I ignored him. It was exactly the sort of obvious gesture someone entrusted with sensitive information might attempt, and exactly what I found so irritating about him. Subtle attempts to relay information in this setting only invited trouble. He'd put not only No. 21 on alert, but probably No. 6 as well.

But he prattled on like a fool, not a care in the world.

"Finally, I'd like to ask Captain Cactus to provide a word of encouragement before we commence," he said. "After all, you did such a good job easing everyone's nerves with your stories. Attentiveness like that is the mark of a fine leader."

That comment caught me off guard—not just the realization that Cactus's earlier clowning had been for the benefit of the group's morale, but that Black was the one who'd observed a fact that I missed. Considering the instructor's appalling carelessness, I hadn't thought him particularly attuned to his soldiers' needs.

It seemed he wasn't an entirely unqualified leader. And neither was Cactus.

Not that it concerned me. The extent to which Cactus and Black were suited to their roles had no bearing on my mission.

It was a trivial detail—one that could be safely discarded from my mind the moment I acknowledged it.

"Let's all make it back alive and safe. No matter what!" Cactus proclaimed.

As I listened to everyone cheer in response, I had a strange feeling—one that was difficult to put into words.

Let's make it back? To where? M Squadron's fate was already decided. The three Resistance members were deserters. Not a single person here had any place to go back to.

M Squadron wasn't even meant to evacuate the stranded Resistance members in the first place; the distress signal and the mission surrounding it was just a sham. They'd been told they were being sent to the Mountain Zone to identify the source of the signal and assist anyone found on site, but their "mission" was just a pretext to have M Squadron rendezvous with their eventual assassin. Me.

The Resistance members were just extras on the stage.

But as soon as the thought entered my mind, I felt disgusted with myself for having it.

"No. 2!"

I pulled myself back into the moment. The squadron members and Resistance androids were nowhere to be found. The only ones who remained were me, caught up in my superfluous thoughts, and No. 9.

"Here. Don't forget to put this into your supply tank."

" . . . Put what into my supply tank?"

"This! The water, remember? I brought it just like I promised. Hurry, before it gets a bunch of dust in it."

Remember? Remember what?

Ah. Right. He'd run off earlier saying he was going to fetch me some water. He seemed worried about me running out during a fight and being unable to function.

"And just so you know," No. 9 said, looking me straight in the eye, "even Healers have to complete sword training. At least the basics, anyway."

For the first time, I became aware of the intensity in his gaze.

I'd pegged him as a quiet, reserved type, but the way he stared at me now suggested a degree of strength I hadn't anticipated.

"So, uh . . . let's do a good job together at the airfield." He smiled at me.

I was caught by the radiance of his smile. For a moment, I found myself frozen in place, unable even to nod in response.

But No. 9 didn't seem bothered by my lack of response. He dashed off, leaving me alone.

I needed to get going. I was in Team C as well. I couldn't afford to arouse suspicion. I needed to act normal.

I stood and began to follow No. 9. A small beep stopped me. The timing was almost uncanny, as if the SSU had been waiting for this moment to pipe up.

"What is it?"

Its low, tinny voice announced, "Alert: Four hours have elapsed since scheduled mission completion time."

"There have been complicating factors. Request extension of time allotted for mission completion."

Right now, there was too much going on at once. There was no way I could execute my mission without the squadron quickly realizing what was happening. If Command had a problem with that, maybe they should've considered what kind of situation they were dropping me into. Nobody told me I was going to have to carry this order out behind enemy lines.

Or . . . on second thought, maybe that was deliberate. Maybe in the chaos of our escape, the perfect opportunity would present itself.

Allowing yourself to become attached to your squadmates could prove a real obstacle when it comes time to kill them.

Black's words replayed themselves in my mind. It was irritating to think I'd received advice from *Black*. Though at first his words seemed nothing more than a casual comment, now they were haunting me like a curse. The sense of unease within me was growing.

"Extension denied. Proposal: Eliminate YoRHa Experimental M Squadron immediately."

Great. Nobody was going to cut me a break.

"Understood," I muttered to the SSU.

Then, to myself, "Keep your emotions out of it."

I had to dispose of anything that could get in the way of my mission, and unnecessary feelings were at the very top of the list.

[Log Entry: No. 22 / Airfield—Control Tower Approach]

The control tower seemed so far away. In actuality, it was only a few hundred meters—I could've sprinted the distance in no time. Yet it still *felt* impossibly far away, thanks to the dozens of machines occupying the stretch of ground before us.

In a situation like this, No. 21 would have instantly been able to rattle off the exact distance to the tower, accurate to the millimeter, and then tell me that as long as I was able to take down X number of enemies every Y period of time, I'd reach the tower in T minutes S seconds. He'd have given me the facts in hard numbers and told me that I didn't need to worry.

"First off, we gotta eliminate the enemies near the tower." No. 4's voice seemed the very definition of composure.

In contrast, when I responded, "Understood," my voice quaked like a frightened child's. No. 21 wasn't by my side. That alone was enough to fill me with fear. This was the first time we'd ever had to operate apart from each other.

No. Enough. I couldn't rely on No. 21 forever. I had to grow up.

When we first rolled off the production line, we'd both been like little children. Our memory banks were free of any data beyond the preinstalled settings, and we had yet to begin our training. It was so much fun simply being together, I think we spent every moment smiling ear to ear.

But as we looped our way through the rounds of study and tests, No. 21 became more and more clever. Stronger, too. I felt like I was barely keeping up, running with everything I had just to stay at his back. But even then, things were all right. As long as I kept chasing after my twin, that meant that I was growing, too. And if I had to chase after him forever . . . Well, that just meant we'd always be together.

So when had things changed? At some point, I wasn't hoping to simply follow in his footsteps anymore. I wanted to walk beside him. I wanted to be able to protect him like he protected me.

No, no, no. There wasn't time for those thoughts now. I needed to concentrate on my shooting. The enemy still hadn't noticed us. We needed to act while we had the initiative. I lined up a machine in my sights. I wanted to make each kill with one clean shot.

But the moment I fired, everything changed. Now the machines were alerted to our presence. We'd expected as much, of course, but we hadn't anticipated how swiftly they'd react.

"Erm, the enemy appears to be closing in!"

Lotus didn't need to tell me. It looked like the machines had calculated our firing position nearly instantaneously. If No. 21 had been here, I'd have been able to snipe from farther out, but on my own, this was as great a distance as I could manage.

I needed to finish them off before they reached us, but they were moving too fast. There were too many of them, and they were packed too tight. I was having trouble lining up another clear shot.

I panicked. "I-I'm not gonna be able to make the calculations in time!"

"Take a deep breath." No. 4's voice was steady.

Approaching enemies were falling one by one: No. 4 was shooting with perfect accuracy. I was awestruck. How was he managing at this distance, and when there were so many of them?

"Halve the resources you're allocating to aim correction," he directed, "Rely on instinct for the rest."

"Y-yes, sir!"

No. 4 was right, of course. With the enemies packed this tight, even if my shots were slightly off I'd still likely hit *something*. It was going to be all right. I could do this. I just needed to concentrate on thinning the machines' numbers. We needed to get to the tower quickly so we could neutralize the flying units. The airspace had to be safe by the time No. 21 commandeered the transport.

Just then, I heard Phlox say, "Let's go, Cap."

"Huh?"

"Decoy duty. We'll move out wide on both flanks and harass the enemy. It should take some heat off the YoRHa snipers."

"Don't. It's too dangerous," No. 4 began, but over his shoulder, I saw a pack of machines closing in.

"No. 4! Watch out!"

Half aim. Half instinct. I silently repeated No. 4's words and fired. The enemies clattered lifelessly to the ground. No. 4 had turned to fire, too. I felt as though I'd only managed half as many kills as him, but still, a victory was a victory. It did leave me uneasy about how well we'd manage if the next group of machines was larger, though.

"Yeah, we definitely wanna split the herd up." Phlox was as calm as ever. The way he announced his plan, you'd have thought he was stepping out for a casual stroll.

"We don't have as much punch as you guys, but if all we gotta do is draw attention, I think we'll do just fine. Not to mention, we've got a secret weapon. Isn't that right, Cap?"

Cactus piped up with a lively, "You know it!"

What was this secret weapon? I wanted to ask, but I was too busy firing at more approaching machines. Phlox and Cactus took off at a full sprint in the direction of the enemy horde.

"Are they . . . gonna be okay?" I asked Lotus, who remained behind.

"Yes, yes. Nothing to worry about."

It did little to reassure me, considering Lotus's usual threshold for concern.

"Earlier," Lotus said, "I outfitted their weapons with a virus. Hrm. Yes. It's quite effective against machine lifeforms, you see."

I recalled our approach to the cave during the initial rescue operation; we'd found it surrounded by autoturrets made from virus-infected machines. I certainly had my questions about Lotus's personality—whether he took things seriously or was just a lazy bum—but when it came to engineering, I had to admit he was at the top of his game.

"It's delivered via their bullets, yes. Any machine struck by one will be, for lack of a better word, *zombified*. They'll transform into autoturrets, firing on anything in range!"

The way Lotus said it, I didn't think he was trying show off. His invention seemed to bring him genuine delight. Implanting viruses and modding machines wasn't a job to him so much as a hobby. He was into it for the personal enjoyment.

Lotus made to continue explaining the modifications, but No. 4 interrupted. "Hold up.

"*Anything* in range?" No. 4 asked. "No distinction between friend and foe?"

"Oh. Erm . . ."

From some distance away, we heard a shriek from Cactus, along with an angry shout from Phlox.

"Loootuuus!"

Undoubtedly, the two had discovered the same detail firsthand.

As I'd feared, Lotus's net contribution to the op was close to zero, if not squarely in negative territory.

"No. 22."

"Yeah?"

"Let's not waste the chance. We take 'em all out. Now."

No. 4 was right. This wasn't what Lotus had promised us, but the machine offensive had admittedly deteriorated into a state of chaos.

"Got it!"

And there was only one way for me to help: take down as many enemies as possible. The more kills, the better. We'd exterminate the lot of them and seize ourselves a transport. This would be the time we made it back alive. This mission would end with our escape to safety—the same me and the same No. 21 that existed right now.

Half aim. Half instinct. Still repeating my newfound mantra, I kept shooting to kill every machine in range.

There were so many enemy units, I began to wonder if there was any need for me to be scouting at all. Just behind me, No. 3 barreled along the machine-infested runway, blade gleaming with each strike. The runway was so packed, he could have just swung his sword in circles with his eyes closed and he'd still be taking down machines.

First, I had to find us a route to the transport. Once we reached it, we'd get ourselves inside while cutting down any reinforcements that tried to swarm in. Then No. 3 and No. 6 would head back out, keeping the area around the craft clear while I hacked the thing's controls. Once the craft was ours, we'd alert Teams A and C to make their way over. We'd all been briefed on the plan.

"Graaaaaaah!"

I saw several machine bodies go flying through the air as I heard No. 3's battle cry. Once more, I found myself in awe of the physical strength he had to possess in order to swing his huge sword around so freely.

"Take this! And *this*! C'mon! I'm right here!"

Another mob of machines swarmed No. 3, as if goaded on by his taunts. His giant blade drew one more wide arc, and the entire group was neutralized, heads smashed or cylindrical trunks stove in. They flew backward, smashing into the next wave of oncoming machines.

"Hah! That all you got?!" No. 3 yelled. "Hell, I could keep this up all day! How about a challenge?!"

Unfortunately, the machines obliged him. A new group crashed down from above—ground units ferried in by flying machines high up in the sky. It played out exactly as No. 4 had always feared: No. 3 had a bad habit of letting his attention wander every time he finished something off.

"Shit!"

This time, it wasn't No. 4's bullets that brought No. 3 back from the brink of defeat. The newest machine assailants clattered lifelessly at the M001 unit's feet, and I saw No. 6

standing cool and composed with sword in hand. He, too, had finished off an entire group of enemies with one smooth action.

"Could you please stop yelling?" he asked. "It's so vulgar. You don't have to holler like an ape every single time you swing your sword."

"Oh, shove it, you stuck-up bastard." No. 3 growled in response.

No. 6 ignored him and turned to me. "Which way next?"

"Four incoming from the north. Big ones!"

"You heard him, No. 3. Let's get to it."

"Yeah, I'm standin' right here! You don't have to tell me!" No. 3 turned to the north and started running. "And it's No. 3, *sir*, to you!"

The well-worn phrase elicited a snort from No. 6.

"I'll think about it . . . if you manage to survive, that is."

No. 6 looked like a predator about to pounce on its prey, practically licking his lips at the prospect of taking on the big machines. Slaughtering enemies almost seemed to bring him joy, like he'd never get enough of it.

No. 3 was the same way. Whenever he began swinging that huge sword, leaping to and fro, it looked like he was dancing. He dragged enemies along with the tip of his blade, then beat them into the ground, letting out another of his "vulgar" cries, grinning the whole time with almost manic glee.

Yeah. These two would do just fine. They'd give me exactly what I needed.

Hardly a few minutes had passed before the four large machines were four piles of lifeless scrap strewn across the battlefield.

[Log Entry: No. 9 / Airfield—Back Lines]

From the way the sky looked, I thought it might start raining at any moment. Ashen clouds were rolling in on an unpleasantly warm wind. I recalled a document I'd read explaining that storms in the Mountain Zone were a lot more intense than those in open terrain. I hoped there wouldn't be thunder. I hated thunder.

We crept among the shadows of fallen trees and great boulders scarred by machinegun fire, slowly making our way forward. Team C's only responsibility was to get aboard the transport safe and sound, and in order to accomplish that, we needed to do everything we could to avoid encounters with the machines.

We didn't have No. 21 with us to give warning of enemies closing in on our position, or No. 22 to pick off those machines with deadly precision. I had no idea how we'd fare if our team found itself cornered into a fight.

I knew that the instructor would do his best to protect me, but even then, I worried that No. 2 might have to absorb hits on my behalf. No. 2 wouldn't hesitate, either. He'd do whatever it took to keep me safe. I felt certain of that. It only made it all the worse to think of him hurt or killed for my sake.

"This . . . from Team . . . reporting in."

No. 4's voice sputtered over the instructor's SSU. The wireless transmission itself was coming in uninterrupted, but No. 4's words were almost impossible to make out over a background of gunfire or some other racket.

" . . . Control . . . power lines . . . ccessfully destroyed."

The roar of an explosion accompanied this last statement. Then another, and yet another. I figured it must have been the sound of flying machines crashing to the ground as they lost flight guidance.

"Good work. Head down the runway to the transport and stand by," the instructor ordered.

I looked down the runway, too. Dead machines littered its length; nothing seemed to be moving. Beyond the trail of carnage sat the transport. No. 3 and No. 6 had secured us a clear path.

"We should hurry, too, sir!" I said. "Before enemy reinforcements arrive."

This was our chance. Sensing no machines lurking in the surroundings, I started to run straight for the transport.

"No. 9! Stop!"

The sudden shout froze me in place. Had I failed to notice a lurking enemy? No. That didn't seem to be the case. So why had the instructor ordered me to stop?

"Sir?" I asked, turning around. I quickly looked around once more, but I still didn't see any sign of an active machine.

The instructor had drawn his blade. I could hardly remember the last time I'd seen him with his sword out.

I flicked my gaze to No. 2, who had been right behind me. It didn't seem like anything had happened to him, either. What was the cause for alarm?

"Sir?" I repeated.

"Keep your guard up out there." The instructor's face was rigid, his tone flat.

"Y-yes, sir. Of course."

Something wasn't right. I could sense the tension emanating from the instructor as clear as day. It was almost frightening, in a way. A part of me wanted to flee, to put as much distance as I could between me and him.

"Sir! This is No. 21, Team B!" The transmission blared from instructor's SSU.

I was grateful to hear No. 21's voice. It was coming through loud and clear, a stark difference from No. 4's broken messages. Maybe it was because Team B would have been much closer to us than Team A.

"The enemy is regrouping on our position. As soon as I've got the transport's engines running, we need to take off. Please get here as soon as you can!"

"Understood."

When I looked up at the instructor again, he seemed back to his usual self: strict, but calm and collected.

"Let's move," he said, glancing at me and then No. 2, as if sizing us both up. For the briefest moment, I thought I saw the disquiet return. Was it just my imagination?

I didn't have time to find out. Both the instructor and No. 2 took off running toward the transport. I followed their lead, unease and confusion still swirling within me.

The inside of the transport was eerily quiet. When Lotus claimed the machines didn't give these things a second thought as long as no androids were aboard, I thought he was full of it. But given the state of the craft, it seemed true enough.

Still, the machines weren't stupid. They'd installed one hell of a lock on the cargo bay door and had also outfitted the interior of the craft with a series of bulkheads, each also locked. It was a hassle every step of the way. Not that I had to deal with it. That was all on No. 21.

So we had to hack each lock, and then open the bulkhead before we could proceed to the next one. We went on like that for a while, making a snail's pace through the transport's interior. By the time we reached the door to the control room, who knew how much time had passed?

"Another lock?" No. 21 groaned, then set to work on the panel next to the door. All I could do was stand there looking at No. 3's dumb face and wait. I didn't like it, but it's not like I had a choice. No use for a couple of Attackers when there weren't any enemies in sight.

"You almost done?"

No. 3 peered over to where No. 21's hands were furiously tapping away. Hmph. Like he had the first clue whatever it was our Scanner was doing. Could he *get* any dumber?

The door began to slide open. After a few centimeters, it ground to a halt.

"Dammit all to hell!"

Apparently, they'd doubled up on locks for this last door. A lot of forethought for a bunch of machines.

No. 21 shoved one hand through the small crack between door and frame, while continuing the hack with his other hand. He was pretty sick of this game, too. Or maybe he was feeling the pressure with No. 3 standing over his shoulder, because now he was trying to force the thing open.

Tiny sparks sputtered from the panel. No. 21's face contorted with effort.

Mmm . . . I hadn't known he could look like that. A faint groan escaped his clenched teeth. I saw irritation and panic and anguish, all bundled up into a delectable whole. A slight shiver passed through my body.

For a while now, I'd wanted to have our Scanner all to myself, the two of us alone in a room, my hands upon him. No. 22 certainly had his own allure, but now I wondered if No. 21 might be even more fun. Always walking around with that cool expression and haughty attitude. He was probably the type that started acting shy the moment you had him cornered.

"Got it!" he exclaimed.

The panel under his free hand crackled and spat out new sparks, much greater in number and size. That was our signal. The door was sliding further open. No. 21 shoved himself through the gap, and No. 3 was in so fast after him, he might as well have been riding the Scanner's back. Still no sign of hostiles beyond, or anywhere else in the transport, for that matter. I made a point of sweeping my eyes around once more before following No. 3 inside.

The control room was a lot bigger than I'd expected. Both the forward wall and center floor had large viewing screens mounted perfectly flush with the surrounding construction. Apparently, this heavy transport we'd chosen was a pretty recent model.

Ah. Right. I recalled Lotus's explanation of how the area had fallen to machine control just four years ago. Not exactly ancient history.

No. 21 planted himself at the main control terminal, his fingers busily tapping away.

Such long, slender fingers.

"Think we can get 'er to fly?"

Could No. 3 not keep his mouth shut for one damn minute? I wanted to watch those delicate fingers in peace. I wished the ugly brute wasn't with us at all, in fact.

"Almost there. If I can get this thing to issue us a key, we're as good as airborne."

The wall screen lit up, and the one on the floor blinked on

to show a map of the airfield. Did this mean we'd successfully seized control? All we had to do was wait for Teams A and C now?

I'd gotten my hopes up too soon.

A guttural cry erupted from No. 21's throat, and lines upon lines of gibberish streaked across the screens.

I had a sinking feeling about what I was seeing.

"Hey! What's the matter?! What happened?!" No. 3 yelled.

Did he really need to ask? Of course he did, the bolthead. And now, because he *had* asked, No. 21 felt compelled to answer. He squeezed the words out, voice laced with pain.

"An . . . enemy . . . logic virus . . . It was a trap!"

I knew it. Everything had been going far too smoothly. Relying on a bunch of locked doors with no guard detail in sight? The enemy never skimped on security like that.

The logic virus wasn't our only problem. One corner of the ceiling popped open, and a swarm of machines dropped in. If the damn things had been here all along, it would've been nice if they could've cut the games and shown up at the beginning. It would've made the journey inside a lot less boring.

Us Attackers finally had work to do. Three swings of my blade, and three machine heads went flying. They offered no challenge—were these models tailored to fight Resistance androids? They had superior numbers for sure, but killing them was easier than squashing bugs. If this was all they had, maybe I'd have been bored even if they had attacked earlier.

Still, it looked like the machines had defeated us.

"Guess that means mission failure," I said. "What a joke."

This was it. The end of the line. If we couldn't gain control of the transport, we didn't have a hope in hell of making it out alive. And now the enemy knew what we'd been up to. The Resistance members wouldn't be escaping the area, and us YoRHa units would all be annihilated—*again*. What a disappointment. Nothing to do but laugh.

I was in for a surprise, though. No. 21 seemed to be hanging on.

"No . . ." he said. "It's . . . not . . . over . . . yet!"

His fingers resumed their dance across the terminal, an order of magnitude faster than before. He seemed to be searching for something.

The symbols filling the screen changed. They blinked, then began clearing from the screen at the same speed they'd appeared. Just watching it made me dizzy.

"Gotcha!" No. 21 exclaimed.

I wanted to ask what he'd found, but didn't. He had enough on his mind as it was, and I wouldn't be able to understand any explanation he tried to give me. I wasn't cut out for that console crap.

The screens flicked brighter, and a short string of characters appeared dead center in each of them. Bright white. In the next moment, they all turned into zeroes.

Heh. Look at him go.

The white symbols vanished, and No. 21 crumpled to the floor.

"Tr...transport control...secured. All that's left is...takeoff..."

His voice trembled as he spoke. I could hear him gasping for air.

No. 3 dashed to the console. "On it," he said.

But, as I suspected, takeoff wasn't going to be that simple. The instant No. 3's hands touched the controls, an alarm blared.

"The hell is it now?!"

Please. Wasn't it obvious? Our plan was blown wide open the second the backhack started. Now every machine in the area knew we were in here trying to steal a transport; the nature of their response seemed pretty obvious to me. But, as always, recognizing the obvious wasn't No. 3's strong suit.

"Get ready for company!" I told him. I didn't want to bother, but I threw in some bonus explanation for his benefit. "The alert. All the machines are gonna be headed this way."

If *that* wasn't clear enough for the idiot, I'd stick my sword straight through him.

No. 3 responded with one of his typical crass outbursts. "Shit!"

I looked down and realized the floor screen still displayed a map of the runway. I hadn't even needed to go to the trouble of explaining. The transport was surrounded by those all-too-familiar blinking red lights—a lot more of them than I was going to bother trying to count.

Fortunately for us, at that moment Team A happened to burst into the room. They'd made it to the transport with impeccable timing.

"What's the status?!" No. 4 demanded, a sharp bark that reverberated throughout the control room. He'd been the first inside, with No. 22 on his heels. After a bit of a delay, the three Resistance members filed in, too.

Well, how about that? Team A had completed its mission.

No. 3 shouted back in the most obnoxious way possible, "We've got control of the transport, but now all the machines are swarmin' in on us! No. 21's hurtin'. Got spiked when he hacked the system!"

"Understood." No. 4 said. He turned to No. 22 and added, "Let's go. The machines aren't gonna lay a finger on this ship."

The two dashed out only for Team C to come tumbling in—with a whole host of machines in tow. No. 3 stepped away from the console and gripped his sword.

"Sir! The helm's all yours! C'mon, No. 6, let's deal with these chumps!"

"I don't take orders from *you*," I sneered.

Ugh. He really pissed me off. Was there anything worse than being ordered around by the biggest dimwit ever? I'd figured out what was going on with my own two eyes, and I understood the situation *far* better than he ever would.

I drew my sword and leapt into the hallway. Time to mow down every machine stupid enough to head for the control room. No time for clean, thorough kills. Right now, it was a matter of quantity. Keep the machines out, no matter what.

I wrenched open the emergency hatch to hurl partially incapacitated enemies out onto the runway. Get them off the transport. That was enough. Not like any of them would be able to follow us once we were in the air.

The whine of the transport's engines rose to an earsplitting roar.

Dammit. I had to hurry.

Black shouted over the intercom, "Initiating emergency takeoff procedures! Everyone hang on tight!"

I kicked the last bucket of bolts out the hatch, then sealed it shut. A little close for comfort, but I'd made it.

About a microsecond into my sigh of relief, I realized I was sliding backward along the deck. I grabbed hold of a handrail before I slammed into some unforgiving surface. I stayed like that, holding on for dear life as gravity relinquished its hold on my body.

[Log Entry: No. 2 / Heavy Transport—Cargo Bay]

My SSU had started up with its infernal beeping again. I was ready to whack the thing with my opposite hand. I only held back because hitting it wasn't going to do much good.

I knew why it wouldn't shut up. This was its way of pressing me to act. Hurry up and eliminate the YoRHa Experimental M Squadron. Yeah, so maybe two full hours had passed since takeoff, but it wasn't like I'd forgotten my mission.

The hell was I supposed to do? The opportunity hadn't presented itself. There hadn't been a single decent moment to strike since we got in the air.

The best opportunity of the day had been back on the runway, during that final dash to the transport. No Attackers. No Gunners. There couldn't have been a more ideal moment to sever the squadron's lifeline. But Black had spoiled my chance. If I'd begun the executions at the airfield, he might have lost his opportunity to get out of enemy territory, so it was probably his "subtle" way of requesting that my mission wait until *after* we'd secured the craft. That wouldn't have been a big deal, if not for the dearth of opportunity following.

We sprinted down the runway and got ourselves onboard, but the only thing waiting for me was a fight with a whole bunch of machines. It was a confusing mess, and I'd learned just how much of a pain in the ass it was to fight as a "Type D."

When things finally quieted down, we were already taking off. A short while after that, we'd finished our climb and leveled off. For a while, we watched the skies just to be certain the enemy really hadn't been able to pursue us. By the time we were finally satisfied there was no threat and the tension aboard the craft began to ease, two hours had passed. I slipped out of the control room, and that was when the SSU started its obnoxious beeping. Once again, the thing had been waiting for a moment when I was alone.

I had to admit, the current conditions looked promising. For the next while, most of us were free to do as we pleased, and plenty of squad members were probably wandering around or resting in the cargo bay, trying to relax a bit after spending the past several hours on edge.

If most of the squad members were on their own, it'd make short work for me. It would be a trivial task to kill them one by one—most of them would probably fall dead before they realized I was there. And here in the transport, I'd have no trouble hiding the bodies. There were plenty of dark corners and empty containers in the cargo bay.

"No. 2? Is something wrong?"

Without warning, No. 9 called out to me from behind. I hurriedly silenced the beeping alarm.

"Huh? No, I'm fine."

"Is it your wrist? Has it started to ache?"

"What? Oh . . . yeah. I almost forgot about it."

No. 9 must have misinterpreted my motion to quiet the SSU as a gesture toward my injured wrist.

"It's doing all right. Feels better than ever, in fact."

"I'm so glad to hear that."

And he did sound glad, from the bottom of his heart. Why would something like this make him happy? Aside from the fact that happiness was the last thing he should be feeling right now. The hand he'd been caring for would soon be the one to strike him down. In tending to me, he'd only sharpened the blade that would end his own life.

"Weren't there some injuries when we were at the airfield? I'm sure the other squad members need your attention more than this little sprain of mine."

"I've already finished attending to everyone."

He smiled. Just a hint of pride shone in his eyes.

"No. 21 was hit the hardest today. He's recovering now. The instructor's sitting with him."

He had no idea I was about to undo all of his hard work, and that his labors to treat the squad were in vain. As the Healer, he would have to be the first to die.

"No. 2? Are you sure you're okay?"

I searched for something to say, unable to bear his expression of concern. I wanted to change the subject. I wanted to talk about anything other than me.

"Hey, so . . . do you ever think about what you might wanna do in the future? You know, when the war's over?" I asked.

Great. Of all the topics in the world, I had to land on that. The sudden question seemed to take No. 9 off guard. Of course it would.

His eyes widened for a moment, and then he laughed.

"What do you mean, 'when the war's over'? It's been going on for thousands of years. What makes you think it'll end soon?"

I didn't. Not really. It was just a meaningless question that somehow found its way out of my mouth as I scrambled for something to say.

But I ran with it, adding, "Just hypothetically."

The war was like my mission. Unyielding. Unchanging. There was as much a chance of it ending tomorrow as there was of me ever seeing release from my duty.

"Hmm . . . Well, let me think . . ."

He was actually trying to give me a straight answer. No. 9 took everything seriously, even inane little questions like this one. So sincere. So kind. I almost felt as if I . . .

"Travel," No. 9 concluded. "I guess I'd want to see the world . . . Take in some beautiful sights for a change, you know?"

Travel? Why? M Squadron had been dispatched to all sorts of locations. At least, that's what I'd gathered from the reports. But he wanted to spend his precious time journeying around the world? It didn't make sense.

Apparently, my skepticism was obvious. No. 9 followed up

with, "I guess that must sound kind of odd to you, huh?" The corners of his mouth turned up slightly, as if he was trying to form another smile. But this time, he wasn't quite able to accomplish it.

It wasn't like him. What was troubling him?

He explained. "The squad's been ordered to lots of different destinations on the surface, but in the end, all we see are ugly, torn-up battlefields. So, what I meant was, I think I'd like to see some of the beautiful places the world has to offer."

His voice was cheerful, as if trying to push away the reality of those ugly, torn-up battlefields he'd been forced to observe. He always carried himself like that—bright, happy—even though I knew his outlook on life was anything but. Alone, far from the front lines, he understood better than anyone the plight into which M Squadron had been thrust.

My question, then, was unintentionally cruel. I was sorry I'd asked it, and I wished I could ask for his forgiveness.

"Just imagine. The islands in the south, or canyons with walls of red rock," No. 9 continued. "Oh! And I'd like to see the ruins of the old world, too. The remains of what humanity built."

He turned and looked out the window, trying to make it seem casual. Beyond the glass, there was a brief break in the clouds, and we saw something glittering far below. What was it?

"Look, No. 2!" he exclaimed. "It's the sea!"

Ah. Light from the sun reflecting off the surface of the water. I realized it was the first time I'd looked down upon the ocean from on high. The last time I was thousands of meters up in the sky, I'd been encased in a descending escape pod, all my processes suspended.

No. 9 continued to gaze out the window as if fixed in place. I wanted to stand beside him. I wanted to look out across the ocean together, to murmur to each other about the beauty we saw, pointing at the things we noticed each time the clouds parted, and laughing together at nothing in particular.

. . . Where the hell were these thoughts coming from?

My right hand brushed against the hilt of my sword. The moment I felt the familiar contours and material of the grip, my chest grew tight. Uncomfortably so. My heart was beating rapidly, though it had no reason to do so. My hands were slick with sweat.

What was going on?

My hand curled around the grip, but my fingers lacked their usual strength. I tried again, forcing them this time. My chest continued to tighten, to an unbearable degree, so I allowed my sweat-soaked hand to loosen.

Were my internals acting up?

No. That wasn't it.

I knew what this was.

"It sure is beautiful down there," No. 9 said. "I hope maybe someday I can stretch out on a beach, listen to the waves, and enjoy a good book."

"Yeah. Sounds nice . . ."

But his dream would go unrealized. The war could end tomorrow, and I'd still have to rip away every desire he'd ever had. It was my duty.

I had to get on with it. I needed to hurry. Further delays would not be tolerated. I needed to end No. 9's life now, while he stood before me, back exposed.

"What is the meaning of this, No. 21?!"

A shout from Black suddenly echoed from beyond the far bulkhead. I quickly took my hand off my sword. No. 9 whirled around in surprise, and I was glad I'd reacted in time. He hadn't seen me beginning to unsheathe the blade.

"Let's go see what it is," he said.

I nodded and followed him. My opportunity had been foiled by Black once again. But this time, I felt no strain of irritation. If anything, I was relieved.

It perplexed me.

[Log Entry: No. 21 / Heavy Transport—Control Room]

The instructor had noticed far sooner than I expected. He'd picked up on the slight discrepancy in the flight course just moments after we leveled off and switched to autopilot.

"Looks like we've got . . . some kind of error in the program," he'd said.

He hadn't mentioned a word at takeoff, simply leaving me to pilot in peace. I'd begun to hope my adjustments might slip past his notice until we were closing in on our destination. But he wasn't nearly that dull.

"Let's shift to manual control and run a scan for problems in the autopilot," he suggested.

"No need to do that, sir." I glanced at No. 3 and No. 6 as I spoke. "It's not an error. The course is intentional. This transport won't be taking us to base camp."

The instructor looked puzzled. I shoved him away from the console, catching him completely off guard. He offered little resistance as he staggered backward, then recovered himself and shouted, "What is the meaning of this, No. 21?!"

No. 3 and No. 6 both unsheathed their weapons and circled around to the front of the console to keep him away.

I looked the instructor in the eyes. "I'll say it once more. This transport will *not* be taking us to base camp."

Concern was on the faces of all three Resistance members, sitting against one wall. They didn't quite seem to comprehend what was happening, but they'd sensed the danger in the air. Not that it mattered. Their inferior strength made them a non-issue. I'd let them live, so long as they didn't get in my way.

"The hell's going on?" No. 4 asked, guns drawn. Unlike the Resistance members, I was certain he'd grasped the situation immediately. But he didn't fire. He was probably just being careful—positioned as I was, an unlucky shot could damage the console and impair the transport's flight. It was the kind of caution I'd expect from No. 4.

"YoRHa Experimental M Squadron is an elite force, providing decisive victories in any location to which it is dispatched, paving the way for the Army of Humanity to win the war. That's what they told us, right?"

Considering we'd been designed as an improvement over the already successful female-type models, it stood to reason that M Squadron's achievements should be even greater. In fact, we'd been told that we *had* to do better.

"But the reality is that we've suffered defeat on every battlefield we set foot on. We lost our lives over and over. It didn't matter what we tried. Victory always eluded us."

I'd first grown suspicious of that fact ages ago. But for a long time, I'd lacked the certainty I needed to act.

As the Scanner, I was tasked with devising the ideal strategy for each and every mission. My focus on the facts showed me how reckless our operations really were. So I'd begun asking to have requests forwarded to Command to call off the operations. I hadn't simply proposed retreat once or twice; I'd asked constantly. But my requests were routinely and thoroughly denied.

Each time we relived the nightmare of annihilation, I took the blame upon myself: we'd lost because *my* strategy had been flawed. I figured I needed to gather more information to do better the next time. Soon, I was referencing every piece of data I could get my hands on, looking for that one elusive key that would keep us alive. I knew it had to exist.

In truth, it never had. Not in the beginning, not now, not ever.

"And that's how it was always supposed to be," I continued. "We were *supposed* to fail. That's what they were anticipating."

"What's the point of sending us in just to fail?"

No. 4 asked the question. No. 3, standing beside him, was the one to answer.

"It's a stress test. A proof of concept. They wanna see how bad things can get before the male-type YoRHa models stop bein' able to win."

Precisely. They'd intentionally sent us into situations where success was impossible.

In the deepest corners of the main server, I'd stumbled across that truth. I dove in hoping to find a means to ensure our survival. I hadn't asked for authorization; I was too pressed for time and couldn't wait for Command approval. And the haul from my little hacking experiment just happened to be an unbearably cruel truth.

The instructor spoke up. "That's not true! Command had the highest expectations for us. We're the most advanced squadron there is. The best of the best. We've got the capabilities to achieve victory even under the harshest conditions . . ."

Expectations? Capabilities? That was one way to word it. Had Command believed they could string us along forever with their sweet lies? How asinine. I wanted to laugh in their faces.

"It makes no difference!" I replied. "It doesn't change the facts!"

There was nobody here stupid enough to believe those lies anymore—nobody except maybe No. 3. In fact, that was why I'd gone to him first, blowing the truth wide open to see how he'd react. I wished the instructor had been there to see the Attacker's face the moment he realized everything he'd been taught was a lie.

"We were their immortal squadron. As long as that didn't change, they could continue throwing us into battles with the odds stacked against us. We'd just go on dying, again and again . . ."

Once killed, we could be brought right back. It didn't matter how many times we died—at least not to Command. They'd shut their eyes to the patent truth of the pain and fear those deaths would bring us.

"Guinea pigs. That's all we were to them. They sent us to die, and they weren't going to stop until we managed to produce a victory."

And maybe not even then. Maybe Command would have had us go on until they decided the experiment was no longer valuable.

"Instructor Black," I said, "allow me to express my thanks. I should let you know that when I was inside the server I read through the messages you exchanged with Command. I'm sorry I intruded on your privacy, but it was a relief to know how hard you fought for us each time Command issued orders for the next cruel, senseless mission."

Among all the deceit, that had been one happy surprise. I'd

assumed the instructor simply abided by whatever Command dictated, but he'd been better than that. He had scrupulously passed along every request we made to have missions aborted or reinforcements sent in, knowing full well those requests would be ignored.

"We would be happy to have you along with us, sir, if you so choose."

I could have arranged to have him killed during the earlier confusion. The battle at the airfield had certainly been chaotic enough to facilitate it. But I wanted this opportunity to ascertain the instructor's intentions. It was also a small token of gratitude for his arguments on our behalf, to the limited extent he'd been able to make them.

"I cannot."

A pity. I'd suspected as much. I'd owed him the courtesy of asking, though, and now my debt was paid.

The instructor was out. It was decided.

No. 3 extended his left hand to No. 4, the right still clutching his sword.

"C'mon. Join us."

"And go where? There's nowhere to run."

He dismissed No. 3's invitation, then turned to look at me and No. 6. The poor fool knew nothing. Yet he still believed he might convince us to abandon our plan.

No. 6 started laughing. It was a slow, throaty chuckle. *He* knew where we could run. The fact that I offered us a future was the only reason he was onboard with my plan.

"Think, you idiot. The other half of the earth. The nightlands—a whole vast expanse that never sees the sun. If we make it there, we'll be well beyond the Bunker's reach."

No. 4 would know as well as we did that YoRHa Squadron Command had no jurisdiction over the nightlands; they'd have no authority to pursue us.

"We're the best of the best. The newest, most powerful combat androids ever produced. There's no one else out there to stop us."

I didn't know what types of androids oversaw the other side

of the world. But I'd never heard anything to suggest they were any sort of cutting-edge models. What I *did* know was that they had their hands full operating the dragoons. They wouldn't have the time or the manpower to waste on tracking down a handful of deserters.

The instructor leveled his gaze at me. "You'll never get away with it."

"Sorry, sir, but I'm not asking for your opinion. This is a mutiny. The squadron's members get to decide for themselves."

My eyes met No. 22's. He was the third to learn of my plan, after I'd spoken with No. 3 and No. 6. He'd always been timid. Just hearing the word "mutiny" had caused him to tremble, and in the end, I hadn't been able to get a clear answer out of him.

"Let's go, No. 22," I said. "Together."

His gaze wavered. I couldn't fathom why he would hesitate. If he found the decision too frightening, I was more than happy to make it for him. All he had to do was nod.

"What's going on?! What happened?!"

No. 9 and No. 2 burst into the control room. They must have heard the instructor shouting from the other side of the bulkhead. No. 2 appeared calm, but No. 9 glanced about the room with obvious unease.

"Perfect timing," I said. "No. 9, we're going to be taking a little trip to the far side of the earth."

"What?"

"Real sorry, but I'm gonna have to insist you come along. We wouldn't be able to back up our data without our precious Healer."

Now I'd forced No. 22's hand. With all of the other members of M002 spoken for, he could no longer refuse. I knew he lacked the resolve to be the only one to stay behind.

No. 9 still hadn't grasped what was happening. No. 6—his movements swift as ever—slipped behind the Healer to apprehend him. It happened so quickly, No. 9 didn't have a chance to resist.

"Mmm," hummed No. 6. "You smell delicious."

He buried his face in No. 9's hair. The Attacker's weird behavior continued to baffle me, but I'd known that when it came time, he was the one most suited to securing No. 9 quickly and without any fuss.

"Get your hands off No. 9."

No. 4 aimed his guns at No. 6.

"Lower your weapons," No. 3 warned. "You know damn well a Gunner doesn't have a chance against an Attacker at close range."

Now it was a question of whether No. 4 would heed his companion's advice. He was stubborn. Inflexible. But if we had to deal with him, we would.

Ultimately, I was more worried about the other, much bigger threat in the room.

I turned to look at No. 2.

"It looks like your time's finally come. We had to fight eventually, right?"

No. 2 drew his sword smoothly and without the slightest noise. No. 22 shouted something to me, but I ignored him. I was focused solely on No. 2, my eyes locked with his.

"That's right," I said. "I know all about you."

There, in the depths of the server, I'd scoured every classified document I could find. Among them was a description of a killer, a YoRHa model designed for the express purpose of eliminating its peers. That was my introduction to the seventh member of our squad—our final "comrade," who in truth was to be our assassin.

Even his name, No. 2 Type D, was a lie. His real designation was Type E. Not our Defender, but our Executioner. And he'd arrived under explicit orders to slay all members of M Squadron.

"Your true designation, and your mission, too," I added. "Everything."

And with that, the battle was on. No. 2 sprinted toward me, blade held ready. I'd anticipated that he would first target No. 9; perhaps he'd opted for new tactics when he saw the Healer guarded by No. 6.

So if not the squad's beating heart, then at least its calculating mind. A wise move.

I pivoted, avoiding No. 2's slash. Although I lacked the combat power of my peers, my capacity to evade attacks was nothing to scoff at. A Scanner running recon on the front lines needed to be able to look out for his own skin as he navigated the thick of battle.

I prepared to avoid a follow-up strike, but No. 2 instead ducked low to the ground, just as No. 3's giant blade whistled through the air where his head had been. The attack came from his blind spot, but the Executioner evaded it easily. No. 3's blade, failing to connect with its intended target, continued on in a great arc. It seemed to move in slow motion; I realized we were all powerless to stop it. Finally, it lodged with a sickening crunch into one of the control room's walls.

A piercing alarm filled the room, along with a booming message from the autopilot system.

"Hull breach detected. Cabin pressure falling. Initiating automated descent."

The transport shuddered violently.

Phlox shouted, "Lotus! Take the helm!"

I couldn't have said whether Lotus responded. No. 2's blade came swiftly. I saw it bearing down on me, understanding all too well the death it would soon bring.

There was a loud clang.

"Heh! Not bad for a scrawny lookin' shrimp."

No. 3 had saved me yet again. His blade caught No. 2's at the last moment. Without a word, the Executioner shifted to address the renewed threat. There was a whirlwind of steel. I heard No. 9 call out, pleading with No. 2 to stop. No. 4, sensing an opening, barreled straight for the Healer.

"Like hell you will! No. 9's not going anywhere!" No. 6 sensed it, too, and soon he and the Gunner were exchanging blows.

I drew my own sword and slashed at No. 4. I had no delusions about overpowering a model specialized for combat, but I could at least help No. 6.

Behind me, I heard the shrill clangs and scrapes of No. 2 and No. 3's swords. Similar noises came from No. 6 and No. 4 as they continued to fight right before my eyes.

Where was No. 22? I scanned the room and found him standing stiff as a board against one wall. I saw his lips move slightly.

Stop it.

Stop it? How? It had to be done. Surely he understood that.

I opened my mouth to call him over, when suddenly, No. 6 slipped by me, aiming his sword at No. 2's exposed back. No. 4 made to follow, but he was no match for No. 6's speed.

No. 6 slashed once, and I saw No. 2's shoulders jerk in pain. A raucous laugh erupted from No. 6 as he prepared to follow with a killing blow. But the second strike did not find the Executioner's flesh: between No. 2 and the Attacker's blade leapt none other than our precious Healer.

"No. 9!" I screamed.

He crumpled to the ground, but only for a moment. He managed to sit back up, his face twisted in pain. I felt weak with relief. He was hurt, but the injury wasn't serious.

My relief soon gave way to rage. How could he do something so foolish?! Had it been some kind of gut reaction, made before he'd had time to think?

No. 3 exploded in anger, "Dammit, No. 6! Stick to your own fight!"

No. 6 paid the outburst no mind. In fact, he seemed to be enjoying himself. His lips curled into a malevolent smile as he declared, "Strikes from behind. Two against one. They're the tactics of cowards, and I absolutely *adore* them."

He turned his blade on No. 3. I couldn't believe it. Was he in his right mind? But No. 3 showed no trace of hesitation. He raised his sword confidently, as if the two had been on opposing sides from the start.

Why the hell were No. 3 and No. 6 going at each other? It made no sense.

"Stop!"

But no one was listening to my attempts to restore order.

The battle had devolved into a free-for-all. No. 2 jumped in among the Attackers' exchanged blows, and No. 4 was there, too, kicking and flailing. And then No. 6 turned away from No. 3 and was rushing back toward No. 9. No. 4 slammed into the Healer, hurtling him to safety.

This was bad. At this rate, we'd fail once again.

No. 6's sword carved a deep gash in the floor where No. 9 had been standing. Another piercing alarm filled the control room. This was the same blade that had sent countless machines to their graves with ease. Against it, the transport's bulkheads and decks may as well have been made of paper.

"Critical fuel loss detected," the system announced. "Aircraft stability controls reduced to fifteen percent capacity."

The transport jerked violently. I caught a glimpse of Lotus wrestling the control stick with everything he had. But the craft continued to shudder. We were still falling.

"Altitude decreasing. One hundred twenty meters."

Cactus and Phlox ran to assist Lotus.

"One hundred ten meters . . . One hundred meters . . ."

I could feel our descent quicken. The entire craft jerked and shuddered unpredictably, yet the melee inside the control room raged on. One portion of the airframe began to groan and creak.

"Eighty meters . . . Sixty meters . . ."

Not one of them stayed their swords. They were fools to the last.

"Forty meters . . ."

"Twenty meters . . ."

And with that final automated announcement, the world went dark and silent.

YoRHa Boys Ver. 1.05

CHAPTER 6

[Log Entry: No. 9 / Forest Zone—Transport Crash Site]

SOMETHING REEKED OF BURNING.

It was quiet, with long stretches of silence punctuated by strains of birdsong.

Where was I?

I opened my eyes and looked around as best I could without moving my head. Eventually I made out some kind of rift in the darkness. Beyond it, I saw the bright green hues of surface flora.

That was when it hit me: it was *too* quiet. Over the past few hours, I'd grown accustomed to a constant drone filling my ears—the transport's engines.

Right. We'd crashed.

I tried to lift myself up, only to awkwardly flop to one side. One of my arms didn't seem to be working. When I tried to force it to move, a searing pain ran through my shoulder. It was a bad sign that I'd sustained serious damage.

Still on my side, I used my functioning arm to pull out my field repair kit. There wasn't much light to see by, so I had to feel my way through the contents of the kit, visualizing the items one by one. Fortunately, I had a clear memory of how everything was arranged.

I pulled out an analgesic injector and plunged it into my damaged arm. After a moment, I tested the arm, finding I was able to bear some degree of movement. But even just righting my body left me short of breath.

I placed my good hand on some twisted, unidentifiable piece of wreckage, using it to pull myself to my feet. I recalled the burning smell I'd noticed on first waking and looked around.

Nothing nearby seemed to be on fire. I strained my senses for any hint of danger—any subtle sounds or unusual variations in temperature.

I didn't perceive any immediate threats. Or at the very least, I didn't need to worry about any encroaching flames or impending explosions.

"Can anyone hear me . . . ?" I ventured.

The back of my throat felt funny, as if it were swollen or constricted. Had I inhaled a lot of smoke?

No . . . That didn't seem to be the case. I was sure about the earlier burning smell, but my surroundings didn't show any traces of a fire significant enough to impact my respiratory systems. Maybe I was just imagining the feeling in my throat.

What about my squadmates and the Resistance members? Was everyone all right? I looked around once more, eyes somewhat adjusting to the faint light streaming through the gashes in the transport's hull. I could tell the ship had come to rest at an uneven angle. In fact, considering the extent of the damage I observed, it seemed nothing short of a miracle that the craft hadn't blown apart or gone up in flames on impact.

I heard a faint scraping noise, followed by a hoarse whisper.

"No. 9," someone said.

"No. 22?" I asked. "Is that you?"

I could see a lone silhouette slowly rising in the dim light of the control room wreckage. There was no doubt. It was No. 22. When he spoke, his voice rasped like mine, and I finally deduced the cause; we must have inhaled particles thrown into the air during the wreck. Not good. I'd have almost preferred smoke. We needed to find our way to the outside and get fresh air as soon as possible.

"Where are we?" No. 22 asked.

"Looks like we've landed in some kind of . . . forest," I said. "But that's about as much detail as I can offer."

I'd seen the green of trees through the fissures in the hull and heard the chirping of birds. For all that had gone wrong with our flight attempt, at least we hadn't crashed into the ocean.

"Any sign of the others?"

"No. I . . . haven't seen anyone else."

In all likelihood, the other units had been hurled from the transport on impact. Given the shredded state of the hull, it was certainly possible. The fact that No. 22 and I were still inside was undoubtedly a result of chance. "A little good luck," as humans might say.

"Can you walk?" I asked.

I held a hand out to him, only for a dull ache to work its way through my arm. The injection would have fully taken effect by now; apparently it had only managed to lessen the pain, not eliminate it completely, a sign that I must have been hurt quite badly . . .

"Yeah. I think I'm okay," he replied.

I felt silly for offering help I couldn't provide. He extended a hand to me instead.

"Sorry. Thanks."

In the end, we limped along arm in arm, supporting each other's weight as we found a way out of the transport. True to my initial observations, we had crashed in a dense forest. The transport's trajectory was marked by a trail of snapped and charred trunks. Smoke still billowed from a few of them. The earlier burning smell, then, had been a mixture of transport debris and smoldering vegetation.

I peered around, carefully checking the area for anyone collapsed on the ground or flung into the branches of surrounding trees. But I didn't see any of the others.

"Hello? Can anyone hear me?" I shouted, then strained my ears for a response.

None came. I wished No. 21 was with us. He'd always been able to pick up even the faintest black box signals; those were exactly the skills we needed in a situation like this.

But I made certain not to say the thought aloud. No. 22 was undoubtedly already anxious about his missing twin without my bringing the subject up. In the wreckage of the transport, when he'd asked me about any sign of the others, I knew he was really asking if I'd found No. 21.

There was a sudden metallic groaning and creaking behind us. No. 22 and I looked at each other.

"Is . . . is somebody there?" I asked.

One of the portholes on the transport's downward-facing side came flying off, frame and all. A figure tumbled out of the breach, clothes torn and hair disheveled. I intuited who it was at once. When he stood up, my breath caught in my chest. A faint alarm rang in a corner of my mind.

"No. 21!"

My hand caught the Gunner's arm. "Don't."

No. 21's knees jerked spasmodically. I recognized something about the way he stood—there was a clip like this among the video footage I'd watched as part of my Healer training.

"Wow . . . I feel great. No pain at all," said No. 21.

He tilted his head and flexed his right arm. The arm twitched repeatedly, a clear sign of atypical signals being passed to his drive systems; the question now was whether he was aware of what was happening.

"Why does everything look so . . . red?" he wondered aloud.

So it had already spread to his sensors. There was no doubt in my mind now.

"No. 21? What's wrong?"

The Scanner turned to look into his twin's concerned eyes.

"Huh? Do I . . . kNOw yoU?"

No. 21 tilted his head further, until it rested on his shoulder at a sickening angle. His glowing red eyes did not blink. They simply continued to stare.

"Hey! Snap out of it!"

No. 22 again tried to dash toward his twin. I threw my arms around the Gunner to hold him back.

"Stop! He's . . . he's infected with an enemy logic virus!"

No. 22 started to say something, but I didn't hear it—every sound in the vicinity was drowned out by the terrible, maniacal laughter coming from the infected No. 21.

[Log Entry: No. 3 / Forest Zone—1,800 Meters Northwest of Transport Crash Site]

The fight. That was the only thing running through my head. Arrogant little shit. I wanted to crack his skull wide open.

And I didn't give a damn if cutting down No. 6 meant I'd be accused of fratricide or endangering the mutiny or whatever. I didn't have room in my head for that crap. Hell, it was just the way my brain was wired. Nothing much I could do about that.

"Shit . . . I gotta hurry and . . . find him."

Huh? Wait. What was I thinking just now?

Did I hit my head in the crash or something?

I remembered a bunch of snapping sounds, right after I was sucked out of the transport, like branches breaking right next to my ears. By the time I made sense of it and realized I was dropping straight into a forest, my body'd already slammed against the ground. Figured I was as good as dead.

"Where am I?"

What was I trying to do again? And where was my sword? Oh, yeah. Right here in my hand.

"No time. I gotta . . . "

I'd been looking for something . . . Wait, no. Some*one*.

Dammit. Why wouldn't my head work right?

"Where . . . am I?"

I . . . I'd started to say something, hadn't I? Like, with my voice. No. That didn't seem right.

"Got . . . ta . . . hurry . . . "

Where was I? What was this place? I saw a forest. Trees. Dark. Light.

Red.

. . . Oh.

So that's what was going on.

I'd finally figured it out. Hell, when things got this bad, even I could catch a clue. Just wished it hadn't taken me for-god-damned-ever. Was getting kinda fed up with how stupid I was.

Someone called out to me. "No. 3!"

I remembered the voice. It belonged to No. 4. Everything

came into focus. I remembered it all. Yeah. I'd been searching for No. 4.

"You . . ."

The instant he saw my face, he lost his words. Hmph. No surprise there.

I looked at my hands. They were shaking and jerking around, but I wasn't the one moving them.

"How long?" asked No. 4.

"Beats me," I replied.

Not like it mattered. Who cared when or where I'd been infected? But No. 4 was always focusing on the strangest details, and no wonder—the guy was dumber than a rock.

Still, I tried to give him an answer. "Guess it must've been . . . when No. 21 hacked the console aboard the transport. He was hit with a logic virus and . . . Yeah. I remember some weird noise over the comms."

He clicked his tongue and muttered, "That means No. 6, too."

What? Why was he talking about No. 6 now? What the hell did that jerk have to do with anything? Oh. Right. He was probably saying No. 6 must've caught the virus, too.

"Look," he said, "I'm gonna forget about the whole mutiny thing for the moment, seeing as we've got a much bigger issue on our hands. I want you to shut down all routines immediately. Get your black box into lockdown mode. If you don't, the virus is gonna keep eating away at your mind until you lose it for good. Once that happens, the machines'll have you."

Man, he was talking a lot. That was No. 4 for you. But . . . he had a point. Couldn't stay like this. I should probably . . .

"Nah," I decided. "Forget that."

I hurled my still-unsteady fist at him, putting all my weight into the blow. Punches were all I got. Couldn't grip a sword with the way I was shaking.

"Man, I've waited a long time for this. Just you and me, all alone."

No enemies. No allies. Mano a mano. But what was with the gloomy look on his face? Ah, hell. He was always like that.

Probably thinking about how I was even more useless now than I was before.

"You've been lookin' down on me since the day we first met," I spat. "Always outdoin' me, as an Attacker or a Gunner! And you knew damn well you were better with a sword than those guns. You only backed outta the role 'cause you figured Attacker was the only thing I stood a chance of bein' decent at."

"Gotta have the best people we can get in every role. Makes for a more efficient squad." He was stone-faced as he said it, his features locked down tight. Looked like he wasn't ever gonna show his hand. Not even at the bitter end.

'Cause here he was, still going on about that "best people in every role" crap. Efficiency. Hmph. Did he seriously think I couldn't see through that bullshit?

"Like hell that's what this is about," I told him. "You felt sorry for me."

How was that for accuracy, huh? Knew I'd hit dead center of the target.

I added, "And I bet you don't have the first clue how alone that made me feel."

I'd believed we were brothers-in-arms. I was never gonna surpass him, but I figured we could at least keep fighting side by side, watching each other's backs. That was all I'd really wanted. That was what it meant to stand together on the battlefield as squadmates, wasn't it? But No. 4 had denied me even that.

My right arm was still shaking. I couldn't make it stop. I balled my left fist up as tight as I could and punched him again. I couldn't let my right have *all* the fun; my left wanted some of the action, too.

"I just wanted to be treated like an equal! That's all!"

"That's enough, No. 3."

There was a dull pop, and the shaking in my arm stopped. Finally.

Now we could settle this. Now we could fight.

"Whoo! My bODy feels light as a feather . . . "

The pain was all gone. I felt great.

"It's an early symptom of the infection. Your limiter stops functioning, and you aren't able to register the load stress on your own frame anymore. If you don't shut yourself down, the virus'll move on to your drive systems next."

"Sounds pretty nice, actually."

It'd be worth it—even if didn't give me much time.

"If my limiter's down," I said, "that just means I'll be faster than ever, yeah? I can pump out more power, too. So here's my chance to be on your level. Hell, if I get to be your equal in a fight for one damn second . . . I don't think I need another thing outta life."

I drew my sword. It felt light. *I* felt light, like I'd grown a pair of wings or something.

This feeling. This moment. It was all I'd ever wanted.

I raised my sword and pointed it at No. 4. "I'm gonna whip your smug ass if it's the last thing I do!"

His lips mouthed, "Damn fool."

It was the first time he'd ever shown a glimmer of something resembling emotion.

[Log Entry: No. 6 / Forest Zone—900 Meters Southeast of Transport Crash Site]

Enemies. Nothing but enemies in every direction, as far as the eye could see. No matter how many of them we took out, there were always more. That's how it had always been, from the moment we touched down on our first descent to the surface. We were forever surrounded by enemies.

But I hadn't disliked that, y'know? Slice them up, smash them, pound on them until they were a pile of scrap. Repeat ad infinitum. To be honest, I kinda loved it.

Didn't care much for the dying part, though.

When the transport started losing altitude, I felt disappointed; out of all the ways I'd died until then, it seemed like a pretty pathetic way to go. So when I got sucked out of the ship and found that I'd not only survived the fall, but that I'd been

thrown right into the middle of a huge machine army, well . . .
let's just say I wasn't disappointed anymore.

So many enemies. So many things for me to kill.

I stabbed, I slashed, I crushed. It was fun. So much fun.

Why didn't machines scream when they died, though?
That was my only real complaint. Would've been nice if they
learned to talk like humans, and started crying and screaming and moaning. I liked to imagine hearing them wail "iT
hURtS!" or "hELp MeEE!" or "wHY? i HaVEn't DonE aNY-
tHinG wROng!" as they looked at me with loathing in their
eyes. It'd be a lot better than now, when they just fell apart
without a word.

Huh?

Did I hear a scream?

Or was I just hearing what I wanted to hear?

No. There it was again. It was a voice I knew. One of those
Resistance chumps, shouting, "Heeelp!"

I had to hurry. Had to kiLL any machine that got in my way.
I'd beat every last one of them into the ground. I'd crush them!
Heh.

Ah. There they were. The instructor, along with the three
Resistance androids. They were surrounded by enemies,
fReaking out. Looked like they were backed up to the edge
of a cliff. No way out. The machines had these kills in the bag.
DaMmit all!

One of them . . . Cactus, was it? He was the one whose pathetic scream I'd heard, and he was still at it. "Heeeeelp!" The
instructor was putting up his best fight, but he diDn'T stand a
chance with three useless androids weighing him down. Phlox
seemed to be helPinG as beSt he could. And Lotus, well, this
encounter was way out of his league. But I'd always known
that.

What was I doing? CoUldn't stand around watching forever,
could I?

I charged straight into the horde surrounding the four, ripping machines up left and right. Ah, it didn't get any bEtter
than this.

Except . . . it was over all too fast. What a shame. It was almost like the machines flung themselves onto my naked blade. It didn't leave me satisfied at all. The machines around here were way too weak.

"Huh? What just happened?!"

The three Resistance androids stood with their jaws slack, looking from me to the piles of machine scrap now littering the ground.

"No. 6 . . . !"

The instructor managed not to gape moronically, but I wasn't a fan of the expression he had on his face instead. It was the way people looked when they were relieved to find someone alive and well. That sentimental crap didn't suit him.

But I knew how to fix it.

"Wh . . . ?!"

Now he was staring in disbelief at my knife lodged in his shoulder. Yeah. That was much better. I liked that look. sUr-pRise and pain all miXed up into one. I was glad I'd kept that spare throwing knife around. I hoped he didn't get the wrong imPreSSion though; it WaSN't like I'd been holding on to it just for his sake.

"Mmm . . . Feeling rEAL good."

Huh? That was odd. My aRM was tWiTcHiNg.

"Did I slam it into something?"

I gave my arm a good hard shake. There. All better.

But the instructor was still looking at me.

"No. 6!" he gasped again, this time all gravely concerned or whatever. The heLL was his deal? What a laugh.

"It's a logic virus, isn't it? You're infected," he said.

What of it? Had it seriously taken him this long to figure it out? A little late, yeah?

Our mutiny had failed. I knew damn well what that meant. Command had sicced their Executioner dog on us. Anything short of a trip to the back half of the world meant we didn't have a future. And when we'd tried to make the trip, we failed. In other words, we were fucked. We always were. 'Course, our resident genius No. 3 couldn't even figure that much out.

I turned my attention back to the instructor. "What makes you think I give a shit?"

Really, what a riot. But that was enough chitchat. It was time to move on to somEthiNg fun.

"Let me tell you what's going to happen next," I said. "You're all going to suffer, until eventually I decide to let you die."

I swung my blade hard. Put all my strength into it. There was a shriek.

No. That wasn't what I was looking for. Not at all what I wanted to hear. Damn Cactus. Old fart. Why couldn't he shut up? The scream I was after right now wasn't anything he could give me.

"No. 6! Stop this!"

"You want me to stop, huh?"

We were getting closer: right voice this time, but it wasn't making the right sounds. I didn't want an order from the instructor. I wanted a scream. Or he could beg. That would be nice, too. C'mon. How long was he going to make me wait?

"M Squadron's done for. How's that make you feel, sir? All your hard work down the drain."

I readied one more hard strike. Had to be careful not to cut the chest or the throat, though. It'd be a real letdown if this ended quick. So I'd aim low. Yeah. His legs. That could be nice.

Ooh. Look at him go. Quick as lightning. Managed to avoid the slash by a hair. But it cost him his balance—flopped right down on his ass. Real embarrassing, yeah? Mmm. Looked real vulnerable down on the ground like that. This wasn't half bad.

"Why?!"

The shout came from an unexpected direction. Huh? What was Phlox's problem?

"If you wanted to kill us, why go to the trouble of rescuing us?!"

Geez. Looked like we had another wiNNer in the intellect department. And here I'd thought PHloX was the most put-together of the bunch.

"Haven't figured it out, huh?" I decided to do him a favor. I'd break it down for him. "I'm doing it because it's fun."

I pivoted away from the instructor, instead bringing my blade down on Phlox. What better way to learn than a hands-on demonstration? The anger filling his face shifted to confusion for a moment, before his features crumpled in pain.

"How's it feel? Hurts, right?"

Hmph. Seemed he wasn't able to answer my question. He fell and lay there on the ground, not attempting to move in the slightest.

"I want you to know, that cut was just for you. I aimed it very carefully to cause you the most amount of pain I could."

In order to ensure someone experienced pain, care had to be taken to keep them conscious. The tRicK was to avoid any undue damage to the internal units. Better to maximize attention to the skin and muscles. That was where most of the pain receptors were found. Keep cuts shallow and have them extend as long as possible. That aBoUT summed it up.

Oh, another tip: avoid cLEaN cuts. The more jagged the wound, the more intense the stimulation of the surrounding receptors.

"When I see someone doubled over in pain or breaking down in tears, that's pure pleasure for me. I can't get enough of it."

Phlox was facedown. I kicked him over onto his back. This wasn't going to be any fun if I couldn't see his pretty mug.

"I like having power over people. I like looking down on them and laughing at how pathetic they are."

I stamped a foot down on his fresh, gaping wound. I bet it hurt. It did, didn't it? I bet it was pure agony.

"I want to watch as they lose all hope in the face of overwhelming power. That delicious moment when I can see despair creeping into their eyes."

But the damn machines didn't show anything. It didn't matter how much you cut them up or crushed them; thEy didn't let out a single scream. If something didn't scream when made to suffer, that meaNt it didn't *feel* anything.

Same thing when they were the aggressors—machines

didn't react when androids were in pain, trembling and begging for their lives. They didn't *experience* the joy of seeing faces twisted in agony, a mess of tears and snot and blood.

"And you're telling me I should throw that all away? Let the machines kill you instead?"

He honestly thought I'd give that joy up to a bunch of uninspired robots that couldn't put a damn thought together if their lives depended on it?

"What a waste! What an absolute waste!"

I turned to check on Cactus and Lotus. The two were sitting in place, trembling, but I wanted more. I needed to hear them cry. To wail. This fun belongEd to me and me alone!

"Eeny, meeny, miney . . . moe!"

I stabbed my index finger up against Cactus's nose. A wheezing sound escaped his throat. Hmm. Still not quite there.

Ah. I knew what I could do. I could lop off one of those two little ears. That'd get things moving, wouldn't it?

Yeah. That's exactly what I'd do.

"Don't even think about it!"

Oh, for . . . The instructor couldn't leave well enough alone, could he? Another couple centimeters and my blade would've been peeling Cactus's ear right off. How did he figure it out, anyway? Were the tHoughts in my head leAkiNg?

The instructor had thrust his sword at me right as I'd bent down next to Cactus's head. Had he been waiting for a moment when my guard was relaxed? I mean, they did say that birds of prey were most vulnerable right at the moment when they stooped to strike. Come to think of it, it was the instructor who taught me that.

Now he was trying to circle around to my left. Did he think he was keeping himself on my weaker side? Hmph. Nice try, but obvious moves like that only worked on the training ground. Real fights were a whole different game.

"I know your secret, sir."

I slid my sword against his, disarming him. His blade went spinning off to the side. Then I swung low to sweep his feet out from under him. Too easy. What a laugh.

"You're not actually a YoRHa unit. You're just a plain old android, reinforced a bit for extra strength."

He was down, but he still reached one hand out, straining for his fallen sword. Mmm. Struggling in vain. Good stuff. I'd have to give him a little reward for pleasing me. I thrust my blade through the back of his right hand, pinning it to the ground. Now he didn't have to do anything but lie there like a good little instructor.

"It all comes down to whether or not you've got a black box. That lovely little high-output reactor core? That's the mark of a YoRHa. Makes all the difference in the world, y'know?"

Now it was time to *really* enjoy myself . . .

Unfortunately, there was another unwelcome interruption. One measly bullet grazed the side of my neck. It didn't have a chance in hell of properly hitting me, and it wouldn't have made a damn bit of difference even if it did. Against YoRHa models, Resistance weapons might as well have been loaded with training rounds.

DaMn Phlox. How was he still moving?

"C'mon," I said. "Now you're just getting on my nerves. You don't aCtUaLLy think some pathetic Resistance android is going to take on a YoRHa model and win, do you?"

He was weak, and he was slow. He couldn't evade my attacks, which meant I could hit him as many times as I wanted. Why, I cOuld evEn . . . retrace the wound I gave him earlier, running my blade along precisely the same path to deepen the cut. See? Just like that.

Ah. Now he was making a nIcE face for me. All scrunched up, wet with sweat and tears and snot and drool.

Next, how about the heel of my boot on his nice rosy cheek? I was doing this for *his* sake, to be nice. He couldn't breathe very well with his teeth clenched tight like that. He needed to open his mouth to let the air in. Yeah. Just like that. Deep breath out.

"Cut it ooooout!"

Ugh. The annoying old fart had spoiled another beautiful moment. Here Phlox was, making such a preTty sound for me, and Cactus had to drown it out with his yelling. Maybe I needed to shut the captain up first.

I turned, only to find something entirely unexpected. Machines, right in the middle of my playtime. Hadn't I killed these things already? I was sure of it, but they seemed to have bounced right back up off the ground.

Someone shouted, "Fire!"

And then bullets were flying at me from every direction at once. After a moment, I recognized the voice as Lotus's. So the machines had to be some kind of trick he'd worked up. But before I could address that issue, I needed to do something about these bullets. Unlike the pathetic toys the Resistance carried, the guns that the machines were armed with packed a punch, and they shot plenty fast.

I deflected the bullets with my sword, sending them right back at the machines. It took a moment, but I finally managed to destroy them *again*.

What a chore.

When it was over, I turned back to face the Resistance androids. "A bunch of hacked machines all programmed to fire on me at once, huh? Nice tRIck."

Lotus stood stock-still, eyes wide as saucers.

"Yes, well, I . . . wasn't expecting that. Did you just . . . erm . . . knock every bullet out of the air?"

"Not quiTe," I sneered. "A few of them managed to hit me."

SomEthing warm trickled down from my forehead to my cheek. Dammit. Getting shot by the machines *hurt*.

"Guess I better pay back the favor."

I brought my sword down for a quick swipe at Lotus, who was still standing stiff as a board. I was hoping maybe he'd shriek or turn away or run in circles or something. But he just took the blow and flopped down to the ground. C'mon. Really? I'd barely scratched the guy. I was being *so* careful to avoid any vitals.

"Hey. Get up. I haven't killed you yet."

I grabbed him by his face and lifted it up near my own. It was so puny. I could've crushed it right there.

"Hmm. What kinda pain do you deserve for ruining my perfect features?"

His skull creaked and groaned between my fingers. If I flexed them a little bit harder, maybe his brain unit would come splurting out one side. But if I did that, it'd all be over in an instant.

"How about I sever your arms and legs, and keep you alive to watch? But not all at once. I bet we'll have more fun if I hack away at each of them one centimeter at a time."

Yeah. That sounded good. I'd start with his right hand. To an engineer like him, nothing would be more terrifying than the thought of losing his dominant hand.

"Lotus!"

"I am getting *really* sick of you, old man. Wait your turn!"

I gave Cactus a light kick, but he went flying off nearly two meters. How weak couLD you get?

"How . . . how . . . *dare* you mess with my men! Graaah!"

The hell? Suddenly he was breaking out this hotheaded crap. It reminded me of No. 3 and all his irritating stupidity.

Next, Cactus started slamming his fiSTs against me. Even the lacK of efficiency reminded me of M Squadron's resident moron. But this was even worse, really—the Resistance captain wasn't hurting me at all.

"You just don't know when to stop, do you?"

I kicked him once more. This time, he flew about three meters.

But he *still* struggled back to his feet. This was exactly the kind of tHing I hated about idiots like him and No. 3.

The captain screamed as he rushed in again. "How . . . how . . . "

"Huh?" he paused in confusion. "I don't hurt at all. And . . . why's the world gone all red?"

Phlox's eyes widened. It was likE he was so surprised, he forgot all about his pain. Ugh. And here he'd been making such a nIcE face for me. Now he was calling out all grief-stricken or whatever. "Cap! No! Don't tell me you're . . . !"

I mean, it *was* grief, at least. Kinda nice in its oWN way.

Cactus started going on about his arm. "It's . . . it's nOt dO-inG what I tell it to . . . ! Hee hee. Ah ha ha!"

His head tilted to one side, and his entire body began to tremble.

"Seriously?" I smirked. "You let yourself get infected, old man? How laME! How totaLLy pAtheTic!"

What a laugh. Here he was, planning to go down in a blaZE of glory, and it turned out he'd been infected with a virus. He was laUGhing like some kind of lUNaTiC as he fired. Man. How stupid could you get?

"No! Cap!"

Phlox sounded like he was about to burst into tears. The old man continued spraying bullets at random and laughing.

On second thought, maybe it wasn't so random. Cactus was aiming for Phlox and Lotus, backing them up to the edge of the sheer drop. Hmm. Maybe Cactus wasn't so bad now that he was infected.

But hang on. That rifle he was firing . . . To a YoRHa unit, it was about as effective as a toy, but it hit plenty hard enough to kill old models. Did he realize what he was doing?

"Cap! Please! Get a hold of—"

Aw, jeez. Cactus hit 'em both. Phlox and Lotus got whacked by their now-infected captain and went tumbling headfirst off the side of the cliff.

I guessed he was probably coming for me next. Except . . . The hell? Now he had his barrel aimed at himself. What was he trying to accomplish? It didn't make any sense. What kind of infected android felt *guilt*?

Damn. He shot himself. He actually did it. One blast straight to his throat.

He wobbled for a moment, then fell off the side of the cliff to join his two dead comrades. I GueSSed he must've retained some tiny sliver of consciousness right up to the end.

It was absurd. I couldn't hold back the laughter.

"Hah! Imagine that. Losing your mind to a virus, going after your comrades, then offing yourself. All nice and tiDy, like some kind of cleaning dRoNE. Doesn't get any more convenient than THaT!"

Ah, how funny. But at the same time, what a loss. The three Resistance members had finished themselves off. Hmph. Those kills were supposed to be mine. Now where was I going to get my fun?

"Well, instructor, looks like it's just you and me," I mused.

I turned back to face him. At some point, he'd gotten his hand free. He must've managed to pull my sword out. Heh. He was trying pretty hard. But I sure wished he could have doNe it when I was watching. Why keep all that eXCruCiaTing worK a secret? Oh well. We'd just have to make up for it now.

"We're going to have a real good time together."

At long last, I had him all to myself.

[Log Entry: No. 2 / Forest Zone—1,200 Meters Northeast of Transport Crash Site]

It was the second time I'd been dragged back from the depths of darkness to the waking world. The first was when I was pulled comatose from the escape pod. It hadn't been particularly bright in the cave, but it had been plenty noisy.

This time—my second experience—was comparatively quiet. And it was a lot brighter. When I opened my eyes, I saw the sky; it seemed I was supine on the ground. Some manner of dark shadow blotted out one portion of blue. No, not a shadow . . . something green. Vegetation of some kind. When my eyes managed to focus, I realized it was a tree with huge, spreading branches.

I had a vague memory of the transport losing altitude fast, ultimately crashing into the Forest Zone. A huge gash had formed in the hull—probably because we'd been foolish enough to start fighting onboard. I must've been sucked outside, sent plummeting to the ground alone.

I attempted some gradual movement in my arms and legs. Considering the height of the fall, my injuries seemed trivial. I sat up. The movement left me a little dizzy, but it wasn't anything debilitating. A few minutes would be enough to recover and have myself restored to normal.

I soon confirmed that my auditory processes were functioning fine, too. It was kind of a disappointment, actually. It might've been nice to go without hearing for a while, just so I could shut out one particularly unwelcome sound: my SSU seemed very excited by my return to consciousness and was beeping nonstop.

I blearily told it, "SSU. Knock it off. I hear you."

"Alert: Eight hours thirty-six minutes have elapsed since scheduled mission completion time. Proposal: Eliminate YoRHa Experimental M Squadron immediately."

"You just can't let that go, can you? Have you been paying *any* attention to what's been going on?"

Was Command out of their minds? Surely they had to be aware of the attempted mutiny. And then there was the transport's crash landing—at this point, it was unclear if any of the squadron's members were alive. But they were still hassling me about carrying out my mission? It was absurd.

"Alert: Refusal to comply with direct orders issued by Command will be punished with black box overload and consequent disposal of unit No. 2 Type E."

Seriously? Straight to death? I hoped that wasn't a joke, because I wasn't laughing. If it was a real threat, it seemed a little harsh, if you asked me. Though I didn't doubt they'd follow through with it.

"Proposal: Eliminate YoRHa Experimental M Squadron immediately."

Great. So Command had come up with a joke in the worst possible taste, and now I got to listen to my SSU deliver the terrible punchline over and over. It was completely twisted. Everything was falling apart.

"Someone up there's got a real sadistic sense of humor . . . "

A dry, rasping sound tickled its way up my throat. I'd thought this comedy couldn't get any lower, but apparently we'd bottomed out and looped right back around to hilarious, because now I was laughing. Me. The jester at the center of the whole damn farce.

"SSU, provide last-known coordinates. I'll start my search for the squadron members."

I looked down at my palms. The tape on my right wrist was smeared with dirt and starting to come undone. I softly touched it with my left hand, then set off walking through the forest.

[Log Entry: No. 4 / Forest Zone—1,800 Meters Northwest of Transport Crash Site]

I'd faced the sharp edge of No. 3's sword plenty of times, both up on the Bunker and here on the surface. I knew all his techniques, inside and out. I knew all his bad habits, too. In fact, on balance, I probably had a better read on the next move he'd make in any given fight than he did himself.

But right now, I wasn't able to read anything. He still brought his blade crashing down with all his might, but the openings I expected to see after weren't there. I tried faking a few stumbles, but he wasn't taking the bait.

You've got a bad habit of letting your attention wander every time you finish something off.

You can't afford to hesitate when you go in for the kill.

How many times had I leveled those remarks at him? Now here I was, mulling over my own words. This was a No. 3 with focus and precision, who guarded every opening and pressed every opportunity he saw.

I twisted away one moment too slow, and his blade connected with my gun, knocking it from my grip. Unlike every other time we'd fought, No. 3 continued to press, rather than celebrating his small victory. I realized I might not find the moment I needed to draw my backup weapon.

"C'mon! Quit playin' around and fight me for real!" he spat, backing up and lifting his sword overhead in a high guard. It was a solid stance. He looked ready for anything I might throw at him.

No. 3 glowered at me. "Forget the gun. Draw steel."

I'd lost count of the number of times we'd practiced close combat, sword versus pistol. It was thanks to all that experience that I knew I had to switch weapons or risk defeat. My handguns weren't going to cut it against the new No. 3.

So I drew my sword.

When No. 3 saw, he grinned from ear to ear. He looked utterly ecstatic. I understood then how badly he wanted this, and it stirred in me a sadness more terrible than I could bear.

"You really are a damn fool," I told him.

All this time, I'd believed we were fighting the same foe—that we stood on the fields of battle both facing the same way. We were supposed to be brothers-in-arms. So why was he pointing his blade at me now, lips curled with delight? Was this what he'd always truly desired?

"Nothin' I hate more," he said, "than hearin' you talk like you already got the fight in the bag."

He gave a roar, and his monstrous blade gleamed as it swept in. I lifted my sword to parry and succeeded, but it was like holding back a falling boulder. How was he putting so much force into the blow? His sword was huge, but not *that* huge.

The last time we'd fought sword on sword, we'd been training on the Bunker. It was before I got reassigned to the Gunner role, when both of us were still Attackers.

At the time, the ratio of wins had been in my favor. But that was only because I was careful about keeping my weaknesses with a sword hidden. I figured that once No. 3 learned to recognize his own shortcomings and developed the skills to compensate for them, we'd find ourselves on even footing in short order. But no matter how many times I tried to point him in the right direction, he refused to listen.

As it turned out, my evaluation was spot-on. With his flaws and bad habits ironed out, No. 3 was a tough opponent. No matter where I tried to strike, he was ready to block the blow. And his attacks were coming in from directions I hadn't even considered. We locked blades, jumped back, then instantly covered the distance to strike again. It was a perfectly even match.

A different kind of smile touched No. 3's lips. I'd only seen it once before, though the memory stayed with me. It was a day not long after we rolled off the production line, when we sparred for the first time. As our swords crossed, he'd had a look of pure delight on his face. No misgivings. No doubts. Just uncomplicated joy in the fight.

I wouldn't have guessed that the second time I'd ever see that smile, we'd be fighting to the death. Irony if I'd ever known it.

But his pleasure, along with our even match, soon dissipated. The virus continued to creep its way through No. 3's systems. He let slip a laugh that was more insanity than joy, and the hand gripping his sword began to tremble. His drive systems were beginning to fail. The end was near.

The next blow I parried deflected his sword to one side. I went in for a strike. It connected, sending No. 3 flying backward, sword still gripped tight in his hand.

But it wasn't the end. He stood back up, a creepy smile plastered to his face, his shoulders twitching. I swiped at his feet, knocking him down before he could lift his sword. He managed to stand again, so I knocked him down once more. He lay still only a moment before defiantly struggling to his feet a third time.

I'd cut him up something fierce. His internal units were showing through the gashes on his chest and abdomen. But he was still trying to fight, a faint grin lingering on his face. His sensors would be completely shot by now. Maybe he didn't even register the feel of my blade against his skin anymore.

"Why?!" I shouted. His consciousness was probably long gone, but I couldn't hold back the question. "Why didn't you infect me?!"

I drove my blade into his right shoulder with all my strength. His huge sword went clattering to the ground, and his right arm fell limp at his side, its muscles severed.

He remained on his feet and tried to stagger toward me. A few unsteady steps revealed the truth: walking was now beyond his battered body. He fell to his knees, for what was probably the last time.

"You could've easily given me the virus," I cried. "It's inside you! Fighting in close like this, all you had to do was reach out!"

I wasn't expecting an answer. To be honest, I didn't need one. All I really wanted was—

"What . . . kind of victory . . . would that be?"

He lifted his head and looked into my eyes. There was a different kind of smile on his lips now. Softer.

So he'd been clinging to consciousness after all. That would explain how stubborn he'd been about getting to his feet no matter how many times I knocked him down.

"Yeah. Guess so . . . " I offered.

The virus had spread to every part of his body, but he still clung tenaciously to his mind. He could have given in. He had to have known it'd be easier that way. 'Course, I guessed easy was never what No. 3 was after.

His eyes, still locked on mine, continued to glow hellfire red. But I didn't see madness in them anymore.

" . . . I got a favor to ask," he said.

Consider it done, I wanted to reply. But I couldn't get the words out.

He deserved an answer. We'd lived with far too few words between us. It was why we'd believed we understood each other, when in truth we hadn't known a damn thing.

I swallowed and tried again.

"Consider it done."

As No. 3's eyelids fell shut, I gently slid my blade straight through his heart.

[Log Entry: No. 9 / Forest Zone—Transport Crash Site]

No. 21 was weaving unsteadily from side to side. This, too, was a textbook symptom of logic virus infection: degradation of motor functions.

"Whoo! I'm feeling *good*! *So* good, No. 9!"

I heard a rifle report. No. 21's body went flying backward.

"I'm sorry," No. 22 whispered, finger still trembling on the trigger.

I knew the two had been together since they rolled off the line. I couldn't begin to imagine how difficult this was for No. 22. Here he was, forced to take out his twin with his own two hands.

But he wasn't afforded any time to dwell on the fact. No. 21 rose back to his feet and started shambling toward us again.

Apparently, the rifle shot hadn't been enough to keep him down. I'd seen the round hit and watched as No. 21 was thrown backward on impact. In fact, I could see the charred hole in his uniform now.

Conflicted as No. 22 was, he was a Gunner. He didn't miss.

So the reason this wasn't over had to be the infection. It must have deadened the Scanner's sense of pain—yet another classic symptom of a logic virus.

"It doesn't hurt!" No. 21 exclaimed. "It doesn't hurt at all, No. 22!"

He tilted his head in apparent surprise.

"Huh?" he continued. "No. 22. Right. That's your name. The twin model manufactured with me."

The Scanner gave a sinister grin. "But you failed your aptitude tests. You couldn't cut it as an Attacker and ended up as a Gunner instead. Ah, poor, poor No. 22."

His comment reminded me of something that had nagged at me before, not long after we all first met. We were on the Bunker, talking. No. 22 had introduced himself to No. 6 as a Gunner. It confused me at the time, since I was certain I'd heard before that he was an Attacker, but I filed it away as my own failure to properly record information.

Apparently, I'd been correct all along.

No. 21 pointed a finger at his twin and erupted in shrill laughter.

"I always pitied you, you know? So frail. So vulnerable. No. 22, the little crybaby, too weak to survive without my protection."

I turned to No. 22 and pleaded, "No! Don't listen to him!" I didn't want him to hear those words.

"That's not No. 21!" I cried. "He's not himself anymore!"

But the Gunner didn't pay any attention to my warnings. He let out a bloodcurdling cry, firing wildly in No. 21's direction.

I thought he might go on like that, riddling his twin with bullets until every internal unit had been shredded into tiny fragments. No. 21 had stopped his awkward shambling—he'd taken several direct hits already, easily enough to incapacitate him under normal circumstances. But suddenly he began weaving and dodging, skillfully evading his twin's continued fire. I took it as a sign that his combat instincts were somehow still intact, in spite the fact that the infection would have now spread to the majority of his body.

"N . . . Num . . . b-b-b . . . r Twen . . . twenty-two . . . " he stammered.

He was losing his speech.

No. 22 kept firing, as if now doing it merely to drown out the words. The bullets tore into No. 21, but he continued to stumble forward.

"LeT'S bE . . . tOgETher . . . "

As his infected twin drew near, No. 22 began to back away. He tripped and fell to the ground.

"wON't yoU . . . cOMe wITh mE . . . ?"

The Gunner struggled to get back to his feet, but No. 21 was closing in. I had to do something, before I lost another friend to the infection.

"Hey! No. 21!" I yelled.

As the Scanner swiveled his head in my direction, I barreled in from the side and dropkicked him with all the force I could muster. I didn't know what I was doing. I just knew I had to keep him away from No. 22.

"Stay away! He's trying to infect you!"

I drew my sword. I wasn't well-suited to close combat. But under normal circumstances, neither was No. 21—that was why I figured I might have a shot. I had to take No. 21 down. I refused to let him cause his twin any more pain.

No. 22's the only combat model here, and he's non-functional. I'm telling you, there isn't a combat strategy in existence that would give a single Healer and a single Scanner a fighting chance against these odds.

I could practically hear No. 21's voice, repeating the words he'd said that day in the trench, and I realized that day wasn't nearly as long ago as it felt . . .

You just concentrate on bracing and firing. I'll worry about the aiming.

He'd always been the one to take our hands and lead the way—me, with my difficulties in combat, and No. 22, with his somewhat timid disposition. Among the M002 units, No. 21 was the de facto leader, and he was someone I'd always felt I could rely on.

Now here I was, swinging my sword at my comrade and close friend—or what was left of him, at any rate. I figured he might evade my awkward attack, but just as my blade sliced toward him, he seemed to falter.

I realized that No. 22 must have fired again, hitting his twin in the leg to ensure my blow landed. It was a perfectly aimed shot—just the kind of precision he had always excelled at.

In my mind, I offered another apology to No. 22. I'd meant to save him from further anguish. But it turned out this was another task I was too weak to manage by myself.

At the very least, then, I'd try to bring the fight to a swift end. No. 22 continued firing, further slowing his infected twin's movements. With each shot, I struck yet again.

I wasn't sure how many times we repeated that awful loop, but finally, No. 21 collapsed to the ground. I heard a long, high-pitched beeping sound—it was the alarm meant to indicate that his heart had stopped. My breath was so ragged and heavy, it nearly drowned the sound out. I felt like my chest unit might collapse in on itself.

"Why . . . ? Why did it have to be like this . . . ?" I murmured.

Behind me, No. 22 was sobbing. Neither of us liked combat, but the anguish and pain we felt now came from something far worse than that aversion. I knew No. 22 would be hurting even more than I was—the situation was far more bitter for him. But there was nothing I could do about it.

No. 21 often claimed, playfully, that he and No. 22 were two halves of a whole. If that were true, No. 22 had just lost his other half. I had no idea how to console him.

I was still standing there, unmoving and useless, when the unimaginable occurred.

No. 21 sprang back to his feet.

"How . . . ?"

How is this possible? I wanted to ask. He should have been dead.

I'd heard once that among the machine lifeforms, some units exhibited an extraordinary capacity for self-recovery, and sometimes even were able to resuscitate themselves, given enough time. With the virus having spread through his entire system, No. 21 was essentially one of the machines now. Had the infection increased his ability to regenerate, too?

"Look out!" I shouted.

But he had already closed in on his twin. No. 22 bore the full brunt of the blow, flying through the air and then slamming down onto the ground. It happened almost instantly. There was no way he could have avoided it.

No. 21 looked around in confusion.

"Huh? No. 22? WheRe'd yOu Go . . . ?"

He seemed unable to parse the fact that his attack had sent No. 22 hurtling away. In fact, he seemed unable to spot No. 22 now, writhing in pain in the dirt and grass. His sensors must have been barely functional.

"comE bAck . . . ! i'M So loNEly . . . "

No. 21 continued to look about himself, an uncertain frown on his face. His eyes rolled back in his head, and he began shuddering unpredictably.

The sight was disturbing in the extreme. Still, to me, he somehow had the appearance of a sobbing child unable to find his way home.

"WheRe . . . arE you, N . . . num . . . bER twEn . . . ty-tWo . . . ?"

Eventually, he located his twin and began shambling over.

No. 22, still in pain from the earlier attack, was unable to move. I jumped between them, ready to protect the Gunner at all costs.

"Don't!" he protested. "You have to . . . You have to get away, No. 9."

"nOOoooO!"

I held up my sword. My legs trembled. The aches radiating throughout my body reminded me of my own injuries, and I understood why No. 22 had insisted I get away. But . . .

"It's my responsibility to keep the squadron safe," I said. "I won't run, no matter what."

I leveled my blade at No. 21. But I never got a chance to strike. Before I managed to take my first step, he'd already closed the gap between us. His speed was astounding. I found myself rolling across the ground, unaware of what exactly had happened—not even of what part of me he'd hit.

But I did know I was in pain. It was a tight, strangling sensation. I found it hard to draw breath.

No. 21 stood above me with the eyes of a beast ready to claim the life of its prey.

I had to keep fighting. I had to hurry. He'd kill me if I didn't. But my sword was gone. He must have knocked it from my grip when he rushed me.

I squeezed my eyes shut, preparing for the fatal blow sure to come. After an unbearable pause, it still hadn't arrived.

Trembling, I opened my eyes and looked up. No. 21's face was contorted in pain, his body frozen in place. I saw a spray of red coming from his back, and the final ripples of a shock wave dissipating behind him. Who had unleashed the attack?

I slow lifted myself up and saw my savior standing before me, sword unsheathed.

"No. 2?"

ReD. So much rED. So pREtty. So fUn.

"Sir! Sir! Hey, sir!"

What a spoilsport. Here I was, calling for him to respond, and he wouldn't say a word.

Oh. Wait. Maybe he *couldn't* respond. Maybe his jaw was clenched too tight to move.

"Are you listening, Instructor, sir?"

Yeah. See, it wasn't LikE I wanted an actual answer. This might be even bettER, in a way, watching him start to say something but falter, unable to get the words out, face twisted in agony.

"Do you get it now? I *adore* this kind of play."

I admired the many strokes, the many dozens of strokes, my sword had drawn across his flesh. I'd sliced him up real good. His skin hung in tatters from his cowering frame.

Did he want me to make him hurt more? He did, didn't he.

"Just to be clear, this iSN't the virus talking."

He might've wanted to believe my actions were a result of the infection. I didn't want him to get the wrong idea.

"I've *always* adored this."

Wasting machines on the battlefield was fun, of course. But what really got me going was the sight of my comrades squirming in pain and agony. There were a few other things on my bucket list: I wanted to snap No. 21's pretty little fingers. I wanted to make No. 22 cry until his voice gave out. I'd had those fantasies for a long time. I just hadn't spoken of them.

"See? I was right, wasn't I? You *did* believe it was the virus making me act this way. Making me *violent*."

Bzzt! Wrong answer. Better luck next time. I mean, I could see why he might have thought so. Logic viruses were weapons, after all. Their whole point was to get androids to eliminate each other.

So what I wanted to know, then, was why the hell the guys

in R&D thought it was a good idea to outfit me with a personality that made me act like one of the enemy's weapons.

I'd heard people with certain . . . *predilections* like mine had existed among humans, too. Maybe that was about as much thought as they'd put into the decision. Who knew?

"I think I would've done this whether I was infected or not, y'know? I've always wanted an intimate moment alone with you . . . Oops. I mean, a moment alone to *torment* you."

I sure wished he'd respond. Just a word or two would be nice. Something like, "Stop this!" And then I could tell him, "Now, now. Don't forget the magic word. You have to ask me *nicely*." He needed to learn some manners; I'd teach him how to address me properly. And then, I'd carve him up some more.

"C'mon. Order me around like you used to. Or are you just being quiet because you haven't had enough yet? Is that it, sir?"

His legs were already so sliced up, I was out of pLaces to cut. His arms, too. I'd have to move on to his face next. So that begged the question: which should I stab out first, his right eye or his left?

There was a rush of movement. The instructor thrust his sword at me. My eyes went wide.

"You're still able to move?!"

It took me a moment to regain my composure—not that I'd lost it for long. Whew. That was unexpected. Still, the instructor's attack was poinNtlEss. He'd managed to lodge his blade in my left arm. Thanks to the virus, it didn't hurt. Hell, I hardly felt it go in. And it wasn't like damage to my non-dominant arm was going to interfere with my sword strikes.

"Pathetic. You do realize that isn't evEN gonna slow me down, right?"

Was he still trying to struggle in vain? Had I not sliced up his sword arm thoroughly enough? Right. Well, I'd just have to do him the favor of roughing it up a little m—

"SSU. Initiate scan."

"Huh?"

I felt something course through my body, wriggling and

crawling as it made its way through my system. What had he done to me?

" . . . the hell . . . is this . . . ?!"

"I've instructed my SSU to run a full-body scan on you, using my sword as a conduit."

His weapon? So he hadn't aimed to kill? Any hit woRked for him, as long as it connected?

After another moment of experiencing the tingling sensation, I figured it out. This was that diagnostic tHInG he'd done the day we first received our . . .

No. Wait. Something was different this time.

"My . . . my body isn't . . . !"

I tried to move my limbs, but they wouldn't budge. Back at base camp, thE diagnostic had tickled. It made me feel goOD. But THiS time felt different; I didn't like iT.

"Forgive the delay," the instructor said. "I needed some time to reprogram the routine."

He'd collapsed back onto the ground. Clearly the attack had required all the strength he had left. He let out a deep sigh—it almost sounded like he was relieved.

What the hell was he talking about?

"I had to improvise a little," the instructor continued. "It's now configured to overload your black box."

My SSU began a countdown. "Ten seconds to detonation."

Shit. He was telling the truth.

"Why would yOu do that?! The explosion will—"

Kill you, too, I meant to say, but my words were cut off by the SSU. "Seven seconds . . . "

If my black box detonated, the blast radius would be enormous. There would be no escape.

"Don't worry. When I see that a student of mine is struggling, I stay with him until we fix the problem."

"Three seconds to detonation."

"Make it stop! Make it stop make it stop make it stop make it stooooop!"

My cries did nothing to halt the countdown.

Everything went white.

"No. 2?"

His voice rasped and trembled as he called my name. I didn't need to look No. 9 over to know how badly he'd been injured.

"Hello, No. 9."

Those blows were meant to be delivered by *my* sword. *I* was supposed to be the one to make him draw his last breath.

"It's No. 21! He's—"

Infected, he clearly meant to finish, but I cut him off.

"Answer me one question."

I sensed movement at my back. The infected Scanner was struggling to his feet. It seemed I'd have to use more deadly force if I was going to keep him down.

"If I were infected by a virus and lost my mind . . . If I became your enemy . . . " I began.

No. 21 rushed at me with a bloodcurdling scream.

I turned to parry the blow, which was far more powerful than I would have expected from a Scanner model. His limiter must have been forced offline as the infection progressed.

I stepped forward, quickly covering the space between us, my sword held parallel to the ground to deliver a rapid strike. I slashed him once, and again, then zeroed in on his neck: that would be the quickest way to disable him. My blade again found flesh, and his vital fluids cascaded from the wound. But he was still moving. I hacked at his neck again—two, then three more blows just above the clavicle. I finished with a shock wave, sending him flying back.

"Ngraaaaah! It hurts! YOu'rE hUrtInG mEeeEEEeeEee . . . !"

No. 21 fell to the ground, writhing and groaning. His senses were dulled, but that didn't mean he was completely impervious to pain. I'd have to do what I could to stimulate his receptors to the greatest extent possible. The goal was to divert resources: more time spent processing the pain meant slower movements—at least slightly—and, more importantly, reduced focus.

For the moment, No. 21 remained unable to stand. I watched,

hoping he might stay down for good, praying I'd done enough damage for him to simply black out and cease functioning. I needed to avoid a drawn-out fight—it wasn't about saving myself the trouble so much as minimizing the chance of the virus spreading to No. 9 and No. 22.

I was getting a crash course in how powerful infected units were; their strength was truly off the charts. Faced with a long encounter, there was a small but ever-looming possibility that I'd fail to defend the two M002 units—that I wouldn't be able to keep No. 9 safe.

I didn't want to think about what would come after that. I drowned out my thoughts by shouting at the top of my lungs.

"No. 9! If I lost my mind, would you kill me?"

His face crumpled. Though his eyes were hidden by his visor, I suspected they were filled with tears. I hated having to ask something so cruel.

"Why would you . . . ? I could never. I . . . I'd refuse. I'd find a way to help you. I swear it."

I was sorry for making him cry. But I needed to hear those words.

I silently thanked him. Aloud, I simply replied, "Good. I was hoping you'd say that."

It was enough. It was all I needed.

After a moment, I added, "I hope . . . you never change. I hope that kindness always stays with you."

I smiled at him. It was the first genuine smile I'd ever given anyone. I realized it would also probably be my last. But if I'd never crossed paths with No. 9—if I'd never come to know him—my life would have ended without being able to have even that.

No. 21 pulled himself to his feet yet again, screaming with rage. It seemed that draining his vital fluids wasn't going to be enough; his body must have adapted to replenish any portion lost at an alarming rate.

"kiLL . . . KiLL! nUmbEr twO . . . mUst dIE!"

He leaped toward me, his movements those of a wild beast. He was fast. I stepped into the attack; this time, I aimed for his gut. I would've preferred to go straight for his chest, but he wasn't going to give me the opening.

I slashed low across his torso. If fluid loss wasn't going to keep him down, I'd destroy his abdominal unit. I doubted he'd manage self-recovery for that as quickly.

"gEt OUt oF my wAY!" he screamed.

I shifted to stabbing, darting thrusts into his stomach every chance I got. But he still wouldn't stop.

"NuuUmmBBBeR twOOO! AgRRaAAAah!"

His hands clamped onto my sword arm to keep me from skewering his chest. I reached out with my left hand, grabbed his neck, and squeezed.

"Stop!" No. 9 cried. "Don't touch him! The virus . . . It'll spread!"

I was well aware of the danger of direct contact. But I couldn't allow this to drag on any longer. And to be honest, I no longer cared. My decision to keep No. 9 safe meant a direct violation of my orders. Whether I died here in the forest or not, my fate was already sealed.

Still, I knew exactly what to tell him.

"It'll be all right. I'm a Type D, remember? I'm resistant to viruses."

He never doubted a word I said to him. He would still believe me now.

No. 21 struggled to break free. I tightened my grip on his neck, and his hands moved to my left arm, clamping down so tight I wondered if he might crush it. An awful, wrenching, high-pitched sound came from my arm. Searing pain ran up its length, straight into my brain. But I did not let go. It would all be over soon.

I heard someone screaming, and realized it was me.

There was a dull snap. My left arm was broken, the pain so intense I had trouble drawing breath. No. 21 twisted his body in attempt to flee, and for the briefest moment, I saw my chance. His guard was down. My sword plunged straight into his chest.

"NgrAAaaaAAAah!!"

He swiveled back and clung to me as he screamed. Was he planning to self-destruct? The full force of the explosion would tear us all apart, unless . . . I could get him over the side of the cliff before us.

No. 22 yelled, "Look out!" as I threw his twin away from me with all my might.

As No. 21 flew backward through the air, I saw his eyes move, and for just a single moment, they connected with those of No. 22. Despite the red glow of his pupils, his gaze in that moment seemed quiet. Serene. All trace of the madness gripping him vanished, and, though it might've been just my imagination, he seemed to manage a faint smile right as he slipped over the edge.

It was all over as soon as I'd processed it. No. 21's body exploded in a pillar of flame, the roar and heat of the blast sweeping over us like a great wave.

I was hurled to the ground, clinging desperately to a consciousness that wanted to slip away. I heard No. 22's wail of anguish. I turned, wanting to see whether No. 9 had found safe cover, but it was hard for me to make out anything at all.

Finally, the flames subsided, and the dust thrown up by the explosion began to settle. Relative silence returned to our portion of the forest. No. 22 continued to sob quietly, and I looked around once more to find No. 9. He was slowly sitting up and didn't seem to have sustained any injuries from No. 21's self-destruction. Relief flowed through me.

I didn't have time to waste lying on the ground. I began to lever myself upright, too, when the awful truth sank in: despite my slow, labored movements, I was completely free of pain.

I needed to hurry. There was one last thing I needed to see done.

"No. 2?! Are you all—"

"Stay back!"

I held up a hand to stop No. 9, who had begun rushing toward me.

I stood up. Good. It seemed I still retained ambulatory control.

"Don't come near me," I told him.

My drive systems were hanging on by a thread, but the only overt sign so far was my broken left arm, which occasionally twitched of its own accord.

"No! It's not true! It can't be . . . !"

He seemed to be on the verge of tears.

Once more, I was sorry. I would have given anything to allow him to go on smiling.

"You said it yourself," he sniffled. "You're a Type D model. You're outfitted with a barrier to deflect any kind of virus thrown at you . . . "

Since he was unable to do so, I smiled for him. "You're so kind, No. 9. So gentle. But you're too naïve. You can't go on believing everything you're told."

I hoped he could see the sincerity in my smile. I hoped it might lessen his sorrow as we made our way through this.

"I want you to know the truth about me. I'm a safeguard. I exist as a solution in case any YoRHa unit tries to betray Command. My real designation is No. 2 Type E. An Executioner model."

I watched the fine muscles of his throat work as he swallowed convulsively.

"I was created to kill you all. I was meant to be your assassin."

"Th . . . that can't be right . . . Tell me that's not true."

I couldn't see his eyes under the visor, but I imagined them wide with surprise. Good. Better that than sadness.

"I have to admit . . . I envy you, No. 9."

There wasn't much time left. The infection was spreading through my systems at an alarming rate. The virus I'd contracted from No. 21 must have been some kind of new variant.

"Instead of fighting enemies, you get to spend your time helping your allies. I envy the person you are, too . . . your straightforward, pure nature."

My chest felt tight. But I had to get the words out. I had to let him know how I felt.

"Me, on the other hand . . . From the moment I came into existence, all I've done is learn how to kill. I've lived my life telling nothing but lies. That's why, when I see you, I . . . "

My cheeks were wet. Was . . . was I crying? It seemed the tightness in my chest wasn't from the virus alone.

"When I'm with you, I feel like maybe my soul could be saved . . . "

I remembered the way he'd wrapped the tape around my hand, explaining how he was trying to help me recover. Afterward, I'd felt like that hand, long sullied, had somehow been purified. It had pained me to think of dirtying it once more.

"SSU!" he shouted. "Halt internal clock for the processor in No. 2's black box. Proceed with virus inactivation and elimination from—"

It wouldn't help. Inside me, I could feel how rapidly the infection was spreading. I knew how bad it was, and so did he. Even the SSU understood the futility of the request, replying with a simple "Unable to comply."

I checked my systems. Yes. I'd apparently lost 67% of myself to the virus. That sounded about right.

"Shut up! Just do what I say!"

I hadn't known he was able to raise his voice in anger. Here I was at the bitter end, still learning new things about him.

"Corruption of unit No. 2 black box at 78% and rising. Loss of consciousness in two minutes. Proposal: Destroy YoRHa unit No. 2 Type E immediately."

No. 9 screamed in fury at the tinny voice. He tore the SSU from his arm and threw it to the ground.

I understood that feeling. How many times had I wished to do the same to mine? The devices certainly were annoying. I would have laughed if I could.

"Ah, No. 9. You really are naïve. But it makes me happy to know how strongly you feel."

"I'm not letting you die!"

He seemed intent on treating me, even though he knew it was futile.

If anything, it was exactly like him to try.

"No. 22," I called. "Take care of No. 9 for me."

I reversed my grip on my sword and brought the tip to my chest. I knew I should do it now, while No. 9 was still far enough away.

"Goodbye, No. 9," I said.

The world was stained red, but the only thing in my eyes was him.

[Log Entry: No. 4 / Forest Zone—Northwest of Transport Crash Site]

I continued on through the forest in search of the transport. I'd lost No. 3, but that didn't change the fact that there were things that I needed to get done. If anything, his death made them all the more pressing.

I was heading southeast, coaxing my exhausted legs along. I estimated I had about 800 meters left to go. I wondered where No. 6 and No. 21 had landed, and whether they were alive or dead.

Guess it must've been . . . when No. 21 hacked the console aboard the transport. He was hit with a logic virus and . . . Yeah. I remember some weird noise over the comms.

That was what No. 3 had said. So if the two were in fact alive, they'd be infected, too. I'd have to fight them.

If so, the next question was whether I could take down two more YoRHa units in my current state. The wounds I'd sustained while fighting No. 3 were more serious than I wanted to admit. If a few of those strikes had landed a little to one side or another, they could've spelled my doom.

And aside from the sword wounds, there was my own mounting fatigue. Every joint in my body cried out in pain. I'd pushed myself too hard. But if I'd put in any less effort, I wouldn't have survived to be standing here thinking about it. Victories didn't come much closer than that.

Here's my chance to be on your level. Hell, if I get to be your equal in a fight for one damn second . . . I don't think I need another thing outta life.

In the end, No. 3 got what he wanted. This pain was proof enough of his strength. Damn fool. I wished he could've been here to enjoy it . . .

And what about the squadron's other members? With our Scanner infected, those of us left on the surface would have a tough time finding each other.

With that, a thought occurred to me: I could turn on my distress beacon. The Bunker would be able to pick up the squadron's black box signals. They were too stingy to ever send us backup, but maybe they'd at least consider relaying my squadmates' coordinates.

A gust of wind carried with it the stench of burning: I must've been downwind from the remains of the transport. Turned out I'd picked the right direction to walk in, after all. But thanks to the densely packed trees, I still didn't have visuals on the crash.

The forest would be one hell of a place to run into machines . . .

I'd just had the thought when I caught a bit of movement out of the corner of one eye. Nearly stopped my heart.

It turned out to be Cactus. The captain was sitting against the base of a broken tree. I started to call out to him but caught myself. Something seemed off. I drew my sword instead.

His arm was twisted at an odd angle and twitching unpredictably—not exactly things you'd see from an android operating normally. Worse, his buddies Phlox and Lotus were on the ground next to him, unmoving. Had he taken them down? Had he been infected by a virus?

He noticed me and panicked, throwing both arms into the air.

"Whoa! No! No, no, no! This isn't what it looks like!"

His right arm continued to shake.

"It's not a virus!" he exclaimed. "We went over the side of a cliff! The fall messed up my arm."

If that was true, then how was he going to explain the two corpses?

He seemed to notice the shift in my gaze and began furiously shaking his head.

"They're not dead! Honest! They're just unconscious from being hit with a few training rounds."

I looked at them more closely. It took a moment to see, but the chests of the two fallen Resistance members were rising and falling evenly. They were breathing comfortably. In fact, it seemed Lotus was even snoring. Huh.

I looked back at Cactus. His eyes were their normal color.

"Shot them with training rounds, you said?"

"Things were looking bad. I had to pretend I was infected. A coward's gotta do what a coward's gotta do, y'know?"

He didn't offer to tell me who or what had necessitated the ploy. I didn't ask. Phlox and Lotus were recovering, apparently in pretty good shape. The fact that they were safe said enough for me.

"Well, damn."

With this latest source of tension defused, fatigue suddenly hit me. I leaned against one of the great sentinels of the forest and felt like I might slide right down to the dirt and just rest for a spell. I hadn't noticed until now, but I'd apparently been on edge for too long. I was mystified by how relieved I was to see Cactus and his friends safe and sound.

Cactus asked, "Where's your buddy? Y'know, the other big guy. No. 3."

I shook my head in silence. The captain understood not to press any further. He simply parroted my earlier comment. "Well, damn."

It was quiet. The wind through the trees continued to carry the reek of burning. We sat for a while like that, not speaking, until Cactus finally mumbled, "Looks like we managed to survive . . . "

Not too long ago, it might've been something any of us would've said with a smile. Speaking for myself, at least, survival had been the goal. I'd thought endlessly about how No. 3 and I could improve our tactics on the battlefield . . . Because better tactics meant a better chance of both of us making it out alive.

But No. 3 was dead now, and I'd been the one to kill him.

I grunted a reply. "Looks like."

It was just as Cactus said. We'd managed to survive.

I looked up at the sky, allowing myself to have a sentimental moment, but a burst of noise came in over the comms to ruin it.

"This is the Bunker. YoRHa M Squadron, do you read me?"

It was an operator. Well, I'd be damned. Sometimes pigs did fly. I didn't know how things worked for other squadrons, but in our case, direct contact from the Bunker was all but unheard of. Everything we got came relayed via our instructor.

So if the Bunker was contacting us directly now, that probably meant . . .

"This is YoRHa M Squadron, Gunner No. 4. I read you. Go ahead."

"Whew! Am I glad to hear you. We're sending backup your way. I don't know what's going on, but we can't get through to the M Squadron instructor."

The operator all but finished my thought for me. Either the instructor had met his end in the crash, or he'd sustained serious injuries and ceased functioning. And given that the instructor wasn't a YoRHa model . . . Well, for him, "ceased functioning" was just a fancy term for "dead."

The operator interrupted my grim musings. "Oh! 2B? Yes, ma'am. We've confirmed approximate coordinates for M Squadron just now."

Apparently, she'd patched someone else in on the call.

"Understood." The new voice was that of a female unit. I didn't recognize it.

"Commencing support operation," the stranger continued.

And then the operator was gone, and I was on a direct line with this mystery android.

"M Squadron No. 4, do you read?" she asked.

"Loud and clear."

"This is YoRHa Squadron No. 2 Type B. I'm headed in your direction to provide support. What is your current status?"

"No. 2 Type . . . B, you said?"

I couldn't help but query the designation. I'd never heard of a Type B before.

"It's a newly introduced all-purpose model, meant to supersede the Attacker and Gunner roles."

An all-purpose model, huh? I figured the "B" must've stood for "Battle." Sounded like the Attacker and Gunner designations had just become obsolete.

Always outdoin' me, as an Attacker or a Gunner!

He'd spat the words out at me like a cobra spits venom. No. 3 had been almost obsessed with the two designations we'd been forced to split. And now neither of them meant a damn thing.

What the hell had he died for, then?

"Sounds like your whole squad's up for reassignment," the stranger said.

He'd died for nothing. That was what. Hell, not a single thing we did meant anything at all, not anything we'd done since the beginning, and not anything we could do in the future.

Reassignment? That didn't mean jack shit. It didn't matter where they put us. Nothing made a damn bit of difference.

I mumbled to myself, "Well, there it is. Our squadron's a failure . . ."

The comm link was still open. Somewhere in the background of my awareness, I could hear her demanding that I relay my present coordinates, then after a few seconds, demanding again. I stayed silent on the line. Not that it'd cause her much grief. The Bunker could pinpoint our location and send the info her way easily enough.

In the end, nothing would have changed. It wouldn't have mattered if No. 3 had survived or if I'd died. The fact that any of us had been alive at all didn't change a damn thing about the world.

I cut the transmission and pulled the visor from my eyes. Still leaning against that great big tree, I skimmed my gaze up the trunk, all the way to the top.

The sky sure was blue. Damn pretty color.

[Log Entry: No. 9 / Forest Zone—Transport Crash Site]

For some time after No. 2 self-destructed, I found myself unable to move. I didn't want to think. If No. 22 hadn't been with me, I might've sat there forever and refused to leave.

But No. 22 had sustained some heavy injuries in the fight with his twin. He needed attention. That was what convinced me to stand back up.

Once I was beside him, my hands going through the familiar movements of my tasks, I started to feel a little better.

"Somebody's sending out a distress signal," No. 22 said, peering at his SSU. "It's a YoRHa code."

So there was at least one more of us still alive. If that was the case, I needed to go provide help. That was my job, after all. As long as I was still alive, I'd go on treating everyone's injuries—even if M Squadron itself was no more.

"Can you get a fix on the source?" I asked.

Maybe they weren't far away. Maybe they were close enough to be within visual range, and we just hadn't noticed. I took a casual glance around, not really expecting to be so lucky, when a glimmer caught my eye. Something on the ground was reflecting the sunlight.

"What's that?" I wondered aloud.

I didn't really have any sense of what I might find, but before I knew it, I was on my feet, walking over to pick whatever it was up.

"It's . . . it's No. 2's SSU . . . "

It must've flown off his wrist when he detonated. Or maybe he'd lost it during the fight with No. 21. I didn't know which, but in any case, I was impressed to find the SSU without a scratch on it, considering the intensity of the earlier events.

As I held it, I thought of the wrist it was meant to rest on. No. 2's hands were slender yet very strong. But those hands and their owner were gone now. All that remained was the SSU, miraculously unharmed.

"SSU," I ordered. "Delete all data pertaining to No. 2."

When I issued the command, No. 22 looked at me with surprise.

"This is for the best," I said.

As long as No. 2's data remained on the server, Command could always try to salvage him. But would that make him happy? He'd been in such torment over his mission. I didn't think he'd want to be revived only to have to live as an assassin once again.

The order, however, went unexecuted.

"Unable to comply," replied the SSU.

It was hard for me to swallow what the device said next.

"All experimental data is to be reported to the Council of Humanity. Deletion of specified data cannot proceed without direct approval from Bunker Command."

And there was more. The SSU's preprogrammed response continued. "Project conclusions are as follow: Application of Attacker, Gunner, and Healer systems to be reevaluated. New dedicated support unit to be implemented upon completion of development. Future YoRHa combat androids to be manufactured with a primary emphasis on female models; despite improved attack strength, male models determined to exhibit poor organizational cohesiveness. Following final field operation for Experimental M Squadron, all assigned units are to undergo a full reformat."

A reformat? As in, they were going to wipe our consciousness data?

That meant the lives we'd led were to be blotted out entirely—even mine and No. 22's and that of whoever was sending the distress signal. The three of us had managed to survive only to face extinction. In effect, this was no different from the countless annihilations we'd suffered before.

And this time nobody would be coming back. Not even me.

In a way, I guessed it meant I would finally join that inner circle of squadmates from which I'd long been excluded.

"All male-type YoRHa models are to be repurposed as Scanners. The Type E model will not be allowed to return to the Bunker until all project objectives have been completed."

Its answer finally complete, the SSU fell silent, and for a while afterward, I stayed quiet, too. Until this point, I'd lived oblivious to the truth. I hadn't doubted anything—not the training I'd received on the Bunker, and certainly not the words of our instructor. I'd entertained some vague reservations about the way Command went about things, but those had never, I realized, bloomed into true doubt.

"He was right . . . We really were just guinea pigs . . . " No. 22's voice was choked up.

An enemy logic virus had spelled the end for No. 21. But ultimately, it didn't matter. Had the infection never occurred, he would have eventually been snuffed out along with the rest of us. It was only a matter of time. We were test subjects, lab rats to be sacrificed once the experiment had run its course.

You really are naïve, No. 2 had said.

What had he been feeling when he said those words, shouldering the lonely burden of truth?

No. 2's SSU beeped, as if acknowledging my silent question. "No. 9?"

I gulped. It was No. 2's voice. *You're alive?! Where are you?!* I wanted to shout, but something told me to hold back.

"I hope you're the one listening. This message was meant for you."

Ah. It was a recording. He wasn't alive. This was just a file containing the sound of his voice. All the same, I wondered where and when he'd found the time to record it.

"I've been lying to you since the beginning," the recording continued. "It looks like I'll end up paying for that with my life. But I want you to know I'm not lonely. Not even a little bit."

"No. 2 . . . " I whispered.

"There's a question that's been bugging me for a long time. It's about our souls. As we die and get remade, over and over, I wonder where they go. What happens to them?"

Our souls? I'd never stopped to think about anything like that. I'd been so wrapped up in saving everyone, in bringing them back to life, I didn't have time for much else. That was why No. 2's earlier revelation had caught me so off guard.

I really was naïve, wasn't I?

"Anyway . . . No. 9, I'm sure you've made a copy of my data to keep inside yourself. I'd like you to delete it, please."

My hand flew to my chest. He'd seen right through me. He

must have sensed that I'd try to keep a secret copy of him to carry with me.

When I told the SSU to erase his data from the server, it was because I hadn't wanted him to be revived and forced to live as an assassin again. But the local copy was for me; I wasn't going to let Command get ahold of it. I'd intended to carry it with me in the hope that someday, somehow, I might find a way to see him again—not as a Type E, but just as No. 2, the person I knew.

"You don't need to hang on to it," the recording continued. "I have a feeling we'll be able to see each other again soon enough. So, until then . . . Goodbye, No. 9."

Did he truly think so? Would the two of us be reunited someday, even without my saved copy?

It occurred to me that in all likelihood, I would soon be wiped from existence, too. I supposed holding onto his data for as long as I lived didn't really mean much if I wasn't going to live long in the first place. So I decided to trust him. I decided to trust *in* him, that someday we might be able to see each other again.

"Look," No. 22 spoke up. "It's the sun."

I looked up at the sky. At some point during the turmoil, the wind had finished driving the clouds away. We now stood under a vast expanse of blue overhead, bathed in the brilliant light of the sun.

I wished he could have seen it, too.

I would have liked to take his hand and go walking together through this world of light.

"No. 2 . . . " I whispered again.

His voice had already fallen silent, the recording finished. He was gone, though my yearning to see him was not. I believed that someday, the two of us might be together once more. And when that happened, maybe we'd find ourselves somewhere bright and warm, just like the place where I now stood.

I quietly tightened my grip around the SSU he'd left behind.

YoRHa Boys Ver. 1.05

EPILOGUE

"THIS IS THE BUNKER. YoRHa M Squadron, do you read me?"

The message came in over my SSU shortly after I'd finished listening to No. 2's recording. I was still trying to process everything I'd just learned, and it had me maybe a little more on edge than I needed to be. So I didn't respond right away.

"YoRHa M Squadron, please come in. Are you there?"

I recognized the operator's voice. I'd heard her over the comms before. She had a calm, collected manner, though her words felt cold somehow.

"Sorry," I replied. "This is Gunner No. 22. Go ahead."

"Please report status and coordinate data for current location."

"Two survivors: units No. 9 and No. 22. Two casualties: units No. 2 and No. 21. Cause of death: logic virus infection followed by . . . self-destruction."

When No. 21 had attempted to catch us in the blast radius of his self-destruct explosion, No. 2 intervened, knocking him over the edge of a cliff. And then No. 2 had also self-destructed, though his act was a selfless one meant to save us from the threat of infection. He'd plunged his own sword into his chest and thrown himself off the side of the same cliff.

But the operator didn't ask for the details. "I see," was her curt reply, and she left the matter at that.

"Um . . . " I ventured. "Are there any other survivors besides us?"

"Contact has been established with Gunner No. 4. A backup unit is en route to his position."

"And . . . anyone else?"

"Current status of squadron members other than you two and No. 4 is unknown."

I started to ask about the Resistance units but stopped myself. They were deserters. No reason to get Command involved, even if those three had survived. I felt certain they'd scurry off well before our backup arrived, leaving no trace of where they were headed.

"Please stand by at your current location for rendezvous," continued the operator.

"And after that?" I asked. "What's going to happen to us?"

"After recovery by the backup unit, I'm told you'll be returned to the Bunker for repairs and reoutfitting."

The words from No. 2's SSU flashed through my mind. *A full reformat.*

"I . . . see. Understood, ma'am."

The experiment had run its course. All survivors were scheduled for disposal—No. 4, No. 9, and me, too. Now that I knew the truth, I wondered if maybe we'd have been better off escaping like No. 21 had wanted. Maybe I should have agreed to his plan.

I remembered how he said that he'd always pitied me, and how No. 9 had been so desperate to protect my feelings, shouting, "No! Don't listen to him!" But I already knew what No. 21 really thought of me. I'd realized it a long, long time ago.

And his words were all true: I *had* failed as an Attacker, and No. 21 *was* far more accomplished than me. I'd always been aware of my inferiority. I'd always known that my twin looked down on me. Of course he would.

How could I not know what he thought of me? We were twins. He knew me better than I knew myself—just like I knew him more thoroughly than he ever could.

So when he was taken over by the logic virus and said those things aloud, it was kind of a relief, to be honest. It showed me that even though he'd had those thoughts, he was embarrassed by them. He didn't want to say them out loud for fear of hurting me. That was how much he cared about me.

If the virus hadn't undermined his self-control, he'd have probably kept those thoughts to himself until the day he died, all to let me hang on to the little pride I had left. That made me happy.

It also made me realize that I should have—

"No. 22? Is something wrong?"

"Huh? Oh. No, I'm fine."

I hadn't even noticed No. 9 lower himself to the ground beside me. I figured he must've heard my exchange with the operator. That was probably why he was speaking in an unusually hushed tone.

"Sounds like we're the only three left."

The instructor and No. 3, along with No. 6, No. 21, and even No. 2 . . . They were all dead. Pretty soon, we'd be gone from this world, too.

I should have agreed to No. 21's plan. I didn't care anymore that it violated orders. I didn't care whether it was right or not. I should have gone with him because he was my twin and I loved him.

"No. 21 . . ."

I wondered where he was now and what had become of his soul. I wanted to be by his side again, and soon.

Everything feels still somehow, almost like when it's snowing . . .

Who waS it that said thosE words? I cOuLDn't rEmeMber. But the words seEmed very . . . vErY . . . f . . . ? Fo . . . foNd? What waS "FonD"?

I wAs aT the bottom oF thE sea. I kNew thAT mUch. And, um . . . TherE hAd beeN an explosion. I was throWn far awaY. I remembeRed. BefOre, it wasN't thE sea. It . . . it was a . . . a fo . . . foReSt. It huRt. VEry muCH hurt. And I could nOT move. I rolleD. I wAS liKe a stone. RoLLing.

When I oPeNEd mY eyes, machines were carryinG me. We were goINg far. Very faR, FAr aWAy. dEEp in tHE sEa.

I wanted him to come back. I was so lonely.

I Did noT wAnt to be aLoNE!

It was cOld. Few SounDS at the boTTom oF the sea. I diD noT waNT to be there . . . Not aLONe. I wAS sUpPOseD to . . . to have **** bEsiDe me.

I cRieD.

A bIG machine cAme. A vERy . . . very . . . biG mAchine.

LeT'S be tOgeTHer. LEt's go togethER.

leT's . . . Oh. I aM soRRy. I was wRong. YoU arE nOt it. wE tried toGeTHer, but You aRe noT it. The toGeTHer I waNT iS thE togeTheR i WanT is . . .

I . . .

I . . .

WHo is "I"?

WhO Am I? WhAT iS tHIs pLaCE? wHY iS hE NOt hErE?

T . . . tw . . . TwEn . . .

N . . . Num . . . beR . . . twentY-two . . . ?

WHEre aRe yOU? I aM cold. PleASe . . . bE neXT To mE.

tWEnTY-tWo? whO iS tHAt? Who aM I? wHo ArE YOu? i dO nOT kNOw.

bUT . . . I wAnT iT hERe . . . I want . . . nUMbEr . . . tWentY . . . twO . . . ?

NumBer 22. RiGHt. ThAt'S your naMe.

Come hERe. I'm coLD. NumBEr TwENty-tWO, nUMbER tWEnTY-two, numBEr twEnTy-tWo . . .

. . . sHoULd I go to yOU? It wILL be wARM beside YOu. I WiLL gO.

NUMbeR TwENty-twO. Where aRE you? RiGHt now. I wiLL huRRy. I will bE witH You . . .

FLASHBACK

"THIRTY SECONDS . . . "

The countdown had begun.

Looking back on it all now, time limits had always been a big part of my life. From the day I rolled off the line, through my training and assessments, and through my missions and duties afterward, time had always been relentlessly counting down. Maybe it had to be that way. Maybe it was because I was always meant to be an instructor.

And you want me *for the job?*

That's how I'd responded when Commander White promoted me to the position. I was confused, to be honest. I knew about the project's previous experimental squadron, and rumors about the formation of a new one had been circulating around the Bunker for some time. The female-type YoRHa androids had proved to be a huge success. The next squadron was to be composed entirely of male-type models, and we were all excited to see what they could do.

The army's most cutting-edge weapons, YoRHa units had demonstrated an unprecedented degree of combat proficiency. Operating costs were soaring, but so were hopes. We still needed to prove their viability in actual combat, but once that data was in hand and we'd ramped up to full-scale production, we believed the YoRHa models might prove to be the key element we needed to turn the tide of war.

Monumental expectations would rest on the shoulders of this new squadron. And the person they tapped to lead it was *me*? It seemed improbable. Something about the situation didn't sit right in my gut.

Why the hesitation? I certainly hope this isn't because of a lack of confidence. There was a hint of mockery in Commander White's tone, which I remember feeling a little perturbed by.

I can assure you, that is not the case, I said firmly, shaking my head.

The squadron is composed entirely of the new models, she said, *and despite your enhancements, you're certainly no YoRHa unit. I suppose it's reasonable to feel ambivalent about guiding students with capabilities far exceeding your own. However, I would remind you that it's not particularly unusual for students to surpass their mentors. It happened frequently enough in the schools that existed in human civilization.*

I was well aware of the fact. My hesitance was due to something else—namely, why I in particular had been chosen.

Rest assured, the commander added, *you won't be expected to engage in combat. The only ones fighting will be the YoRHa units. Just stand there on the back lines and look dignified.*

In fact, it's rather important that you don't *fight. In any case, the enemies will be well out of your league. We wouldn't go so far as to prohibit you from engaging in a battle at all, but just be aware that we're expecting you to keep intervention to a minimum.*

I'd never heard the commander talk to this extent before. So maybe it was the flood of information she was providing that made me forget to ask one more crucial question: why was she not taking charge of this new squadron?

The previous experimental squadron—the one composed entirely of female androids—had been led by Commander White herself. If, for example, her choices as squadron leader had led to failure, I might have been understood the decision to place the next squadron in someone else's hands. But the previous one had been a resounding success. So why fix something that wasn't broken?

In the end, I didn't ask, and found myself accepting the post.

Commander White nodded her approval. *Very good. You are hereby assigned sole responsibility for YoRHa Experimental M Squadron.*

What do you mean, "sole responsibility"?

Exactly as it sounds. I will of course retain final authority, and all missions will be issued directly by me, but beyond that, the squadron is entirely in your hands. Surely that's a more preferable arrangement than my hovering over your shoulder, evaluating every decision you make?

That's very considerate of you, ma'am.

It did occur to me at the time that she might be trying to distance herself from M Squadron. Rumors were floating around that Commander White vocally opposed the plans for a squadron of male-type androids, and that ultimately, her concerns were rebuffed by the Council. Perhaps that was the reason why she preferred not to lead the squadron herself.

But in the end, rumors were just rumors. It was impossible to say whether the stories I'd heard had been exaggerated, or whether they were true at all, so I placed little faith in them. I figured I should just be grateful that Commander White had promised not to meddle in my new daily affairs.

It wasn't until much later that I realized her non-involvement was a means of self-defense.

"Twenty-five seconds . . . "

As soon as the countdown began over the loudspeakers in the shooting booth, No. 3's accuracy noticeably decreased. He began firing as rapidly as he could, his finger pulling nonstop on the trigger.

The rules of the test stated that all rounds had to be fired within the given time limit, including those in the spare magazines scattered across the booth's countertop. Given that requirement, No. 3's reaction was understandable. He'd decided to sacrifice his hit rate in exchange for speed, concentrating on getting all his shots fired instead of worrying about target accuracy. It wasn't necessarily a wrong decision, but it wasn't a right one either.

On the surface, the test appeared challenging but doable, given sufficient effort. The reality was that the time allotted to each shooter would be just shy of what they would need. In other words, the number of rounds provided—extrapolated based on previous test results—was intentionally a little more than what the examinee could physically fire off in time.

In fact, the test had little to do with measuring shooting proficiency. It was a way for me to better understand my students, by presenting them with an unachievable goal. I wanted to see how long it would take them to realize they weren't going to make the time limit, and what course of action they'd choose once the truth became apparent.

No. 4 quickly perceived the problem. Figuring it out really only required a calm and logical analysis of three things: the number of shots fired in the first few seconds, the total remaining rounds, and the time limit.

If I or another assessor had been with them during the test, the examinees probably would have stopped once they realized what was happening, in order to express their confusion to us and ask us what to do. So I made sure that each unit would be completely alone for the duration of the test, on the pretense of eliminating any potential distractions.

What would my students do when faced with an impossible task, with no one to turn to for answers or advice?

No. 4's solution was to fire off as many rounds as he could

at his normal rate, while preserving—and, in fact, slightly improving—his accuracy. He'd probably interpreted the test as an assessment of what he would do when surrounded by more enemies than he could handle. It was a conclusion that precisely fit his nature.

When his time ran out, his unfired rounds numbered almost exactly as I'd predicted. Every shot he fired had hit its target.

In contrast, No. 3's target accuracy dipped below 30%—but in the end, his unfired rounds numbered fewer than I had estimated. When his time expired, he slammed his fists down on the counter repeatedly, shouting, *Dammit! I was this close! Just a few seconds more!* He was so preoccupied with the frustration of failure, the idea that the task could be impossible hadn't even crossed his mind. That, in turn, precisely fit No. 3's nature.

I posed the same challenge to the other members in the following days. The results were varied, a reflection of the diverse personalities filling the squadron's roster.

The moment No. 21 saw the number of rounds provided, he concluded that the task could not be completed given the time constraint and his own skill level with a gun. He didn't even pick the weapon up. He assumed there must have been some kind of mistake and exited the firearms training area.

No. 6, like No. 4, realized the problem within the first few seconds. But he differed from No. 4 in his reaction: instead of trying to adapt to the situation, he gave up. But he didn't walk away like No. 21, either. He carried on for the remaining time, shooting languidly, the expression on his face making it clear that he just couldn't give a damn.

When No. 22 took the test, he began looking slightly confused about halfway through but soldiered on, keeping up his rate of fire until the timer ran out. Most likely, he had begun to suspect the task was impossible but lacked confidence in his own conclusion.

No. 9 appeared to notice the issue approximately halfway through the exam, as No. 22 had. However, he responded quite differently. He grew anxious, pulling the trigger as rapidly as he could, undoubtedly believing that if he tried hard enough, he might just make it through. But lacking the combat skill of No. 3, he failed to display an unexpected increase in speed. His performance was well in line with what I'd anticipated.

I had wanted to know how each of my students would react when faced with an impossible task. After the tests were complete, I knew. However, I'd failed to apply that knowledge. If only I'd . . .

No. Best leave it be.

After all, hindsight is always twenty-twenty.

Actually, come to think of it, that had been right around the time when No. 4 requested reassignment.

He claimed it was a matter of "having the best people we can get in every role." And he wasn't wrong: he would make a far more capable Gunner than No. 3. But I accepted his request mostly because it was what he wanted, and I didn't see any particular reason to deny him.

I thought that would be the end of it, but the decision seemed to make waves among his fellow squad members. Some time later, No. 21 came to me, eyes bright with curiosity, to ask, *Is it true that No. 4 switched roles from Attacker to Gunner?*

I was taken aback. I'd known that Scanners were naturally curious, but I hadn't thought No. 21 would take an interest in something that seemed so minor. No. 4's reassignment was not a matter of secrecy, and No. 4 himself hadn't asked me to keep the matter private, so I told No. 21 the truth.

That slightly odd turn of events aside, No. 3 and No. 4 were progressing through their training right on schedule. Suddenly, I found myself concerned about the *other* M001 unit, who was lagging far behind.

I'd been informed since the beginning that because of the special nature of No. 2's duties, he would likely require significantly more time than the rest to complete his training and calibrations.

And I was aware of his true designation: No. 2 Type E. I knew that his real purpose was to destroy other YoRHa androids. I'd been told it was a safety measure, to prevent the dissemination of YoRHa model specs if one were to be incapacitated on the battlefield and seized by the enemy.

But when it came to No. 2's training, although I was nominally his instructor, I found it quite difficult to observe his development. Command kept me informed of the general progress of his training and calibrations, but I soon learned that there was a great deal of red tape to clear before my superiors were going to allow me to observe him in action. Everything about him was top secret.

Ultimately, I contrived a plan to make use of his atmospheric entry test. Given the costs of operation, usage time for the descent training units was always strictly managed. All I had to do was be present in the hangar immediately before or after No. 2's scheduled testing window; I'd run in to him for certain.

No. 2. When I called out to him in the hangar, he quietly turned to face me, exhibiting no outward sign of surprise. He proceeded to salute me, his expression flat and revealing nothing. In a reversal of what I'd intended, I was the one to be caught off guard by my orchestrated encounter.

No. 2's model had the form and features of an adolescent boy, just like all the M002 squad members. At the same time, there was something very different about him, though I'd have been hard-pressed to say exactly what it was.

Unnerved, I simply ended the encounter by saying, *Ah, it's nothing important. Carry on.*

He bowed once, spun away from me, then dashed to the flight unit and deftly hopped inside. The silence and absolute precision with which he moved was another surprise. His was the grace of an assassin.

To be honest, when I'd first read the report on him, I wondered if he was up to the task. A Scanner or Healer like No. 21 or No. 9 would pose little trouble for him, I assumed, but I had my doubts about whether he'd be able to overpower the squadron's Attackers and Gunners. I knew his frame was reinforced beyond the specs of the standard YoRHa models, but that didn't change the fact that there was a considerable difference in size between No. 2 and androids with adult male frames. As No. 3 and No. 4's instructor, I'd witnessed the incredible physical capabilities of the two larger M001 units.

It was a needless worry. I could tell immediately that No. 2 was far more powerful than the others, just by the way he'd stood before me. I suspected that the delays in his calibrations were caused by the difficulty of *concealing* that degree of strength. And, of course, No. 2 would have needed additional time to familiarize himself with the duties and behavior of his Type D cover.

The Executioner model itself was no secret: the fact that such androids existed was common knowledge. But when deployed alongside a predetermined group of potential targets, the designation was typically concealed so as to prevent unnecessary alarm.

Thus, the fact that No. 2 had been assigned as a Type E rather than a Type D was telling: his targets were decided, the fate of Experimental M Squadron sealed. The only reward that awaited M Squadron at the conclusion of the experiment was disposal. Death at the Executioner's hands was to be their cruel end.

"Twenty seconds . . . "

The memory of another particular countdown haunted me even now.

We're not gonna make it, No. 22 had cried, voice shaking so badly I could hear it over the comms. He was nearly shrieking, which wasn't surprising—reports from the front lines were rarely issued in calm tones. No. 3 tended to bellow, No. 6 and No. 21 tended to be sullen. Even the ever-cool No. 4 would hurry his words.

Silence followed No. 22's despairing cry, and just after that came a distant sound like an earthquake tremor. The Goliath had self-destructed. Mission complete.

The operation had called for the elimination of a massive enemy discovered near the coast; our plan was to hack it and force it into self-destruct mode. That was about the only viable option we had against that particular target. Small-arms fire tended to not even scratch machines of that size.

However, we'd been left with far less time than anticipated, a span of mere seconds from triggering the Goliath's self-destruct mode to ignition. No. 21, in charge of the hack, and his escorts, No. 22 and No. 3, had all been caught in the blast.

Some 340 seconds prior to the explosion, No. 6, who had also been assigned to the vanguard, was rerouted to stop the enemy's approaching reinforcements. He died keeping them at bay.

When No. 9 arrived on-site to recover the bodies, guarded by No. 4, I immediately opened a comm channel to Command.

Commander, permission to discuss my earlier report?

She cut me off with a curt, *Denied.*

Though I referred to it as a report, the contents were more like an outright protest. I'd gone on at length, detailing the absurdity of our latest orders and demanding that the mission be called off.

The squadron's missions cannot be altered.

But Commander, it went exactly like the previous operation. The entire squad—

Was annihilated? Yes, we know. The present outcome falls within acceptable parameters.

We're allowing them to suffer in vain? *Sending them into battles they can't win, forcing them to fight like animals desperate for their lives—you're telling me that's all part of the plan?*

This wasn't a training exercise. The squadron wasn't being tested in the safety of a shooting range. They were on a field of death, staring down hordes of deadly machine lifeforms.

The commander was growing impatient with me. *I hope you haven't forgotten the purpose of the experiment, Instructor. M Squadron endures so that all future YoRHa squadrons might flourish. The sacrifices made by these six units will save hundreds, if not thousands of android lives. It's unfortunate, yes, but it is unavoidable—in fact, it is* prudent.

My six, then, were the subjects of a stress test—a proof of concept. The Council wanted to know how bad circumstances could get before the male YoRHa androids failed to deliver. A thorough understanding of the razor-thin line separating victory from defeat would enable them to utilize future units in the most efficient manner possible.

I was being told it was a necessary evil. This was the gamut we had to run to ensure that our immense investment delivered practical results. I understood the logic. When the sacrifice of Experimental M Squadron was weighed against the great number of YoRHa units likely to be produced over time, it was evident which way the scale would tip.

But for me, knowing the ill-fated six firsthand, it was not an easy argument to swallow.

I countered with, *If you refuse to allow us to abort or withdraw, then at least provide us with backup.*

Denied. Don't you understand? Outside support would render the entire experiment meaningless.

But . . .

It is the will of the Council.

And that was that. Once the Council of Humanity's name was invoked, there was no further room for argument. Its decisions were absolute, never to be overturned.

There's one other matter, Instructor. No. 2 has completed his calibrations. He'll be descending to the surface within the next few days. Expect further details from me soon. Over and out.

Commander! I haven't finished—

But the transmission had already been cut.

Over the following days, I persisted, stubbornly attempting to contact the commander. Each time, I was rebuffed, and before the operator cut the connection, she gave the same short response. *The commander wishes to remind you that sole responsibility for M Squadron rests in your hands, Instructor.*

I finally understood what the commander truly meant by "sole responsibility," and what she had been so desperate to avoid.

Still, I refused to give up. I sent numerous messages to the commander, denouncing the harsh conditions the squadron was forced to endure. I wrote of the members' lowered morale and the unavoidable toll on their mental states. I shared how the squadron Scanner, tasked with devising our operational strategy—and thus by far the most versed in enemy numbers and likely outcomes—had begun frequently asking me to submit requests to have missions reconsidered. The list went on.

All of my messages went unanswered.

"Fifteen seconds . . ."

I remembered No. 4's transmission in the Mountain Zone with surprising clarity. Perhaps it stuck with me because it marked the point of no return—both for Experimental M Squadron, and for me.

Fifteen seconds to breech.

His report issued from the fray was terse. Extrapolating from the few words, I knew he meant fifteen seconds until they finished clearing all the machines and proceeded to blast their way inside the cave.

We'd been fortunate; the enemies in the immediate vicinity were weak and easy to deal with. Thanks to that, the mission could continue despite the minor injuries sustained early on in the trench by No. 21 and No. 22.

The rescue operation in the Mountain Zone was something of a departure from the stress tests we'd gone through thus far. Of course, the squad members weren't aware of that fact. I simply said that we had information regarding a soldier from a local base stranded in enemy territory, and that M Squadron had been asked to perform the extraction.

This time, Command wasn't trying to evaluate how dire a situation the squad could handle. The real purpose of this mission was to rendezvous with No. 2. I'd been informed that the distress signal emanating from the cave was that of No. 2's escape pod. The story of the local soldier was merely a pretense.

No. 2, after launching from the Bunker, was intercepted by the enemy upon atmospheric entry. He was forced to board an escape pod for an emergency descent, but he got unlucky: it would have been difficult for the pod to touch down any deeper in enemy territory.

Escape pods were standard equipped with sensors and programs to locate the best possible landing site—i.e., whatever location in range that showed the least amount of enemy activity. But the equipment aboard No. 2's pod seemed to have malfunctioned. Or perhaps the enemy attack on his craft had been so intense that he was forced to abort the scan and manually enter a trajectory.

However, the most curious detail came after touchdown: the escape pod seemed to have *moved* from its landing site. A follow-up scan showed the pod inexplicably located inside a cave several dozen meters away from where it had come down. Since the pod possessed no means for overland travel, we concluded that someone, or something, had carried it inside the cave. Unfortunately, the cave was surrounded by enemy signatures—hardly a safe location.

Recovering No. 2 was going to be dangerous. To make things even worse, it seemed the machine lifeforms in the Mountain Zone were particularly adept at learning: soon after we commenced the operation, a horde of enemies launched a surprise attack on our back line, where No. 9 was supposed to be well out of harm's way. If No. 3 and No. 4 hadn't sensed something unusual happening and gone rushing back to help, the squadron could have suffered a debilitating blow.

Once the situation was under control, we began our approach to the cave.

I issued my orders. *No. 6, I want you in front to secure us a route in. No. 22 will provide cover. No. 9 and No. 21, stay close behind them.*

They responded in unison. *Understood, sir!*

No. 6 rushed forward with swift, easy movements.

In contrast, No. 22's feet still dragged slightly with each step, and No. 21 looked a bit unsteady as he ran alongside No. 9. They'd been the ones to get hit in the earlier surprise attack.

Still, they soldiered on, determined to complete their mission, unaware of the YoRHa android they were soon to meet and the sinister role he was meant to play. How would they have reacted if they knew that the one they'd been injured trying to save was the Executioner meant to seal their fate?

I recalled how No. 6 had mumbled, *It'd save us all a lot of trouble if this "distressed party" could just kick the bucket.*

Little did he know, the implications went far beyond that. No. 2's death would have saved M Squadron's lives—but only for a little while. I assumed that a copy of No. 2's consciousness data was retained on the Bunker's server. So even if he were to die, Command would need only to shove his data into a new body and send it to the surface. M Squadron would enjoy a few more moments of life, but the outcome would not change.

I hadn't anticipated that our arrival at the cave would be quickly followed by an enemy bombardment, or that we would find ourselves face-to-face with actual local soldiers. But despite the string of surprises, No. 2 was successfully recovered, the true mission objective achieved.

No. 3, No. 6, and No. 21 were wary of the seventh member of the squad and the unusual timing of his arrival. No. 4 and No. 22 adopted a wait-and-see attitude. Only No. 9 welcomed him without any trace of reserve.

As for me . . . I did not want No. 2 with us. Though I was his direct superior in theory, he had his own orders to follow and operated under a separate chain of command.

You're not authorized to know when my mission is scheduled to begin.

His words to me were icy. He clearly wanted nothing to do with me. It bothered me, and maybe that was what fueled my immature decision to shoot back.

Allowing yourself to become attached to your squadmates could prove a real obstacle when it comes time to kill them.

I regretted the words as soon as they left my mouth. I regretted them because I knew they embodied my own desire: I wanted No. 2 to grow attached to his squadmates because then he would be unable to kill them. I wanted him to grow attached because *I* had grown attached. I was their instructor, and they were my students. It was meant to be a transient relationship, but in our short time together, they'd become important to me.

Their disposal was a decision that had been in place since the beginning. To put it coarsely, our relationship was that of lab animals and their caretaker. I wasn't supposed to feel anything for them.

Yet I did.

I did not want to see them killed. I wanted them to go on, to flourish after the experiment as an ordinary squad, one of many among YoRHa's forces. I wanted them to finally know fulfillment, dispatched on missions appropriate to their number and abilities—missions that, if difficult, were in no way impossible. The six had their faults and idiosyncrasies, but I felt certain that utilized properly as a squad, they would astound us with the victories they achieved.

Once I'd reached that conclusion, I understood what their survival meant to me.

I again tried to visualize the moral scale: six units on one side, hundreds or thousands on the other. On paper, M Squadron was an insignificant handful, dwarfed in importance next to the multitudes of YoRHa soldiers yet to come. But the units making up that handful were my students. To me, the faceless, nameless thousands could never compare.

Perhaps the ability to dispassionately weigh the fate of six units before one's eyes against that of thousands unseen was the mark of a leader suited to stand at the top. Commander White would be able to do that. But for me, it was impossible.

That wasn't to suggest I was any better of a leader on the ground: to the squadron members, I was just a puppet relaying orders from Command. No matter how much they pressed me to have missions aborted or reinforcements called in, I did nothing. There was nothing I could do. So, to them, it made no real difference whether I was there or not.

At the cave, we encountered another leader: Cactus. And while he appeared to be as ineffectual as I was, in time I would find that there could be no leader more diametrically opposite to me than he was.

At first, I'd thought he was the laziest and most incompetent officer I'd ever laid eyes on. Anything remotely technical, he dumped on Lotus, and any time there was need for tactics or decision-making, he relied completely and unabashedly on Phlox. He did even less for his men than I did for mine.

That, I reasoned, was the sorry face of the deserter—the rot that dereliction wrought on a man who had fought many long years for the Resistance's cause. So I was disgusted that he was going around still calling himself a captain.

But when I looked more closely, I realized I was wrong. Though Cactus and I appeared to serve no purpose to our men, our contributions as leaders were vastly different. Phlox and Lotus seemed to relax simply knowing that Cactus was nearby. It didn't matter whether he did anything in particular; just his presence was enough to put the other two at ease. And I'd learned firsthand how difficult it was to ease the minds of those in your charge.

And I believed—though this was mere speculation on my part—that if faced with the choice between the few and the unknown thousands, Cactus would not hesitate in the slightest. He would choose the few that he'd come to know. This, too, was the mark of a leader.

In fact, I'd complimented him on it once, telling him, *Attentiveness like that is the mark of a fine leader.*

The comment brought a vaguely uncomfortable expression to Cactus's face. I wasn't sure why, but maybe it revealed how oblivious he was to his own effect on his men.

Where Cactus could easily choose, I had failed: I was unable to commit myself either to the few before me or the unknown thousands.

That particular failure aside, were there other ways I could have done more for my men? Could I have been more attentive to the directions in which my students were heading?

Surely I could have foreseen the danger of Scanner No. 21's persistence as he labored to devise a perfect strategy. In his constant search for data, it was inevitable that he'd finally overreach and stumble upon something he wasn't meant to see. Or maybe I could have predicted his incipient rebellion. When No. 21 believed a task was impossible, he walked away from it, refusing to participate any longer; did that not indicate a tendency to disobey orders he disagreed with? I'd witnessed this during my shooting range assessment, yet I let it pass unaddressed.

If only I'd paid more attention to him. If only I'd recognized the danger in time. I couldn't help but dwell on such regrets, though doing so could never change the fact that I'd failed to stop him.

Sorry, sir, but I'm not asking for your opinion. This is a mutiny. The squadron's members get to decide for themselves.

He'd said it decisively, without the slightest shift in his usual demeanor or tone.

And that wasn't all. No. 21 had realized the truth about No. 2, as well.

It looks like your time's finally come, he'd said. *We had to fight eventually, right? That's right. I know all about you.*

Even if I'd somehow been able to prevent the mutiny, the squadron's end would have been much the same: androids killing androids. Squadmates killing squadmates. The transport could have flown true, headed straight for base camp rather than the other side of the world, and the only difference would have been who wound up killing who.

No. 2 had tried to act even before we stepped aboard the transport. As our three-man team circled toward the runway and waiting ship, No. 2 had constantly positioned himself so that No. 9 stayed in his field of vision.

He'd intended to kill No. 9 before takeoff, and then board the transport as if nothing had happened. If questioned by the others about No. 9's absence, he could have claimed the Healer was wounded, taken to rest and recover in one of the ship's berths. Then, for the remainder of the flight, he'd have carefully stalked the rest of the squadron, taking them down methodically, one by one. That, I felt certain, was the essence of his plan.

The only thing he'd failed to account for was my reaction. I was expected to look on in silence as No. 2 carried out his mission, not uttering a word when he crept into No. 9's shadow.

Instead, I'd shouted. And not just that—caught up in the moment, I'd inadvertently drawn my weapon.

I was a fool, unable to choose, unable to act decisively. Yet there I was, meddling in others' duties.

No. 2 was able to sheathe his sword before the Healer whirled around. We resumed our dash toward the carrier, No. 2's façade of innocence still effective enough to keep No. 9 from suspecting anything. I, however, felt no sense of relief; I knew I'd only postponed the inevitable, and that No. 2 was already watching for his next opportunity.

The mutiny plotted by No. 21, No. 3, and No. 6 ended in failure. None of the other squadron members willingly joined in, and the transport, their critical means of escape, had ultimately crashed.

Still, my duty was not over—not after the mutiny attempt failed, not after M Squadron had collapsed into chaos, and not even after I was thrown from the plummeting transport to land deep in the forest, uncertain whether any of my students had survived.

I was alive, and so were the three Resistance members who had joined our flight from the Mountain Zone.

And we'd found ourselves right in the middle of a large group of hostile machines.

Cactus, Phlox, and Lotus hadn't meant to get involved in any of it. They'd come across No. 2's escape pod by chance and were dragged into our struggle as a result. Aside from their status as deserters, they were free from blame, and they'd certainly done nothing to deserve the situation in which they'd found themselves. Thus, I had a responsibility to see the three of them to safety.

To abandon my fellow androids was unthinkable, and more importantly, I felt responsible for the trio's plight. The transport had crashed because of my students' disgraceful conduct.

I fought, defending Cactus, Phlox, and Lotus at my back. But the enemy's numbers were great, and we were at a significant disadvantage in terms of location: the sheer drop of a cliff was just behind us. Soon, we found ourselves surrounded and pressed right up to the edge.

But an unexpected deliverance changed our fortune. No. 6 appeared, broke the enemy line, and then singlehandedly exterminated every machine in sight.

Except it wasn't a deliverance. No. 6, as it turned out, had not come to save us.

On approach, he hurled a throwing knife at me and began to laugh aloud. His eyes were stained red with the telltale glow of a logic virus infection.

Let me tell you what's going to happen next, No. 6 had said. *You're all going to suffer, until eventually I decide to let you die.*

No. 6 was powerful to begin with; his skill in close combat was exceptional. Once the virus forcibly deactivated his limiter, there would be no stopping him.

It all comes down to whether or not you've got a black box. That lovely little high-output reactor core? That's the mark of a YoRHa. Makes all the difference in the world, y'know?

It was true. I didn't have a hope of besting him physically. All of No. 6's combat data was there in my mind, and so I knew every habit and shortcoming he exhibited in a fight, but he still effortlessly disarmed me and knocked me to the ground. That was when I learned what it truly meant to guide a student with capabilities far exceeding one's own: it was to know impotence and despair.

No. 6 had whirled away, his bloodthirsty blade again trained on the three Resistance members. Phlox put up a fight, and even Lotus managed a clever counterattack using the scattered remains of the machine lifeforms. But they could not stop No. 6.

In the end, Cactus was infected, and he turned his weapon on Phlox and Lotus. Though his consciousness was gone, his sense of duty as a captain seemed to remain; sensing what he'd done to his men, he then turned the gun on himself, firing and sending himself plummeting over the cliff's edge.

The pain of having involved those three innocents and inadvertently sentencing them to death tormented me far worse than any wound No. 6 could inflict.

But I knew that if the infection was allowed to progress, my student would continue to cause other androids harm.

Well, Instructor, looks like it's just you and me.

I had to stop him, no matter the cost. But how?

We're going to have a real good time together.

How could I ever hope to overpower No. 6?

. . .

When I came to, he was shouting for my attention. I must have blacked out for a while, probably due to massive loss of vital fluids. Or perhaps my AI had been overloaded by the nonstop pain. My sensors were struggling to cope with the sustained, intense stimulation, and if the onslaught lasted much longer, I assumed my mental capacities would fail well before my physical ones did.

"Sir! Sir! Hey, sir!"

He was laughing—the laughter of madness—as he continued to slash at every inch of my flesh. I found myself in too much pain to move, much less resist. He'd obviously devoted a lot of attention toward figuring out how to deliver his attacks so as to inflict the greatest possible degree of agony.

"Are you listening, Instructor, sir?"

I had to do something. I had to stop him. No. 6 had been outfitted with an aggressive, brutal nature—an attempt to boost his effectiveness as an Attacker. Once he was finished with me, he would continue to seek out new targets. He would butcher his comrades until his body was physically wrecked and unable to function.

I couldn't bear the thought of more victims. But my mind was sluggish. I wanted to focus on the moment, but I kept meandering over events of the past. My consciousness must have been starting to slip.

"Do you get it now? I *adore* this kind of play."

I recalled him standing somewhere else, smiling and announcing that there was "plenty of other stuff" he could handle, too. That must have been when he introduced himself to M001 on arrival at base camp.

"Just to be clear, this iSN't the virus talking. I've *always* adored this."

Yes, I imagined so. No. 6 had revealed his unusual predilections quite some time ago. That, too, was when we were still at base camp, shortly after I'd presented the squadron with their Support System units.

No. 6 had raised his hand. *That diagnostic you initiated. It tickled. Felt kinda good even. Permission to have that run that on me again, sir? Maybe we could do it in private this time?*

The diagnostic.

The Support System . . .

A sudden idea began to coalesce through the haze blanketing my mind, but before I could grab hold of it, a searing pain coursed through the left half of my body. He'd cut me again. I was still feeling the strikes, though I had little sense of where in particular they were landing.

But I couldn't give in. Not yet. I had to stay conscious. The first inkling of an idea had been nearly in reach—some way to stop No. 6. What was it?

"I think I would've done this whether I was infected or not, y'know?"

It was somewhere among the words he'd spoken . . . Something he'd said that triggered something my brain . . .

It all comes down to whether or not you've got a black box. That lovely little high-output reactor core? That's the mark of a YoRHa. Makes all the difference in the world, y'know?

The reactor core. The SSU. The diagnostic routine.

That was it.

Could I pull the plan off in my current state, and without No. 6 noticing? I didn't know. But it was the only option I had left, so I had to try.

I began to reprogram the routine . . .

No. 6 suddenly bent over me and peered into my face. Had he already seen through me?

"I've always wanted an intimate moment alone with you . . . Oops. I mean, a moment alone to *torment* you."

No. Thank goodness. The only thing on his mind was what kind of pain he could deliver next. He was a child completely absorbed in a new toy.

"C'mon. Order me around like you used to."

How was my sword arm? It seemed to be responding, if just

barely. I carefully reached for my weapon, making sure No. 6's eyes were focused elsewhere.

"Or are you just being quiet because you haven't had enough yet? Is that it, sir?"

I thrust my sword at him, pretending to put all my effort into the physical attack itself. It was difficult to summon enough strength, but the blade managed to lodge in his left arm.

No. 6 grinned, mocking my efforts. "Pathetic. You do realize that isn't evEN gonna slow me down, right?"

Yes. He was right. And it didn't matter. I only needed a conduit. I yelled out for my SSU to initiate the scan.

"Huh?" No. 6's brow furrowed with suspicion, but I knew his expression would quickly change.

" . . . the hell . . . is this . . . ?!"

"I've instructed my SSU to run a full-body scan on you, using my sword as a conduit."

He froze. The program was designed to serve as a virus scan and lent itself well to the initial rewrites, which would keep him locked in place.

"Forgive the delay," I said. "I needed some time to reprogram the routine."

Relief flooded my body. My muscles, long tensed, suddenly went slack. I sighed, which caused a strangling pain in my chest, but it didn't matter. I had to hang on only a little while longer, and then all the pain would be gone.

"I had to improvise a little," I told him. "It's now configured to overload your black box."

"Ten seconds to detonation."

His face was twisted in consternation, all traces of his haughty attitude now gone. After No. 21, No. 6 was the quickest thinker of the bunch—he'd have swiftly worked out what I'd done and how I'd done it.

"Why would yOu do that?! The explosion will—"

Of course it would kill me, too. I had no intention of being the only one in the squadron to go on living.

"Seven seconds to detonation."

Derived from the cores of machine lifeforms, the black boxes were as destructive as they were powerful; an overloaded core created an enormous explosion. Fortunately, we were 900 meters away from the transport's crash site. I didn't have to be concerned about any of the other squad members getting caught in the blast.

"Don't worry. When I see that a student of mine is struggling, I stay with him until we fix the problem."

All I wanted was to faithfully discharge my duty.

. . . No.

I wanted to act like a proper instructor. At least for once. At least at the end. That was all.

"Three seconds to detonation."

"Make it stop! Make it stop make it stop make it stop, make it stooooop!"

His face went stiff. Though he'd experienced death on the

battlefield many times before, the death that awaited him now was different. There would be no return. He would never live again. His consciousness, his memories, and everything about him would vanish for all eternity. I understood why he would be afraid.

Summoning my last bit of strength, I extended my hand to him. But he was just out of reach. I'd wanted to reassure him, to place a comforting palm on his shoulder. Instead, being there with him at the end was the best I could do.

Finally, I'd been able to make my choice. I did not choose the unknown thousands. I chose the six that I knew. It was the first and final thing I could do for my beloved students.

The voice of the SSU marked the end of my last countdown.

A TREASURE HUNT IN 1194X

"HEEEELP! SOMEBODY HELP MEEEEE!"

Cactus wailed at the top of his lungs, but the wind and crashing surf drowned out his cries. He looked to his side to find Phlox shouting, too.

". . . something, Cap . . . ?"

You say something, Cap? That was probably what he'd asked.

Cactus bellowed back, "Nothing! Just forget it!"

But his words again failed to reach his companion's ears. Phlox mouthed "Huh?" and Lotus, clinging to the raft just as desperately as the other two androids, wore an identical look of confusion.

In the distance, the surface of the sea continued to heave, another great mountain of water building up, its peak rolling ever closer. At first, when the waves were just beginning to grow heavy, Cactus had been fascinated, eager to observe them up close. But the novelty had quickly worn off. Now each time the surface of the water rose and tumbled toward them, he could only shriek in fear.

"Oh my gosh! We're all gonna die!"

They all knew what was coming next: the sickening lurch as the raft dropped off the other side of the wave. They'd experienced it plenty of times already. Cactus screwed his eyes shut, wondering how many hours he'd endured being rocked to and fro by the terrible wind, rain, and rolling waves. He was now richly regretting the decision to set out to sea; if he'd known this would be part of the experience, he never would have left dry land.

A fair amount of time had passed since their narrow escape from the Mountain Zone. After that, they'd traveled inland for a while, their purpose, as always, to search for treasure.

At one point, they'd found themselves riding about in the "Lotus Tank," a vehicle haphazardly modded from the remains of a Goliath-class machine lifeform. That, incidentally, had been Lotus's new craze for the past while: naming everything he came up as the "Lotus whatever."

The tank had lasted all of two days and change before blowing up spectacularly, right in their faces. And then they'd moved on to the "Lotus Tank Mk. II," which blew up during its initial test run, and then the "Lotus Tank Mk. III" . . . Lotus was really committed to the naming scheme. At least, Cactus reflected, his creations had made for a lively journey.

Still, for all the trouble and time spent, they had yet to come across one measly bit of treasure. They'd pressed on, stubbornly walking until they arrived at a place with a view of the sea. And that was when one of them had declared that they ought to set out on a voyage across the water to see what they might find. Cactus couldn't remember if he was the one to suggest it, or if it was Phlox. But that was beside the point.

If they were going out on the water, they needed an appropriate mode of transportation. So Lotus drew up plans for a small watercraft, which he referred to as a "raft." When Cactus saw the result, it didn't inspire much confidence.

A raft, as it turned out, was an extremely traditional and widely used means of waterborne conveyance throughout human history. But the construction was worryingly simple: the body consisted of a number of logs lined up and firmly bound together with wire. In the center was a smaller, perpendicularly oriented log from which Lotus hung a large, triangular piece of cloth that waved in the breeze. The cloth appeared to serve as the raft's sole decoration.

Cactus had to give some credit to the cost-efficient design, but he suspected that the raft afforded no more than the bare minimum of safety when it came to a sea voyage.

Still, things hadn't been too bad for a while after they shoved off, when the "Lotus High-Speed Engine" had still been functioning. The sky was a vast, clear expanse, and they were making a quite pleasant, rapid headway of twenty-four knots.

But in their third day at sea, things took a turn for the worse. Without warning, the engine broke down, and they began drifting aimlessly.

Cactus also broke down, just a little. He grabbed Lotus and shouted "Hey! What's the holdup?!"

"It, erm, appears to be a problem with the engine. Could be the salinity, yes . . . There's a very high concentration of salt in seawater. Or perhaps it's the high concentration of *water* . . . "

"Can't you just fix it up real quick? Y'know, like you always do?"

"No, no. Not possible, I'm afraid. Lack the necessary parts, see?"

"I thought you brought spare parts along for the voyage?"

"True. Very true. Did have the parts, until *someone* dumped them overboard."

" . . . Huh?"

"The box. The one you hit the shark-type machine lifeform over the head with. Remember? Just the other day? Our full set of engine spares was packed neatly inside."

Lotus glowered at the captain, and Cactus found himself trying to avoid the accusatory stare.

And bad luck proved to come in threes, as the weather suddenly deteriorated. Cactus and his companions looked on in shock as the sea went from a calm, flat expanse of blue to a raging tempest of towering liquid mountains and vertiginously deep valleys. The hapless raft was left to ride out the storm, one moment rising several meters and the next plummeting back down.

Eventually, one particularly monstrous wave lifted the raft high, high above the surroundings—far higher than any wave before. They hung there at the apex for a brief moment, their stomachs the first to sink.

"Oh, no. Oh, no. Oh no no nooo!" Cactus yelped.

The dread had scant seconds to sink in before they were all deep underwater, their poor raft overturned and floating away. Cactus flailed for air, but darkness swirled in.

"C'mon, Cap, wake up already!"

The next thing Cactus heard was Phlox's impatient voice. His eyes opened to the blinding light of the sun.

"Huh . . . ?" he murmured. "Oh! Whew . . . It was just a dream. Phlox, it was so terrible. A nightmare, really. I thought for sure I was going to—ahhh . . . *ah-choo*!"

As his sneeze subsided, Cactus realized he was drenched from head to toe—and freezing cold because of it.

Phlox shook his head. "Wasn't a dream, Cap. We went overboard. Washed up here."

"And . . . where exactly is 'here'?"

Phlox shrugged. "Good question."

It was certainly no southern isle. The vegetation lining the water was not tropical but temperate. Cactus glanced out to sea and saw numerous concrete structures poking their dilapidated heads from the water's surface. They must have been the remains of some city from the era of human civilization—a city of quite considerable size, though now largely lost to the water.

"Uh . . . Where's Lotus?"

"Where do you think? Out collecting junk like always. But this time we should probably be thankful. Seems we lost all our weapons when we fell from the raft. Lotus said he'd whip up whatever he could with what he could find. Wouldn't want to be caught empty-handed, y'know?"

Cactus patted his jacket pockets. Phlox was right. All his spare magazines were gone, along with the handy folding knife he'd taken to carrying on his person. The sea had swallowed every one of his belongings—even the small pouch of coins he'd tied around his waist.

He felt his shoulders slump in defeat.

"Guess our treasure hunt turned into a real disaster."

"Hey, we've still got our lives. Gotta be thankful for that, right?"

"Heh. I guess so."

"And besides, our luck will turn around eventually. C'mon. Got something to show you."

Phlox began walking, and Cactus obediently followed. His boots sank into the ground with each step; the composition of the soil was perplexingly loose. After a while, the two reached a rather shoddy-looking cottage that was leaning to one side. Phlox stopped in front of it.

"Why don't you sit here and rest for a bit? I'm gonna circle the area and make sure our perimeter's safe."

He added, "Oh, and don't you dare think about going off on your own. You never know when you might run into a machine. C'mon, Cap. I wanna hear you say it. You promise to stay here?"

"What am I, a kid?"

When Cactus balked, Phlox gave an exasperated sigh.

"I worry like this because you're *not* a kid. What kind of adult goes wandering off, always ending up stuck in some dangerous situation? Remember that time—"

"All right! All right, already! You've made your point!"

Just don't forget this when you *start yelling for help*, Cactus thought sourly, *'cause I'm gonna stay put right here, exactly like you told me to.*

"Look! *Look* at this big haul! The machines here are nothing like I've ever seen before! Absolutely marvelous parts to salvage. Yes, yes, and in such abundance!"

Lotus hadn't shut up from the moment he got back from his scavenging excursion. Phlox, who had returned at about the same time, was hardly able to get a word in.

"And listen to this!" Lotus babbled on, "The machines here? They're walking all over the place!"

Phlox raised an eyebrow. "Uh . . . yeah. We've seen the machines moving around before, buddy. It's what they do. Why is that so—"

"Not moving! *Walking!* With legs!"

"We've seen plenty like that, too."

And they had—ones that scuttled around like insects, with dozens of tiny legs. There had been machines like that in the Mountain Zone. In fact, those particular machines had troubled the trio to no end.

But Lotus decisively shook his head. "Not like that! I'm talking *two* legs, one alternately placed in front of the other in bipedal ambulation—the same means of locomotion that developed among the early ancestors of humans! Do you understand?! This is new! The machines have progressed! They're attempting to tread the same evolutionary path as mankind!"

Yeah, right, Cactus thought. *And what next? Language? Were the machines gonna up and start saying, "Good morning"?*

Before Cactus could voice his rejoinder, however, Phlox piped up.

"Well, speaking of unusual machines, I guess I did see something pretty weird today."

Lotus stared at him eagerly, hanging on every word. "Yes? Yes, what was it? A new physical configuration?! Some kind of novel behavior?!"

"Both, I guess. Kinda transfixing, really," Phlox responded.

"In what way?!"

"Well, it's kinda hard to pin it down to one thing. Just weird in general, y'know? Like—"

"Not *that*! In what way were you *headed* when you saw it?!"

"Oh. Uh . . . over that way, I guess? But it was hours ago. I really doubt it's . . . Hey! Lotus!"

But Lotus had stopped listening as soon as Phlox pointed out the direction. He went dashing off.

"Great. Should've known better than to get him worked up," Phlox said dryly. He hauled himself to his feet. Stern words weren't going to be enough to get Lotus back now. They'd have to give chase before they lost sight of the engineer.

As they turned to go, Phlox pulled out an object. "Oh, Cap? This is for you."

"What's that? A steel pipe?"

"Not gonna do much, I know, but at least it's better than finding yourself bare-handed."

Cactus had to agree. The trio had lost every last weapon and piece of equipment to the terrible waves. Cactus had woken up without so much as his trusty pocketknife. And Lotus, after offering to make some new armaments for them, had become so caught up in the novelty of the area's machines, he forgot all about his promise. Not that this was the first time Lotus had let his curiosity get the better of him. Anticipating the possibility, Phlox had made a point of picking up a few steel pipes spotted during his patrol.

Crude weapons now in hand, they glanced back to find Lotus scrambling up a cliff.

"Oh, come on!" Phlox groaned. "How'd he get all the way up there?!"

Flustered, Phlox broke into a sprint. Cactus, a bit resentful to be breaking his petulant vow to stay put, followed behind.

They were exhausted, but they'd somehow managed to scale the imposing cliff, and they'd caught up with Lotus, too. There was no trace of any odd-looking machine at the top. The engineer's curiosity had apparently fizzled out when his mad scramble yielded no prize, and he'd plopped down on a spot of ground near the ledge.

"Phlox!" he chided on seeing his companions. "I demand an explanation! I haven't found a *trace* of this so-called transformer of yours. Not one!"

"Whoa, whoa, I never said the thing could transform."

Cactus recalled Phlox claiming he'd been *transfixed* by the sight of the odd machine. Apparently, Lotus, in his enthusiasm, had misinterpreted it as a claim to have seen the enemy *transform*.

Lotus glared at Phlox. "You did too say that!"

"C'mon. What do you want from me . . . ?" Phlox lamented, bringing a palm to his forehead.

"I was there when he said it," Cactus jumped in, "and I can confirm that Phlox made *no* mention of a transforming machine hanging out at the top of a cliff."

He was trying to offer Phlox a helping hand. It was a rare reversal of their usual roles—the kind of situation that probably came around once in a century at best. But Phlox shook his head.

"Well . . . it *is* true that I saw it at the top of a cliff, Cap."

"Seriously?! I was giving you a way out!"

"At any rate," Phlox continued, not paying Cactus's offered help any mind, "the thing was moving incredibly fast. I figured it was long gone by the time I mentioned it."

At that, Lotus's eyes regained their sparkle.

"Incredibly fast, you say? Really?!"

Phlox had unintentionally reignited the fire of Lotus's curiosity.

"Come on! We have to go find it!" Lotus declared. "I simply *must* see this ultra-fast transforming machine of yours!"

He began to dash off again, but this time, Phlox managed to clamp a hand on the engineer's collar. He clearly wasn't anxious to play a second round of their earlier game.

"All right, all right. We'll go. *Together*. But first, we need to think about water. We gotta find a clean source so we can fill up."

At that, Cactus realized the last time he'd had anything to drink was aboard the raft, before the storm set in. Their purification equipment and spare tanks were undoubtedly at the bottom of the ocean.

And the fact that they'd just scaled their way up a cliff wasn't helping: Cactus was acutely aware of how much strength he'd used up in the climb. Without a water source, it was only a matter of time before they ran out of energy completely.

"Fresh water . . . That's gonna be a tall order," Cactus murmured.

There was nothing in their surroundings other than decaying human skyscrapers. It didn't seem at all a place where they might stumble across a spring or river.

But, at the very least, they'd begun to head inland. It seemed reasonable that potable water would be easier to find the more distance they put between themselves and the sea.

"Well, let's get looking, then," Cactus said, and after clapping a hand on Phlox's and Lotus's shoulders, he began to lead the way.

They'd been walking for ages, it seemed, finding nothing more than one massive, half-toppled building after another. For a while, they'd entertained the hope of finding an old well—surely other Resistance androids would have dug one if any had traversed the area in the past. But they had no such luck; it seemed the land might not be suitable for well-digging.

The sun beat down, reflecting off the asphalt for double the agony. Cactus felt as though every trace of moisture was about to evaporate from his body.

"W . . . water . . . " he croaked.

"Dunno how much longer I can go on, Cap . . . "

"I'm done for . . . *done for* . . . !"

The three were on the verge of collapse when an unmistakable sound reached their ears.

They looked up.

"Is that . . . a river?!" Cactus exclaimed.

It was the sound of running water—of that much, they were certain. And they'd all heard it, so that ruled out hallucination. Cactus had his doubts about finding a real, true-blue river in the concrete jungle surrounding them. But it did, at least, sound like a considerable quantity of liquid.

They ran with what little strength they had left, making directly for the source of the noise. It occurred to Cactus that the concrete jungle was showing some hints of green: trees lined the buildings with outstretched branches, and clumps of tall grass grew underfoot. For such a quantity of plants to flourish, surely there had to be a stable source of water nearby.

"It *is* a river!" he exclaimed.

Under a raised platform that had probably once served as a road, a narrow strip of water wound its way among the thick concrete pillars. On reflection, Cactus decided that "river" was probably a bit too generous: it was shallow, and the paltry amount of water it carried would have been difficult to describe as particularly clear. Given the amount of time unpurified water took to run through their onboard filters, drinking from the stream would be a fairly inefficient means of refueling. But Cactus figured this was no time to be choosy.

The three approached the water's edge, then froze on noticing a sudden flash of movement. Rather, Cactus and Phlox stopped. Lotus, for his part, seemed ready to make a mad dash toward what they'd seen: several machine lifeforms were standing just upstream.

In a way, it was intriguing. The machines looked as if they'd come to the stream to play. They stood in its shallows, splashing each other. There were three of them—puny things with cylindrical torsos, round little heads, skinny arms, and stubby legs. Their appearance and the way they moved about was almost comical, and they exuded none of the ferocity of the machines that occupied the Mountain Zone.

But machines were still machines.

"L-let me go!" Lotus sputtered, as Phlox quickly pinned his arms behind his back and began dragging him away. "Just look at them! They're adorable! Oh, please, please let me mod one!"

Lotus squirmed to get away, and his cries grew louder. Cactus clamped a hand over the engineer's mouth, fearing what might await them if they were noticed.

To their good fortune, the three machines didn't seem to pay them any mind. They simply continued to splash about in the stream. Maybe, Cactus reflected, they weren't particularly alert to noises made by androids.

Out of caution, they withdrew to the safety of the nearby buildings, intending to put some distance between themselves and that particular stretch of river. Lotus, distraught at being torn away from the enticing new machines, had to be half-pulled, half-dragged along. But they soon realized that the three machines at the stream were not alone. Others lurked about in the shadows cast by the great skyscrapers, pacing down the wide boulevards that traversed the city and prowling the grassy plazas punctuating the urban sprawl. Suddenly, the machines seemed to be everywhere.

Every time Lotus spotted one, he threw a new fit, demanding he be allowed to capture it, and Cactus and Phlox had to calm him down all over again. They'd gone through the absurd routine several times when they realized they were lost and had no idea how to circle back to the river they'd worked so hard to find.

"We're really screwed now, aren't we?" Phlox said.

Cactus rasped, "Don't speak. Waste of energy."

Even vocalizations increased their fuel consumption, if only slightly. Still, Cactus had to admit it was minor in comparison to the strength they wasted in the constant struggle to keep Lotus from dashing off. And he was still feeling the exhaustion from climbing the cliff earlier . . .

Just recalling the ordeal was tiring. Cactus's body felt heavy, and his vision grew dim. If he'd known things would get so bad, he figured, he would have stayed on the coast, gulping down the turbid seawater. He chastised himself for failing to find some other hypothetical water source along the way—one that was cleaner and not infested with machines.

He was busy lamenting their situation when Phlox muttered, "I hear water."

Cactus felt sorry for him. This time, it was definitely a hallucination—a sign of how thoroughly his comrade's auditory processes had deteriorated.

But a moment later, Cactus spotted something several meters ahead that glittered in the sun's relentless rays. He couldn't believe it. Was Phlox right? Had they managed to stumble upon water a second time?

The three hobbled forward, arm in arm to support each other's weight. As they emerged from between the buildings, the world opened up to reveal water, precious water, stretching for meters in every direction. It was a large pool, and from crevices in the sloped hill on its far side, little waterfalls were gushing forth in all their glory.

"We're saved!" Cactus exclaimed.

They splashed their way across the pool, hurrying to the nearest waterfall to scoop the precious liquid from it with cupped palms.

Just as they began to carry the nectar of life to their mouths, a stern voice sounded at their backs.

"Hey."

Then again.

"Hey. I wouldn't do that if I were you."

They turned to find a woman toting a rifle.

"You don't wanna drink that stuff. There's a pretty good chance it's contaminated."

What do you mean? Cactus tried to ask, but he found himself unable to speak. His hands hung centimeters from his mouth, the water they held so tantalizingly close. What ironic timing for his energy reserves to run dry. His vision faded, and then he was no longer in the waking world.

"Dieeeee!"

Cactus felt a harsh thump on his forehead, along with an explosion of sparks. He jolted awake to find Lotus wielding an oddly-shaped lump of metal in his hand.

"Lotus!" he griped. "For the last time! When you're waking someone up, be—"

Gentle, he meant to finish, but his mouth clamped shut when he saw the stranger. She was looking on, clearly unimpressed by the scene unfolding before her.

She *was* a stranger, but Cactus recalled the large pool of water they'd found in the city ruins and how someone had appeared just as they were about to drink. This must've been the same woman who had provided the warning.

"Seems we dodged a bullet, Cap."

"Huh?"

"The pool. She says there's a dead machine further up-stream. A Goliath."

"Ah . . . So that's what she meant by contaminated . . . "

Cactus recalled once sitting through a lesson about the characteristics of machine lifeforms. Many of them were known to emit substances that were toxic to androids—and they could continue to do so even after they'd ceased functioning. In fact, most such machines remained a source of potential infection long after they'd kicked the bucket. Cactus, Phlox, and Lotus had been moments away from gulping mouthfuls of the water without so much as a rudimentary treatment. They really had dodged a bullet.

Their savior now peered over at Cactus with a concerned look.

"How are you feeling?" she asked. "Can you move?"

"Huh? Oh, uh . . . yeah."

With some help from Phlox, Cactus managed to sit up. His vision was back to normal, and he felt no trace of his earlier weariness. It seemed the woman had refueled his tank while he was out cold. He felt, quite honestly, on top of the world.

"I'm fine," Cactus said. "Thanks to you, that is. You really saved us."

He turned, slowly surveying his surroundings. They seemed to be in some sort of encampment. He could tell that much at a glance. The place was bustling, with soldiers walking to and fro, equipment stacked under tarps, and boxes full of various materials lined up on the ground. The camp appeared to be a major base of operations.

"I'm guessing . . . you must be in charge around here," Cactus ventured.

That, too, was obvious at a glance, really. There was something about the woman—almost an aura she exuded—that put Cactus on the defensive. This was a rival leader.

"My name is Anemone," she said. "I'm the leader of the android Resistance that controls most of this territory."

He'd hit the nail right on the head. Not that it was easy to miss, Cactus reflected, for someone with as keen an intuition as himself.

"Oh, uh . . . We're . . ." Cactus faltered. "Jeez, how do I put it?"

"Treasure hunters, or so I hear," responded Anemone.

Cactus mentally sighed. He felt certain that it was Lotus who let their story slip. Phlox was cautious; he wouldn't have given details away so easily.

"Well, the thing is," Cactus said, "that's just our cover story."

An outright claim to be hunting for treasure would likely arouse suspicion, and Cactus wasn't eager to have their status as deserters brought to light.

"The *real* reason we're here is, uh . . . a top secret mission. Very hush-hush, see?"

Phlox rolled his eyes and muttered, "Oh, for crying out loud . . ."

Cactus pointedly ignored the reaction, asking Anemone, "By the way, you wouldn't happen to know of any good places around here to look for tr—I mean, uh . . . any places where lots of androids and machine lifeforms have fought? Y'know, like old battlegrounds?"

Combat sites were, in effect, goldmines. Lotus could mod the enemy remains they found into weapons, and if they were especially lucky, they'd come across stray bits of android equipment. And, of course, sites of particularly large battles had far greater potential to yield items of exceptional value.

"Old battlegrounds?" Anemone tilted her head.

"It's geographical information of critical importance to our top secret mission. We'd really appreciate any help you can offer."

"Sure. I think I know just the person who could help. I'll see that she gets in touch with you."

"And, um, maybe you could spare some water and basic equipment . . . ? Y'know, to help ensure the success of the mission!"

Phlox elbowed Cactus in the side, mumbling, "Don't push our luck."

But Cactus steadfastly pretended not to notice.

After enjoying a nice, long break and procuring water and equipment thanks to the Resistance camp's generosity, Cactus and party set off.

"Hey, Cap? Don't you think we're imposing a bit much? Maybe we oughta dial it back."

"Now, now. It's important to help each other out in times of need."

"Uh-huh. So we're helping them, too, huh? Funny. Kinda felt like a one-way thing to me."

"Nonsense! That's all in your head!"

"Speaking of which, I'm positive Anemone saw right through our story. She had to suspect we're deserters, but she just waved it away as everybody having their own problems to deal with. She just seems really, I dunno, open-minded and . . . understanding, you know? I can see how she got to be in charge around these parts."

"Great. Good for her."

To Cactus, hearing Anemone praised so thoroughly was like having his own credentials as a leader called into question. He didn't like it. Not one bit.

"*Anyway*," Cactus said, eager to change the subject, "let's get going. We gotta get on with our hunt. Treasure, ho!"

He pointed the way to the Desert Zone. Anemone's soldier, apparently quite familiar with the local topography, had told them that if there was any treasure to be found, it was probably in the sands.

It was a little embarrassing, to be honest. Cactus had thought his cover story was pretty clever, but Anemone had seen right through it. Before sending the soldier over, she'd apparently explained, "We've got three visitors searching the area for treasure. Maybe you could give them some ideas of where to look."

As Cactus mentally kicked himself for his failures, they traversed the patches of grass and dirt between the buildings.

They continued to catch glimpses of machines, but they'd learned that the area's enemies were not hostile, so long as you didn't get too close to them or launch the first attack.

"I reeeally want to mod one . . . Just look at them. So demure. Such good little machines . . . "

"Yeah, maybe from this distance. But you heard Anemone. Get too close and they'll be more than happy to take a swipe."

"Not a problem! If they come after us, I'll simply shoot them with one of these bullets! They're outfitted with a virus, you see, and—"

"Ack! Please, no. *Anything* but that."

Back in the Mountain Zone, Cactus had seen quite enough of Lotus's virus-loaded bullets and the zombified machines they spawned. Just thinking about the episode had his hair standing on end.

"But . . . but . . . I haven't modded *anything* since we washed up on shore. Not one single machine! Pleeease let me!"

It was true that Lotus's engineering skills had saved their hides during countless enemy assaults. But right now, there was no enemy they needed to engage. Cactus was perfectly happy to go on without riling up any machines and spoiling their safe and pleasant walk through the city ruins. He racked his brain for some way to focus Lotus's attention elsewhere.

As if reading his captain's mind, Phlox piped up. "Hey! There's that thing I was talking about!"

Nice one, Phlox! Cactus mentally flashed him a thumbs-up.

Phlox had even pointed a finger at some imaginary object way in the distance. Classic distraction technique. Still, Phlox seemed really dedicated to the charade. He continued to point and shout, "Look! Over there!"

Cactus finally realized it wasn't an act. Phlox was actually pointing at something.

He followed the finger to find an unusually shaped machine in the distance, zooming along at considerable speed. It wasn't as fast as, say, one of the enemy's flying units, but it was still pretty quick.

The mysterious machine suddenly turned and began barreling full speed in the trio's direction. It zipped by just to one side, and as it passed, they became aware of a strange, high-pitched noise.

"Get baaack heeere!"

Lotus, eyes gleaming, tried to give chase, but the mysterious machine was far too fast. Its bluish frame soon vanished in a cloud of dust kicked up as it rolled along.

"What in the world was *that*?" Cactus wondered aloud.

Phlox lifted both palms in an exaggerated shrug; he had no idea, either.

"Like I said. Some kinda weird machine."

They hadn't encountered anything like it before. Not in the Mountain Zone, and not during their journeys across the inland plains.

"Still, something about it seemed kinda familiar . . . " Cactus mumbled.

"Really? I'm pretty sure I'd remember something as strange as that."

"Hmm . . . I just get the feeling it's a lot like something I've encountered before."

If the thing hadn't been moving so darned fast, Cactus figured, he might've been able to pin the resemblance down. All he'd been able to get a handle on was that the mysterious machine was blue and kinda rectangular—and that it was blaring an odd, continuous pattern of sound. The sound, too, seemed to tickle some deep, long-neglected memory in his brain.

"Ahhh, how I would love to mod a machine like that," Lotus announced. "I really hope it comes back . . . "

Lotus stared after the machine, a look of intense longing on his face. Cactus stood beside him, gazing in the same direction.

Then, for a moment, Cactus thought he'd figured it out . . . only for the epiphany to slip right through his fingers. Whatever the thing reminded him of, the memory was just out of reach, which only made it all the more frustrating.

"Man, it's on the tip of my tongue . . . What *was* it . . . ?" he murmured.

The sound was so distinctive. In fact, he was so close to

figuring it out, his ears were playing tricks on him. He could still hear it—so clearly, in fact, it was almost eerie. And it was growing louder . . .

"Huh?! It's back!" Phlox shouted.

The strange, blue rectangular machine appeared again, blaring its rhythmical noise. It drew close, and this time, they realized it was carrying some kind of cloth fluttering from a stick.

"Waaaaait!" Lotus shouted, again desperately giving chase, and again failing to get anywhere near it. The mysterious blue machine vanished into the distance again, this time headed out past the city ruins.

"That sound . . . It's kinda like . . . *music*, don't you think?" said Phlox.

Cactus considered the description; yes, an emission of sound using defined frequencies, alternating at regular intervals with organizational intent. The sound from the mysterious machine certainly did fit the definition of "music."

And with that, the old, old memory finally came dislodged. It floated up from the deepest recesses of Cactus's mind, and an overwhelming wave of nostalgia washed over him.

"The bargain day sale!" he exclaimed. "The one in the market street! That's it!"

"Uh . . . *what*?"

"It's a scene I remember—a part of my pseudomemory!"

Cactus had finally put his finger on it. He knew the machine's appearance and the music it played because of the memories implanted inside him—his individual pseudomemory, sourced, as for all androids, from the archives of human civilization.

The pseudomemories were buried deep in the memory banks of every AI—so deep, in fact, it was hard for androids themselves to distinguish them from their own organically formed memories. Cactus's understanding of the topic was limited, but he'd heard the purpose of the simulated memories was to allow androids to think and act more like humans.

And apparently, each android's pseudomemory was chosen at random; for some individuals, it was a complete mismatch in terms of gender or age. The memories weren't necessarily happy ones, either. Some androids lived their lives burdened by the pain or sorrow of the scenes they happened to carry with them. Fortunately, Cactus's own pseudomemory was decidedly innocuous—so innocuous, in fact, that it was a little boring. He'd nearly forgotten about it altogether.

"I *knew* it sounded familiar!" Cactus continued. "There was this little truck parked outside the shop just across the way. It looked just like that blue thing that's been zooming back and forth. See? My brain was right!"

The truck in Cactus's memory had been decorated with pink flowers and silver tinsel streamers. A tall, rectangular banner jutted from one side, on which were written the words "Bargain Day Sale." There were decals, too—red stickers that each read "Insanely Low Prices!"

The shop it belonged to sold an assortment of intoxicating fermented beverages, and each day the truck was taken out for deliveries by the proprietor, an old woman of seventy years.

"Wow . . . That really takes me back. I wonder if the old lady's still doing all right? Er, I guess she's probably dead now. It *has* been about ten thousand years . . . "

"Speaking of which, who were you in that pseudomemory of yours, Cap?"

"Oh, well, I was apparently a—"

Cactus's answer was drowned out by a new burst of the strange music. The mysterious machine was back to remind Cactus of the market street and its never-ending bargain day sale yet again.

Now that he had a third chance to hear the melody, he was catching more of its nuances. He could hear what might have been a voice mixed in among the tones—the sound of someone singing. He'd thought it was the exact same tune as the one that was in his pseudomemory, but now he realized that certain parts of the melody were different from the song he knew. The music was similar, but not quite the same.

As the machine zoomed off into the distance again, the pitch of the music seemed to twist and warp until it finally vanished.

A pair of strange words flashed into Cactus's mind with no apparent context: "Doppler effect."

"Maybe the machines are continuing to learn . . . Like, they've evolved again or something," Phlox offered.

"You think so?"

"Well, what else could it be? I mean, a machine that reminds you of a pseudomemory? We've—"

"Never run into anything like it before!" Lotus jumped in. "Just think! Machines imitating android memories! A marvelous evolutionary step, yes! Why, a trio of steps, really! They're bounding up the evolutionary stairway! We simply *must* capture it for study!"

Lotus rolled up his sleeves and set right to work. First, he started pulling a wire taut across the ground, and then he began digging a hole . . .

His fervor went beyond reignited curiosity. The engineer's hands were moving so quickly, Cactus wondered if he'd been outfitted with some kind of accelerator. The captain was beginning to feel apprehensive about whatever might come next.

Would Lotus be able to stop the mysterious machine? It obviously had a good amount of power and acceleration. In fact, Cactus reflected, it was unclear whether there was a single machine that kept zooming around in circles, or if there were several of them, all identical, traveling over the same stretch.

In any case, the peculiar music was soon back, along with its *tra lee lah lee laaah* sounds, which Cactus thought might be "lyrics."

"Hey! It's almost here again!" Cactus announced. "You gonna finish in time?!"

"No need to worry! I'm already done!" Lotus announced. He stood and immediately jumped to the side of the road.

"Come on, Cap! Hurry!" Phlox said, grabbing Cactus's arm and tugging him along so fast, the world began to spin.

"Hey! What's the big idea?!"

"Get down!"

Just before Phlox shoved his head down against the dirt,

Cactus caught a fleeting glimpse of the mysterious machine being tripped up by the wire and spinning wildly through the air.

Cactus, too, ate dirt, and just as he was about to complain about how unnecessarily rough Phlox was being, a blast wave washed over them.

It seemed Lotus had planted a landmine.

The engineer's calculations were quite precise: he'd prepared the tripwire, then determined exactly where the speeding machine would slam into the ground, burying the landmine there with pinpoint accuracy. Cactus found himself impressed with the thoroughness of Lotus's work, given what little time he'd had. Once again, Lotus had outdone himself.

"Novel machine lifeform defeated! Another has fallen to my landmine!"

Lotus twirled around in a little victory dance as he approached the machine, which now lay immobile on its side— or so they'd all assumed. Suddenly, it popped up into the air and righted itself before settling back down.

"Ow! Owowowowowwwww . . . That was really mean!"

Lotus froze in his tracks, eyes as wide as they could go. Cactus couldn't have stopped staring if his life depended on it.

"D-did the machine just *talk*?!" he cried.

The thing immediately responded, "No! I'm not a machine lifeform!"

So it claimed, but to Cactus's eyes, it certainly looked like one: a round head set atop a body fashioned of metal. The features on this one's face were admittedly somewhat different from the enemies they'd seen before, but overall, Cactus felt certain the strange being displayed all the hallmarks of being a machine.

"My name's Emil. I run a shop here in the city ruins, selling cheap, high-quality items to any android who happens by."

Cactus's eyes grew wider still. "You sell to androids? So . . . does that mean you're friendly?"

"Yes! Of course! Which is why I wanna know what the deal with the landmine is! Now my frame's all bent up . . . "

Cactus considered this new information. If the strange being wasn't an enemy, then access to archives describing human civilization seemed more plausible. That might explain the thing's truck-like appearance, as well as the music it played as it zoomed around, so similar to the music from the market street of his simulated memory.

It was hard enough to believe that a machine lifeform could speak, Cactus reasoned, and harder still to believe one could speak so fluidly.

Lotus seemed to have reached the same conclusion. "All right," he conceded, "so you're not a machine. But that makes you some kind of unidentified lifeform, yes?"

The engineer had edged closer to the strange being calling itself Emil. He was now stroking its spherical head with a look of longing.

"Ohhh, how I would love to mod you . . . "

"K-keep your hands to yourself, please! If I got taken apart, who'd run my business?!"

"Just a *little* modding. Just some teensy, tiny changes, yes?"

"No way! I'm really busy, okay?! I've got over a hundred loyal customers waiting on me today . . . Okay, well, that might be a little bit of an exaggeration. I don't exactly have any regulars yet. But still . . . !"

Emil began to slowly back away from the three Resistance members.

"I had plans this afternoon, you know? I needed to go stock up on merchandise, since I'm all sold out of broken batteries and dented sockets. But now thanks to you, I've gotta stop at home to fix up my frame!"

"Hold on. You're selling *broken* batteries?"

To Cactus, it was beginning to sound like this Emil character dealt in rather questionable wares.

Phlox, however, had a different reaction. "What other kinds of stuff do you stock? Any chance we could get a list?"

"You wanna buy something?! That's great! Thank you so much!"

"No, uh, what I meant was . . . if we happened to find some

of those busted batteries and sockets and whatever, could we sell them to you? I mean, it sounds like it's a lot of trouble for you to go out and restock by yourself, right?"

"Oh! I see. You're saying you'd like to be my suppliers?"

Phlox and Emil began a rapid, animated discussion, with offers and counter-offers traced in the dirt and furiously wiped away.

"How much are you willing to pay us?"

"This is what I can afford."

"C'mon. How about just a little more?"

"No, no, I'm serious. My margins are tight enough as it is."

Exasperated, Cactus shouted, "Okay, that's enough! We are *not* here to start a business. We're on a *treasure hunt*! We're not interested in scavenging for junk like broken batteries and dented sockets all day just to scrape together a few measly coins!"

Phlox and Emil whirled around in unison. Their shouted response came in perfect sync, too. "Excuse me?!"

Both began to storm toward Cactus.

"What's so bad about scraping together a little extra cash?" demanded Phlox.

"Yeah!" Emil added. "Low margins, high turnover is the golden rule of retail!"

"I think *you're* forgetting the power of a little *change*, Cap!"

"Absolutely!" Emil continued. "If you don't know how to save on the small stuff, you'll be crying whenever the big stuff rolls around! Respectfully speaking!"

With the double-team of scolding, Cactus couldn't get a word of defense in edgewise.

"I . . . ! Um . . . ! I'm sorry, all right?!"

But he resented the accusations. He didn't have a problem with change. In fact, he never belittled coins. Why, just that very day, Cactus had bent down to pocket a few coins he'd seen on the ground in the Resistance camp.

"Well, Mr. Phlox, I think we have an agreement."

"Put 'er there. I'm counting on the best deals you can give us, hear?"

"But of course, friendo! Oh, and, uh . . . I guess I should let you know that my home is underground. Waaay underground, in the farthest reaches of the deepest cave you'll find around here. It's a pretty steep drop, so please be careful when you stop by!"

And with that, Emil trundled off, his battered body squeaking and creaking as he went.

Cactus wondered how in the world Emil managed the "steep drop" to get into his home, especially given his current state. It looked like the next fall he took would see him go up in flames. How did a truck get up and down a cliff, anyway? Though Cactus knew it didn't have a thing to do with him, he couldn't help but feel a bit concerned.

"Well, whatever," he decided. "Now, let's *really* get on our way. Treasure awaits us. Treasure, here we come! Onward, to treasure!"

"Onward, to batteries, sockets, bolts, nuts, coils, and screws!"

"Onward, to mods, mods, mods, and more mods!"

Cactus and his two companions set off toward the desert, each with his own goal firmly in mind.

Cactus didn't want to waste another second in their search for treasure, but things just wouldn't go according to plan. They'd found themselves stuck at the entrance to the desert due to a major sandstorm said to be on its way. No one was being allowed in.

"No use getting your panties in a twist. Sit down and relax. The storm'll pass when it passes."

That was the advice of the woman who had explained the situation to them. She'd introduced herself as Jackass and had begun blatantly sizing Cactus and party up, not showing the slightest trace of reserve as she looked them over.

"Hey, I recognize those frames," she said. "You guys must be from out west. One of the European squadrons or something?"

"Y-yeah . . ." Cactus replied. "But, uh, we're on a top secret mission, see? Can't share too many details about ourselves, so, um . . ."

"You don't say. Top secret, huh?"

Inside, Cactus was sweating bullets. She was sharp. If she was able to recognize their models and the region from which they hailed at a glance, who knew what else she'd pick up on.

He figured Phlox was probably on his guard, too. Of the three, only Lotus continued chatting away with the woman. He seemed to get on with Jackass quite swimmingly.

"Your rifle!" he exclaimed. "That's a custom job, yes? I almost mistook it for standard issue, but, oh, look at all those lovely mods . . . A lightweight replacement frame and everything!"

"You can tell, huh? Yeah. Built this baby from the ground up. Went striker fired, with a nice tight spring."

"Fascinating! Simply fascinating!"

The two appeared to be birds of a feather. Lotus and Jackass went on like that, huddled over Jackass's weapon, their rapid speech filled with all kinds of technical terms that didn't mean a thing to Cactus, along with the occasional exclamations of "Mods!" and "Science!"

First Phlox and Emil, and now Lotus and Jackass. Considering how well his comrades got along with the locals, Cactus was beginning to think the city ruins could prove a pleasant home for the three. He mused for a moment about setting down roots there if their search for treasure ended in failure. Maybe they could even join up with the local Resistance.

Phlox interrupted his thoughts with a casual, "Hey, Cap?"

"Yeah?"

"It's about what you said earlier . . . "

Like Cactus, Phlox seemed to have found himself without much to do as Jackass and Lotus chattered away.

"What did I say earlier?"

"The stuff about your pseudomemory . . . I wanted to hear more about it."

"Huh? Haven't I talked about it before?"

"I only remember you mentioning that you ran some kind of restaurant."

"Yeah, an udon shop."

"Oo . . . don . . . ? What's that?"

"It's this food you make by mixing flour with water. You knead it real hard like this," Cactus explained, the heels of his hands emphatically working the air. "And then you roll it out flat, and finally, you cut it into thin strips," he said, using the edge of one hand to rapidly slice his imaginary dough.

The pseudomemories were, admittedly, fake. But given the way they were installed in the AI, it was as if the recipient had experienced the episodes firsthand. So, despite the fact that Cactus had not once eaten udon in his entire life, he knew the taste of the noodles so intimately, it felt like he was finishing off a bowl right there as he shared his story with Phlox.

"And then you pop 'em in a bowl and pour some *tsuyu* in there," Cactus continued. "You gotta make it right, though, with plenty of flavor from the *dashi*. And then you top it all off with chopped green onions and a big, round *maruten*."

"Slow down. *Tsuyu*? *Dashi*?"

"*Tsuyu*'s like a soup. It's flavored with stock made from stuff like dried fish and kelp. That's *dashi*. Real good stuff. Savory. Makes your mouth water."

Cactus knew that his added explanations only opened up more questions in Phlox's mind. Androids didn't eat fish or kelp. They didn't have a need to ingest anything resembling "food" in the first place.

Jackass unexpectedly turned toward him, clearly fascinated and bursting with questions.

"Hold up. What was that about fish and kelp? I gotta hear more about this."

Cactus hesitated. "I mean, what else is there to say . . . ?"

He was surprised by how thoroughly his story had captured her attention—she'd put her discussion with Lotus on hold.

"The stuff about dried food. I'd heard of *grilled* fish before, but I didn't know people dehydrated the things. Was that some kinda delicacy or something?"

"No, it was pretty common. I think every home in my area

had a stock of bonito flakes and dried sardines on hand. Oh, and dried mackerel, too—that was a breakfast staple."

"Really?! As in, they'd eat fish *every morning*?!"

It was, of course, an anecdotal account, limited by the parameters of Cactus's simulated experience. There was no way to say if *every* human routinely ate fish for breakfast, or if trends might have varied considerably between different regions and neighborhoods.

"And what about that other thing you mentioned? The *maru*-whatever. I've heard of onions before—they're a few species of interrelated plants, right? But that other thing's news to me."

"*Maruten*? It's made of ground, mashed fish. You press it into a round shape and fry it in oil."

"You're shitting me. *More* fish?!"

Unlike Lotus, Jackass's interests seemed to extend beyond machines and weapons. She was getting so worked up just talking about fish, it was almost disturbing. Next, she wanted to know every kind of fish Cactus could "remember," and every possible way to prepare them as food. She wanted to know if it was true that humans sometimes played a game in which everyone ate pieces of poisonous fish and waited to see who remained alive at the end. Her questions went on and on.

But it wasn't an unpleasant exchange. In fact, Cactus reflected, it was kinda nice having someone completely enraptured by the things he had to say, firing off questions like a machinegun and hanging on every word uttered in response.

And the more Cactus talked, the more invested he became. He found other things he had once known but nearly forgotten, floating back up from deep in his mind.

" . . . And another thing! There were these events called 'food challenges.' I remember a real official-looking one being held at my little restaurant, and the contestants showing up with a big TV crew in tow. Couldn't believe how many cameras they managed to shove inside the place. And the contestants just started doing their thing, shouting stuff like, 'Condiment change!' and someone would run over with some new topping they could use, or 'Finished!' and a guy with a stopwatch would hit the button and record the time."

"Okay, you've lost me."

"They were trying to see how much food they could pack into their guts within a given timeframe. It was a form of competition. Crazy, really. You wouldn't believe how much food a human stomach could hold. I'd set out these enormous pots filled to the brim with udon, and the contestants would slurp them all up in a matter of minutes. You'd have thought they had black holes inside them."

"Huh. Sounds like a kinda . . . weird form of entertainment."

"I think it was part of human nature. If you told them there was a limit, they just had to try and push it."

He remembered one particular customer, as clear as if he'd seen her just the previous day. She'd scarfed down *thirty-three* bowls of tempura-topped udon, explaining that she was trying to set a new personal best.

"Limits, huh? Yeah. I get that," Jackass said, nodding enthusiastically. "I'm into pushing boundaries myself. Well, not *me* so much. I like to run *other* people through challenges to see how they do. Gotta get my hands on that juicy data somehow."

Jackass suddenly pulled out her rifle. Cactus's stomach sank when he saw her eyes. Something about them looked all too familiar . . .

"Huh? Hey! What're you—"

Gunfire cut Phlox's yelp short. He fell face-first to the ground, clutching his chest.

"Phlox!" Cactus shouted. He glared at Jackass, "What the hell do you think you're doing?!"

"Relax. It's just a tranquilizer dart. I want to tinker with his frame and AI for a bit while he's out. I'm dying to figure out what makes you guys tick."

Jackass angled the gun toward Cactus.

"H-hang on! Can't we talk about this?!"

It was the same sparkle he saw in Lotus's eyes whenever the engineer was about to start modding a newly discovered machine. This woman was bad news. They needed to get away. Far, far away.

Cactus felt the slam of the dart. He dropped to the ground.

"Whaddya say, Lotus? Wanna gimme a hand for science? I figure this kinda stuff is right up your alley."

Cactus sensed Jackass right above his head. He felt her hand brush against him. This was his chance.

"Graaaaah!" he yelled, lunging upward to steal her gun.

At least . . . that's what he intended. Jackass just swept his feet back out from under him, and he fell right on his ass.

"Damn. You're still kicking?" Jackass marveled. "You got some kinda resistance to sedatives? This just got way more exciting."

"No!" Cactus protested. "You've got it all wrong! Your dart just happened to hit my coin purse. There isn't a single interesting thing about me, I swear! Modding me would be the most boring thing imaginable!"

Had they survived the high seas only for things to end like this? Was Cactus going die at the hands of some inscrutable woman, his body tinkered with to who knew what end?! Had his life meant anything at all . . . ?

"Dieeeee!"

He heard an all-too-familiar shout and saw Lotus smash a rock over Jackass's head. The woman groaned and slumped to her knees—she might've been an android, but a strong blow to the skull still had its merits. It'd slow the functioning of her brain unit, at least.

"Behold my latest invention, the Lotus Smoke Grenade Mk. II Rev-A!"

There was a dull thump, and thick black smoke began billowing outward, obscuring everything in sight. Cactus had never been more thankful to have Lotus as his comrade.

"Great work!" he exclaimed. "Now let's get outta here!"

He hefted Phlox's unconscious body over his shoulder and began to run, Lotus in tow. They ran for all they were worth—which, if you asked Cactus, was plenty: if there was one thing the trio did better than anyone else, it was running away.

They ran and ran and ran some more. When they'd run for what felt like an eternity, Cactus risked a glance over his shoulder, only to find that there was absolutely no one in pursuit.

"How unlucky can we get?" Cactus heaved a sigh, only for a jolt of pain to run its way from the base of his spine to the top.

"Owww . . ."

"I told you, Cap, you gotta relax. Tense up any muscle on your body right now and you're gonna be feeling it everywhere."

They'd managed to get away. But in lifting his unconscious companion and sprinting to safety, Cactus had once again thrown out his back.

"C'mon, now," coaxed Phlox. "Deep breath, then let all the tension out of your arms and legs."

Now it was Cactus who was being carried by Phlox. The embarrassment was hard to bear, but he tried his best to put it out of his mind. He knew he should be thankful they'd made it safely out of the terrifying encounter at all.

Beside them, Lotus fumed. "Modding androids. Hmph!

"I want to mod *machines*!" the engineer continued. "Tell me, how could anyone be so indiscriminate as to start tinkering with their own kind?! What a complete lack of self-control!"

It was a rather unpersuasive argument, Cactus decided, given how little self-control Lotus managed to demonstrate whenever a machine lifeform passed before his eyes.

Of course, acting indiscriminately against those who were supposed to be your comrades . . . That, he had to admit, was on an entirely different level. The woman known as Jackass was a terribly dangerous android, indeed.

And if that was how Jackass behaved, what about her commanding officer? Was Anemone even worse? Cactus could hardly believe that just a few hours earlier, he'd been daydreaming about joining up with them.

At least Emil didn't seem so bad.

"But I guess," Cactus mused aloud, "as reckless as Jackass was, she didn't come close to those YoR-whatever guys."

He'd almost been killed at the hands of YoRHa Experimental M Squadron's No. 6. *That* had been a miserable situation. "Unlucky" couldn't even begin to cover it.

But then again, No. 6 had been infected by a logic virus. Cactus figured he probably ought to cut the guy a little slack . . . or maybe that was just the healing power of time. Maybe Cactus only felt that way because he'd lived to tell the tale.

After a bit more reflection, Cactus concluded that the YoRHa guys were not, in fact, bad people. Instructor Black had, after all, fought to the bitter end to keep Cactus and his companions safe.

And that day at the airfield, No. 4 and No. 22 had kept Phlox and Cactus safe when they'd been running around in circles, chased by enemies near the control tower. No. 9 had tended to Cactus's injured back, and No. 3 seemed to be an all-around good guy.

No. 21 had plotted that dreadful mutiny, but without his reconnaissance work and strategies, they wouldn't have made it out of the Mountain Zone in the first place. As for the android that came out of the mysterious container, Cactus never really had a chance to get to know him, but he'd pinned him as someone with a good heart. He recalled the hints of sadness that would appear in No. 2's eyes when he believed nobody was looking.

"Erm . . . I don't know about that," Lotus opined. "Those YoRHa people were all sorts of trouble. In fact, androids in general are just downright *scary*."

Phlox rolled his eyes. "Don't forget that you're an android, too, buddy."

The two began to argue, prompting a new line of thought in Cactus's mind. Lotus's assessment made sense. The three of them were deserters—and cowards, to boot. Of course they'd be frightened of Resistance groups, and of YoRHa Experimental M Squadron, with its top-of-the-line androids. Units like that fought endlessly for the sake of their war, never showing the slightest trace of hesitation. Really, they just didn't have much in common with Cactus and his men.

"All right, that settles it," Cactus announced. "I'm ready to head somewhere far away, where there's nobody else, and we can live out our days without a care in the world. We'll score some treasure, get filthy rich, and—"

"Cap? Remember that advice I gave you earlier, about being discreet? Y'know, dressing up your words?"

"I'm talkin' *big moolah*! Raking in the loot! We're gonna have so much cash, we'll be making it rain!"

"Cap! Are you even . . . Wait. You're doing this on purpose, aren't you?"

"Hey, a coward's gotta dream what a coward's gotta dream."

Cactus imagined a place where there was no need for killing, and where nobody would have to die. He longed for the day when he might visit that paradise.

"C'mon, let's get searching."

Cactus turned his head—carefully, so as not to disturb his back. Behind them, the endless rows of skyscrapers had faded away in the distance, leaving not a trace to be seen.

Jun Eishima was born in 1964 in Fukuoka Prefecture. Her extensive backlist includes stories set in the *Final Fantasy, NieR:Automata,* and *Drakengard* universes. Under the name Emi Nagashima, she has also authored *The Cat Thief Hinako's Case Files*, among other works. In 2016, she received the 69th Mystery Writers of Japan Award (Short Story division), for the title *Old Maid*.

Yoko Taro is the game director for the *NieR* and *Drakengard* series.

Toshiyuki Itahana is an artwork and character designer at Square Enix. Major works include *Final Fantasy IX, Chocobo's Mystery Dungeon*, and *Final Fantasy Crystal Chronicles*. He also designed the characters Devola and Popola for *NieR:Automata*.

Stephen Kohler is a translator of narrative fiction, games, novels, and comics, including such titles as *Witch Hat Atelier, Magus of the Library,* and *Final Fantasy XV: The Dawn of the Future*. He lives in western Japan with his wife and daughter.

Cover Illustration: **Kazuma Koda**
Interior Illustrations: **Toshiyuki Itahana**
Japanese Edition Design: **Sachie Ijiri**
English Edition Design: **Misha Beletsky**